Color Me Blind:

A Divine Love Story

Published By

This book is a work of fiction. Names, characters, places and incidents are either the product of the author's imagination or used fictitiously. Any resemblance to actual persons, living or dead, or to actual events or locales is entirely coincidental.

Copyright © 2013 by Gwendolyn Melinda Michelle Evans

All rights reserved. No part of this book may be reproduced in any form without the expressed written permission of the publisher, except by a reviewer.

Global Multi Media Enterprises (GMME)
PO Box 3727
Tallahassee, FL
850.396.2665

Visit my website at: www.gwendolynevans.wix.com/gmme

Email me at: gwendolynevans21@yahoo.com

ISBN: 978-0-9891460-0-5
LCCN: 2013937146

Cover photo courtesy of: Bigstockphoto.com
Cover creation by: GMME

Acknowledgements

I would like to thank God. He is so amazing and I am so grateful to know Him and serve Him. Without Him NONE of this would be possible. Not many people get to live out their purpose, so I'm amazed that every day I wake up I get to do this!

I want to thank my editor Yanela Gordon for her selfless kindness in assisting and directing me. Thank you for believing in me and my purpose. You make my words the best version of themselves. ☺ Consider this our "paper texting" and I will need to order one roll to go. It's just a TURKEYYY!!!! LOLOLOLOL ~ Love ya girl!

I want to thank my parents for taking the time to read this in its infancy. I appreciate the love and support you both continuously give me without hesitation. I'm so blessed to be able to call you mom and dad.

I want to thank my P.I.C. (☺) Ileana Guerrero for listening to the "audio version" of this novel all night (LOL). You've been an awesome support system and in case I don't say it enough, THANK YOU for being my TRUE friend and lending help and support whenever I need it. Nothing you do for me goes unnoticed. Love you Ma Sylvia!!!

I would like to thank my cousin Howard for his endless support and help as my unofficial PR rep. You're awesome and I love you for continuously cheering me on.

I gotta give a shout out to the best church ever, Family Worship and Praise Center, and our Pastor Cyrus Flanagan. This church has changed my life and knowing you Rev has changed my perspective on what it means to truly be a Christian.

To my Tally fam who motivate me all the time to keep doing what I'm doing. Joshua, Maleah, Sharvis and Chantiel, I love you guys to no end and I'm so excited about what we are building together. We need a name for our dynasty people and a theme song! Forever and always #teamsundaydinner

Elder Sharvis Whitted for keeping me biblically in line, I appreciate you big bro. Michelle Griffin for once again making my book debut a masterfully crafted event, I love you girl. Crystal Baker, you're awesome! Ericka, you rock!!! Angela, I'm grateful for you honey!

To all my family, friends and church members, thank you for your endless support and encouragement. I want to thank my readers for continuing to support me and I promise Monday Madness is on the way!

Dedication

I thought by the time this book came out I would have a permanent special someone in my life to dedicate it to. That was not the case but then I realized that I already had someone *permanent* and *special* in my life, the Almighty God. He is the Creator of all things and the love of my life. On this risky walk of faith I have seen God's love for me in ways that I could never imagine. He has seen the very worst of me and yet He still loves me. He brings out the best of me and allows me to share it with the world in a very amazing way.

He cares about every little detail of my life and is always there when I need Him. It's just like any other relationship. There's fussing and crying...well I fuss and I cry and He remains the same, faithful. He patiently waits out my tantrums and then when I'm quiet, He speaks. Sometimes He just waits for me to remember who He is and all that He's done. He has been everything to me. In my darkest hour when there is no one around He's *always* there, He's *always* listening and He's *always* working it all out for my good. I can honestly say there isn't a human being on this planet who can love me like that.

Like Paul I am convinced that neither death, nor life, nor angels, nor principalities, nor things present, nor things to come, nor powers, nor height, nor depth, nor any other created thing, can separate me from the love of my God. But the best thing...the very best thing is that the love He has isn't just for me. It's for you too if you are willing to accept His son Jesus as your personal Lord and Savior. It is the *ultimate* love affair and one you will never regret!

What Readers Are Saying about "Surviving Sunday"

Once I started reading, I couldn't put it down.

All I can say is awesome book.

WOW....A MUST READ.

From the beginning I was hooked. Misplaced my book and I was going crazy...

This book can definitely be a tool to win lost souls in a new way. Genius author! :)

This book had me laughing, crying, pissed off and on the edge of my seat!

I look forward to hearing more from this young lady. #devotedfan!

I really enjoyed the approach Melinda took to help the reader understand the spiritual battle that rages around us. Her goal to do so reminds me of CS Lewis' Screwtape Letters...

It's not predictable and it is everything you want in a good read and more. I'm looking forward to the series!

It's been a long time since a book kept my attention. I almost felt this book was about my life in some strange way.

Surviving Sunday is filled with suspense, humor, and the Holy Ghost. The story line allows you to become involved with the characters as if it was you.

The book was not only entertainment, but as a sinner who was already considering giving their life to Christ, and you having the gift of painting the picture of the work of angels vs. demons in this book has given me a hunger to want to serve and give my life to Christ. I read the "ABC's" of salvation at the end of your book and I have given my life to Christ.

∞∞∞

...One of the scribes came and heard them arguing, and recognizing that He had answered them well, asked Him, "What commandment is the foremost of them all?"

...Jesus answered, "The foremost is, 'Hear, O Israel! The Lord our God is one Lord;

...And you shall love the Lord your God with all your heart, and with all your soul, and with all your mind, and with all your strength.'

...The second is this, **'You shall love your neighbor as yourself.' There is no other commandment greater than these."**

~Mark 12:28-31 (NASB)

∞∞∞

Love is patient, love is kind *and* is not jealous; love does not brag *and* is not arrogant, does not act unbecomingly; it does not seek its own, is not provoked, does not take into account a wrong *suffered*, does not rejoice in unrighteousness, but rejoices with the truth; bears all things, believes all things, hopes all things, endures all things. Love never fails...

~1 Corinthians 13: 4-8 (NASB)

Part One:

Elementary School

(Jacksonville, Florida ~ 1994)

Chapter 1: A Bond like No Other

Blake and Jasmine sat on his bed playing video games after school on Friday afternoon. Normally Jasmine would never be staying the night because her mother didn't think it was proper since Blake was a boy. Jasmine's parents had to go see about her grandmother who fell ill.

Her three older brothers were caught up with practice for their various sports and all manner of things. Her mother didn't want to leave her nine year-old-baby at their irresponsible teenage mercy. Blake on the other hand was an only child. He and Jasmine had been playing together since they were two. Growing up across the street from one another was like fate's way of positioning them for a lifelong friendship that only got stronger with every passing year.

Blake sat on his twin bed. His dark blue eyes gleamed with anticipation as he played the game. He pushed his wavy dark brown hair away from his face as the levels got more intense. They were lanky nine-year-olds in the fourth grade. His white skin had a slight tan, hers the color of creamy peanut butter.

They had already finished their homework and were waiting for Blake's mother to come home from the store while his father was somewhere in the house working on his second or third whiskey. Jasmine wasn't her usual self. Her mind wasn't really on the game. Her big brown eyes were not focused on what she was doing as she ran her hand through the mass of big, untamed black kinky curls.

Blake noticed her lack of interest and said, "Come on Jaz, what's wrong?"

She blew a curl out of her face, "Nothing."

Blake paused the game because she sounded really down.

He turned to face her, "What happened?"

She knew she could tell Blake anything.

"I just get so tired of people picking at me."

"Who was picking at you?"

She pouted.

"These dumb girls were saying all this stuff about my hair. They were calling me mop head and dust bunny."

"Don't worry about them. They're just stupid girls. Who cares what they think?"

"Well even if you don't care what they think it still doesn't feel good to always be the one people are talking about. And that little brat Marsha that likes you always picks at my nose, saying it's so big it covers my whole face."

"Ewe, I don't like her. She annoys me."

Jasmine laughed, "Good because I don't like her either. I think she's just jealous because you're my friend."

Blake studied her sad face for a few moments. He had always been fascinated with her hair. Her hair was like her, free and uncommon. He wished he could be that free. It was so wild, but on her face it always looked somehow that every unruly curl was in the exact place it should be.

He asked, "Wanna hear a secret?"

Jasmine's mood perked up.

"Sure."

He smiled that crooked smile she loved and whispered, "I think your wild crazy curly hair is awesome. I always just want to play with it. It looks so cool."

She laughed, "Blake that is the dumbest thing I've ever heard."

He blushed a little but asked, "Well since I've always wanted to, can I touch it?"

"My mom told me not to let anyone touch my hair."

He looked disappointed, "Oh, okay."

"But maybe just this once, it will be alright."

He smiled, put down his controller and ran a hand through her heap of curls.

He said, "Their soft and my hand didn't get stuck like I thought it would."

She laughed, "White people are so funny."

He poked her, "I don't know anybody with hair like yours so I was curious."

She started to feel better about her wild hair.

- 11 -

Blake leaned in and sniffed the curls, "They smell like coconuts."

She laughed again, "You're silly, but thanks. Can I touch your hair?"

"I don't care."

She ran both her hands through his thick mane of dark brown waves.

"It don't feel nothing like mine."

She sniffed at it, "And it don't smell as nice."

She grinned. He stuck his tongue out. They laughed.

He said, "I'm sure those stupid girls are just jealous 'cause their hair looks just like everyone else's and yours don't."

She never really thought about it like that.

He continued, "And as far as your nose, I mean it's just a nose. Yeah, it's a little bigger than mine, but it fits your face. It's not too big. Mine is straight and yours is round at the bottom."

Jasmine frowned, "Well that didn't sound like a compliment Blake."

He rolled his eyes and then an idea came to him to put her at ease.

He kissed her nose and said, "Your nose is perfect, just like you."

She blushed, but before she could say anything his father's shadow entered the room. They were unaware he had been standing at the door watching their little show and tell.

In a larger than life booming, drunken voice he said, "What the hell are you two doing in here?"

Blake jumped up, "Nothing dad. We were just talking."

His speech was slurred and his dark blue eyes were unfocused. His dark brown hair was disheveled. Blake knew that look. He was scared for Jasmine more than he was scared for himself because he knew his dad didn't like her. He was suddenly wishing badly for his mom.

"It didn't look like you were just talking to me. Don't you think for one second that you and this little nigger will ever be more than just friends. That is if I let you stay friends."

Jasmine rose slowly to her feet. She was scared. He was yelling. He smelled like alcohol. She knew he didn't like her. She wished now she had told her mother that he didn't like her. If she had maybe they wouldn't be there alone with him now.

Blake instinctively stood in front of her. The loyalty he showed her set his father off. His hand came from behind him holding a belt. He grabbed Blake by his shirt and shoved him aside. Blake hit his head on his dresser and was momentarily dazed.

Jasmine screamed and turned to run, but he grabbed her by her hair and threw her to the ground. When she hit the floor the belt hit her across the back. She screamed and tried to crawl away. He swung the belt again and it got her arm and her face. Now she just whimpered.

Her screams brought Blake back into the moment. He jumped at his dad, swinging his tiny fists and hitting him in the back. His father simply shoved him back as he continued to yell at Jasmine screaming all manner of racist rants and expletives.

This time when Blake got up he didn't try to stop his dad. His first thought was to protect Jasmine. He got in between them and covered Jasmine with his body. They were in a corner of his room up against the wall. Jasmine was crying. Blake was screaming and crying for his dad to stop taking the brunt of all the licks the belt lashed.

Out of nowhere he heard his mom's voice. It was cold and calm.

"If you strike either one of those babies again I will blow your head clean off your shoulders."

His father froze as he stared at his wife. Blake looked up at the anger on his mom's face and the fear on his father's. To his mind she looked like an avenging angel. Her golden blonde hair framing her face and her gray eyes were filled with rage. His mom held a 12-gauge shotgun aimed point blank at his father's head.

She said, "Blake, you get Jasmine. Go to my room and lock the door."

Blake begged, "Mom no, please no. I don't want to leave you."

Her voice was matter of fact.

"Blake do not argue with me. Take Jasmine and go. Lock yourselves in my room and don't come out until I come to get you. Do you understand?"

"Yes ma'am. Come on Jaz, we gotta go."

They got to their feet and moved as fast as their beaten bodies could take them up the stairs to his parent's room.

Frank Jessup raised both his hands and said, "Lisa, what are you doing?"

Incredulously she asked, "What am I doing? No, what are you doing to those babies?"

"I'm sorry. I was drinking. I saw them kiss and I just got so upset. I don't want my son with *her*. Just please put the gun down."

"You need to get out of this house. If you don't leave right now on your own two feet, you're going to leave in a body bag."

She backed up to let him pass. She held the gun on him until he gathered his keys and the door was shut behind him. She lowered her weapon and rushed to the door to lock it. She was breathing so hard she thought her chest would explode. She ran to the phone and shakily dialed 411 for a locksmith. She got the number. When she was satisfied that they were on their way, she grabbed the shotgun and hurried upstairs to see about the kids.

Chapter 2: Revelations

When she knocked on the door to get them to unlock it her adrenaline was starting to ebb as fear was starting to seep in. She had no idea what had gotten into her husband. To strike his own child in such a manner, but to strike someone else's was insane.

She knew her husband was not a fan of black people, but she didn't know he could take that out on a poor innocent little girl. Then her mind started to catch up with her actions. She wondered if this was an isolated incident or had he done this before and she was none the wiser.

Blake opened the door. His face was red as well as his eyes. She saw the bruises showing up on his legs, arms and face. Her heart broke. When she looked at Jasmine sitting on the floor by her bed, the poor child looked like she was in a trance as she sat curled up shaking.

A terrified Blake asked, "Mommy are you okay?"

"Yes, baby I'm fine and your daddy's gone. He won't be coming back anytime soon okay."

She went to Jasmine and picked her up.

"Jasmine baby, look at me. Are you okay?"

Jasmine just buried her face into her bosom and wept.

Lisa stood and held out her hand for Blake.

"Come on baby, let's go in the bathroom. Let me see what's been done to you guys."

She saw that Jasmine's jaw line had a welt that was bleeding. She sat Jasmine on the toilet and told Blake to sit on the edge of the tub. She took a deep breath to steady herself to be strong for the kids. She tended to Jasmine first pulling off her shirt to look at her back. All that could be heard was their quiet sobs.

She had to lift up the little undershirt she was wearing beneath. She wasn't bleeding, but she had welts everywhere. She wanted to scream. How was she going to tell this child's mother what happened to her?

She put some peroxide on her jaw and put a Band-Aid on it. She looked at Blake and pulled off his shirt. His back was much worse and to her horror she'd seen old bruises that were healing.

She grabbed his face and said, "Blake Jessup, you tell me the truth. Has your father ever hit you like this before when I wasn't around?"

His blue eyes swam with fresh tears as he nodded his head. She looked over at Jasmine and she shook hers. That was it. That was the last straw. She put her head in her hands and cried. The pain and tears ravaged her and made her body shake. Blake hugged his mother and Jasmine reached for his hand. He pulled her in and hugged her too. He knew he had to take care of his girls.

When his mom stopped crying she said, "I'm sorry. I'm so sorry baby. I didn't know. I would never ever knowingly stand by and let anybody hurt you, no matter who it was. Do you understand?"

He nodded.

"Blake, don't you ever keep anything like this from me again. If anyone, I don't care who it is, you tell me. It is my job to protect you and even though I failed this time I promise you I will never fail again."

He nodded.

She looked at Jasmine, "Awe baby, I am so sorry this happened to you."

Jasmine asked, "Are you going to tell my mommy what happened?"

"Yes sweetie, of course I will."

"But what if she won't let me see Blake anymore? I really don't want that, so maybe you don't have to tell her."

Lisa's heart broke for their little friendship.

"Sweetie, I have to tell your mother because if something like this happened to Blake and your mom didn't tell me I would be very angry. She is your mother and has a right to know. I promise you I will do everything in my power to make sure you and Blake can still be friends, okay."

She nodded.

Lisa needed a minute to figure out what to do, but she had to get the kids settled. She was amazed at how they were handling this better than she was. To have the presence of mind to protect their friendship after something like this had been done astounded her.

She said, "I tell you guys what. Jasmine, why don't you get cleaned up and get in your pajamas and then Blake you get cleaned up and put on yours. You guys use this bathroom and then you can get in my bed and watch TV all night. I'll go order a pizza. Jasmine, we will tell your parents about this tomorrow when they get back and we'll deal with whatever we have to deal with."

She kissed both of them on the cheek, glad that their tears were beginning to dry up. She went downstairs to get Jasmine's overnight bag and Blake some night clothes when she heard the doorbell. She dropped everything and went back to the hallway to get the shotgun where she left it. Through the peephole she saw it was the locksmith. She hid the shotgun behind the door and opened it.

She let in the locksmith and told him to change all the locks in the house. He said it would take about an hour. She just hoped he would be done before Frank decided to try and come back to the house. She prayed he would stay away long enough for her to at least get Jasmine out of harm's way. She was so afraid of what her parents were going to do but she couldn't deal with that now.

She ordered the pizza then took the kid's clothes upstairs along with a few VHS tapes for them to watch. She remembered what Frank had said, that he saw them kiss. All she needed on top of this was the two of them experimenting with each other.

When she walked into the room she said, "Hey guys, I need to ask you two a question. I want you guys to tell me the absolute truth okay."

They nodded.

"Your dad said he saw you two kissing. Is that true?"

Jasmine looked scared.

Blake said, "No mom. I was playing in Jasmine's hair and then I kissed her on her nose. Then dad came in and started yelling."

She didn't know how to interpret that, "Okay baby, I need you to explain that."

He let out an exasperated sigh and Jasmine giggled.

"Mom, okay look, some stupid girls were picking at Jasmine about her hair and her nose. I told her that I thought her hair was really cool and her nose was perfect. So to make her feel better I kissed her nose, no biggie. Geez."

He took the "Lady and the Tramp" out of her hand and asked, "Hey Jaz, wanna watch this one first?"

Lisa stood there staring at her son. That had to be the sweetest thing she had ever known him to do. She realized that maybe they really did care about each other more than any of them realized. She really hoped they wouldn't be forced to end their friendship. She adored Jasmine. She was the daughter she never had. She was such a sweet girl and she knew Blake loved her.

"Hey guys, I need to go down and stay with the locksmith. The pizza should be here any minute now."

After his mom left Jasmine asked him, "Blake, how come you never told me your daddy hit you?"

He couldn't look her in the eyes.

"So my dad spanked me a couple times. You get spankings too, I saw."

Yes, that was true. It made her think about the time her mom popped both of them on their bottoms when they were five because they broke her blinds. Then there was the time his mom popped both of them on the hand when they were six because they broke her favorite cookie jar.

"Yeah, I get spankings but not like that. My mommy doesn't yell and curse and she never hit me that many times. Plus with a belt she usually hits me on my bottom, not in my face."

Blake turned away from her, but not before she saw the tears run down his face. She turned his face back to her and wiped his tears away.

"I'm sorry that happened to you, but you shoulda told me. I'm supposed to be your best friend."

He sniffed, "I knew that you wouldn't wanna come and play over here. He isn't like that all the time, just when he drinks and when mom's not here."

She couldn't stand to see him crying. A tear rolled down her cheek.

"Jasmine, I'm sorry I never told anyone, maybe if I did you wouldn't have gotten hurt too. I'm so sorry my daddy hit you."

Jasmine still felt the stings from the beating, but there was something else of greater concern to her.

"What are we gonna do if my mom says I can't play with you anymore. I don't wanna stop being your friend 'cause your dad is mean."

Blake didn't want that either. Jasmine had just found out his worst secret and she still wanted to be his friend. She didn't turn on him like he thought she might. He didn't want to lose her either because she was his very best friend in the whole wide world.

Blake said, "If they say we can't be friends, then we can run away."

"Run away? But where are we gonna go?"

"I don't know, but you don't want them to keep us apart do you?"

Jasmine said, "Of course not, but if we're gonna run away we have to be smart about it"

"What do you mean Jaz?"

"Well, we gotta find money and we gotta find a place to go that they can't find us."

He nodded, "We need to make a plan tonight though because tomorrow they might separate us for good."

She hugged him. He kissed her nose and they laughed.

Lisa sat on the sofa and all that could be heard were the sounds the locksmith was making as he turned her house against her husband. She finally had a moment to herself to cry. What was she going to do? She loved her husband and she meant every vow she made to him. Yes, she had to protect her child, but her husband needed help too.

She knew his drinking was getting heavier, but she didn't know he had turned violent. Their marriage had been solid up until the last couple of years. Now that they had hit a bump she didn't want to give up on him without giving him a chance to get better. What she didn't know was if she could ever trust him around her son again?

She had no idea what to do. The locksmith called out that there was a pizza guy at the door. She wiped her tears and went to get the pizza. She paid and tipped the guy. The locksmith told her he was finished. After she got the keys and paid him she went through and double checked all the doors. She headed upstairs with the pizza.

When she walked in the room the TV was playing "Lady and the Tramp" and Jasmine and Blake were in her bed facing each other, holding hands, asleep. Too tired to go back downstairs, she placed the pizza on the dresser and climbed in the bed wrapping her arm around both of them and wished for sleep to come.

Chapter 3: The Getaway

Lisa hadn't found sleep the night before, but that was irrelevant because the sun was up letting her know it was okay to stop trying. She had worried all night. She worried about the lasting effect this would have on the kids. She worried about her husband and if he was still alive. Did he wrap himself around a tree?

She hadn't even thought about the fact that she was sending a drunken man to operate a vehicle. She hadn't thought about the innocent on the road. She had only thought about protecting her son and Jasmine.

She wondered if he would ever be in her life again. She wondered if her son even wanted to see him again. She wondered how many times he'd abused their son right under her nose. She wondered what it said about her maternal instincts that she hadn't known.

She worried that Vanessa would rip her eyes out as soon as she saw the marks on her baby's body. She had a mind not to even defend herself because if the tables were turned she would likely try and do much worse. Mostly, she worried about what the children worried about. She sincerely hoped they could figure out a way for them to still be friends. She looked at their sweet sleeping faces. They were still holding hands.

She took this opportunity to get up, get showered and get dressed. She had what would likely be the most difficult day of her life to look forward to. Jasmine's parents should be home by noon. She felt a little better after she'd showered. She put on a pink sweat suit and sneakers. She pulled her hair back in a ponytail and decided against makeup. It was just one of those days.

She was startled when she heard the phone ring. She rushed quickly to the side of the bed before the phone woke the children.

She picked up the phone, "Hello."
There was silence.
"Hello."

"It's Frank."

Her heart sank.

"Frank, where are you, are you okay?"

He chuckled, "It depends on what you mean by okay. My wife pulled a gun on me and kicked me out of our house."

Her temper was quick and cool. Her sympathy was nonexistent. She walked out of her bedroom so she wouldn't wake the children.

"You listen here you bastard, you are lucky I didn't pull that trigger after what I walked in on. What the hell were you thinking? Are you so unhappy that you have to take your racial frustrations out on a nine-year-old who has never done anything to you except be a friend to your son? To the son you claimed to love but have been beating behind my back scarring his body and his mind. If you come back here I promise you I will pull that trigger."

She hit the off button and leaned against the wall to calm her nerves. What was happening to her world? How could it be crumbling all around her? What was wrong with her husband?

"Mom? Mom?"

She took a deep breath and went back in the room.

"Hi baby. How do you feel?"

He rubbed his eyes, "I'm okay. Why were you yelling mom?"

She closed her eyes and let out a frustrated sigh.

"I was talking to your father sweetheart. We are just having a really hard time communicating right now."

In a panic he asked, "Is he coming back?"

"He won't be back until he's better. If he doesn't get better then he won't be back okay."

"Okay."

The phone rang again, Lisa snapped, "What!"

"Uh hello, Lisa. Is that you? This is Vanessa."

Lisa cringed, "Vanessa I'm so sorry. Please excuse my rudeness. Are you guys heading back in town?"

"Actually we're home. I was going to come and get Jasmine."

Lisa wanted to panic. This didn't give her anytime to think.

She said, "Actually she is still sleep. I will get her up and bring her over because there is something I need to talk to you about."

"Oh okay, well that's fine. See you in a few minutes."

"Okay, bye."

Lisa hung up.

Blake was starting to shake Jasmine awake.

"You guys go brush your teeth and wash your face. Just throw on some shoes so we can get this over with."

"But mom we're wearing our pajamas."

"Baby please, just do what I asked."

He didn't respond, just pulled a sleepy Jasmine out of the bed and headed to his room. Lisa took a deep breath and said a silent prayer for some help.

∞∞∞

Lisa rang the doorbell at Jasmine's house. She held the hand of a sleepy Blake who held the hand of an even sleepier Jasmine. Vanessa's pretty brown face had a puzzled look when she answered the door because the kids were not dressed but since Lisa looked a little worn she decided to table her comment. They spoke their pleasantries and Vanessa bent down to kiss Jasmine's cheek. She was alarmed by the bandage.

She asked, "Baby what happened to your face?"

Lisa jumped in before Jasmine could reply, "Why don't you guys go in the kitchen and eat a bowl of cereal while I talk to Vanessa."

They gratefully obliged and practically sprinted to the kitchen. Vanessa looked after them and then locked eyes with Lisa.

"What's going on Lisa? How did Jasmine get hurt?"

"Uh, can we sit down?"

"Uh no, you can tell me what happened to my baby's face!"

Lisa wanted to run. Instead she took a deep breath and said, "Last night when I got home from the store I walked in on my husband beating Jasmine and Blake with a belt."

Vanessa let out an exasperated, "What!"

"I know, I know. I put him out the house and I tended to the babies. I didn't know. Blake told me last night that his father had hit him before but I never knew about it. He'd never hit Jasmine before last night though."

"Is that supposed to make me feel better?"

"No, of course not. Vanessa, I'm so sorry. I know you left your child in my care and I failed to protect her."

"What could they have possibly done to make him beat them?"

"He said he saw them kiss, but it doesn't matter. What he did was inexcusable."

"That little boy of yours was kissing my baby?"

"Okay now wait a minute. They weren't kissing like that. He kissed her on her nose. Frank took it out of context."

Vanessa just stared at Lisa, so she explained why Blake said he kissed Jasmine on the nose. Vanessa was heated. She knew better. You could never trust white people. They would always show their true colors. She was fond of Blake, but she was about to cut this off before it got any worse.

Justin came into the room due to the commotion, "What's going on?"

Vanessa practically yelled out the recap of what Lisa had confessed. A look of strong concern spread over his face.

Justin was a spiritual man and he never jumped to conclusions. He could feel the Holy Spirit giving him a sense of peace. He knew he had to take a different approach to what was going on. There was something bigger at stake. He tuned in to listen to the spiritual guidance.

Justin asked, "Where is your husband now?"

Lisa said, "I put him out of the house and I had the locks changed. I honestly don't know where he is. I told Blake he wouldn't be back if he didn't get some help for his drinking and anger issues."

Vanessa was livid, "I don't care what kind of help he gets. My baby is never setting foot in that house again. As a matter of fact you can get Blake and get the hell out. You're lucky I don't press charges on that bastard you married."

Lisa tried to calm the situation down, "Listen I know this is bad, but we can't stop them from seeing each other. That's the one thing they asked me is to make sure they could still be friends and Frank will get help."

Unable to stop herself Vanessa slapped Lisa. Justin jumped to grab his wife. He told her to calm down. Lisa grabbed her cheek and accepted the slap. In any other situation she would have returned the gesture but the guilt she carried made her unusually passive for the moment.

Lisa warned, "Vanessa, keep your hands to yourself."

Vanessa replied, "Do not defend that racist prick to me. Did you think we didn't know he doesn't care for black people? We aren't that stupid Lisa, but if I had known he would have the gall to put his hands on my child she would have never set foot in that house. My child will never see any of you again."

Jasmine and Blake overhead everything as they sat at the table with their untouched bowls of cereal. Once the yelling escalated Jasmine grabbed his hand and pulled him to the pantry.

"Okay Blake we are gonna have to run away. My mom is never gonna let me see you again."

She opened the pantry door and grabbed a grocery bag.

She said, "Help me get some snacks."

They filled the bag with cookies, chips, crackers and juice boxes. Then they took the back stairway up to Jasmine's room.

They ran in, but she didn't close the door all the way. In her rush she didn't notice. She sprinted to her closet and pulled out her little pink suitcase and she grabbed her book bag.

Throwing everything on the bed she said, "Don't just stand there, we have to hurry."

"Okay what do you want me to do?"

"You start getting clothes for us?"

"For us, Jasmine I can't wear girl clothes!"

She let out a frustrated sigh, "Blake we don't have time to go back to your house. Plus you're always calling me a tomboy so just get some of my clothes that can pass for boy clothes too."

He looked at her like she was crazy. She grabbed him and pulled him to her mirror.

"Look at us B. We're almost the same exact size. I'm just taller 'cause my hair."

"Jaz, I really don't wanna wear girl clothes and what about shoes?"

She looked down at their feet.

"We will just wear the sneakers we have on now. Come on, we have to hurry."

He asked, "Okay well what about money?"

She grinned, "My brother Shawn keeps his money in his sock drawer. One time I saw and he has other monies besides one dollar bills."

Blake's eyes widened.

"Jasmine that's stealing!"

"I know, but we will just leave a note that says we're sorry. When we get older we can find a way to earn money and pay him back."

"Jasmine, we are gonna get in so much trouble."

"Not if we don't get caught. I know it's wrong, but we don't have no choice and we need to hurry."

"How long are we gonna run away for?"

That was something she hadn't thought about. She pondered it for a moment then said, "For two years and then everybody should be okay by then."

Blake thought that was a really long time but said, "Okay Jaz. I trust you."

He kissed her on her nose and they laughed. They continued to pack clothes and put the snacks into her book bag.

Outside her room door her sixteen-year-old brother Shawn had heard every word of their plot. He just happened to be walking out of his room when they ran by and he wanted to know what they were up to in such a hurry.

Not only was he was pissed that Jasmine knew about his stash, but that she was planning on stealing it. On the other hand it made him kind of proud that she had found a way to think on her feet. He thought Blake was a cool little dude and he didn't have a problem with him. He realized them running away had something to do with all the yelling going on downstairs.

He left them to finish their escape plan and went to tell his other two brothers to go outside and watch for them as they made their exit, but not to let them go any further than the end of the street. He headed downstairs to talk to their parents. He saw his dad holding his mom and Mrs. Lisa holding her face. Whatever was going on it was bad because he was sure his mom hit her.

"Hey guys, guys," he yelled.

They all looked over at him.

"I don't know what happened, but whatever it is it made Blake and Jasmine decide to run away."

They looked at him like he had two heads. He explained to them what he'd overheard. Vanessa was just outdone.

"That sneaky behind little boy has convinced my baby to run away with him? I knew he was a bad influence."

Lisa was okay with Vanessa taking shots at her, but not at Blake. She put her finger in Vanessa's face, "Now you wait just a minute."

Shawn interrupted them both, "Actually Jasmine seemed to be the brains behind the operation and Blake was the muscle. She had him doing all the heavy lifting."

Justin couldn't help it, he had to laugh. He could just see the two of them trying to get away all because their friendship was in jeopardy. Vanessa looked at him like she wanted to slap him too but she wasn't crazy. Lisa laughed because while they were ready to rip each other to shreds their nine year olds were plotting a getaway.

Shawn joined in and Vanessa snapped, "I'm going upstairs to put a stop to this mess."

She stomped off upstairs and Justin said to Lisa, "Why don't you have a seat and let's just see if we can get to the bottom of this."

Vanessa came running down the stairs, "Their gone! They aren't anywhere upstairs!"

Lisa and Justin got to their feet.

Before panic could ensue Shawn spoke, "Calm down, I sent Michael and Kevin out there to head them off in their escape."

The front door opened with Michael dragging a red-faced Blake by the collar with a pink suitcase in his hand. Kevin was pulling an irate Jasmine by one arm. The other was dragging her book bag behind her. They released them once they were inside and stood guarding the door. Jasmine and Blake were petrified. They knew they were definitely in deep trouble now.

Chapter 4: Can't We All Just Get Along

Justin took control of the situation, "Okay, now let's just all calm down. Everybody take a seat."

Everyone obliged. Blake sat with his mom in a brown leather chair while Jasmine sat between her parents on the matching love seat. The three teenagers took a seat on the sofa that completed the set.

Justin asked Jasmine, "Why did you guys run away?"

Jasmine was in tears, "Because you guys won't let us be friends. It's not our fault his daddy is mean. It's not fair daddy."

Lisa's heart broke for her. She held on to Blake tighter.

Justin replied, "Well no, I guess it's not your fault, but honey what Mr. Jessup did to you and Blake was very bad. We are just concerned for your safety."

"But Mrs. Lisa was really nice. She cried too and she said she wouldn't let it happen no more. And she had her gun. She's not scared of Mr. Jessup."

Justin realized what Lisa must have gone through in order to pull a gun on her own husband to protect her offspring. He felt so bad for his baby girl. He could literally choke the life out of Frank for putting his hands on his child, but he didn't have a problem with her and Blake being friends.

Vanessa spoke up, "Jasmine, I'm sorry that you are going to lose your friend, but your safety is more important and we simply cannot allow you back over there."

Lisa begged, "Vanessa, I know this is horrible and I would probably feel the same way if the tables were reversed, but isn't there something we can do? We can't punish them on top of what they've already been through."

Kevin inserted himself, "Yeah ma that is kinda messed up. I mean I don't know all that happened but those two have been running around here terrorizing us since they were rug rats, but they're good kids. It wouldn't be right to separate them. They don't even play with anyone else."

Vanessa threw her hands up, "I appreciate everyone's sentiment, but life is full of hard choices. They will just have to learn at a young age how to deal with them."

Blake turned into his mother's bosom and quietly began to cry. Jasmine was hysterical with her tears and buried her face in her father's chest. He comforted his daughter as best he could and then made an executive decision based on what the Holy Spirit was guiding him to do.

"Okay, here's what we're gonna do. Lisa, Blake will be welcome over here anytime he wants to play with Jasmine, but for the time being she's not allowed at your house. I know a couple of the counselors in town. I will give you some numbers so you can do what you need to do to get your husband some help. At the earliest possible convenience I want to have a *talk* with Frank."

Vanessa attempted to protest, but Justin cut her off.

"Vanessa, the situation has been dealt with. It's time to accept that."

She bit back whatever it was she wanted to say. Her husband was a quiet non-confrontational man, but when he made a decision that was that. He turned his attention back to Lisa.

"You're not going to be in this alone. We have been neighbors for a long time and we consider you a friend. We will help in whatever way we can to get your family back in one piece. Thank you for being honest with us about what happened and for doing what you had to do to protect our daughter."

The boys knew their father had said the final word on the matter and there would be no more fireworks, so they got up to leave the room.

Vanessa knew her husband and he would do everything he could to help that drunken bastard. There was no need for her to fight it. She would never admit it, but deep down she was grateful that Blake and Jasmine would be able to still be friends. She discerned Blake would always have Jasmine's best interests at heart even though she didn't want to believe it. She knew all too well what it was to have your innocence snatched too soon and be thrown head first into reality.

She stood up and reached for Jasmine's hand, "Come on baby. Let's go clean your face."

Jasmine took her hand.

"Come on Blake you too."

Vanessa extended her other hand. He looked to his mother to see if it was okay. Lisa nodded.

Vanessa said, "Lisa why don't you go start breakfast for them. I'm sure they haven't eaten anything yet. I can't imagine they ate last night."

Lisa smiled. Vanessa could be as mean as a snake or as sweet as a Georgia Peach. She knew it was her way of apologizing because no one but Vanessa Monroe cooked in her kitchen. Lisa's way of accepting it was by going into the kitchen and throwing something together.

In the kitchen Lisa took out eggs, butter, bacon and pulled grits from the pantry. Vanessa had the children sitting at the table and gave them paper towels to clean their faces. She pulled Jasmine out of her seat and took her over to a corner in the kitchen to examine her to see what all had to been done to her. She wanted to curse when she saw the welts on her baby's skin. She went over to Blake and pulled up his shirt and saw his was ten times worse. His were old and new. When she realized why he had so many more she wanted to cry.

She asked him, "Did you try and protect Jasmine?"

He nodded. She grabbed him and hugged him as tears ran down her face. This little boy was just determined to work his way into her heart no matter how hard she tried to resist.

"I'm sorry baby. I'm sorry this happened to you. Thank you for what you did for Jasmine."

She reached for Jasmine and held them both. Her tear-filled eyes met Lisa's and her heart ached for her. She'd never been a fan of Frank's, but she couldn't deny that Lisa had always been a great friend and neighbor despite the difference in their skin tones. Jasmine's wounds would heal likely by the end of the day, but the scars that Lisa and Blake had may just take a lifetime to heal.

She released the kids and asked them, "Are you guys okay?"

They nodded.

Jasmine asked, "Are we gonna get in trouble for trying to run away and for taking Shawn's money?"

Vanessa laughed, "Under the circumstances we will let that go, but if I ever catch either of you stealing anything again I will break every one of your fingers off. Do you understand?"

In unison they said, "Yes ma'am."

She continued, "If you ever want to talk about this don't be afraid okay. You can talk to me or Lisa or my husband okay."

They nodded.

She asked, "Y'all hungry?"

They both nodded vigorously.

She smiled, "Okay I'll go help Lisa with breakfast."

∞∞∞∞∞

Three weeks later Justin parked his truck and walked into the obscure bar far off from the main road. He had been helping Lisa look for Frank by using his contacts at the police station. They found him but before he let Lisa know he wanted to have a private man-to-man conversation with Frank. Justin didn't like confrontation but when it came to his baby girl all of that went out the window.

He opened the heavy wooden door. His senses were assaulted with cigarette smoke and country music. The first thing he noticed was he was the only dark spot in the bar. He wasn't concerned about it though. He came there for one purpose and one purpose only.

He looked around trying to spot Frank. He saw couples dancing on the dusty make shift dance floor. There were several patrons at the bar tossing back shots. He spotted Frank in the very back sitting at a table alone.

As Justin approached Frank he ignored all the stares he received from the other patrons. Frank's head was down. He was staring into his beer mug like it had the answers to life's enigmas.

Justin casually pulled out a chair and took a seat. Frank was so drunk it took him a second to realize someone had joined him. Moments later he looked up. They stared at each other not saying a word for a long while.

Justin finally spoke up, "You don't look well Frank. Your wife has been looking for you."

"Mind your business Justin and get the hell out of here. This isn't exactly the kind of place you should be frequenting."

"I don't plan to stay long."

Justin reached into his jacket and pulled out a revolver. He sat it down on the table casually and looked Frank dead in the eyes.

Frank was visibly disturbed. He wasn't necessarily scared of the gun just shocked by such a bold statement from a man as peaceful as Justin.

Justin said, "If you ever touch my child again I will kill you. Understood?"

Frank stared in disbelief for a few moments.

"Listen Justin I'm..."

"I don't care. There is no need for a discussion. I just need to know that we understand each other."

Frank sat back in his seat and took another sip of his beer.

"We understand each other."

Justin put his gun back in his jacket. He walked out of the bar as quietly as he walked in.

Part Two:

High School

Chapter 5: Temper, Temper

Days turned into weeks, weeks turned into months and months turned into years. Before they knew it Jasmine and Blake were in high school. They were 17 and in their junior year. They managed to stay the best of friends through elementary and middle school even though Jasmine shed her tomboyish ways when she got to high school. She was not into running around outside with Blake anymore, but she managed to still have a love for video games.

She was now into make-up, skirts and high heels. Her new affection for all things feminine bonded her to Blake's mother. She had always admired Lisa's beauty. Jasmine thought her mom was beautiful, but she never celebrated it. As a matter of fact she always downplayed it. It seemed to Jasmine as if her mother went out of her way to be plain and not stand out. She never understood why because she loved being a woman and she loved being beautiful. So she went to Lisa to learn all the tricks of the trade.

Lisa had been happy to help. Her relationship with Frank was strained to say the least and she always wanted a daughter. Jasmine so perfectly filled that void for her. With Lisa's help Jasmine had blossomed into a shapely exotic beauty standing five-feet-seven-inches. Her beautiful bushy head of curls had become her trademark. She became captain of the cheerleading squad her freshman year and had maintained her title through her junior year. She was a straight-A student and was experiencing high school to the fullest.

Blake had sprouted up to a lean handsome six-foot-three carbon copy of his dad. His rugged good looks were the only thing his dad ever gave him as far as he was concerned. His popularity rivaled Jasmine's as his talents led him to the football field. He wasn't so shabby in the classroom either. He and Jasmine always competed in their academics, but he was currently beating her by half a point for the first time since they started high school.

Even though Blake was good at football and it helped with the ladies, he didn't want to pursue it beyond high school. He just had a lot of anger that he wasn't in denial about because of his issues with his dad. He figured hitting people legally would allow him to deal with that anger in a positive way. He had his sights set on being a lawyer.

After the incident when they were nine his father was absent from his life for two years while he got help for his drinking. His parents attended marriage counseling during their separation. His mother refused to let his dad come back home until she was sure he was no longer a threat to Blake. He had never laid a hand or a belt on him since that night.

He knew his mother loved his dad with all her heart and he wished he could feel half of what she felt for him, but he didn't. He hated his dad and they pretty much just stayed out of each other's way. It was the oddest thing to hate someone and still want them to accept you, to still want a relationship with them. When they did have to be around each other Blake was always respectful and tolerant. It hurt him that his father never came to any of his games, but he tucked it away along with every other hurt of which his father was the root cause.

When Jasmine finally started coming back to his house they were in high school. Frank treated her with less respect than he would a dead cockroach. Out of all the goals Blake set for himself, at the top of his list was not to be anything like his father.

Jasmine's father had stepped in to the fill the void Frank left. He taught Blake how to throw a curve ball, a spiral, how to fish and how to fix cars. He was the father Blake wished he was born to. He had a great appreciation for Justin Monroe and he would be forever grateful.

Jasmine would tease him that her father spent more time with Blake than he did her. After all his boys graduated and left for college Blake helped Justin fill the void of not having a son to teach things to. Justin tried to teach Jasmine, but her philosophy was as long as Blake knew how to do it she didn't need to know. She considered Blake her other half.

They both had their choice of the cream of the crop when it came to dating. Jasmine was dating the captain of the basketball team, Robert. Robert was six-feet-three-inches and was the color of rich mocha. His hair was always neat sporting deep waves and he kept his face clean shaven. Blake was involved with the class president, Melissa, a perfectly proportioned blonde with dark gray eyes and smooth milky white skin.

They double dated a couple times, but neither of their significant others seemed to appreciate their intimate camaraderie. This was the first time Blake and Jasmine had found blatant resistance to their friendship, other than Blake's father. It was something they weren't prepared to handle because they didn't know any other way to behave.

Blake was in the locker room after football practice. He and Damon were chatting about practice. Other than Jasmine, Damon was Blake's only other close friend. Damon was an army brat that ended up at their high school sophomore year. He and Blake hit it off the first time they hit the field together. Damon was mixed and a stocky five-foot-eleven. His green eyes, creamy brown skin and short curly black hair made him a chick magnet. He embraced his mixed heritage with pride though his features were more prominent from his African-American parent than from his Caucasian one.

Blake said, "Man, you slammed into John like a freakin' truck today. What was up with that?"

Damon cut his eyes over to John and then back at Blake, "He was pushing up on one of my ladies today right in my face."

Blake laughed, "That's cold dude."

Damon shrugged.

Blake said, "You keep it up I'm going to be your only friend."

Damon grinned, "You, me and Jasmine. I'm cool with that."

Blake shook his head.

"Man, these cats are whack. I ain't trying to be down with any of them," Damon confessed.

John walked up to Damon and Blake.

"Hey Damon. Try that mess off the field without coach there to get in between us."

Damon didn't respond, just got in his face. The noisy locker room went silent as everyone turned their attention to the altercation.

Blake grabbed Damon's arm, "Yo, chill out fellas."

Damon continued to stare John down for a few more seconds then backed up.

Damon said, "I already said what I had to say on the field. You can respond anytime you feel like you're up for it."

Blake knew this was about to be ugly.

He stood between them before John could respond, "Come on Damon. It's time to bounce."

John's friends pulled him back and told him to let it go.

As Blake and Damon were getting ready to leave one of John's lackey's said, "Hey Blake since you'll be busy babysitting Damon tonight I guess that makes Jasmine free for me to sample what you're obviously tapping on the side. I know she ain't satisfied with you white boy!"

The locker room erupted in laughter. Blake's temper went from zero to 100 in a finger snap. It was now Damon's turn to stop Blake from plowing his fist into somebody. He knew Blake was very protective of Jasmine. When Damon reached to hold him back he was surprised by how strong Blake was. He almost wasn't able to keep him under control.

Blake said, "If I ever catch you anywhere near Jasmine I will kill you."

Blake's face was so calm and so serious that Damon thought he might actually mean it. The heckler didn't like that cold look in Blake's haunting blue eyes, so he laughed it off.

"Whatever man."

When they were out of the locker room and heading to Blake's truck Damon said, "Dude, you're kinda scary. What the hell was that?"

Blake was still pissed.

"Sorry man, he just pushed a button. I don't play like that about Jasmine."

Since the opportunity presented itself and Damon had always been curious he asked, "And why is that?"

Blake just stared at him for a moment then said, "I don't know why, but I've always known she was mine to protect. I just can't explain it. I won't let anything or anyone hurt her ever again."

To Damon it sounded like Jasmine had been cosmically assigned to Blake. If that were true so much about them made sense. He wanted to ask about the "again" but decided to let it go. They didn't see Jasmine and one of her squad mates, Rachel, walking up to Blake's truck.

Jasmine asked, "Did I hear my name?"

Startled Blake turned to face her.

"Hey Jaz. Yeah you did, but it's nothing to worry about."

She gave him the once over, "B, your ears are red. Who pissed you off?"

Before he could respond John and his crew were headed out to their cars. Instinctively, Blake pulled Jasmine closer to him and watched them like a hawk silently driving his threat home. Jasmine wanted to snatch away. She wasn't a child, but the look on Blake's face was a little intense so she let him do whatever he needed to do. She knew he could be overprotective of her.

Rachel asked, "What the heck happened in the locker room?"

Damon didn't believe in women getting caught in the crossfire of something that was between men.

"Come on ladies, how bout we go grab something to eat."

He looked at Blake to make sure it was okay, Blake nodded. They all piled into Blake's black F150 quad-cab. They agreed on pizza, so Blake headed to the local pizza joint.

Chapter 6: Choices

They walked into the pizza parlor.

"Pizza's on me guys," Damon said and headed to the counter.

Blake, Jasmine and Rachel grabbed a booth. Jasmine and Blake sat with their backs to the door and Rachel slid in on the other side. They were making small talk when Damon came over carrying drinks.

Jasmine asked, "Okay guys, seriously, what was the tension in the parking lot about and Blake why did you grab me like a child?"

Blake rolled his eyes, "Jaz, can you let it go for me please? All you need to know is that I handled it."

He kissed her nose. She saw the plea in his eyes and decided to let it go.

Rachel changed the subject, "So do you think you guys are ready for regional's coming up."

Damon smirked, cocky as usual, "Of course we are." He slid an arm around Rachel smooth as always, "You wanna be my personal cheerleader?"

Blake and Jasmine both rolled their eyes as Rachel began to blush. Jasmine would have to remember to tell Rachel to run because Damon was the ultimate ladies' man. They ignored the now private conversation that was starting between Rachel and Damon.

Blake asked, "Hey, did you take good notes in Economics today?"

Jasmine responded, "I sure did, but it will cost you."

"Come on Jaz, you know I'm good for it."

She laughed, "No boo, boo, you still owe me for the last set of notes from Anatomy."

He gave her his best puppy dog face and then kissed her nose again.

She giggled, "Okay fine, I'll make you copies, but the next two sets of notes are on you."

"Deal."

They were in their own world and were oblivious that Melissa and a couple of her friends had just walked in and witnessed their *friendly* exchange.

One of Melissa's friends said, "See that Melissa, I told you they had a thing going on. I know you're not going to let him get away with that."

Melissa couldn't hide the embarrassment creeping up on her face. She thought Blake was a good guy. She didn't have a reason not to trust him when he said they were just friends, but the way he was carrying on with *her* in public was not cool.

The other friend asked, "So what are you going to do?"

Melissa wanted to cry. She wasn't the confrontational kind, but she didn't want to lose face in front of her friends. She and Blake had been dating for almost a year and they had real feelings for one another. She was so tired of hearing about Blake and Jasmine.

"He is making a fool out of you. If I were you I would confront them both."

Melissa took a deep breath and walked over to their table with her two friends in tow giving her a boost of confidence.

"Blake what the heck is going on?"

Her shrill voice caused everyone to stop their conversations and stare at her.

Blake was genuinely surprised to see her, "Hey babe, what are you talking about?"

"I'm talking about you sitting here flirting with "your best friend" like I don't exist."

Blake was genuinely lost. He was trying to avoid losing his temper. However, Melissa causing a scene for no good reason didn't sit well with him.

"Okay, you need to calm down. I really don't know what you're talking about. I'm not flirting with anybody. We're just having a pizza."

Blake could feel Jasmine about to say something. Without looking at her he laid his hand on hers and shook his head. Jasmine rolled her eyes and sat back. Melissa didn't miss their unspoken communication. It only made matters worse.

"Whatever Blake. I just saw you kiss her!"

He looked at her like she was missing a screw.

He stood up, "Let's go outside Melissa. You're causing a scene."

He reached for her hand, but she snatched it away from him and that put him on the defensive.

She left her two friends and followed Blake outside. They both gave Jasmine dirty looks.

Jasmine said, "Y'all better back off. I'm not the one."

Damon laughed, "Girl you are crazy."

Jasmine just rolled her eyes.

Rachel said, "I got your back Jazzy."

Jasmine gave the two guard dogs the once over and said, "Thanks, but I won't need it."

Jasmine had gained a reputation freshman year after she decked a junior with her right hook when he grabbed her butt at lunch. With the dismissal they walked off to find their own booth.

Outside, Melissa stopped just beyond the entrance door.

Blake said, "No, in the truck."

She spat, "I'm not getting in your truck."

"We are not about to have this conversation in front of all these people."

He walked off and headed to his truck. Melissa reluctantly followed. When she got in the truck she slammed his door.

He snapped, "What is your problem. I haven't done anything."

"Don't try and act so innocent. I saw you with my own eyes Blake."

"What did you see?"

"I saw you kissing Jasmine in public like she was your girlfriend."

He wanted to scream.

"You can't be serious Melissa. You saw me kiss her on her nose. You have seen me do it before, so why are you throwing a fit all of a sudden."

"This is not all of a sudden. I told you I don't like how close you two are."

"And I told you that you were just going to have to get over that. She is my best friend. I've known her since I was two."

"So I'm just supposed to accept how humiliating it is that you're being seen with her in public making me look like a fool?"

"You look like a fool because you're going around yelling at me in public places like you have lost your mind."

She looked as though she wanted to slap him. What was with everybody today pushing his buttons?

∞∞∞

In the pizza parlor, Damon asked Jasmine, "Are you gonna eat that?"

She pushed her plate toward him, "No you go ahead. I'm not hungry anymore."

Rachel asked, "What's wrong?"

"People suck, so I lost my appetite."

Damon laughed, "That's cool, 'cause I found it."

Rachel laughed a little too hard. Jasmine rolled her eyes as the two continued to flirt. Her mind was on Blake. She didn't want to be the cause of problems between him and Melissa. She knew Blake genuinely loved Melissa and she hoped they could work out their differences.

Damon eyed her as she pouted. He wondered if she understood why Melissa was so mad. He knew there was nothing going on between her and Blake. He didn't really understand why though because he couldn't imagine any two people more perfect for each other than his two friends.

∞∞∞

Inside the truck it had been uncomfortably silent for several minutes.

Blake said, "Look Melissa, I love you and I want to be with you. Can you please stop trying to make something out of nothing? Jasmine is my friend, you're my girlfriend."

If tonight was the only incident maybe Melissa could forgive it and move on, but it wasn't. Countless people had told of her seeing Blake and Jasmine somewhere together. Though she never heard about anything physical between them the fact remained that he spent too much time with another girl. He had more than enough opportunity to do whatever he wanted, she was his neighbor. She was exhausted with trying to defend herself against the rumors. She had no idea what took place when she was not around and she was tired of wondering.

With tears in her eyes she looked into Blake's, "I love you too, but it's time for you to prove that you love me."

He looked at her confused, "What do you mean prove it?"

"I mean make a choice. It's me or Jasmine. You can't have us both."

For the second time that night his temper returned. He punched the steering wheel. Melissa jumped. His sudden reaction scared her. He was heated. Melissa had been the first girl he was in love with. It hurt him deeply to know she had such little faith in him and that his word meant nothing to her.

He had always treated her with kindness and respect, so this demand that he sever ties with his oldest friend caught him off guard. He found himself in unfamiliar territory. There was no doubt in his mind that he loved Melissa, but he absolutely could not see himself not being Jasmine's friend because Melissa was insecure.

Blake said, "I'm really sorry you feel that way, but I'm begging you to please reconsider what you're asking me to do. I don't want our relationship to end, especially over such a stupid reason. Please don't make me choose."

She couldn't stop the tears now, "Well looks like you've made your choice."

"Jasmine and I have been through things that you could never understand. She has always been there for me. What kind of friend would it make me to just abandon my best friend because you told me to? She's my friend. I care about her. She is not a threat to you so I don't understand why you're doing this."

"I hope you and Jasmine are very happy together. Goodbye Blake."

She opened the door and slid out. He called her name. She turned to face him.

Against his pride, he begged, "Please don't do this."

Her response was the click of the door shutting in his face. It disturbed him that he wanted to cry. He hadn't cried since he was a kid. He wasn't about to open that door back up. Something inside him broke and contempt for the opposite sex began to take root. This was the last time a woman would ever stomp on his heart.

Minutes later he saw Jasmine, Damon and Rachel heading towards the truck. He was really mad now because he just realized he didn't even get to eat any pizza and his hand hurt from hitting the steering wheel. Damon opened the door and they climbed in.

Jasmine touched his arm, "Hey B, are you okay? Melissa didn't look too happy when she got out."

He shrugged her hand away, "I'm fine."

She knew him well enough to let the offense go. The car ride to drop off Damon and Rachel was filled with silence. He dropped off Rachel first and then Damon. When Damon got out of the truck Jasmine climbed into the front seat.

She said, "Okay Blake cut the BS and tell me what's going on."

He looked at her. He wanted to tell her to leave it alone, but he knew it was pointless. Besides she was the only person he could tell anyways.

"She told me I had to choose."

Jasmine was confused, "Choose what?"

"Choose between you and her."

She sucked in her breath, "Oh. But why?"

"I honestly wish I knew. I mean if this is because she saw me kiss you on your nose then to hell with her. I don't have anything to prove. I have never cheated on her or disrespected her in any way."

Jasmine felt sick, but what could she do? She understood his side better than hers because she would never choose someone over him either.

"I am so sorry Blake. Is there anything I can do?"

"No, I think you've done enough."

That offended her, "Okay, whoa! I haven't done anything to deserve your attitude."

He mumbled a curse word in anger.

"You're right Jaz, I'm sorry. I'm just not a big fan of your gender at the moment."

She softened because she knew he was really hurting so she swallowed her pride. She pulled his right hand off the steering wheel and held it. He squeezed hers, and somewhere in his heart he knew he'd made the right choice. He wouldn't regret it, but it didn't help with the pain.

He pulled into Jasmine's driveway, put his truck in park and turned off the ignition. She looked over at him puzzled.

"You wanna come inside or something?"

He shook his head, "Maybe we could just sit here for a little while."

She knew they both had serious homework to do and it was getting late, but she said, "Sure."

He reached down and grabbed her hand again.

She asked, "You wanna talk about it?"

He shook his head, "Just sit here with me while I process it."

She nodded. They sat there in silence for almost twenty minutes.

Finally he spoke, "Jasmine this hurts like hell."

Her heart ached so badly for him and since she knew he wouldn't but needed to, she let her tears be his tears.

"I'm so sorry Blake. What can I do?"

"Just keep being you."

She smiled, "I can do that."

He said, "For the record, I'm done with the whole love thing."

"Blake don't say that."

"I am so serious. You can have this crap. It's not for me."

"It's your first broken heart Blake give it some time."

"There won't be a second, you can bet that. From now on you're the only woman in my heart. I *know* you will never hurt me."

She laughed, "Okay, me and you against the world."

He managed a smile. She pushed his hair back from his face and kissed his temple.

"Come on inside. We can eat junk food while we do our Economics and Algebra homework. I'm sure it will take your mind off it for the time being."

He took in a deep breath, kissed her nose and then wiped her tears away.

"You're right. Economics will definitely replace this headache."

Part Three:

College Years

Chapter 7: Scared Stupid

Jasmine, Blake and Damon all graduated from high school and got accepted to the University of North Florida in Jacksonville. Jasmine was pursuing business administration, Blake, English with plans for law school.

Damon was still undecided, though he was leaning toward architecture. College was a whole other realm for each of them. There were new people, new experiences and new responsibilities. Their new lives didn't always make time for them to hang out the way they used to.

The first semester of college breezed by in no time. Damon and Blake still hung out with some consistency, but he hadn't really spent much time with Jasmine. When he wasn't studying or in class he was hanging out with some pretty young woman enjoying the freedom of being a perpetually single man. This was how he coped with his heart break.

Jasmine and Robert never made it through high school for reasons she never cared to remember. She had been dating a young man for the past couple of months and she spent most of her spare time with him. She and Blake kept in touch via email but they always seemed to be too busy to hang out with any regularity. She missed him, but she had a life of her own. As smart as she was she hadn't managed that new life very well and found herself in a disturbing predicament.

Blake and his newest lady friend were tipsy and stumbling into the apartment groping each other practically joined by the lips. They made it through the front door, but he was struggling with his room key because he had her pressed up against the door. When he dropped the keys she laughed, but was still tugging at his clothes.

Finally after what seemed like forever, he unlocked the door and they tumbled in barely keeping their balance. He pushed her down onto the bed as she laughed, but her laugh was cut short and turned into a scream because she felt a body beneath hers.

Jasmine yelped as she was suddenly awakened. She tried to focus on her surroundings. Through her blood-shot-swollen-from-crying eyes she could barely make anything out. Blake hit the lights to see what was going on. He cursed. He loved Jasmine but she really had some pretty inconvenient timing. They had explicit rules not to drop by unannounced on the weekends.

His libido was being watered down and his alcohol-laced buzz was fading. Now he was just fuming.

"Jaz, what are you doing here?"

She was still struggling to focus on the sudden light in the room as the young lady stood with her arms folded and a scowl on her face.

"Who is this girl in your bed Blake?"

Blake waved her off, "It's just my friend."

He hadn't really paid any attention to Jasmine. When he could finally get past his anger and really looked at her, his heart dropped as did he, to his knees by her side.

"Jaz, what's wrong? What happened?"

She was disoriented and trying to leave. She didn't mean to be there when he brought someone home. She couldn't say she actually knew what day it was.

"B, I'm sorry, I didn't mean to be here. I'll leave. Just call me tomorrow."

She looked into the fiery eyes of his date, "I'm so sorry. I just needed to talk to Blake, but it can wait. Please don't let me ruin your evening. I'm leaving right now."

As she searched around for her shoes Blake stared at her dumbfounded. He realized she was shaking. She looked ragged, like she had been crying for days. When was the last time he saw her? It had been a few weeks because classes were hectic. He really had just been too busy with his life to hang out. He had never seen her look so bad and it scared him. What could be wrong?

He remained there in shock as she finally got her shoes on and headed out the door. He got off his knees and sat on his bed. The young lady knelt in front of him and began kissing his face.

She said, "Now that almost ruined my buzz."

For some reason that irritated him beyond reason, "Would you just stop, okay? My friend is obviously in some kinda trouble."

"Weren't you listening? She said she was fine and to call her tomorrow. Now can we please get back to us?"

"Did she look fine to you? God where is your compassion?"

She looked at him annoyed, "Compassion for a complete stranger?"

He stood up causing her to tumble back.

Thoroughly incensed that her evening was about to be ruined she yelled, "What is your problem Blake!"

He shook his head, "You need to leave. I'm sorry, but I have to go see about Jasmine."

He fixed his clothes and began looking for his keys.

She was irate, "Are you kidding me? Obviously she is a little more than a friend. Who is she Blake?"

"She is my oldest friend and I can't think about sex right now knowing she could really be in some kind of trouble."

"I know you are not about to leave me for that stupid nig..."

His eyes were blue ice, "Don't you even finish that. Get the hell out of my room and lose my number."

"I'm sorry I didn't mean it. I'm a little drunk. Can we just start over?"

He held the door open and rudely gestured for her to walk through it. He heard the slew of expletives as she headed for the front door, but he could care less. He had to see about Jasmine.

Chapter 8: The Truth Hurts

Blake was driving so fast to get to Jasmine's apartment it didn't even register to him that he was slightly inebriated as he flew through the city in the wee hours of the morning. He was so thankful to make it there in one piece and without a ticket. He parked in front of the apartment she shared with her roommates. There wasn't a single light on, including the porch light.

He didn't want to knock because it was nearing 3 A.M., so he walked around and tapped on Jasmine's window. He had tried her cell, but it kept going to voicemail. He tapped for what seemed like hours but in reality it was only five minutes. Then her light was on. She peered through the blinds. He pointed towards the front door.

Moments later she opened the door. The person staring back at him looked even worse than she did earlier. He didn't think that was possible.

"Jaz, what is going on?"

More tears fell as she said, "Nothing Blake. Why are you here?"

He pushed his way in closing the door behind him.

"Because you look like the poster child for an anti-drug ad and you obviously cannot control the tears that are running down your face."

She turned away from him in frustration wishing he would leave and wishing she hadn't allowed herself to be so stupid.

"Blake, just please go. I can't deal with this right now."

He ignored her as they walked into her room. He let out a frustrated breath. He swore he could feel the depression in the room practically leap on him. That's it, he had enough. He grabbed her by the shoulders and got in her face.

"Jaz, I'm not playing. You are going to tell me what the heck is going on and you are going to tell me now."

Having been able to finally get a good look at her he asked, "Jasmine, is that a bruise on your face? Did somebody hit you?"

She thought she was all cried out but apparently not as a new rush of tears began cascading down. She grabbed him and held on for dear life. He brought her over to the bed as they sat. He waited out the tears knowing her like the back of his own hand. This part had to come first.

After the tears were done she looked up into those gorgeous blue eyes that were filled with fear and pain and whispered, "I'm pregnant Blake."

He blinked, and then just stared.

"Say that again."

Her voice had a little more strength now that she had finally said it out loud.

"I'm pregnant."

Of all the things he had imagined and there had been some pretty bad things, this was not paramount on the list. He had no idea what to say. Jasmine was such a responsible person. How could she let this happen?

So he just asked her, "Jasmine, how could you let this happen?"

"I don't know Blake. I mean it was only one time. Now that bastard is saying it's not his and I'm just trying to trap him. He told me I better get rid of it. We sorta got into a very heated argument and he hit me. I tried to kick his balls into his throat. He won't be making any more babies anytime soon. Blake I don't know what I'm gonna do."

Now all he felt was anger topped off with some hate for that excuse of a man she was dating. Everything in him wanted to find him and kill him with his bare hands. What kind of a man would not only walk away from his kid but put his hands on a woman in anger? He knew Jasmine was a virgin so to him that just made it more despicable. He tried to calm himself and think.

"Jaz, what is it that you want to do?"

She snapped, "Didn't I just say I don't know. I can't a have a baby and finish school. I can't have a baby and not be married. I can't have a baby from a man who put his hands on me and who doesn't want it."

Her tirade began to fizzle out as she whimpered, "Blake, I cannot have this baby."

It finally clicked that she was heading toward abortion and even though it was an obvious option, his thinking was more along the lines of stay in school or leave school. Not if she would have the baby, but when she would have the baby.

He grabbed her face, "Jaz you can't kill this baby."

She snatched away, "Don't you judge me. Don't you dare judge me! I have been agonizing over this for a month now and I can't do this. I cannot tell my parents I was stupid enough to get knocked up on my very first time which wasn't even that great. I cannot finish school and raise a kid on my own. I cannot see him dating other women while me and my bastard child are struggling to make ends meet because I have to work full time and go to school full time and be somebody's mother full time."

She let out a frustrated scream and Blake just sat quietly and let her rant. She got down on her knees and faced him.

"B, I never thought that I could ever kill my baby, but you have no idea how I feel right now and I just can't do this."

He hurt for her but he had to be true to himself, "Jaz, I think that's a bunch of bull and I'm not saying that it won't be hard but that just can't be your final answer. You won't be by yourself Jaz. I'll be here."

She stood as she rolled her eyes, "Yeah right Blake, you'll be here. We don't even see each other but maybe once every other week as it is and that's in passing. Every time I see you you're with a different girl, living your life and having fun, and that's fine but this isn't your problem it's mine."

"Jaz, I love you and I'm not going to bail on you because I'm boning some chick. One thing has nothing to do with the other. I'm not naïve, but come on there has to be a better solution than killing an innocent child."

She couldn't handle the way he was making sense.

"Blake, just stop okay because you know what one day you're going to be married and you're going to have kids of your own and I'm sure your wife isn't going to want the little black bastard child tagging along on family picnics."

His temper was red hot and it was fast. Before she could utter another word he was in her face.

"Don't you dare bring race into this Jaz, after everything we've dealt with. Don't you belittle this friendship to black and white. I am not my father Jasmine. I am not him!"

The hurt in his eyes shamed her because she pushed that button on purpose.

"I'm sorry Blake but like it or not our friendship is changing. It's been five months. We barely know anything about each other anymore. You have a life and I have this mess I made of mine. I'm sorry I came to your house. I wish I had never told you this so that I could do what I needed to do without seeing that look of disappointment on your face."

He felt pangs of guilt hit him. She was right. Once they got to college they kind of headed in their own direction. If their friendship had remained intact would she be in this situation or would he have been able to warn her away from this guy who he knew was no good for her?

It also hurt him to know she regretted sharing her secret with him. They had shared just about everything since they were snot-nosed kids. What was happening to his world? When did being friends with Jasmine become so difficult? Why did he pull away from her? If he was honest with himself he knew it was because Jasmine would never approve of his current behavior. He didn't want to hear her chastising him about his promiscuity.

His temper was ebbing so he reached out and pulled her into his chest. He laid his cheek on the mass of curls that he loved to play in. He just breathed her in to steady himself, the scent of coconuts bringing back childhood memories. Jasmine had been his rock for as long as he could remember. Now it was time for him to be hers.

"Jaz, just let me think for a minute okay."

She held on and nodded. She missed her friend and it hurt to think that their friendship was taking a turn that would send them off in different directions forever. She didn't want that. She didn't think she could handle that. Blake lifted her chin with the tip of his fingers.

"Jaz, I love you and I'm going to love this kid. We can figure this out. Just please don't do this. You have always been there for me and you never gave up on me. I would never bail on you when you were in need. Even if your need was a lifelong one."

She avoided his eyes, "I already have an appointment first thing Monday morning."

That irritated him, but he tried not to let it show.

"Okay Jaz, that gives us three days to come up with a plan that doesn't require you to keep that appointment."

She started to shake her head.

He grabbed her face, "Jaz, please just let me take the next three days to figure out something. We can do this. We can make this work. I'm not saying it will be easy, but it is doable. People have unexpected babies every day."

He touched her belly, "Please don't do this Jasmine, please. I'm just asking that you exhaust every other option."

A seed of hope began to plant itself in Jasmine's heart. She didn't want to kill her baby, but she didn't see any other way except to undo what she had accidentally done.

"Okay Blake, I can't promise you anything, but we can take the next three days and see what we come up with."

He kissed her nose and gave her one last hug. He felt like he had some breathing room finally. He wasn't a praying man, but he muttered something akin to help me God.

Chapter 9: The Nail in the Coffin

It was Saturday and Jasmine hadn't talked to Blake for the last 24 hours. She knew this was how he thought so she hadn't expected to hear from him, but something was weighing heavy on her heart. She knew Blake to be a man of his word. If he said he was going to be there for her he would, even if it hindered his future but she didn't want that. She would never be okay with his life suffering because of her bad decision making skills. So while his support was necessary she needed the support of her parents.

She woke up early and tried to make herself look normal and happy. She had to pile on the make-up to cover the hideous dark circles under her eyes. She put on a gray jogging suit and some sneakers. She grabbed her purse and keys and headed out for the hour drive home to the other side of town.

Being left alone with her thoughts haunting her did not make for a great road trip. The first song that played on the radio was, "Zion" by Lauren Hill. She couldn't take the guilt and made up in her mind that she was going to tell her parents about the baby that way she would have no choice but to keep it.

She pulled up in the driveway admiring her parents' beautiful home. She looked across the street at Blake's parents' house but his mother wasn't out on the porch. She would make sure to go over and speak to her before she left. She used her key to unlock the door. She hadn't called to warn her parents. She didn't have the guts but she called out when she entered and dropped her overnight bag by the door.

"Ma, I'm home?"

Her mom came from another room and waved at her, "Oh hey baby," but kept nodding her head as if the person on the other line could see her.

Jasmine mumbled, "Well great to see you too mother."

She followed her mother into the kitchen and tuned into her conversation, "Girl she ought to be ashamed coming home knocked up and embarrassing her family like that."

Jasmine's heart stopped. She couldn't believe what she was hearing.

Her mother continued, "Mmmm-hmmm girl, I wish my child would come home pregnant, and I heard she don't even know who the father is."

Her mother laughed, "Girl you ain't never lied."

Jasmine was nauseous. She ran out of the room before her mother could see her crying and ran right into her father.

"Wait. Slow down honey. What's the matter?"

She was startled, "Nothing daddy, I just don't feel well."

He eyed his baby girl, "You don't look so well. Sit down baby."

"No daddy, I really just want to go upstairs to my room."

He nudged her to sit, "Wait sweetie. What's got my beautiful baby so upset?"

She wanted to tell him, but after hearing her mother's obvious disdain for unwanted, unplanned bastard children the words got caught in her throat.

"I'm sorry daddy, I can't. Please don't tell mom I was upset. I just need to lie down for a little while."

He stared into her eyes as if he could see right through to her soul. He knew something heavy weighed on her heart. He was never one to push though. He always let each of his children come to him on their own. He didn't pry. His wife did plenty of that for the both of them.

Jasmine desperately wished just this once he wouldn't let her leave until she spilled her guts by default, but she knew there was a better chance of a purple moon popping up at noon.

He kissed her on the forehead, "Go lie down sweetie and when you've calmed down come tell me all about it."

She nodded relieved and disappointed.

"Yes daddy."

As she got up to walk away he grabbed her hand.

"Jasmine, no matter what it is you can tell me. We can figure it out together."

One look in his eyes and she knew he meant it. She nodded and headed to her room.

∞∞∞∞

A couple hours later Jasmine woke from her tear-induced nap. After she splashed water on her face she went to hunt up her dad and tell him what was going on. She found him sitting at the kitchen table with her mother. She caught the tail end of the conversation.

"Rachel should know better than to get knocked up. I mean didn't she ever hear of birth control. If you're stupid enough to be having sex that's the least you could do."

"Come on now Vanessa. Why are you judging that child so harshly? She is young and she made a mistake. A baby is not the end of the world."

"Hmph. I tell you what, no child of mine better come in here talking about they got a baby on the way. Her parents saved for years to send her to college and she just threw it all away because she couldn't keep her legs closed."

"It's not the end of the world."

"No, it's just the end of her life as she knows it."

Her father shook his head. She was about to flee the scene when her mother spotted her and smiled.

"There you are baby. Come sit down and tell me how you've been."

Her father gave her the once over and was about to ask her how she was feeling when she gave him a slight shake of her head. He understood and backed off. He kissed them both on the forehead and headed out to sit on the porch.

Jasmine stared at her beautiful mother for a moment before answering. She had her mother's peanut butter complexion but her dad's big brown eyes. Her mothers were black and heavily lashed, which served her well since she never saw her mom's face made up.

"I'm good mama. I just wanted to get away for the day. How are you?"

"Sweetie, you look a little worn, are you sure you're okay?"

"Yeah, just you know finals, so little sleep, and lots of studying."

Her mother brushed her cheek with her fingertip.

"Well just be glad all of your worries revolve around studying. Rachel Phillips is having a whole boatload of problems that you would not believe."

Jasmine squirmed.

"Yeah I heard you and daddy talking about it."

Her mother stood and kissed her on the cheek.

"Well, I'm just glad that is something we don't have to worry about because we raised our daughter right."

Jasmine wanted to crawl through the floor.

"You hungry," her mother asked.

She shook her head no as the tears threatened to come back with a vengeance.

"I'm going to go sit with dad on the porch," she managed to squeak out.

"Okay, tell him I'm making him a peach cobbler tonight because he's so sweet."

Jasmine smiled in spite of herself. She always wanted a marriage like her parents, but she felt very unworthy of love at the moment. Her dad was rocking in his chair on the front porch. She sat in the rocker next to him and neither said a word.

She knew he wouldn't push, and for this she was grateful. She didn't cry this time. She just reached out and held her father's hand. She studied the contrast of his dark chocolate hand in hers. She wondered where the hue of her baby's skin would fall in their family spectrum and if she had the courage to find out.

Justin could feel it through his daughter's skin as well as his paternal instincts that Jasmine was in trouble.

He said, "Baby, whatever it is you can tell me. I promise you we can figure it out. I can't help you if you don't tell me."

Jasmine said, "Dad I will handle this on my own. I'm a grown woman and I can't run to my daddy every time something is difficult. You promised you would never pry."

She'd placed him securely between his word and his instincts, a very uncomfortable place.

He said, "You're right baby. I'm sorry."

Somewhere deep down he knew this was the one time he should have gone against his word and followed his instincts.

Chapter 10: Un-break my Heart

It was Sunday night and Jasmine had just received a text from Blake saying he was on his way over. This was her moment of truth and the butterflies in her stomach felt like they were on caffeine overload. She had come to her final decision and she wasn't budging no matter what influences or fears came her way. She was so scared, but she was determined to stick to her decision no matter how hard it was or what it cost her. She heard her roommate call out that Blake was here.

She went to her door and opened it. She smiled at him. He smiled back. She thought he looked a little worn but he still wore that crooked smile she adored.

He gave her a hug and kissed her on the nose, "Hey Jaz."

"Hey love. How are you?"

"I'm great," he said as he walked in and sat in her desk chair. He figured he would waste no time and just get right down to it.

"Okay Jaz, I think I have this all figured out, but first let me say this. I thought long and hard about the things you said about us and the truth is I miss you in my life. I'm sorry I haven't been a great friend and I'm sorry that you felt like you had to do this alone."

She gave him a watery smile but she didn't want to interrupt him.

He continued, "Now, with that being said, it will take some adjustments but I think we can make it work. I come into my trust fund in a year plus we both have money saved up that we can use now. We will finish out this semester and both find work next semester. In the summer we will get a place with three bedrooms. Our scholarships will cover tuition and we will make sure what we have saved up will cover us for a year."

Now she wanted to interrupt him but he kept talking so fast and with so much passion.

"By that time we will have two years left and my trust fund so we will be fine. We will just be roommates for the duration of school. See it was so simple."

He saw the strange look on her face and continued, "I know, I know what will we do after that? Okay, I thought about that too and it depends on who gets what kind of job offer, but those details can be worked out when the time comes. The bottom line is I should still have enough to buy you and the baby a townhouse or something, that way when you do find work that's one thing you won't have to worry about."

He smiled at her with triumph like he had solved an ancient enigmatic conundrum.

"So what do you think? Oh, and wait, I'm going to put my name on the baby's birth certificate so the kid will know he or she was always wanted. Screw Jeremy, he is such a punk. He better hope I never lay eyes on him," he sneered.

She just stared at him, flabbergasted by his generosity, support and his obvious love for her. She hated herself for the words that fell out of her mouth.

"Blake, I'm having the abortion. That's my final decision."

He goggled at her in earnest disbelief.

"Jasmine, you cannot be serious!"

She didn't respond but turned away.

He grabbed her arm and angrily said, "No, the least you can do is face me. I asked you not to make a decision until after we talked. How can you be so selfish?"

"You can have your self-righteous rant Blake, but you forgot to factor in the emotional toll this will take on everyone involved, people we haven't even met yet."

"What the hell are you talking about Jasmine?"

"I'm talking about your future wife, your future children, whoever there is in my future. What about this baby? How will it feel when the father he has known leaves to go start the life that you have every right to? When he finds out his own father doesn't even want him. No, you're not thinking about that and yeah I may be being selfish, but so are you. You are putting this kid into an impossible situation and making decisions that will affect his life.

At the end of the day the only person to blame for this baby's hurt or your guilt will be me and I'm not having it."

Her response didn't fall on deaf ears, but he couldn't think about his hypothetical wife or kids because the baby was real and the baby was here right now. It deserved a chance to be born. He was so infuriated with Jasmine he wanted to choke some sense into her, so he thought it was best he left.

Jasmine felt the lump in her throat because she honestly thought that he would hate her for the rest of his life, but she had to do what she had to do.

As he walked to the door she called out, "Blake, one last thing."

He stopped but it took him a full minute to turn around and acknowledge her. The cold glare in his eyes confirmed her fears. Her friend was lost to her forever despite his earlier heartfelt confessions.

After a deep breath she said, "Blake, I know you hate me right now, you may even hate me forever but I'm going to ask you for one last thing and you never have to speak to me again."

He just stared waiting for her to get to the point.

Her voice cracked, "Can you please go with me. I have to be there at nine." Her voice cracked more now. "I need someone to be there with me to drive me back home. There isn't anyone else I can ask. I would never ask you to do this if I had another choice."

His hateful stare broke her heart.

"Please Blake, I need you and I'm scared."

He felt his face flush so he didn't think he had to verbally explain to her what was going through his mind. He turned his back to her and then a pang of guilt hit him as he thought back to the words he had just spoke to her. Then he remembered all the times Jasmine had been there for him.

During the most shameful depressing times in his life she was there. She never judged the way he dealt with his pain, not once. She didn't agree with his desire to have a relationship with his intolerable father. He couldn't blame her, but she was always there trying to support him in any way he needed.

It enraged him to no end to have to say it but between his teeth he said, "I'll be here to pick you up at eight."

With that he slammed the door. The finality of it made her jump. Jasmine lay across her bed and mourned for the friendship that was irrevocably broken. It was just one more thing in her life that was affected by one stupid moment of irresponsibility.

Chapter 11: Defining Moments

Blake hadn't slept much the night before so on top of being outraged, hurt and anxious, he was sleepy. Today he would definitely be a man of very short patience. He pulled up to Jasmine's apartment and blew the horn. It was something he never did. He always went to the door to pick up a woman, any woman, but chivalry was low on his list of priorities today. His mother would skin him alive if she ever found out.

He waited a few moments and then sent her a text because he still was not in the mood to talk to her. Moments later, she came out wearing a black track suit and a black baseball cap. Her wild curls were straightened and drawn back into a bun. That was different. Her face was stoic and void of make-up. Her face always seemed to be highlighted, never overdone though. Now her bare expressionless face made her look like a frightened little girl. He could feel his heart softening just a little bit. That added to his resentment.

She slid into the car and spoke a soft, "Good morning."

He didn't respond, backed out and took a sip of the coffee she had placed in the cup holder. The 45 minute ride to the clinic was filled with silence. Each of them sat consumed by their own thoughts. Jasmine was irked that he couldn't even bother to speak to her, but that was the least of her problems. Not only was she about to make a life changing decision, she also had to deal with whatever was left of her soul afterward all alone.

No one but Blake knew, well except for Jeremy, but she was never speaking to him again. She wouldn't spit on his body if it was on fire. Why would she when she was the one who would have lit the match. She had never known hate, but what was forming in her heart for Jeremy must be it.

Blake was trying to have a heart-to-heart with himself and get rid of the disdain he felt for someone he loved so much. It was true their friendship had been challenged by life and life was winning. So he had to decide if he wanted to continue letting life win or did he want to fight for his friendship.

Could he actually live his life happily without Jasmine in it? As mad as he was, if he was honest with himself and left pride out of the equation then the answer was emphatically no. Why would he want to?

When they arrived there were protesters out on the lawn of the clinic, chanting and waving their pro-life signs. As Blake came around the car, his instincts outweighed his ire. He possessively hooked an arm around Jasmine to shield her from the angry mob and took her bag in his other hand. She gratefully hid her face in his chest.

The tears wanted to fall again because of the additional guilt brought on by the strangers yelling and judging her, but she refused. Her tears hadn't helped her all this time. They wouldn't do her any good now. She was determined to stop being so weak and own up to the decisions that she made. After all, she couldn't spend the rest of her life in a perpetual state of crying. She knew it would be easier said than done though.

Blake opened the door to the clinic and guided Jasmine to the reception counter. The atmosphere was morose and lifeless. The décor of pristine white and a drab gray he assumed was meant to keep patients detached and focused on what they were there to do. The pretty, petite receptionist asked what time was her appointment.

Since Jasmine stood there like a deaf mute, Blake said, "9 A.M."

She asked Jasmine, her name and date of birth. Again Jasmine didn't respond, so Blake answered. The receptionist became suspicious as to whether Jasmine was being forced to do something she didn't want to do, if she only knew.

With a hint of an attitude she said, "Sir, I need to hear from *her*. Ma'am are you sure you want to do this?"

Jasmine felt Blake's body go rigid. She knew him and his temper. That caused her to snap out of her daze.

"I'm sorry miss, this is just very hard. It took me a minute to find my voice."

"Are you here because you want to be?"

The receptionist suspiciously eyed Blake. Jasmine felt his hand tighten on hers before he let it go and walked off to have a seat.

"Yeah, I am. It's him who doesn't want to be here."

The receptionist relaxed a little and continued with the registration process. After they were done Jasmine joined him as she waited for her name to be called.

Jasmine wanted Blake to hold her hand through the process, but she knew he couldn't. The clinic would provide someone to be with her every step of the way until she could be reunited with Blake. Jasmine had never let go of his hand from the moment she sat down. He could feel hers tremble in his.

He squeezed hers.

"Jaz, you don't have to do this. I'm begging you, please don't do this? What about adoption?"

She tried to pull her hand out of his, but he held on.

She forced herself to look him in the eye.

With tears streaming down her face she said, "Blake, this is what's best for me. I do not expect you to understand and I do not expect you to agree. Even if you think I'm selfish or you think I'm weak, love me enough to allow me to be flawed. I'm so sorry I hurt you, but look at it this way. After today you will never have to look at me again or be reminded of how disappointed you are in me."

His throat burned with the emotions that shot through him. As hard as it was for her to go through with this, he knew her well enough to know that the regret would be so much worse. He was trying to save her from a point of no return. Before he could respond they called her name. He looked at their joined hands and this time he let go.

Jasmine didn't know if that was his dismissal of her or his acceptance of her choice. As she walked toward the nurse she felt as though she was walking her last mile, but in her mind she had done the mental pro and con list. The cons won. Her heart couldn't be trusted to make this decision, so she used her mind. She used logic. She only hoped her heart could live with the decision her mind made.

As Jasmine left to exercise her right to choose, Blake sat in the waiting area in limbo. He loved Jasmine more than he had ever loved anybody. However knowing she was capable of something he felt was so wrong made him question that love. He asked himself if he didn't agree with someone should it make him stop loving them. He had to decide if this moment was a deal breaker for their friendship?

What did it say about him if he didn't think her worthy of him because she made a choice? He knew he could never agree with her decision. Sure he could understand it, but he couldn't agree with it. He was also concerned if it would change who she was? Would it change who she was to him?

He didn't want to lose his friend now that he had just got her back. He didn't want this to be hanging over their heads forever. Would it be the pink elephant in the room that they weren't allowed to talk about? Would the wedge he already felt between them widen? Maybe they would be forever bonded with a secret they would take to their graves or maybe they would forever be divided in their morals. He wondered if it was her morals that changed or was it just one isolated act of desperation.

Blake wasn't a religious man. He was by no means a praying one. He'd watch his father get up and go to church every Sunday without fail. He'd also watched his dad get drunk every weekend and be the most insufferable man he had ever known Monday through Saturday. So he didn't have much use for church, but was church synonymous with God?

He believed in God, that is he believed in something bigger, something higher than himself, but that was just because it was too depressing not to. Still he found himself at a crossroads in his life and very unsure of what he should do. He reached for what he learned as a little boy in Sunday school. He prayed.

"Dear God, I know it's been a long time and I honestly don't even know if you're there. If you're there I don't know if you'd listen to me. I mean I can't possibly be your favorite creation, but to be perfectly honest I don't really have much of a choice right now. I'm terrified for Jasmine. So if you're there, and if you're real, fix this. Fix Jasmine. She is going to need it. I think I will be okay as long as she is okay. Somehow make it alright. If you can find it in your heart to do that for her then I will find it in my heart to forgive her and I won't leave her side. I'll be a better friend. I promise, if you would just do this one thing for me. Amen."

He was sure the procedure was done by now. He knew she had to be in recovery, but he used the time to sort through his feelings about the situation. An hour later Jasmine walked through the double doors. Her face was stoic again. Even though her eyes were red they were dry. He stood up as she approached him, but before he could speak, she shook her head.

"Can we please just leave?"

He would respect her wishes for silence. He took her bag in one hand and her hand in the other. They walked out.

When they arrived at her apartment Jasmine had the door open before he could put the car in park. Once he turned off the ignition he got out to just stare at her.

"Look Blake, thanks for doing this, but you took me and brought me back so you're free to go now."

He ignored her, got her bag out of the car and took her house keys out of her hand. She didn't have the energy to fight so she just followed him into the house.

He asked, "You hungry? I could cook you something or we could go get something to eat if you want."

"No, I'm not hungry. I'm fine. I just want to be alone, so if you could..."

He continued to ignore her and headed to her room. She rolled her eyes and followed him. He closed her door.

"Jaz, you should probably lie down and get some rest."

She was exhausted and her heart was broken into quite a few pieces. The guilt wasn't unexpected but it was overwhelming. She didn't know how much longer she could hold up. She just wanted him to leave because an, "I told you so," would drive her insane.

When Blake looked in her eyes he knew she needed him but he knew her pride wouldn't let her ask. He went to her and held her. She held on and cried and cried and cried. When he finally got her calm she lay down in the bed and he lay beside her.

He said, "Close your eyes Jaz and try to get some sleep."

She said, "I thought you were done with me."

He pulled her hair out of the bun and ran his fingers through it to make the curls wild again.

He kissed her on her nose and said, "Get some sleep, I'll still be here when you wake up."

She curled into his side and willed her mind to let her sleep. She prayed that he really would still be there when she awoke.

Chapter 12: Friendship is a Gift from God

Jasmine and Blake were headed to meet their friends for Blake's birthday dinner. It was the spring of their junior year and Blake and Jasmine were closer than they had ever been. They knew now there wasn't anything that would ever come between their friendship. Jasmine had found a way to cope with her decision, though it was a long and arduous process. The burden was now a dull distant ache instead of a stabbing pain in her heart.

Blake had been her rock and she was so grateful for his friendship. She would never take for granted the love he had for her. It was unparalleled. Her due date was June 8th. Every year on that fated day she thought she would lose her mind, but Blake was right there with her.

He had taken her to a secluded area of the beach, her favorite place in the whole world. They celebrated the child that neither of them would ever know. Each year she bought her child a little teddy bear or some small toy because she didn't want to show up empty handed on his birthday. She always thought it would have been a little boy.

The ache in her heart on that day was so overwhelming she knew the only reason she was able to stand on her own two feet was because Blake was holding her up. Blake had taken her to the spot on the beach they found when they were kids.

It had big jagged and smooth rocks that formed an odd u-shape. When they were kids they would climb the rocks and chase each other for hours while her dad was surf fishing.

Blake found a little spot behind the rocks, dug a hole and buried whatever present she bought. He made a beautiful a memorial spot with seashells that always washed away when the tide came in. Whenever it was swept away Jasmine let all of her emotions go with the receding water until the next year.

Blake never knew exactly what Jasmine needed or how long she would require this purging process. He was always there to support her whether he had to wipe her tears, hold her hand or just sit there in companionable silence. Whatever she needed he would provide. She had been there for him in his darkest moments returning the favor was his genuine pleasure.

When he used to have nightmares about what his dad did to him he would sneak out of his window, cross the street in the dead of night, and tap on her window. She always let him in. He knew even if it made him come to tears Jasmine would be there without judgment. He'd climb into her twin bed. She'd hug him and lay her head on his little chest. He would play in her hair while he told her about whatever haunted him that night. Playing in her hair calmed him down. The smell of coconuts was like a soothing balm. Jasmine loved the way he played in her hair. It had a calming effect on her as well. It eventually put them both to sleep.

She would set her little Mickey Mouse alarm clock so he would have plenty of time to sneak back home. He had those nightmares until he was 13. Jasmine was always there with an open heart and a strong shoulder to lean on. He admired her strength. Even at such a young age her strength was evident.

Jasmine looked over at Blake and couldn't believe they were 21 already. Time was flying by so fast.

She said, "You're old now."

He laughed, "Uh you were old a month before I was."

"I cannot be bothered with petty details."

They laughed as he pulled up to the restaurant. Blake got out and went to open Jasmine's door.

He said, "You look very pretty."

She said, "I know," and laughed.

He pinched her nose and then kissed it.

She said, "You're not so shabby yourself."

"Did you expect anything less," he replied.

She lightly punched him in his shoulder as they headed inside.

The hostess led them to a table in the back. All their friends were there waiting. Sitting at the table was Damon, Lucy, Carmen and Ahmed. Since sophomore year this had been their motley crew. Lucy was a skinny little bean pole with a fresh pleasant face, shoulder length straight black hair and eyes the same rich hue. Lucy was Vietnamese and had been Jasmine's roommate sophomore year. They hit it off instantly.

Lucy introduced her to Carmen because they worked together as waitresses at a local restaurant. Carmen was average height with an athletic build though she did possess the curves common to her Mexican heritage. She had long dark brown hair that cascaded down to her backside. Her brown eyes sparkled as she greeted Blake and Jasmine with kisses on their cheeks.

Ahmed gave Blake a fist pound and kissed Jasmine on the cheek. Damon and Blake had met Ahmed on the basketball court. Ahmed was about five-eleven with gorgeous wavy black hair. Since he was Middle Eastern his skin was the color of ripe olives and his jet black eyes were pleasantly mysterious.

Their crew was a uniquely eclectic one, but the love between them was as authentic as it could possibly be. They embraced their differences and never took their ethnicities too seriously by always keeping the jokes about stereotypes frequently flowing. Not everyone they encountered could handle the realness of what they shared. As they were catching up Damon's date arrived.

She was a sista with bone straight hair and curves for days, the way he liked them. Her cocoa skin was flawless. She looked around the table trying to figure out how she would get along with this rainbow of people. She and Damon had only been hanging out for a month, but she was already smitten with him like most women he encountered.

He introduced her.

"Hey everyone, this is Stacy. Stacy, this is everyone."

He went through and introduced each of his friends by name. Stacy was nervous and wanted to make a good impression, but she was starting to feel like she might not have anything in common with Damon if these were his closest friends.

She smiled shyly and said, "Nice to meet all of you."

Just then the waiter came up and made his way around the table taking orders. Jasmine eyed Stacy suspiciously and then shared her glance with Carmen and Lucy. They both lifted their water glasses to try and camouflage their laughter.

Damon was a ladies man. He always had a new flavor every month. They didn't waste their time getting to know any of them and they didn't even try to make them feel comfortable. They had gotten burned too many times getting attached to a woman he brought around. Their hearts couldn't take the disappointment anymore.

Jasmine wanted to warn the poor girl and tell her to run as fast as her long legs could take her away from that man. She had yet to meet the woman who could tame him.

Blake and Ahmed always had his back and laid on the charm thick. They gave every one of his women the benefit of the doubt that maybe they would be the one to make the cut.

Blake asked Stacy, "So what is your major?"

"I'm a poly-sci major."

Jasmine asked, "Do you want to be a lawyer or an actual politician?"

As if she was tired of the question she answered a little exasperated.

"I'm going into politics. My family has had a politician in every generation. This time it's my turn."

Carmen caught the hint of dissent in her voice, "Sounds like following in the preplanned script isn't what you're passionate about?"

Stacy consciously made her smile reach her eyes, "Now why would you say that? I can't wait to become a public servant."

Jasmine sipped her water and said, "Well, you definitely have the makings of a politician. You turned on that charm extra sugary sweet in the blink of an eye. I still have to agree with Carmen you don't seem that excited. Life's too short not to do what you love."

Smile still in place Stacy asked, "And what exactly do you know about my life, *sista*? You just met me so don't go there."

Jasmine's eyebrow shot up as she slowly set her water down. Blake knew that she was about to go in hard on Stacy. So did Ahmed and Damon. Lucy and Carmen sat back to enjoy the show.

Damon was quick, "Uh Stacy, don't mind my girls. They always go for the jugular the first time out trying to see if you've got what it takes to stick around. They don't mean any harm."

Lucy said, "Yeah, it took me a minute to get used to it, but they're harmless. Well Carmen is but Jasmine, well that's another story."

Everyone but Jasmine and Stacy released a tension filled laughed. Their eyes were locked on each other.

"If I had known I was going to be interrogated I would have brought my lawyer along," Stacy said sarcastically.

"Honey if you can't handle this table then politics is probably not the smartest decision you've ever made. We represent just about every voting group," Jasmine retorted.

Damon, smooth as ever, laid a soft kiss on Stacy's ruby red lips before she could respond.

Ahmed always the peacekeeper said, "Quick Blake, say something oppressive and redirect the palpable tension."

Blake said, "I oppressed yo mama last night!"

Carmen said, "White people just can't quite pull off yo mama!"

Damon replied with a straight face, "Carmen, half of me is offended."

Lucy said, "Just don't let your black half offend the waiter by not tipping him!"

Blake said, "Luce make sure you calculate the tip so Damon and Jasmine don't have any excuses."

"Uh, that's Chinese people," Lucy smirked.

"Wait you're not Chinese," Ahmed asked.

Lucy threw her napkin at him and responded, "Nope, the people across the street from your uncle's gas station are Chinese."

Damon said, "Oh you mean the one's next to your cousin's nail shop?"

Jasmine redirected and said, "Carmen I'm looking at the dessert menu and I don't see anything on here with beans. Sorry maybe next time."

Carmen gave Jasmine the finger.

She said, "It's okay I checked with the waiter and they're out of hot sauce so we'll both have to tough it out."

Damon gasped, "Now my other half if offended! But Jasmine always brings us a bottle of hot sauce in her purse. Ain't that right Jazzy?"

"Actually it's the hot sauce packets from various fast food joints," Jasmine said. "I'm all out though because Blake used them all trying to support Black History Month."

Lucy asked, "Now Damon what are you going to put on your chicken?"

"I didn't order chicken," Damon lied.

There was a collective smirk and then all of them fell out laughing. When they composed themselves they each pulled out a dollar bill and handed it to Damon.

Damon exclaimed, "Here's my tip!"

They laughed again. It was a game they played frequently. Whoever made them break their flow and laugh got a dollar from each of them. They loved to freak out new people to the group with it.

Stacy stared for a moment slightly thrown off. She wanted to be offended but she had to admire the quick wit and word play. She could tell this was something they did often. Before she could decide how to respond two waiters came out with their food and began distributing it.

When all the plates were settled Stacy was about to dig in when Jasmine said, "Okay y'all, wait, we gotta bless the food."

Stacy caught herself as they all prepared to bow their heads. She wondered if they were going to pray to Jesus, Allah, Buddha or the Virgin Mary. She had no idea what to expect so she quickly said her own silent blessing. She knew the rest of her night would be very interesting.

Chapter 13: The Plan

It was senior year and one month before graduation. The gang had all received local job offers, was ready to go into business for themselves, or heading to their next level of education. They were ecstatic about what the world had to offer.

Jasmine and Lucy had gone to cosmetology school at night the last two years of school. Lucy was a licensed cosmetologist, esthetician and a nail technician. Jasmine was a licensed cosmetologist and esthetician. Jasmine was graduating with a degree in Business Administration and Lucy a degree in Accounting.

Carmen attended culinary school at night and was graduating with a degree in Business Administration and a culinary degree. Damon had a degree in Engineering and was heading toward his masters in Architecture. Blake was an English major and about to enter into law school in the fall. Ahmed was enrolled in an accelerated program and was graduating with a master's in Finance.

Ahmed had been thinking about this for some time so he called a family meeting. He loved the family they had created and knew they would all be friends for life. He knew that at some point things would change when promotions, spouses and kids entered the picture. He wasn't quite ready for their friendship to come to a crashing halt just because they were about to graduate.

He cherished his friendship with each of them and realized he was closer to them than his own family. He had a plan to give them all a great financial start and keep them together. He had of course already sat down with Blake, discussed the logistics and enlisted him to help find the perfect place. Blake had a better eye for that sort of thing than he did.

They were meeting at their favorite place on campus to hang out. It was a nice breezy spring day and Ahmed sat waiting for them underneath the big oak tree near the administration wing.

One by one they all trickled in to their meeting place exchanged greetings, hugs and kisses. When they all assembled, Jasmine was the first to speak up.

"Okay handsome, why you got us out here sitting in the grass?"

Ahmed glanced at Blake and gave him a nod.

Blake said, "Okay guys, all of us pretty much know what's next in life but Ahmed has brought a plan to my attention that would allow us to get off to a great start financially and still get to hang out every day."

Ahmed saw that interest was now piqued and took it from there.

"So you guys know me as the finance major. I wanna make sure we are all making good financial decisions now and setting ourselves up real nice for the future." He received agreeable nods. "So I was thinking that if we all went in together and bought a place that was big enough for the six of us then the bills would be really cheap as well as the mortgage. Instead of paying the monthly balance we will overpay and it would still be affordable. The way I figure, we can get a decent place and pay it off in seven years. Then when it's paid off we can turn it into a bed a breakfast and have residual income for the rest of our lives. What do y'all think?"

He saw the skeptical glances pass around the group. He could literally see the questions running through their minds.

Lucy asked, "So what if someone gets married or gets another job before seven years is up?"

Ahmed said, "Well the good thing is that none of us are in a serious relationship right now so that's a plus. Well except for Blake and Jasmine, you know they've been together since they were in the womb."

Everyone except Blake and Jasmine laughed. Jasmine shot a bird at Ahmed and Blake just shook his head. Damon gave a fist pound to Ahmed as he laughed extra hard.

Blake said, "Anyway, to answer your question, that person still pays their portion of the mortgage so they can still benefit when we flip it at the end of seven years."

Damon said, "I know we all have job offers, and Jaz and Luce are going into business together, but what kind of mortgage are we talking about and how much out of pocket for each person."

Ahmed said, "Okay, so we find a place for about $250,000. If we could get an interest rate at six percent, which is on the high side, then the payment would be about $1,800 a month. That right there is only $300 a piece, but since we want to pay it off in seven years the payment would be about $660 a piece. Now the plan is that we each pay $700. We will eat up the principal in no time paying an extra $2400 a month. With the other household bills of utilities, cable and food each person should not be out of pocket for this house more than $1,000 per month. We make this investment and in seven years it pays off for the rest of our lives."

Carmen said, "Okay, so you have the house as our investment, but what about other investments?"

Ahmed said, "I'm glad you asked. I will be handling each of our investment portfolios. You guys already give me a head start at the firm because I will start out with five clients."

Blake said, "You guys know how good Ahmed is with money so we can trust him to do his part. We just gotta do ours and have a little faith in our brother."

Jasmine said, "Me and Lucy are starting out indebted to our parents as they are loaning us the money to open our salon. I don't want to stretch myself thin and not be able to pay them back. It's hard enough to get a new business off the ground."

Ahmed said, "Trust me gorgeous, I'm gonna make sure our money is right. I know I was born to do this. You and Luce are going to have your salon and it's going to be nice. Give me one year to invest your funds and you two will be paying that money back and making upgrades."

Blake said, "Remember guys, I still have my trust fund. We can have that as a fall back if we ever need it for emergencies or whatever. I'm going to law school and that will be done in three years. Then I'll be working full time. There is more than enough for me to cover my basic expenses and still give us something to fall back on."

Damon said, "Man we can't ask you to put your ducats up like that. I mean I understand taking one for the team but are you sure? I'll be working full time and going to school full time to get my masters. What you guys are offering is ambitions but I can see this working. I just want us to make sure we don't fall on our faces in the first two years."

Blake said, "Man I love you guys. Y'all are my family. I really believe this is going to work and in seven years we won't even be thirty. We will have an investment property. Jasmine and Lucy's salon will definitely be profitable by then. Maybe we will have enough funds to help Carmen open her own restaurant. I haven't decided if I want my own practice yet or even you with your own architecture firm. We could set ourselves up royally."

Lucy said, "Yeah Jazzy and I should have an established and loyal clientele and we can definitely help with funding the businesses. Ahmed do you want your own firm?"

Ahmed said, "Absolutely. But y'all can keep your profits and let me make your money work for you. We can all have our own businesses and an investment property that sleeps six."

Damon asked, "So where are we going to find this perfect property."

Blake said, "I've already found three. We can go and see them all this weekend."

Carmen asked, "What about the down payment?"

Ahmed said, "I've had y'all saving for three years. I know the six of us can come up with it. No problem, right?"

They all looked at each other as if they didn't want to admit to Ahmed that they didn't have it.

Getting agitated Ahmed said, "I know you guys have been saving 20 percent from all income like I've been advising since we met?"

They all laughed.

Damon said, "We got you dude."

"That's not funny. Y'all know I don't play about money and saving for the future."

Damon said, "I'm in."

"Me too."

"Me three."

"Family gotta stick together. Count me in too."

- 80 -

Ahmed smiled, "You guys wait and see. This is gonna be awesome."

Part Four:

Adult Years

(Five Years Later)

Chapter 14: A True Test of Faith

Jasmine came through the automatic doors of the hospital emergency room. She had just come from work wearing a pair of jeans and a red t-shirt. Her red flip flops were flopping loudly as she rushed in. She was beside herself with concern for Blake. When he'd called to tell her his father had been admitted to the hospital because of kidney failure she could hear the fear in his voice.

There was no love lost between her and his father, but her heart ached for Blake. Especially when he told her that he and his mom were being tested to see if they were a kidney match. He and his father had some serious unresolved issues. If he died before they could resolve them she knew it would leave a hole in Blake's heart that he might never recover from.

Her thoughts were interrupted by a soft whisper in her heart, "Take the test for a kidney match."

The whisper was so absurd it halted her quick pace. Ever since she turned her life over to Christ a few years ago every now and then she would hear these whispers. Each time it was giving her direction, but God was trippin' with this one. This was not a direction she wanted to walk in. In her mind she said a resounding, *No!* The conviction hit her so hard she had to stop to catch her breath.

Jasmine was livid.

God are you kidding me? This man hates the very air I breathe and toward him I feel whatever emotion is right before you get to hate. I would probably do a dance on his grave and you want me to get tested to be a match to give him one of my kidneys? That is insane. Of course I'm going to be a match because why would you even bring it up. So this isn't about me being tested, this is about me giving that hateful, spiteful evil spawn of satan a kidney!

Her mental rant halted when she spotted Blake at the nurse's station. He must have come straight from work because he was wearing a gray suit. The crisp blue shirt was unbuttoned at the collar and the tie was missing. His eyes met hers and they looked so worn. She got quickly to his side.

He reached out for her, "Jaz."

Her arms were around him. He felt centered. He felt like he could handle whatever came next now that Jasmine was here. She felt his body tremble as he began to cry on her shoulder. It startled her, so she gripped him tighter. She couldn't remember a time other than when they were kids when she had ever seen him cry.

His father had been the cause of those tears as well. The rest of her resistance melted. She knew she would be donating a kidney to that rat bastard that masqueraded himself as her best friend's father. She held Blake and soothed him until he gathered his composure a few moments later.

He pulled her away from the nurse's station for some privacy.

"I'm so glad you're here Jaz. I can't do this without you."

"I'm sorry I couldn't get here faster. Work was crazy and traffic, but you know what, that's not important. I'm here now and I will be as long as you need me."

He tugged on her curls, kissed her nose and hugged her once again.

"Jaz, no one knows better than you all the crap my dad put me through."

She stroked his hair back from his face and kissed his temple.

"But seeing him like that. I know you've been telling me for years to get everything off my chest. What if he doesn't make it Jaz? What if neither of us is a match?"

"Blake you can't think like that."

"If you saw him you would think the same way. There's so much I need to say to him. Is it selfish to do it now because I was too much of a coward to do it sooner?"

She wanted to weep for him.

"B, you are not a coward and your dad hasn't exactly made you feel comfortable talking to him. Don't be so hard on yourself. Look at it this way, if selfishness is what it takes to get some closure your dad is in no position to judge or call you out about it."

He chuckled, "I guess you have a point. I should probably head back in there."

She smiled, "I should probably stay out here for a while. I mean when I come in the room it can't possibly help his health situation."

He smiled as she'd hoped he would.

"Don't be too long okay. My mom would love to see you."

"Okay, give me just a few more minutes. I need to handle something."

He kissed her hair and breathed in the scent of coconuts.

"Thanks Jaz. I know this isn't going to be easy for you so I appreciate you being here for me, even if you can't be in the room for long periods of time."

She pushed his hair back and kissed his temple again.

"Go. I'll be there shortly."

He turned back and asked, "Jasmine, what does it say about me that I want and need a relationship with a man that vile?"

She walked up to him.

"It says what an amazing man you are and just one more reason why I love you so much."

He walked off smiling and yelled back, "Room 103."

Now that Blake was gone Jasmine could focus on the woman who had been shamelessly hanging on to their every word.

She looked at her name tag, "Hi, uh, Ashley is it? Maybe you could help me out."

Ashley was a tall forty-something blonde with eerily sparkling hazel eyes.

She smiled, "Yes, what is it that you need."

"Wow your eyes are unlike anything I have ever seen."

The nurse smile sheepishly, "Thanks. They're a gift from God."

Jasmine continued, "It's my understanding that the crotchety old man in room 103 needs a new kidney."

A ghost of a smiled tugged at her lips, "Yes ma'am, that's right."

"Okay, so where can I get tested to see if I'm a match?"

Ashley let out a laugh that she disguised as a cough then said, "I'm sorry, what did you say?"

Jasmine smirked. She liked her already.

"Yeah, I need to see if I'm a match because even though I loathe the man I adore his son. Let's just say I have a feeling that I have the power to be of help in this situation."

"Please don't be offended but I'm looking at your big beautiful curls and his deep blue eyes. Then I'm thinking of the man lying in the bed with the same blue eyes fighting for his life. I can't quite understand how you two maintain a successful relationship."

Jasmine laughed, "So you've met our beloved Frank huh? We're not together. We're just best friends. Trust me he's been complaining about that for years."

The nurse gave her a blank stare.

"You two are not together?"

"No, why would you say that?"

"Um, I don't know what would make me say that other than the way he seemed to be basically holding his breath until you got here. I mean he was at my station pacing waiting for you."

Jasmine blew if off as nothing.

"We have been friends basically since God created us. We've seen each other through many things. He just needed to know that I was here, that's all. Don't you feel the same way about your best friend?"

Ashley looked at her skeptically and said, "Yeah, maybe, I guess."

"Besides, his girlfriend is Amber you know the red-head. I thought she was here."

"He didn't greet her like he greeted you. Like I said, he was waiting for you. He told me I would know who you were immediately by your hair and to call him but you got here before he could go back to his dad's room."

Jasmine was ready to move on from this conversation, "So can you tell me what I need to do to be tested?"

"Yes. I'll page the doctor and have him come out to talk to you."

"Could you do me a small favor? Don't let anyone know I'm being tested until we know what the results are."

"Not a problem."

Amber was heading toward the nurse's station but Jasmine's back was to her. She didn't see the way Amber rolled her eyes. It didn't escape Nurse Ashley's attention though. She smirked to herself. Something was definitely up between ebony and ivory, whether they knew it or not.

Amber tapped Jasmine on the shoulder, "Hey there. I see you *finally* made it."

Jasmine turned around, "Yeah. It was crazy trying to get here. You know I'm trying to prolong my entrance. I want to keep the room drama free as long as possible."

Amber plastered on a fake smile, "I just came out to get some ice."

Jasmine had tuned Amber out thinking about whether she could really give this man her kidney. Her mom would have a cow.

She saw Amber wave at her, "See you later."

Jasmine turned back to face the nurse.

The nurse smirked and said, "Mmmm-hmmm."

Jasmine genuinely was lost and asked, "What?"

Nurse Ashley chose to ignore it and said, "The doctor should be here in about ten minutes."

Chapter 15: What Lies Beneath

Jasmine met with Frank's doctor so she could discuss being tested as a possible kidney match. She didn't know how long it would take but she was told she had to be tested for a blood match, tissue match and cross-matching. She didn't know what all of it meant but she did know it sounded like too much to go through for satan's first born.

Dr. Williams was a fifty-something mixed race man that had features more loyal to his Anglo Saxon ancestry but his skin tone told the rest of the story. After he discussed all the medical jargon and the process of being a donor he sat back in his chair with his hands steeped on his chin and got silent. The way he looked at her he was starting to make her feel weird.

She asked, "Is there something wrong?"

He looked like he was unsure of what he was about to say.

"I don't want to offend you but the curiosity is a bit tempting."

She knew this old man was not about to hit on her. If he did she was about to go slap off.

He went on, "If I can just step out of the professional for one moment and ask, how do you, a beautiful, intelligent and obviously compassionate sista, fit into the family in room 103 that is obviously headed by a patriarch that likely still has ties to the Klan?"

Jasmine let out the breath she was holding with a laugh.

"Oh, is that all?" This she could handle. "Well, I'm the best friend of the son. We've been as thick as thieves since we were ankle biters, much to the chagrin of Frank. Oh, and I adore his mother."

Dr. Williams laughed.

"Oh, so much is starting to make sense now."

She gave him a quizzical look, "Like what?"

"Well, now I understand why the redhead kept cutting her eyes when the son mentioned you."

"Amber was cutting her eyes about me? I can't imagine why. Blake and I are just friends. She knows that. They've been together for quite a while now. She's met my boyfriend. You must have misread the situation."

Dr. Williams looked at her like she was insane. How can someone seemingly so intelligent be having such a stupid moment? He opted to leave it there and get back to the kidney.

"Ms. Monroe."

"Call me Jasmine please."

"Okay Jasmine, I just want you to understand what it is you're doing. This is a major medical procedure, not to mention the emotional aspects involved. I know this ultimately isn't my business, but why are you doing this?"

She mumbled, "Because God has a sick sense of humor."

"Come again?"

"Look, I don't expect you to understand this but trust me when I say I know that I will be a match for him. Even though his life isn't important to me, it is important to someone who I care very deeply about. This is the right thing to do. I'm young, I'm healthy and I will be okay. If I don't help him, Frank won't be."

Dr. Williams had seen a lot of things in the two decades that he had practiced medicine. But this one definitely ranked high on the list of the strange ones. They scheduled an appointment for her to come the next day to take all the tests. He told her it would be two weeks to get the results. Then they could schedule the surgery if she was a match.

She got up to leave when he said, "Just one last thing."

"What's that?"

"What makes you think he will accept your kidney?"

She smirked, "Oh he will accept it because after his initial temper tantrum his pride and vanity will win out. He's too mean to die. I'm sure he knows even the Grimm Reaper doesn't want him."

With that she walked out and prepared to face her arch nemesis.

She walked back by the nurse's station to give herself another moment. She had been here for almost an hour. She knew Blake was going to come and look for her soon. She so was not in the mood for Frank and his antics today. As a matter of fact she figured she would be more likely to give him her kidney if she could just not see him until the surgery. This time the nurse's station was full with nurses busying themselves. She was searching for Nurse Ashley when she felt a tap on her shoulder from behind. Jasmine smiled as she turned to see Nurse Ashley.

"Hey, did you get all your questions answered?"

"Yeah I did. I'm going to be tested tomorrow and I'm trying to get my mind right to go in his room."

Nurse Ashley laughed, "Well blue-eyes came out here asking about you. I told him you had to handle something that came up but said you would be back any minute now."

"Okay thanks. How long ago was that?"

"About fifteen minutes ago."

"I hate lying to him and I'm sorry you had to but..."

"But this is something you had to do because you don't want any hopes to get up until you know for sure. I understand, and I didn't lie. Something did come up."

Jasmine smiled, "You know what? I like you. I hope you like me because I may need an ally when I go down in the trenches."

Nurse Ashley laughed and waved as Jasmine headed to Frank's room.

Jasmine stood at the door and took a deep breath before she entered. She knocked lightly and then opened the door. When she stepped in she saw Frank. He looked so frail and sad. She felt the pity in her belly begin to stir for him. Blake stood up and stole her attention. His eyes were still red and he looked tired.

"Hey Jaz, where you been?"

"I'm sorry sweetie. I had a few things to deal with."

"Is everything alright," he asked with concern.

"Yeah, it's fine, I will tell you about it later."

She saw Amber stand and reach for Blake's hand as he was headed towards her. She was reminded about what Dr. William's said but discharged it as silly. She walked over to Lisa and leaned down to kiss her cheek.

"How are you doing ma?"

"I'm hanging in there baby. Thank you for coming."

Jasmine smiled and turned to look at Frank.

With a wheeze he asked, "What are you doing here? Get the hell out of this room. I don't want to see you."

Jasmine wanted to spit in his face. How can he be that sick and that hateful? He could barely get the horrible words out. His skin was pale and pasty. He looked like the living dead. He had lost at least ten pounds since she had last seen him and his cheeks looked like someone took the air out of them. Before she could respond Blake was at her side pulling her into his arms for a comforting hug.

"Dad can you please just stop it for once? She's here for me. She's here because I need her here."

Hearing Blake's words caused Amber's lips to tighten and her fists to clench. The reaction wasn't lost on Lisa but it wasn't the time to address it. As much as she had hoped Blake and Jasmine would be together, she knew they never would be. As far as she was concerned they were perfect for each other, but if they themselves couldn't see that then there was no point.

Wearily Lisa said, "Frank please, just stop! Can you do that for me please? Do it for me. Jasmine you are welcome here. You are always welcome. Don't let the rants of a mean old man make you feel otherwise."

Jasmine said, "I'm used to it. It's not a problem."

She turned back to Frank and walked up to his bedside. She deliberately placed her hand on his forearm knowing he was too weak to do anything about it. He could see it in her eyes that she did it on purpose.

She smiled sweetly, "Mr. Jessup, I wish you a speedy recovery, but I will leave you with your family now. I'm so sorry to have upset you."

She turned to face Lisa, "Ma, call me later tonight okay."

Lisa smiled, "Okay. Bye baby."

Jasmine waved bye to Amber and asked Blake, "Walk me outside love?"

Amber's cheeks flushed red, but Blake refused to address it as he told her, "Be right back baby."

Blake closed the door behind them as they stood in the hallway. They were back in Nurse Ashley's line of sight, but they didn't notice she was watching. Blake hugged her again and laid his cheek in her mass of curls.

"Thanks for coming Jaz. I thought he would be too weak to argue with you, but I guess not."

She laughed bitterly, "It's okay, but I can't do this today. If you want me to I will stay here and just hang out with Nurse Ashley but I can't go back in that room without spitting in his face."

She thought she was over him. She thought that she was numb to his antics but something very dark was forming in her heart for that man. The truth was it hurt her to the core for him to perpetually show her that she wasn't worthy to be in his presence. It seemed as though he hated her very existence and she couldn't understand why.

It hurt on a primal level to be looked at as less than a human being and it frustrated her that he never even gave her character a chance. It was especially disappointing now knowing what she was willing to give up just so he could continue living out his life of hate. She wanted to cry, but she wouldn't give him the satisfaction. She also didn't want to put anything else on Blake's plate to worry over.

In that moment she resolved to let him have her kidney. Only so she could torment him every single time he saw her. She wanted his evil butt to know that this black woman was the reason he still had breath in his body.

Every time he looked at the scar she wanted him to be reminded of her and she wanted him to suffer knowing it. Her black inferior organ would be giving life to his body. He wouldn't be able to argue with the science that she was now his equal. Her kidney did the same thing his did. She'd be sure to point out that fact on a regular basis to drive him insane.

Blake interrupted her hate-filled vision, "No, you don't have to do that. I'll be okay. I'll see you when I get home. Thanks so much for being here."

She pushed pause on her pain for the moment, "Yeah I think it's for the best because your dad isn't the only one that doesn't want me here. I think Amber had her claws out."

He laughed, "Yeah I caught that. I don't know what that was about. This is her new thing, but most of the time I just ignore it. Does Derrick give you the same hassles?"

"No, he's never said anything to me about it. I think he knows that I'm head over heels for him."

"Lucky you, I wish Amber would realize the same."

"Okay love, I'm going to head to the house. Call or text me if you need anything."

"I know Jaz."

He kissed her nose and ran his hands through her curls.

"Bye B. I'll see you at home later."

He headed back into his father's room. Jasmine saw Nurse Ashley standing by the entrance.

"Ashley thanks for everything and all your help. I'm sure I'll see you again, but if not it was nice meeting you."

Ashley smiled, "It was nice meeting you too and I'm going to tell you this because I think you simply don't know."

Jasmine looked puzzled, "What's that?"

"You two are so very much in love with each other. If you don't believe that look at how he looks at Amber and then look at how he looks at you. When you realize the difference, know that you look at him the exact same way."

Jasmine was used to people reading more into their friendship but she wasn't in denial. There just wasn't anything there and there never would be.

She responded, "Believe it or not, we get that all the time. The truth is we are just friends. We have never crossed that line and we never will. He is with Amber and has been for a long time. I have been with Derrick for about the same. We are both very happy in our own relationships. So I'm afraid I will have to disappoint you like we have to disappoint everyone else. Blake and I are never going to happen."

Nurse Ashley threw her hands up in surrender, "Okay, if you say so."

Jasmine said, "As a matter of fact, I do."

As Jasmine walked out the hospital, Nurse Ashley wondered was it possible to be completely head over heels in love with someone and genuinely not know it? It was out of her hands now and into much bigger ones. She had planted the seeds she had been assigned to plant.

Chapter 16: Love Holds No Record of Wrongs

A little over two weeks later Jasmine received a phone call from Dr. Williams asking her to come into the hospital so they could tell Frank they found a kidney donor, her. Her emotions were all over the place and the only one she could pin down was relief to finally be able to move to the next step.

Dr. Williams said the surgery was scheduled for the next day because Frank was running out of time. Oh my, wasn't that incredibly soon? She hadn't told anybody why but she had made preparations at her salon to be off for several weeks. She explained that she had a family emergency she would need to see to although she still hadn't even told her parents. How would Blake react knowing she kept it from him?

When she stepped out of her office the three stylists looked at her strangely. She assumed too much of her emotions were plastered on her face. There was no way she could change it though so she asked Lucy to come into the office. Lucy excused herself for a moment from her client at the nail station and headed in. Jasmine closed the door.

"Hey, what's going on? You look like that phone call wasn't good news."

"Okay Luce look. I know I've been acting strange and I wouldn't tell you exactly why, just that I needed to take some time off."

Lucy nodded nervously.

"Well, the time has come and I have to leave now to go to the hospital to tell Frank I'm a match."

Lucy looked confused.

"Luce, I'm having surgery tomorrow to give Frank one of my kidneys."

Lucy shrieked, "What! Jasmine are you mental?"

"Shhh. Would you please calm down?"

"Would you please give me a reason to calm down?"

"Look I'm sorry, I didn't tell anybody. I didn't even tell Blake. He is about to find out at the hospital. I didn't want anybody to know until I knew for sure I was a match."

"Jasmine there is just so many things wrong with this picture I don't even know where to begin."

"Look, I know this is a lot to take in but this is just something I have to do. It will have to be discussed later. Please don't tell them until we get home tonight."

Lucy gawked at her incredulously.

"I'm sorry, but I have to go so can you get everything in order here that we've been planning? I'll see you at home. I'm sorry Luce but I have to go."

Lucy threw up her hands, "Whatever Jasmine."

Jasmine grabbed her purse and kissed Lucy on the cheek before she headed out. She said her goodbyes to the staff.

Jasmine arrived at the hospital beyond grateful to see Ashley's smiling face. She was standing near the nurse's station away from the other nurses.

"Well hey there. Don't you look all pretty today?"

Jasmine looked down at her royal blue maxi dress and silver sandals. She smiled, "Thanks."

"Are you here to see blue eyes or his father?"

"Um, both actually. I'm a match."

Nurse Ashley said, "Oh, I see. Well that must be why the doctor is headed this way. Well, good luck in there. I'm sure it will be colorful."

Jasmine smirked, "I promise to give you a play-by-play if I make it out alive."

Nurse Ashley said, "Be warned, the redhead is in there."

Just then Dr. Williams came around the corner and said, "Oh good, you're here. Well let's get this done."

Jasmine kind of winced. Maybe this wasn't the best plan she'd ever had. Amber had been very testy these past couple of weeks.

As they headed down the hallway for the short walk Dr. Williams asked, "Do you want to go in with me or do you want me to tell them we found a match and then you come in?"

"I think the latter is the safest approach."

He laughed, "Self-preservation is likely to win over hate. It will be okay."

Dr. Williams walked in and shut the door as Jasmine stood in the hall biting her nails, something she never did. Lucy would have a fit if she messed up her manicure.

With a smile Dr. Williams greeted Lisa, Blake, Amber and Frank.

"Well folks, I have some great news. We've found a kidney donor and we have the surgery scheduled for tomorrow afternoon."

Frank was too weak to give a verbal response but his eyes showed great relief. Lisa reached out for his hand and began to weep silent tears of gratitude. Blake ran his hands through his hair as Amber rubbed his back.

He asked, "When did this happen? Is it one of us?"

"No, I'm sorry you and your mom were not a match, but we had another donor come in anonymously and get tested. They wanted to remain anonymous just in case they weren't a match. That not being the case I guess now is as good a time as any."

He went and opened the door. A nervous Jasmine walked in and cowardly stood slightly behind Dr. Williams. She stood there all pretty in her dress, flawless make-up. Her big brown eyes met Blake's.

He looked irritated, "I don't understand Jasmine, what are you doing here?"

"Oh, don't you get it? She's your knight in shining armor," Amber said sarcastically before she could stop herself.

Lisa's eyes got wide, "Jasmine, you? You're gonna give Frank a kidney?"

Jasmine slowly nodded her head and Lisa stared blankly then just absently fell back into the chair that was by Frank's bedside. Frank was fit to be tied, but it wasn't much he could do to express it. The newly formed red tint to his face and his eyes going to slits was a slight indication of how he felt.

He managed to get out one word, "No!"

Blake just stood still staring at Jasmine. On the one hand, relief flooded him because his dad was going to be okay. On the other hand he was disturbed because he couldn't understand why Jasmine would do this and why she didn't tell him. She had known about this for two weeks. He didn't seem mad, but he also didn't seem friendly.

He said, "I need to talk to you now!"

He walked out of Amber's embrace and grabbed Jasmine by the arm, pulled her out the door then closed it behind him. He just stared at her, not saying anything. It made her squirm.

"Blake, I'm sorry I didn't tell you. There were several reasons why but none of them mattered because I had to make sure I would be a match. Although I did know it was a strong possibility."

Arms folded across his chest, he asked, "Why?"

Tears began to form but they didn't fall, "Because I can't stand to see you in pain and if there is anything I can do to fix it then that's what I'm gonna do."

Her plea sliced through him and his resistance melted.

He went to her, "Jasmine, I know you love me, but this is too much. We can't just stand here and pretend he's ever done anything worthy of that kinda sacrifice from you."

She had to tell him. She didn't know how he would react to it.

She asked, "Can we please sit?"

They walked over to a couple of chairs against a wall and sat.

"I know you have issues with God and church and all of that, but the truth is Blake I heard it so clearly in my heart the moment I walked through those doors," she pointed back toward the entrance.

He looked at her like she had three heads, "You heard what?"

"I heard the words, take the test for a kidney match. I was stunned and I said no. I wouldn't do anything for that man. Then I felt this pressure on my heart and I knew that was God's conviction. He wasn't really asking me. He was telling me. Then I had an argument with God giving him all the valid reasons why His plan was flawed."

She touched his face. He was just staring at her like he didn't know what to say.

"Then I saw my favorite face in the whole world and I saw all the pain in your eyes. Blake you held me so tight and you cried. Do you realize I hadn't seen you cry since we were kids?"

"But Jasmine."

"Shhh. No, just listen. My love for you made it easy to agree. Then when I went in that room and he was so nasty and hateful my reasons turned very dark. I wanted him to suffer knowing that a black woman saved his life. I wanted him to be reminded every time he saw my face that I was the reason, the only reason, he was breathing. I was tired of him making me feel like nothing."

She looked away from him because she needed a moment. Blake never knew all the resentment she had for his father. She was always so respectful and tolerant of him.

His heart ached for her, "Jaz, why didn't you tell me?"

She smiled a watery smile and continued with no response to his question.

"The truth is, that just made me more miserable. I tried to pray about it, but I was pissed at God for putting me in that position in the first place. I was disappointed in myself because I felt I was no better than your father. I couldn't talk to God, so I let Him talk to me."

"What do you mean?"

She laughed, "I picked up my Bible and I let it fall open. I needed something to get me back on solid ground. It fell open to 1 Corinthians 13."

He remembered that one from Sunday school, "That's the chapter about love?"

"Yeah, it is. It's God's standard for love. I began to read it and I realized the way God wants us to love each other is the way he loves us. I remembered how you protected me from your dad when we were kids. You were willing to take the pain for me. I was reminded of the sacrifice you made for me and the compassion you showed me back when I got pregnant in college. I remembered how you were by my side holding me up until I could hold myself up. I remember how every year on my baby's birthday you held me and comforted me and you never once said I told you so. I know what that cost you. I know that it still hurts you. I know it *still* costs you. I will never take what you did for me for granted."

She saw the emotion storm into his eyes as he looked away for a moment.

"You made a choice to love me and support me even when you didn't agree or didn't understand how I could do it. Blake, I don't understand why you would still want a relationship with your dad and I don't agree that he deserves the chance to be in your life after everything he has done to you. But none of that matters. Love doesn't always make sense. I know you love him in spite of who he's been and I love you. If you need a relationship with him then I want you to have it."

She held his face in her hands, "Blake, I need to do this and you need to let me. I don't know what God is up to but I promise you something good will come from this. I have complete faith and trust."

"How can you be so confident in a God you've never seen?"

"Because I know in my heart without a doubt that God is real and if this is the path He is leading me down then it's up to Him to work it out."

He grabbed her and hugged her so tight she thought she would break.

"I love you Jasmine. I love you so much. Thank you. Thank you."

Amber came out and saw them. Her eyes locked with Jasmine's tear-filled ones. Jasmine thought if looks could kill she would flat-line on the spot. She eased Blake back and wiped her face.

"We should probably go in now and get this fight with your dad over with."

He smiled. She envied how men could hold their tears in check and women never seemed to be able to, or at least she couldn't.

He turned and saw Amber. She was tight lipped.

"Hey baby," he said oblivious to her anger as he walked up to her and hugged her.

"My dad's going to be okay."

She hugged him back not trusting herself to speak. Jasmine's scent was all over him. He reached to open the door. She found her voice.

"You should go talk to your dad. He isn't as happy as you two seem to be."

"It's expected," Blake replied.

"Could you give Jasmine and me just a minute or two," Amber asked.

He kissed her on the lips and walked in his dad's room. Amber closed the door.

Jasmine stood up and braced herself for Amber's obvious ensuing confrontation. She was used to their friendship causing friction for Blake's women but she was more than willing to calmly discuss this with her. Amber strode to her with purpose and a mean mug like none she had ever seen.

"Jasmine, we need to discuss this friendship you have with *my* man. Every time I turn my back lately he is in your arms? I am sick of it. He's mine. If you wanted him you should have decided that long before I came along because I am not just going to roll over and give him up."

The approach shocked Jasmine and infuriated her so she took a step back because she no longer trusted herself to take the high ground.

"Amber, I realize that you have valid concerns. As a woman in her *own* relationship I sympathize with you, but only to an extent. You knew about our friendship long before the two of you got into a relationship. There is *nothing* going on between Blake and me. Understand that this situation is not a normal occurrence. I'm his best friend so there needs to be some understanding on your part as well. It's just natural for him to come to me where his dad is concerned. You don't know the history. The fact remains he loves *you* and he's with *you* so why don't you get your emotions in check."

She got in Jasmine's face.

"I don't need to get my emotions in check. They're justified. You need to get your behavior in check, it isn't. I don't care if you donate every organ in your body to his whole family, you are not his woman. I don't care if you wrote the book on their family history. I don't need you to comfort him. That's my job. If you don't back off I will *make* you back off."

That's it. The gloves were off so Jasmine let her anger win over her better judgment. Jasmine got close enough to her until Amber was forced to take a step back.

"You listen and you listen good. It's not about what *you* need. It's about what *he* needs. You need to accept the fact that he is in love with you. He's already yours, but I promise you if you make him choose he will choose me and there won't be a thing you can do about it. You can take that as gospel whether I give his father my kidney or not. Do not make history repeat itself. You cannot and *will not* take my place in his heart. We're not even on the same level honey. I have a permanent residence in his heart. You currently rent space on the other side of his bed. I suggest you heed my advice because this is a battle you can't win."

Jasmine cut her a look that could melt ice.

Jasmine walked off thoroughly heated and left Amber infuriated to digest her advice. The ache in Amber's heart was breathtaking because somewhere deep down in her gut she knew Jasmine's words were gospel. She didn't want to believe it and she couldn't just walk away. Yes it was a fact that Blake loved her but the truth was he was in love with Jasmine and Amber was in love with him. There wasn't a theory out there that could help her figure out this triangle. She wanted to scream.

Chapter 17: Enough is Enough

Jasmine stood at Frank's room door for a few minutes to calm down. When she looked up Amber was still standing in the hall mad as hell. Jasmine didn't care, she didn't mean to go there, but some people just didn't know when to stop. For God's sake she didn't want Blake.

He was in love with Amber so she should just go be happy and leave her the hell alone. She wouldn't tell Blake. He didn't need two women he loved at each other's throats. If Amber chose to tell him that was on her. The way she was feeling right now she was more than ready to face off with Frank.

When she walked in Blake had his hands up in the air like he was exasperated. Dr. Williams look amused. She heard Lisa pleading.

"Frank, can you just get over yourself. Why don't you for once stop being so selfish. She is giving you a second chance at life. This isn't just about you. It's about your family. Don't you get it, we love you? Do you have that much hate in your heart that you would die for it?"

Frank hated to see that pained look on his wife's face. He loved her so much because she stayed when so many would have left him. The truth was he didn't think he could handle any more guilt because he knew he had never done anything for that girl to feel obligated to help him.

They hadn't noticed her so Jasmine cleared her throat.

"Guys why don't you give me a minute alone with Frank."

Lisa looked down and gave Frank one last plea with her eyes. She hugged Jasmine.

"Thank you baby, I don't know how I will ever repay you for this. Thank you."

Jasmine tightened the embrace, "It's not necessary."

Blake scooted her along, "Come on mom, let's give them a moment."

Dr. Williams followed them out.

Jasmine remained where she was and the look of pure fear in Frank's eyes was more amusing than satisfying. What did he think she was going to do, smother him? She walked to his bed side. His eyes widened with uncertainty.

"You can relax Frank. I'm not here to kill you."

She smiled a genuine smile hoping it would put him at ease.

He croaked out, "Look Jasmine."

For some reason that one word melted some of her anger, he very rarely called her by her name.

"No Frank you look. I'm not here to pretend or play games with you. For the record, you don't like me because you're a racist prick. I don't like you because you're a racist prick, but we both love Blake."

She could swear a smirk tried to form on his lips.

"Yeah that's right, I know in that teeny, tiny heart of yours there is love for your kid even if he doesn't know it. I can't imagine what's going through your head. But I'm guessing you're trying to figure out my motive. Now I admit I had some very shady thoughts for a short period of time. Yeah, I'm going to give you my kidney even though you tried to beat it out of me."

She paused to check her emotions that sprang up with the memory.

"The real reason I'm doing this is for love." Frank looked puzzled. "You can relax, I'm not saying that I love you, but I do love your son and he loves you very much. All he has ever wanted was a relationship with you."

She was shocked to see his eyes swim with unshed tears. She said a silent *thank you Jesus*.

"I tell you what. I will make you a deal. There is only one way that you can repay me for my organ. If you renege on me, I will just have to take it back and don't think I won't Frank."

This time he did smile. He was beside himself to find that he understood why Blake cared so much about her. The girl was fearless.

He managed, "What's the deal?"

"You have to swear to me that you will genuinely form a relationship with your son. You will also put whatever hate you have for me aside and get to know me as a person before you decide you don't like me because no matter what you do Blake and I will always be friends. In order for you to have a complete relationship with him he needs to know that you can at least be civil and respect his choice to be my friend."

He couldn't stop the tears from falling now. Being face to face with the angel of death had a way of putting things into perspective. This young child could not possibly understand the horror he endured that made him the way he is now and he wouldn't want her to. He wouldn't want anybody to. He was tired of the guilt, he was tired of the pain and he wanted to stop hating himself. His family deserved better. Jasmine deserved better. She could have practically been a daughter to him if he'd ever allowed her to be.

Jasmine was stunned. She didn't expect this reaction. Once again she couldn't stop the tears from flowing. To traumatize her even more Frank reached out and grabbed her hand. At his touch something incredible ran through her. She didn't know how to explain it but she felt that this very moment was miraculous.

He reached up with great effort to wipe a tear from her face. She could see the mix of joy and pain on his face. She just stared in amazement. Was she in the twilight zone?

He said, "I am so sorry for everything. You have my word. I promise."

With those words, she released the breath she had been holding since he started crying. His words gave her hope beyond reason that after all these years Blake's heart wouldn't be forced to war with itself over how to love the people in his life. She got some tissue off the table beside the bed and gently wiped the tears from his face.

"I gotta leave you with your dignity Frank. I won't tell anyone you broke down."

Somehow he knew she wouldn't and that simple act of kindness and understanding broke something in him. Something ugly that he thought he would always have to live with. At that moment he was so grateful for her it scared him.

"Well I don't know about you but I'm all done with tears for today. Don't worry. We will have plenty of time to work on our new friendship, but be warned it's inevitable that you will fall head over heels in love with me so get ready to shock yourself."

He didn't think he would fall in love with her but he did think he could learn to sincerely like her. He managed a sad little chuckle. She let out a big laugh for them both.

"Now you be on your best behavior Frank and I'll let the others in. No more tears okay."

He nodded. She went to let his family back into the room.

Chapter 18: Open the Flood Gates

Jasmine headed home to talk to her roommates. She also had to call her parents. Oh dear Jesus, she hadn't told Derrick. Jasmine, how could you be so stupid? She didn't think they would schedule the surgery the day after the results. She thought she would have more time. She couldn't just call him and blurt it out though.

When she pulled into their driveway she took out her cell and sent him a text that she needed to talk to him and it was important. She said she would see him when he got there hoping that would deter him from calling.

They had been at odds for the last week or two and hadn't really been communicating with any consistency. She hoped he would come to her house because she felt she needed home court advantage for this one.

When she walked in the house she was not surprised to see everyone at the table staring at her.

"Lucy, I asked you not to tell them until I got home."

"You are really not in any position to pass judgment right now Jazzy, so come on and have a seat."

Jasmine rolled her eyes, dropped her bag on the sofa table by the door and headed to have a seat. She took a seat next to Ahmed. He was the least likely to hit her. She was tired, she was emotionally drained and she still had yet to deal with her parents and Derrick. She put her head on Ahmed's shoulder. He put his arm around her and kissed her forehead.

Damon said, "So, let me get this straight. You got tested to see if you were a kidney match for Blake's dad even though he hates you. You kept it from all the people that care about you and who will likely have to help you through your recovery process only to tell them one day before the knife ceremony begins. And because of this they don't have time to take off from work to be there with you. Does that about cover it?"

She squirmed again.

"You guys, I'm sorry. This is just something I had to deal with on my own. I didn't make this decision lightly. I didn't even tell Blake, so don't feel slighted like you missed out on a big juicy secret!"

Carmen asked, "Is that supposed to make us feel better? Jasmine, you are having major surgery tomorrow and couldn't be bothered to tell the people who live in the same house with you?"

Jasmine was so over all of this. Dr. Williams was right. She could not prepare herself for the emotional toll this would take on her. She hadn't even been cut yet and it was a little overwhelming.

Before she could respond Blake and Amber came through the door. All heads turned and Jasmine sat up and noticed Amber still wanted to scratch her eyes out by the steely look she gave her. At this point she was not above slapping her. She needed a release. If Amber wanted to volunteer to give it to her by opening her mouth then so be it. Blake would just have to deal. She was being pulled in too many directions emotionally.

Blake was all smiles.

"Hey guys. Good, you're all here. Did Jaz tell you? I haven't been in this good of a mood in a while."

He walked up behind Jasmine's chair and hugged her then kissed her cheek.

He said, "You are the best thing that ever happened to me beautiful."

Jasmine's eyes met Amber's and Jasmine wasn't shocked to see her trembling with anger. The only person who missed it was Blake because his face was buried in Jasmine's hair. Jasmine smirked as if to say, "I told you so." She regretted it the moment she did it though. Her temper was a nasty one that she wasn't always proud of.

When Blake finally released her he said to Amber, "Hey babe, grab a seat and I'll get you a beer. I probably owe you a foot massage for being with me at the hospital all day."

He never looked at her face. If he had his state of bliss would have fizzled into nothing.

Carmen's loyalty was without a doubt to Jasmine. However she felt so bad for Amber because everyone at the table knew

Jasmine and Blake were in love with each other except for Jasmine and Blake.

It wasn't anything physical. It was a perfect intimacy that not many people found. To her way of thinking that was worse than any physical act of infidelity. Time, space and probably even death couldn't separate their bond.

As long as they had known each other there had never been another woman that could hold a candle to Jasmine in Blake's heart. When Amber came as close as she did Carmen thought that maybe he and Jasmine would remain just friends, but now she didn't know.

They were like opposing magnets. It didn't matter how far they were apart or who was standing in between they always found each other. She felt the pity for Amber stir in her belly and that made her think of Derrick.

Carmen asked, "Jasmine what does Derrick think about all of this?"

Jasmine shot Carmen a look that could liquefy steel. She didn't mind the question, but having this discussion in front of Amber was bound to be ugly.

She sighed, "I haven't told him yet."

Amber just stared at her with a satisfied smugness that made Jasmine want to knock her teeth out.

Carmen cut her eyes, "Jazzy, it's one thing for you not to tell us. It's quite another for you not to tell your significant other."

Defensively Jasmine responded, "Back off okay Carmen. Look, what part of I didn't tell anybody do you guys not understand? I didn't think about the surgery being scheduled so soon after the results. This is a decision that I made about my own body. He's not my husband and while I value his opinion he does not get the final say so."

Damon just shook his head. Ahmed was still stuck on why and as soon as an opening presented itself he would ask it. How can she do something so incredibly unselfish for a person who so obviously didn't deserve it? Lucy had already made her peace with it, but she'd had more time to digest.

Lucy knew how much Jasmine loved Blake and she knew the kind of heart Jasmine had. It only made sense for her to do it.

She knew Jasmine couldn't live with herself if she had sat back and let the poor bastard die.

However, she felt it was indeed time for Blake and Jasmine to stop lying to themselves and hurting people in the process. They needed to face their own internal prejudices that clearly kept them from being together.

Blake came back with a beer for Amber.

"Jasmine, how could you not tell him?"

"Look everybody just stop okay. This is between me and Derrick and I will handle it. Thanks so much for your concern, but I got this," Jasmine said exasperated.

Blake sat down and just stared at her.

"Okay Jaz that was weird. Are you okay?"

Amber interrupted before she could answer.

"Blake I need to go home. Can you walk me out?"

He turned to look at her like she had also lost her mind.

"And what's wrong with you?"

She snapped, "Nothing I've been at the hospital all day and I want to go home."

He took another swig of his beer and then stood up to walk her out. Maybe she and Jasmine were both on their periods, but whatever it was he didn't want any part of it.

When they left Lucy said, "So Amber is ready to beat your behind I see. Can't say I blame the girl."

Jasmine rolled her eyes, "Shut up Lucy."

"Truth hurts. Even with my mouth closed it will still be the truth," Lucy uncharacteristically countered.

Ahmed asked, "Jasmine, seriously, why *exactly* are you doing this?"

She put her head down and screamed. Then she looked up into his dark eyes.

"Ahmed the truth is I am in a position to help so I'm going to do it and it's just that simple."

"But how can you do something like this for someone who is so cruel to you?"

She understood his curiosity.

"The day I walked into the hospital I felt it in my spirit to get tested. I knew I would be a match. I don't always understand

God's plan for my life, but I will always follow it. So you see it doesn't matter how this makes Amber feel, how it makes Derrick feel or even how it makes my parents feel. This is bigger than all of that. This is someone's life. This is chance for him to live the next half of his life very different from the first. This is a chance for a family that has been separated for so long to finally come together and enjoy being a family."

Damon asked, "But how do you know he will use this opportunity for that?"

"Because I have faith in the God that I serve, and let's just say Frank and I have reached an understanding. Now if you all will excuse me I'm going to call my parents. Just send Derrick to my room when he gets here. The surgery is at noon tomorrow. I love you all and everything is going to be okay. I promise."

She left and went upstairs to her room.

∞∞∞∞∞

Outside Amber leaned against her car with her arms folded and a scowl on her face. Blake felt like he was missing an important piece to this attitude puzzle.

"Did something happen between you and Jasmine today Amber?"

She ignored his question but asked one of her own. One she hated that she couldn't just ignore.

"If I asked you to choose between me and Jasmine what would your answer be?"

His head snapped to attention. She saw the fury on his face. He could honestly not believe that she was trying to force him to choose. Not this again.

"Why the hell would you ask me something like that Amber? Are you really that egotistical that you would bring that up the night before my best friend and my dad go under the knife? She could die trying to save his life. I could lose her. I'm sorry, but I have just a little bit more on my plate than your ego at the moment."

He left her standing there and went back in the house without a backward glance. She got in her car then broke down and cried. The pain of his immediate dismissal of her gave her the answer she didn't want to hear. A few minutes later she drove home.

Chapter 19: Buried Feelings

Blake came in the house and slammed the door drawing everyone's attention to him and silencing their conversation. Before they could respond the doorbell rang. Blake opened it irate thinking Amber couldn't take the hint.

"What!"

Derrick stared at him like he was on drugs.

"Uh, is there a problem we need to handle?"

Embarrassed Blake said, "I'm sorry man, thought you were someone else."

Derrick nodded and walked in but didn't see Jasmine.

"Where is she?"

Carmen decided under the circumstances she would ignore his rudeness.

"She's in her room waiting for you."

As Derrick headed to Jasmine's room Blake sat at the table. Before anyone opened their mouths he said, "Don't ask."

∞∞∞

Derrick walked into Jasmine's room without knocking. His attitude with her was not the best and having Blake of all people yell at him at the door didn't help. He knew he obviously thought he was someone else but it still irked him. He momentarily put all that to the side when he focused on Jasmine. She was sitting on her bed, phone in hand crying.

"Babe, what's wrong?"

He startled her. She jerked slightly then relaxed when she saw it was him. She wasn't in the mood anymore. She just wanted this night to be over.

"Come in and please shut the door."

He obliged, came in and sat next to her. He put his arm around her and kissed her temple. She eased out of his embrace to face him.

"Derrick I know we haven't exactly been on the same page the last couple of weeks but I need to tell you something."

The look on her face told him he wasn't going to like it.

"What is it?"

"You know that Blake's father has been in the hospital with kidney failure for the last few weeks."

He nodded curiously.

"Well it turns out that I'm a match and tomorrow I am having surgery to give him one of my kidneys."

He simply stared at her opting out of believing anything she said was true. He laughed but she didn't so he got mad.

"Are you serious?"

"Why would I joke about something like this?"

"You would joke about something like this because I can't imagine why in the world you would give that man a kidney."

She was so tired of justifying herself. And after the tongue lashing her mother gave her she didn't have the energy or the inclination to deal with Derrick. She was deeply disturbed because at the moment she had just realized her mother had some severe racist tendencies.

"Look, my reasons are my own. I am so sorry I'm just telling you but in all fairness everybody who needs to know found out today."

"Oh so you're putting me on the same level as everyone else in your life. Jasmine that's just not gon fly."

The eye roll she just couldn't stop set him off.

"You know what Jasmine, I am so sick of you trying to be good enough for Blake's family. Don't you get it? You a nigga. You gon always be a nigga. Them crackers don't care nothing about you. They don't want you in their family because if they did he would have been with you a long time ago. What, you think giving that ungrateful prick your kidney is going to make him welcome you with open arms? Wake up Jasmine, you are living in a fantasy land and frankly I'm sick of watching you make a fool out of yourself to prove you belong."

She couldn't have been more shocked if he had hauled off and slapped her. The pain of what he assumed was going on was like a sledge hammer to the chest. Knowing he thought so little of her hurt and infuriated her to levels she didn't even know existed.

Her reason for doing this was not about acceptance, it was about love, the love she had for her best friend. It was about helping someone in need. Her tears burned away due to her anger.

She calmly said, "Get out Derrick."

"No, I'm not going anywhere while my future wife slices up her body for some racist bastard to get approval. What about our future? What about our children? Did you think about how all of this would affect that?"

She looked at him like he was on crack. How in the hell could he see her as his future wife when he obviously thought she was some lost little black girl with self-esteem issues that would do anything to be accepted by whitey.

Through clinched teeth she said, "Look at it this way. If I die on the table tomorrow none of this will be relevant or of any importance."

The quick look of shock and panic on his face told her the words had hit their mark.

Before he could say anything she said, "Get the hell out of my house Derrick."

His hesitation caused her to scream it.

"Get out!"

He walked out making sure to slam the door behind him.

Derrick felt as though he was walking the green mile as five sets of eyes stared at him. He didn't say a word but he did give Blake a challenging look. Damon saw Blake go rigid. Damon touched his arm and shook his head. When the door shut behind him Blake stood up to go to Jasmine but Carmen caught his arm.

"No, looks like you've done enough. Let us go. Come on Luce."

Lucy followed her.

Chapter 20: Girl Talk

Lucy and Carmen found Jasmine on her bed crying. They both rushed to her side. Carmen pulled her up and held her as she continued to cry. Jasmine was so confused. She knew without a shadow of a doubt that God had directed her down this path. She couldn't understand why it was filled with constant resistance from everyone around her.

Between Amber, Derrick and her mom she was at her wits end. While Carmen rubbed her back Lucy tried to pull her wild curls away from her face before they were matted from all the crying. Her sobs began to slow and she lifted her head off Carmen's shoulders and wiped at her tear-stained face.

"God why is this so hard?"

Lucy was battling back tears. She couldn't stand to see Jasmine so upset.

Carmen said, "Tell us what happened sweetie."

She chuckled, "Where do I begin?"

Lucy smirked, "How bout we start with Amber."

They laughed.

Jasmine told them what happened at the hospital and how she responded to Amber's threats. She could tell by the stunned looks on their faces that maybe she shouldn't have taken it quite that far.

Lucy asked, "Does Blake know?"

"I didn't tell him and I'm not going to unless I have to. I think it would upset him more that she has so little faith in his love for her."

Lucy said cautiously, "But Jasmine, I know you can understand that any woman would have a problem with her man constantly hugging and kissing on another woman."

"Blake doesn't kiss me."

Carmen said, "He kisses your nose."

Jasmine rolled her eyes, "That is something from a long time ago. It's a habit that's completely innocent. It's no different than him kissing either of you on the forehead."

"Okay, well what about his constantly playing in your hair," Carmen asked.

Jasmine thought back to how that started.

"Again, it's something from our childhood. It's harmless. I don't even think he realizes he's doing it. Look, I don't wanna get into it but playing in my hair calms him down. It's hard to explain."

Lucy and Carmen exchanged a look.

"You are so in denial girl, because if I was Amber I would beat you and Blake's behind for trying me," Lucy said.

Carmen added, "And what about tonight? What about what he said right in front of her?"

"Okay, yeah you got me on that one. When he said it she was the first person I looked at. She wanted to rip my face off. The look on my face probably gave her reason to. What can I do, tell him not to feel anything for me?"

Lucy asked, "Do you really think he would choose you over her if she gave him an ultimatum."

Jasmine sighed, "I know he would because it's what I would do. She can't reach every place that I do. I'm sure if I was her I would likely feel the same way, but I can't erase our past and she can't go back and join it. There is nothing physical between me and Blake."

Carmen said, "See Jasmine, that's what you don't understand. It's the non-physical stuff that makes you a threat to her relationship."

"But I can't change that. I mean Blake and I have stopped doing a lot of stuff we used to do together because we are in relationships but we can't stop being friends."

"Well, he knows something is up between you two. Right before you and Derrick, they had some kinda disagreement because he came back in the house beyond heated and told us he didn't want to talk about it," Carmen said.

Jasmine rolled her eyes.

"What happened between you and Derrick sweetie," Lucy asked.

Jasmine sighed, "Well about six months ago I told him I wanted to stop having sex because I always felt really bad afterwards now that I'm trying to live my life right."

Their faces relayed that they understood his side more than hers.

"Look guys, I know you don't understand or necessarily agree with my choice to commit my life to Christ but it is what it is. If he loves me then he'll wait. That sin was a hard one for me to let go of but when I finally found the strength my mind was made up. But that doesn't matter now because I don't really see myself marrying a man who thinks so little of me."

Jasmine told them about the things Derrick said that led to her yelling for him to get out.

Lucy said, "I'm so sorry Jasmine. If it makes me feel bad I can only imagine how you must feel. But you know this is a really stressful situation and maybe he just said things out of resentment because you didn't tell him about the surgery."

Carmen thought that fate had a sense of humor. Evidently Blake and Jasmine needed help cluing in to their own lives. Wasn't it interesting that they were both having major problems in their respective relationships, and that those problems stemmed from their friendship.

Carmen said, "Jasmine, on the one hand I want to say emotions were high. Let cooler heads prevail and blah, blah, blah."

Jasmine nodded.

"And on the other hand..."

Lucy shot her a look that pleaded for her to stop but Carmen ignored her.

"On the other hand I can't in good conscience give you advice on how to work out your relationship with Derrick when I feel very strongly that you're in love with Blake."

Jasmine threw her hands up, "Oh my God, if one more person says that to me I'm going to punch something, or someone."

She gave Carmen an icy stare.

Carmen shrugged, "I'm sorry, I just call it like I see it. There is no sense in you two continuing to ruin other people's lives in this charade y'all continue to play."

"Carmen for the last time, we are just friends. In all the years I've known him, I have never kissed him. He has never kissed me. We have never even discussed it, purposely or accidentally. Nor have we crossed a sexual line. As far as I know I don't even think he is attracted to me like that and I know I'm not attracted to him sexually. I need y'all to read my lips. There is nothing and will never be anything between me and Blake Michael Jessup. That is the last time I'm going to say it. The next time you will be slapped."

Lucy gave Carmen an, "I told you so" look.

Carmen said, "Heifa please. You are lying if you say you are not attracted to Blake. What is there not to be attracted to?"

Lucy said, "True, he is a hottie. I mean the man could be a double for a Greek god with that thick wavy brown hair and those electric blue eyes. Mmm, can you say yum?"

Carmen laughed, "He is quite delicious after some sun. As a matter of fact all three of our guys are hot."

Lucy said, "Yeah, I mean Damon has that smooth brown skin and green eyes and of course that sexy swag. Ahmed gives off that exotic stranger vibe. He's the kinda man you want to meet on vacation. He blows your mind with pleasure and then you come back home and never speak of it again."

Jasmine just stared in astonishment.

"You lil nasty sluts, and no I haven't noticed because I am simply not attracted to white men. Now of course Blake is handsome but I have never had the desire to jump his bones, unlike you two apparently, so sorry to disappoint you. However, Ahmed and Damon are *very* sexy."

They both looked at her like they didn't believe her.

Carmen said, "You're a racist Jasmine. The two dark skinned men are sexy but you're not attracted to the white guy even though he is just as sexy."

She shook her head and laughed.

With a smirk, Jasmine confessed.

"Okay, okay the one thing I have noticed and it's only because it's not a usual trait for them is the man does have some nice full lips for a white boy. If I were ever to date a white man, it would be because there were no black men left, he would need Blake's mouth. But I swear that's it."

They all laughed.

"I'm sorry to disappoint you guys, I love Blake more than I have ever loved another human being but in a strictly platonic way."

Lucy said, "Well, we should get out of here and let you get yourself together. You have quite the big day tomorrow."

They each gave her a hug. After she thanked them for letting her lean on them, they left her.

Chapter 21: Boys Will Be Boys

Sitting at the table Blake was still upset. He didn't appreciate the way Amber came at him about Jasmine. What more did the girl want? He was all hers. She was not about to dictate to him who his friends were going to be. He also didn't know what the hell was up with Derrick but he was always willing to step outside and handle whatever issue he was having with him.

Damon asked, "Man what the heck is going on? I know all of this drama cannot be over a surgery for your dad?"

"Man, Amber pulls me outside to ruin my mood and out of the blue asks me to choose between her and Jasmine. I mean what the hell?"

Ahmed felt bad for him. He was stuck between a rock and his heart but he couldn't say he was surprised to hear it.

Damon asked, "Well can you blame her?"

"What the hell is that supposed to mean?"

Damon shook his head.

"It means what I asked. How you expect the girl to feel when you hug and kiss Jasmine right in front of her and tell her she is the best thing that ever happened to you?"

Blake was about to defend himself when the gravity of what he had done hit him. He muttered his favorite expletive.

Damon said, "Exactly. Man that girl has a right to feel how she feels."

"I am not cheating on her with Jasmine," Blake argued defensively."

Ahmed's calm voice said, "Yeah you are."

Blake looked at him in disbelief.

"Jaz and I have never even kissed let alone done anything else. Besides I don't even see her like that and if you haven't noticed she kinda has a preference for black men."

Damon shook his head.

Ahmed said, "Blake, it's not about sex. It's about the fact that Jasmine comes before Amber and always will. You're in a relationship with her but she's not first."

Blake swallowed hard.

"Jasmine has been a constant in my life ever since I can remember. I can't just walk away from her and I can't change what she's been to me either. I love Amber and I want to be with her but she has to accept Jasmine as a part of my life."

Damon added, "If you and Jasmine just admit what y'all feel for each other then all this mess would be done and over with."

Blake threw his hands up in exasperation. He was so over people telling him what he and Jasmine felt for each other. They never kept secret what they felt for each other. Isn't that why everybody was tripping now?

He said, "I've never lied about what I feel for Jasmine but everyone else doesn't think it can stop there. They think it has to go beyond that to the physical and it doesn't."

Ahmed asked, "So you can honestly sit here and say you're not attracted to Jasmine?"

Damon laughed, "Hell no he can't. Jasmine gives off that exotic vibe. She is hot!"

Blake laughed, "Guys don't get me wrong. I think Jasmine is beautiful but I don't see her like that. I mean, I think all our girls are beautiful."

Damon said, "Yep! Carmen is sexy because she doesn't know how hot she really is."

Ahmed agreed and said, "Lucy's hot too but she's so tiny you might break her."

Damon laughed and pounded Ahmed's fist.

Blake said, "Um, can we focus."

They both laughed again.

"Jasmine is the girl that always steals and wears my sweats. She's the girl that used to run around and play every sport, climb every tree and go on every single stupid adventure I could think of. We did everything together. I loved her because she was fearless. She's not a whiny girl and she's not afraid of her own shadow. Anything I could do, she tried to do better. I see Jasmine as just one of my boys. With really nice tits, now those I have noticed," he laughed.

Damon laughed, "Okay you see her as your homie. I can understand that white boys are breast men, but Jasmine's got a booty that crosses all racial and friendship lines."

Blake laughed, "Um, I'm not really into that sort of thing."

"Man whatever, you ain't gotta be into that to take notice of it when it's in your face. Besides, trust me when I say you can learn to get into that." Blake choked on his beer. "All those times y'all have slept in the same bed together, nothing?"

Blake raised his right hand as if to swear, "Nothing."

He received looks that said they didn't believe him, but it didn't matter because he was telling the truth.

"Well a black man, or should I say a half black man, couldn't always be around that without being tempted to his put hands on it," Damon said.

Ahmed said, "A Middle Eastern man either."

They all laughed.

"Jasmine and I didn't sleep in the same bed often as adults and we don't do it anymore. We're in relationships. We don't purposely try to disrespect the other's relationship. It's all about perception."

"I catch y'all asleep pretty often on the couch," Ahmed said.

Blake shook his head, he just couldn't win.

Ahmed continued, "On quite a few occasions I come home late and find you two lying on the couch. Jasmine's head is on your chest and you have one arm wrapped around her and your other hand in her hair. I'm just saying it looks like a lover's embrace to me."

"If I was Derrick I would whip yo white behind for always having your hands in my woman's hair," Damon chided.

Blake reluctantly admitted, "I love Jasmine's hair. That is one of the things that fascinated me about her when we were kids. Now I will admit, I have a thing for her curls and I love playing in her hair but I swear it's innocent."

They stared at him because that answer wasn't satisfactory.

Blake said, "Okay, so here is the real scoop, again it's something from our childhood. Damon you know all the crap I went through with my dad in high school. Well trust me it started a lot earlier and it was a lot worse. Whenever I was upset playing in

Jaz's hair calmed me down, and that's how we would fall asleep. I guess old habits die hard. I will try to be more conscious of my actions."

"So what are you going to do about Amber," Damon asked?

"I don't know. I guess we will all have to sit down and come to some sort of compromise because I love Amber and I want to be with her."

Ahmed asked, "Does Derrick give her any grief about you?"

"Not to my knowledge. He did ask me if I thought Jasmine would say yes if he proposed a few months ago. I told him to go for it but after tonight I don't know if that's still on the table."

Damon eyed him suspiciously and asked, "So just between us, if you had to choose who would it be?"

The answer hit his heart instantly as well as his head, Jasmine. The answer didn't disturb him but he did wonder what it meant exactly. He couldn't dwell on that now. Instead of flat out lying to them, he simply shrugged.

Chapter 22: A Change is Gonna Come

Jasmine felt very vulnerable as she lay in the hospital gown in the bed awaiting them to wheel her into prep for surgery. She was extremely nervous and had spent every spare minute praying for God to make everything alright.

Her initial thoughts about this didn't lead her to how many people would actually be affected by her decision. Her mom had nearly disowned her saying how stupid she was and how she was ruining her future with a man who loved her by making a selfish decision for someone who couldn't care less about her.

Derrick revealed parts of himself to her that she didn't like. Her best friends were breathing down her neck about some fictional fantasy they had about her and Blake becoming a couple. Amber was ready to actually fight her and over Blake of all people. Her world was spinning so far out of control she didn't know which way was up or down.

"God, I'm trusting you to bring me out on the other side victorious, and could you please touch Frank's heart and un-harden it. Heal him of whatever pain he is dealing with."

Her prayer was cut short as her dad came into her room. She had an hour before surgery and this was the time she got to spend with her family, though she didn't exactly think anyone would be coming.

She smiled at her handsome father, "Hi daddy!"

"Hey baby girl. How you doing?"

She wanted to cry but didn't.

"I'm holding it down daddy. I'm alright."

"Baby, you need to know there are some things you don't understand that your mama is going through. I promise you soon we will all sit down and talk about this and even though she is being stubborn and didn't come in protest, she's been texting me every two seconds asking about you."

Jasmine smiled, "Thanks daddy. Can I ask you something?"

"What is it honey?"

"I know my walk with God is only a couple years old, but if he told me to do this why is it so hard? Why is everybody I love mad at me?"

Her father sighed the sigh of man who had been through many battles and lived to tell about them.

"Baby, if this is what God told you to do then you can't let what you feel based on what you see determine your faith in God. If you know this is God then you need to know the enemy is not happy about whatever God is working out. He will throw every curve ball at you to make you doubt. But you must never doubt that God will come through. You won't always understand while you're in the storm, but when you're out of it God's hand will reveal itself to you more clearly than anything you have ever seen."

His words were like a soothing salve to an aching wound.

"Okay daddy, I know this is what I'm supposed to do so I won't be moved."

He kissed her forehead.

There was a knock at the door. Derrick stepped in carrying a bouquet of pink snapdragons, her favorite. Her father could see she was genuinely shocked to see him and decided to make himself scarce.

"I'll be here when you get back. I love you."

"Love you too daddy, and thanks."

Derrick exchanged greetings with Justin as he exited. He handed her the flowers and despite her desire to stay mad at him she sniffed them. He pulled a chair to her bedside and took a seat. She refused to speak first. He grabbed her hand. She laid the flowers down on the table next to the bed.

"Jasmine, I don't know what to say. Sorry doesn't seem appropriate, but I am. I had some time to think when I cooled off and to be honest this is just like you. I know you couldn't live with yourself if you let him die because of his feelings. You always have to do the right thing no matter what it costs you. That's not a bad thing but sometimes it's a tough pill to swallow. Loving someone who loves as hard as you has its downsides. I don't know what your reasons for doing this is and I'm not really sure they would matter because I still wouldn't want you to do it. But I accept that it's not my choice to make. The way I distanced myself from you after you cut off the sex I guess I can't blame you for not having me on speed dial. Realizing there was a chance I could lose you made me come to my senses very quickly."

He sighed like he had a heavy burden on his heart.

"Jasmine, the bottom line is I love you very much and I want to be with you. I want to work this out. I want a future with you. I know there are some things we need to work out but I'm willing to make the sacrifices if you are?"

She didn't cry. She was all cried out for the moment but said, "Thank you for being here. I appreciate you being honest with me. I love you too. I really do hope we can work out our differences and find our way back to each other."

He stood to kiss her. The kiss was full of passion and she could feel the love he felt for her in it, but she was scared that something had been broken and she didn't know if it could be fixed. She would try her best to make the sacrifices though because she really wanted to be with him. He broke the kiss and stared into her eyes.

Another knock at the door produced Blake. He could tell he was interrupting a private moment and was about to excuse himself. Derrick saw the way Jasmine's face lit up at the sight of Blake and suddenly he wanted out of the room. Blake spoke. Derrick just nodded.

As Blake headed to Jasmine's side Derrick twisted the rod on the blinds to open them slightly because he wanted to see with his own eyes just what was between his woman and this man. He knew they were close but lately he had the feeling they were a lot closer than he originally thought.

Blake and Jasmine were none the wiser that not only was Derrick standing at the window but so was Amber. As always their complete attention was focused on each other. Blake sat in the chair Derrick had just vacated and grabbed Jasmine's hand.

"Hey beautiful. How you doing?"

"I'm a little nervous but I'm okay. How's your dad?"

"He's actually doing well. He's in a much better mood than normal."

She was glad to hear it.

"Looks like I sorta, maybe made up with Derrick."

They laughed.

"Well I went over to Amber's late last night or should I say this morning. We are not seeing eye-to-eye but we're *definitely* making progress."

She swatted his shoulder.

"Your nasty behind went over there and sexed the poor girl out."

He laughed.

"I don't know what you're talking about, but I will say for the moment I am back in her good graces."

He wiggled his eyebrows mischievously and made her laugh. Out of habit he began to stroke her curls. She put her hand on his face.

"What is it love," she asked.

He smiled that crooked smile she loved.

"You know, sometimes it's annoying how well you know me."

She laughed, "Spit it out. I know there is a confession on that tongue of yours."

"Jasmine, I love you so much. I can't imagine loving you more, but then you do something like this and it staggers me. What did I ever do to deserve to have you in my life?"

This time she did cry. Blake wiped her tears with his thumb and then kissed her nose. He kissed the palm of the hand he held.

She said, "I'm familiar with the feeling."

He grinned.

She asked, "Wanna hear a secret?"

He laughed remembering when they were nine years old.

"Sure."

She whispered, "You're my favorite person in the whole world."

He gave her a wide toothy grin that made her laugh.

"Okay, seriously B enough with the mushy stuff. What are we gonna do about Amber?"

"Uh what are we going to do about Derrick?"

She rolled her eyes, "Derrick isn't trying to fight you."

He wasn't so sure about that but he didn't want to upset her so he kept that to himself. He didn't want to talk about this but he knew Jasmine was trying to clear her conscience before her operation.

"I don't know Jaz. If I give her what she wants I'm unhappy and if I don't then she's unhappy."

"I hate that you guys are fighting because of me. I guess she told you about our altercation."

He narrowed his gaze.

"Yeah she did and did you have to go there Jaz?"

"In my defense Blake I tried to take the high road but she actually got in my face and threatened me. You know my temper."

He sighed, because he knew the minute Amber challenged her Jasmine made sure to shut her down and to shut her down hard. Jasmine hated to lose an argument. When she was pushed, Jasmine's words could pack a bigger punch than the right hook he'd taught her.

"I don't know what else we can do. It's not like we hang out a lot now," Jasmine said.

"Jaz, you're going to be in recovery for the next few weeks. I'm not going to leave you now."

"Blake, you are not the only person who can help take care of me."

"Jaz, you've always been my responsibility?"

"Your girlfriend is desperately screaming for your attention and she needs to be your responsibility. I need to be Derrick's. This isn't high school or our first crushes and Amber is not Melissa. This is the first woman who you actually made a commitment to since high school. I can't just let you throw that away."

He let out a deep breath. He knew she was right. They had to do something until their significant others felt secure. He realized letting go of her would be harder than he could ever imagine. How do you trust just anybody with what was most precious to you? He laid his head on her stomach and looked up at her.

"Promise me I won't completely lose you Jasmine. If you make it an official promise I know I can trust it."

She always knew the day would come when they would have to share their lives with others, but the thought of losing him was a pain she wasn't prepared for. She stroked his hair away from his face as he closed his eyes.

"I promise."

She sat up and laid a lingering kiss on his temple.

Blake asked, "Hey how come you always kiss me on my temple?"

Jasmine smiled, "I don't know but I'm doing it now so I'll always be on your mind and you won't forget me since we're breaking up."

She tried to bring humor into the situation but it didn't work. Neither of them could find it funny. The pain of their separation was just beginning.

∞∞∞∞

Amber was fit to be tied as she stormed away from the window. She couldn't hear their conversation but their body language spoke volumes. When she walked into the waiting area she saw Jasmine's father and immediately turned to head back and ran into Derrick.

"Hey, hey, come on now, calm down. Let's just have a seat okay. This isn't the time or the place to honestly express yourself."

She knew he was right but she was very close to not caring. How could Blake come to her last night and make love to her making it clear that he chose her just to turn around and still need something else from Jasmine?

She was a good woman to Blake and she didn't understand it. It made her mad that she couldn't stop her tears. Derrick gave her a sympathetic pat on her shoulder.

"I don't think I can handle this. I just can't. I know he loves me, but not like he loves her. I can't take this anymore. How do you stand it?"

She saw his other fist was clinched. It made her feel a little better. Derrick was fuming. Jasmine was not going to make a fool out of him. He decided it was either him or Blake. He was more than confident Jasmine would choose him. No woman of his would ever be that close to another man.

"I honestly didn't know it was this bad. I mean I knew they were close but they've gone just a bit too far in my opinion. Don't worry. I'll take care of it. After this is all over, Jasmine will be making some changes in her life and you and I will be the beneficiaries of those changes."

Amber nodded. *Finally,* someone was on her side. She left a very irritated Derrick to go wash her face before Blake came back.

Chapter 23: A Pain like No Other

Jasmine and Frank were side by side in their hospital beds awaiting anesthesia. Her heart was breaking because her friendship with Blake was about to change in a way that she knew it needed to, but one that she wasn't sure she could actually handle. Blake was her world and the thought of giving him up was shattering her soul. She *needed* him in her life.

She knew Derrick was a good man. She really loved him, but he just wasn't her best friend. Blake knew the worst of her and accepted her without condition. Maybe Derrick would if he knew but she would never tell him to find out.

Her heart was also filled with joy because she was excited for Frank and everything that life would have in store for him now that he had this new outlook. Her emotions were stretched to capacity in opposite directions.

It hurt her so bad that she wouldn't be able to be there for Blake as his new relationship with his father began. How could she abandon him when she knew he would need her, but that was no longer her job, it was Amber's. Fate was cruel. Leaving him to face that without her made her throat burn.

Weakly Frank said, "Jasmine."

She turned to look at him and managed a smile. He reached out his hand. She grabbed it. No words were exchanged just an understanding that made her genuinely smile. Masks were put on their faces and shortly after everything went black.

∞∞∞∞

In the waiting room sat Blake, Amber, Lisa, Derrick and Justin. Lisa could tell that Amber was very upset and she was sure it had something to do with Jasmine. She honestly felt bad for her because she genuinely liked her, she just preferred Jasmine for a daughter-in-law. However, the way Derrick was eyeing Blake she didn't think he would be letting Jasmine go anytime soon.

Justin saw the same thing. It was something he and Lisa shared. He too preferred Blake for a son-in-law because he had practically raised the young man. He knew, without a shadow of a doubt, the content of his character because he helped put it there.

There had always seemed to be an innate desire for Blake to protect Jasmine. He never could explain it, but he knew it was there. If his daughter was with Blake his mind would always be at ease for her well-being.

He knew his wife preferred Derrick. Even though he hated to admit it, the only thing that Derrick had on Blake in his wife's eyes was his chocolate skin. Vanessa knew Blake was better for Jasmine, but she couldn't let go of her past issues to admit it. It didn't seem to matter anyway. Jasmine wasn't even in the room and Amber seemed to have a death grip on Blake's arm. Oh well, it wasn't in his power to control.

He whispered, "Lord, have your way."

Blake was in unspeakable pain though you wouldn't know it just by looking at him. Having a father that didn't care for him to show emotion taught him how to keep his face void of the truth. He loved Amber. He really did, but it was a violation to his heart knowing that he and Jasmine had to part ways. He knew it was the right thing to do.

It wasn't fair to the other people in their lives, but how was it fair to him and Jasmine? He knew Amber had been crying. It was killing him to know he was the cause. He also knew he was the cure. Amber could never understand him the way Jasmine did because he wasn't willing to open up those scars to anybody else. He didn't have to open them up to Jasmine because she was there when they happened. She even shared a few of them.

He knew Jasmine wouldn't tell Derrick about the baby. Who was going to be with her on their kid's birthday? Wasn't that funny that he still thought of the baby as their kid? The thought of her doing that alone broke his heart. He excused himself to get some air.

He stepped out through the double doors and breathed in the fresh afternoon air. He leaned against the wall willing himself to get it together as he closed his eyes. Derrick walked outside with purpose in his stride.

He stood staring at Blake leaning against the wall.

He said, "Blake, I need to holla at you about a few things."

Startled, Blake opened his eyes and locked them with Derrick's. This was a man who obviously was looking for a confrontation. For the first few moments they both sized the other up. They were eye to eye at six-foot-three-inches. Blake was lean but Derrick knew that was misleading because he was all muscle.

Derrick had him by at least 80 pounds and he was no slouch on the muscle tone either. Blake decided to wait for Derrick to speak first.

Derrick cleared his throat and closed in the space between them so they could have a *private* conversation.

He said, "I think it's time you and I have an understanding where my woman is concerned."

Blake arched an eyebrow but didn't respond.

Derrick continued, "I understand that y'all are so called best friends but you've taken it too far. I do not appreciate your hands in her hair nor the fact that you continually kiss her. Every time I turn around your hands are on her in one way or another. It's inappropriate. She is a woman in a relationship and I'm pretty sure *your woman* would agree."

It was deja-vu for Blake. He and his boys had just had this conversation. Still, he didn't like the way dude was all in his face. He tried to put himself in Derrick's shoes or even Amber's, but all that logic went out the window because it was Jasmine. With her all bets were off.

Blake said, "She might be your woman but she is *my* friend. No matter whom she is with that fact will *never* change. You're disposable, I'm not. I understand that you and Amber are feeling a certain way about this, but we can't change the fact that your perception is not the reality. There is nothing going on between us. I'm really starting to get sick of having to explain myself."

Derrick was two seconds from knocking this cat out.

He said, "Look homie, I'm not about to tell you again. She's mine, stay away from her or else?"

"Or else what? Have you talked to Jasmine about this? Are you sure this is what *she* wants?"

"It doesn't matter what Jasmine wants. This is unacceptable behavior, period. Look dawg, you've been warned and with me you only get one. Next time I'll find a different way to communicate."

Blake was itching to deck him. He reigned in some restraint.

Blake replied, "We both know Jasmine is not one to take orders. It's a good thing the only person that is actually relevant understands that. Ultimately your tantrum is pointless because I *know* I'll never lose her. Can you say the same thing?"

Blake saw Derrick's first clench. He raised his chin and dared him to act on it. Derrick had to control his temper. Now was not the time or the place.

"Like I said, I don't issue second notices."

Derrick walked back into the hospital.

Blake was ready to hit something, anything.

Nurse Ashley walked outside looking for her next assignment.

She spotted Blake and said, "Hey there blue eyes. Guess you're waiting for your girl to get out of surgery?"

She surprised him but then he recognized her.

"Yeah, they're in now. I just needed a bit of fresh air."

She eyed him skeptically. The man looked ready to blow and like he had literally just lost his best friend. Blake hadn't felt the need to keep up the pretense now that he was away from the watchful eyes of Amber and Derrick. For the second time in less than a month he wanted to cry.

Nurse Ashley walked over to him. She put her hand on his shoulder and looked very deeply into his eyes. It was beyond bizarre, but he couldn't really seem to break the stare of those incredibly sparkling hazel eyes.

Her touch sent warmth all through his body and was very comforting. It was disconcerting actually that this stranger could bring him comfort when she couldn't possibly know what was wrong. He felt such a peace overtake him and his anger dissipated.

She said, "I know it's hard to let her go son but trust in the Lord with all your heart and lean not unto your own understanding. In all your ways acknowledge Him and He will direct your path."

Blake swallowed hard. If God was trying to get his attention, He officially had it.

He asked her, "Who are you?"

"Someone who has known you for a long time."

He simply gawked.

She smiled, "All things will be revealed in time."

She walked back into the hospital. He stood there for a moment dumbfounded and then rushed in after her to find out who she really was because she sure as hell wasn't a nurse.

A few steps in he ran right into Amber.

"Hey, slow down. Where are you heading off to in such a rush?"

She couldn't have just disappeared.

He said, "I was looking for someone."

"Who?"

"Never mind, it's nothing."

"Are you okay Blake?"

"Yeah Amber I'm fine. I just needed a minute to breathe that's all," he snapped.

She raised her hands in surrender, "Okay fine. Get your air, whatever I'm going home."

His favorite curse word danced off his lips.

He yelled toward her retreating back.

"Amber I'm sorry."

She turned back and saw how much agony he seemed to be in. She went to him and just held him. She had never seen him so vulnerable. This was a part of him she wasn't privileged to see.

He could feel how much she loved him in her touch and he was grateful for it. It wasn't the same kind of comfort Jasmine gave him, but he was still grateful for it. He thought, *okay God if this is you talking to me then this is me finally willing to listen. I honestly have no idea what to do. Please help me see what I'm supposed to see.*

Chapter 24: Detox

Jasmine had been home from surgery for two weeks. She was very tired but for the most part her recovery was on schedule. Frank's body accepted her kidney without any complications. He was getting stronger every day. Derrick took a week off from work and was by her side the entire week. For the other week her roommates were there for her with whatever she needed.

Derrick took walks with her in between her naps and to all her doctor appointments. They were really starting to get back some of what had been missing in their relationship. She was thankful for all that Derrick did for her, but as much as she loved Derrick, it just wasn't the same. She missed Blake so much it hurt.

She hadn't had a moment alone with him since before the surgery. She did see him after but Amber was practically joined to his hip. They didn't have a moment to talk. She could tell something was seriously bothering him, but they agreed to back off and work on their individual relationships.

She wanted to talk to him about his dad. She wanted to know about his current cases. She wanted to know all the things that she would normally know before the great divide.

There was something good that came out of all of this. Frank was really trying hard to keep his end of the bargain. They made a deal to talk on the phone once a week. Their first conversation was kinda short and revolved mostly around their recovery process. Since Derrick insisted she stay in bed as much as possible she had only seen Blake once. He was headed out when she did.

He'd sent her texts to check on her, but that was it. She imagined this was what an amputee patient went through. They could still feel the limb itching even when it wasn't there. She felt like a part of her was missing.

She'd sent Derrick out to get her some butter pecan ice cream so that he would stop hovering and she could walk around her own house unsupervised. She walked into the dining room to sit at the table just because. She hadn't had a meal anywhere but in her room for two weeks. She was so over the helpless patient act. Carmen came through the door.

"Hey Jazzy, it's good to see you up and out of that room."

"Heeeeeeeyyyyy Carmen! Please come sit," Jasmine begged. "Tell me everything that's going on even if normally I wouldn't wanna hear it."

Carmen laughed and took a seat across from her.

"You ain't fooling nobody Ms. Lady. You are having Blake withdrawals because he hasn't stayed at his own house in two weeks."

Jasmine's face answered for her.

"If it makes you feel any better he had that same look on his face when we had lunch earlier this week."

There was no point in denying it, especially not to Carmen, she smirked.

"I'm going crazy Carmen. I miss him so much."

Carmen got up to take the chair next to her. Jasmine leaned her head on her shoulder.

"How do I do this?"

Carmen felt for her just like she felt for Blake. She had no idea what was blocking their vision from the obvious, but she told her the same thing she told him. Carmen was never one for displaying emotions. With her it was always logic.

"You made a decision to accept the love that someone is willing to give you. You made a decision to move forward with your life. So that's what you're going to do. You're going to move forward and be happy."

"Easier said than done," Jasmine said with a pout, "Maybe if I didn't quit cold turkey. I need to be weaned off him Carmen. I can't talk to Derrick about this. He would flip. The person I would normally talk to about this is the one person I can't talk to. I swear we did not think this through."

"You know what Jasmine, you and Blake are like a carbon copy of each other. Do you want to keep Derrick or give him up?"

"I wanna keep him."

"Okay, then stop whining and deal with it. It's not forever. You will get to see him again."

"It won't be the same though."

With some attitude Carmen said, "Jasmine, suck it up. You made your choice and I'm not going to baby you through this process."

Jasmine put her head down on the table, took in a really deep breath and sat back up again.

"You're right. I'll just have to deal."

∞∞∞

Blake and Damon were having a drink after work. They were sitting at a booth in the back of the crowded restaurant. The look on Blake's face was almost too much for Damon to bear. He honestly felt bad for both of them.

Damon asked, "You miss her huh?"

"Like I'd miss my left nut. Man I don't know how I'm gonna do this."

Damon laughed hard. But he really wanted to choke some sense into him. He honestly didn't know why they couldn't see it.

"Except for when we first started college this is the longest I have gone without talking to her or seeing her. It's really irritating me because people are telling me that I can't see her. I just want to hear her voice and see that smile of hers. I have so much to tell her. Stuff that only she would understand."

"Did you ever try and give Amber the chance to see if she would understand?"

A little defensively Blake said, "It's not that simple."

"Actually it is. If you love her like you say you do it should be that simple."

His friend's words stung.

"I hear you man but some things are easier said than done."

"Look Blake, you know I love you and Jasmine very much but dude, I can only help you if you're willing to help yourself."

Blake took a sip of his drink and pinched the bridge of his nose. He closed his eyes as he let out a hard breath.

"Derrick got in my face about it at the hospital. You were right. He was ready to pound on me."

"I told you that."

"Right or wrong I wasn't about to just sit back and let him hit me because his pride was hurt."

Damon extended his fist for a bump.

"No doubt."

Blake laughed and said, "I can't believe I'm taking advice about my love life from you of all people. You run from commitment like it's the plague."

"I might be trifling in that regard, but if I ever had what you had with Jasmine I wouldn't hesitate to make her mine and accept it for the beautiful blessing it is. I have never seen anything so perfect between two people."

Coming from Damon those words were sobering, but it just wasn't like that. He didn't want to be with Jasmine. He just wanted to be able to keep her as his best friend *and* be with the woman he loved.

Blake said, "Guess I'll just have to play the hand I've been dealt. Time heals all wounds right?"

"So they say."

Blake didn't believe for one second that there was any amount of time that could remove Jasmine from his heart.

Chapter 25: I Miss You Much

Jasmine always tried not to lie to herself so she did deal. It had been six weeks. Today was her first day back at work and it felt great. She and Frank were still having their weekly conversations.

Through him she found out that he and Blake had gone out to lunch twice and regularly had dinner. She was so excited for Frank. He seemed really genuine in his desire to develop a relationship with his son. She wanted to talk to Blake. Not over the phone, not via text and not with his or her warden standing between them.

She was practically wishing just to sit down with her best friend and say, "Hey how you doing?" Was it too much to ask? She had come into the shop a couple hours early to get caught up on paper work and any changes that had taken place.

She was there for about 30 minutes when there was a knock at the door. She had no idea who could be coming to get their hair done this early but she would politely decline. She walked out of her office and stopped when she saw the man in the tailored navy blue suit through the blinds on the glass door.

She rushed to unlock the door. He flashed that crooked smile and she grinned.

She confessed, "I was just wishing for you."

"A little birdie named Lucy text me and said if I was as miserable as you were then I should know that you were coming into the shop early today."

He walked in closed and locked the door behind him. He slid his hands in his pockets not sure what to do with them.

She said, "You look like my next breath."

He responded, "You look like the comfort of home."

"So what brings you by?"

He shrugged then soberly said, "I needed you."

She was in his arms. Hers were wrapped tight around his neck, his wrapped tight around her waist. He ran his hands through those gorgeous black curls and kissed her nose when they released their long embrace. She gently pushed his hair away from his face and kissed his temple.

Blake said, "Come on let's sit, I gotta be in the office in an hour."

He realized how much he missed her smile when she flashed it.

"Okay, on the couch in the waiting area."

She dragged him by the hand to the gray leather sofa.

She said excitedly, "So tell me everything love!"

He laughed, "Where do I start?"

"With your dad, tell me how it's going."

He beamed, "It's actually going really good. We've been to lunch a few times and Amber and I go over for dinner once a week."

"Aww, B, I already knew that, tell me something I don't know."

He looked at her perplexed, "How did you know that?"

So Frank hadn't told him about their conversations.

"I talk to your dad once a week on the phone. It's part of our agreement for us to get to know each other for your sake. That was of course before we banned ourselves from each other," she laughed.

He was stunned. All this time she still found a way to have his back.

"Jaz, you've been talking to him all this time?"

"Uh yeah. You didn't think I would let you go at this alone did you? I had to make sure he was doing his part." He just stared. "Come on B, don't be mad. The man was terrified. I had to help him. I knew it would be a lot for you to deal with and I wanted to help in some way. Please don't be mad, please."

God he loved her.

"How could you know how much I needed you?"

She relaxed, "Because you're in my spirit."

He grabbed her hand and held it.

"Well, the first thing he told me was that there was a reason why he was the way he was. He wanted to tell me but he just wasn't there yet. He asked me to tell him how I felt about him and to be honest."

Jasmine looked surprise, "You mean like everything?"

He nodded.

"So did you tell him?"

"Yeah, I told him that I hated him for a long time more so for what he did to you than to me. I told him I hated how he treated you like a piece of crap just because you didn't look like him. I told him how I was ashamed to be his son and how I always went to your dad instead because he was the kind of father I deserved and just to add insult to injury that a black man was helping raise his son."

"Ouch Blake, how did he take that?"

"Surprisingly well actually. I mean I could tell it devastated his pride but I guess he's trying to make amends. I told him when I got grown though I didn't want it to be like that because although I love your dad and I'm so grateful for him stepping in, I wanted to have that with my own father. I wanted the kind of relationship with my father that you had with yours. He apologized for the beatings too."

She rubbed his arm, "Sweetie, I'm so happy you guys are making progress."

"Oh, you don't know the half of it. We actually hugged for the first time in over 20 years that day."

The next part choked him up and he had to steady himself before he said it.

"What is it Blake? You can tell me."

"Jaz, he told me he loved me for the first time ever that I can remember."

He paused then said with conviction, "I've forgiven him Jaz. I forgave my dad."

She couldn't stop the tears from falling if she was paid to. He buried his face in her neck. She held him and stroked his hair while whispering comforting words in his ear. She knew this was the reason why he was here. She held him tight as he let it all go. She understood now what her daddy meant by after the storm you can see God's hand. The price she paid was well worth it. She had no regrets.

"I am so happy for you love."

After several minutes he pulled away from her and wiped the tears he couldn't manage to keep from surfacing. He felt free.

"Jaz, I've been holding that in for two weeks. You're the only person I could do that in front of. Thanks for everything. This wouldn't be possible without you."

She smiled, "This wouldn't be possible without God."

It made him think of the nurse.

"Hey, you remember the blonde nurse with the amazing eyes?"

"Yes," she said excitedly, "Oh my God, the strangest thing happened. I can't believe I didn't tell you. I had a dream while I was under the anesthesia. It was crazy. You remember when we were little and you used to sneak over to my house at night when you had nightmares?"

He nodded.

"In the dream I had a view of the street between our houses. It was so dark and scary out there. Then I saw you coming from your bedroom window but you weren't alone. Nurse Ashley was holding your hand as you walked across the street. She stood at the bottom of the lattice as she watched you climb up to my bedroom window."

He simply stared at her in disbelief remembering what the nurse had told him.

"When I got out of surgery she was the first person I saw. She whispered in my ear do not be afraid for God has not given you a spirit of fear but of power, love and a sound mind. Then I remembered falling back asleep. When I asked for her later on they said there wasn't a nurse by that name. It was the weirdest thing, but since I had just been heavily sedated I don't think anyone paid me any attention."

"I don't want you to think I'm crazy now," Blake said, "But I think she was like an angel or something."

She looked at him like he was touched, "Or something."

He proceeded to tell her what happened the day of her surgery.

"Whoa that is eerie. Do you think we actually encountered a real angel?"

"I don't know, you tell me. You're the one that's best friends with Jesus, ask Him."

She laughed.

"Well babes, maybe God is trying to get your attention."

He laughed, "Maybe He is trying to get both our attention."

For some reason that statement gave her an itch between the shoulders that she didn't like, Jasmine changed the subject.

"So are things better with Amber?"

"Yeah we're doing pretty good though I am starting to miss my own space. I mean if I wanted to be married already I would propose."

She laughed.

He continued, "But enough about me, how have you been? Did you get the spa day I got for you and the girls? I felt bad I wasn't there to take care of you."

"Yeah I did and thank you so much. We really enjoyed it. You're so good to me." She kissed his temple. "I'm good. Nothing much to tell because I have been on restriction for the last six weeks," she rolled her eyes.

"How's Derrick?"

"He's been amazing actually. A little overprotective at times, but he's redeemed himself."

"You know he wants to propose to you?"

"Yeah, he's kinda been throwing hints."

"Are you gonna say yes."

She smiled, "That's the plan."

She looked happy. He wouldn't tell her about their confrontation. He looked down at their joined hands. She did too.

"I really hate that I can't have my cake and eat it too."

She said, "I miss you too. It's almost unbearable."

"Tell me about it. Is this gonna be what our lives will be like, sneaking around to see each other just to catch up?"

"I know, it sucks Blake but what can we do?"

"I guess there isn't anything to do."

She grinned, "Hey do you remember that time when we were nine and they..."

"...tried to separate us," he finished her thought. "I couldn't forget it if I tried. So you think that's the solution, running away?"

She sighed, "I wish we could love but it's just a nice thought."

Blake laughed.

"We were so serious. I thought they were gonna beat our behinds for stealing your brother's money."

Jasmine laughed. It felt so good to laugh with him.

"But we were gonna pay it back when we got jobs."

"Oh right, at age nine we were going to find work."

They both laughed thinking of their childhood coup. She leaned her head on his shoulder. He put his arm around her and kissed her hair. After all these years it still smelled like coconuts. He started playing in her hair to indulge himself while he had the opportunity.

With a heavy sigh he asked, "Jaz, what are you going to do on the baby's birthday?"

He felt her go stiff in his arms and pulled her in closer.

"I don't know. I've tried not to think about it."

"Do you think you will ever tell Derrick?"

"No, I don't think I can. I don't ever want to tell another soul."

"Jasmine, he is going to be your husband. This is probably something you might want to tell him."

She got defensive, "You mean just like you told Amber about your dad?"

"I'm not about to propose to her, but touché."

"What does that say about me that I can see myself marrying him but I can't see myself being completely honest with him?"

"The same thing it says about me I guess."

She chuckled, "Aren't we the perfect pair?"

"Ha. Yeah, maybe the guys were right about us. Our lives would be easier if we could just be together."

His comment sent a small panic through her. It made him a little uncomfortable that he'd said it. He had no idea where it came from.

He changed the subject.

"The day you had the abortion I prayed for you."

Her head popped up. She looked at him in shock.

He chuckled.

"I know right. See, that's how much I love you. I was willing to talk to God just for you even though I had sworn him off."

She laughed and was very touched.

"What did you pray for?"

"I asked him if He would fix you, make you okay, then I would forgive you and never leave your side."

She was in awe of him at that moment. She laid her hand over her heart.

He continued, "He did His part and now I feel like I'm breaking my promise to God."

"Blake, you didn't break your promise. You have never left my side and I'm grateful. This is just the next phase of our lives. I don't feel like you abandoned me and I hope you don't feel like I abandoned you. I will always be here if you need me. It doesn't matter how much time or space comes between us. We can always pick up where we left off."

He put his forehead on hers and sighed.

"You promised me that I wouldn't completely lose you."

"And I meant it."

"Sometimes it feels like it."

"I know it does sweetie, but even when you can't see me, I'm there. I always got your back. Have a little faith."

He nodded then said, "On the baby's birthday I'll always be there with you if you need me. Both of them will just have to have a fit and we can figure out something to tell them, but I will not leave you to deal with it alone. If you don't want anybody else to know you don't have to tell anyone and you know I'll take it to my grave. Whatever you need, it's yours."

It made her eyes sting. She bit her lip and just nodded. He looked at their joined hands again and saw his gold watch that she bought him years ago for a birthday.

"Aww Jaz, I gotta get out of here."

She nodded and stood up pulling him off the sofa. They just stared at each other for a long moment then he hugged her. She reluctantly broke their embrace and wiped at her face.

"Go. You should go."

"Bye Jaz."
"Bye."
With that, he was gone. She wondered how long it would be until their next stolen moment.

Chapter 26: The Return Home

Another month had passed since Blake and Jasmine had seen each other outside of a few times they had to chat whenever he came home to get more clothes. Even though their conversations were brief she could tell not being in his own space was starting to wear on him. She didn't doubt he loved Amber and wanted to eventually marry her, but she knew him too well.

The fact that this arrangement wasn't on his terms had to be annoying him. He hated to be pushed into doing something but she knew he loved Amber enough to make the sacrifice. It disturbed her that it was getting a little easier to be without him as a constant in her life. It was now a dull ache instead of a heavy weight constantly bearing down on her chest. She felt like they were losing their strong connection.

Her cell phone rang. She sat up in bed and picked it up from the nightstand. It was Blake's mom. She smiled.

"Hey Ms. Lisa. How are you?"

"Hi sweetie. I am wonderful. How are you?"

"I'm pretty good."

"Well sweetie I'm calling because I woke up this morning and decided to have a barbecue. I want to see you. I miss you so much. I know why you haven't been to see me and I understand, but enough is enough."

Jasmine laughed, "Well what's the occasion?"

"Jasmine, you would not believe the changes that have happened since Frank got better. I'm just so happy and I wanted to say thank you for everything that you did to make it happen. I just wanted to have a celebration."

"Aww, that's so sweet."

"I'm going to make it extremely hard for you to say no because I am gonna make your favorite cake."

"Oh, you're gonna make me a caramel cake?"

"Yes, I am."

"Well then I'm there. What time?"

Lisa laughed.

"We're gonna start at about three. Your parents will be here so bring your herd and Derrick. I need to spend some time with my future son-in-law since you and Blake refuse to honor an old woman's wishes."

Jasmine laughed.

"Well I'm sure the roommates will be there since it's free food, but Derrick is out of town on business. He is due back today though."

"Well alright, you can bring him by some other time if he can't make it."

"What do you want me to bring."

"A big hug and kiss for me."

"Okay, let me go round up the gang."

"Bye sweetie."

"Bye."

Her Saturday with no plans was looking up. This worked out great because her last appointment was at noon. She was excited that she would get to see Lisa. She missed her so much. This would also be her first time seeing Frank since the surgery. She didn't know how that would go. Seeing Blake would be a little bittersweet because she knew Amber would block every interaction they might try to have.

It made her think to call Derrick and give him a heads up.

He groggily answered on the second ring, "Hello."

"Hey honey."

"You okay?"

"Yeah I'm fine. I just wanted to let you know about my plans for today."

"What's up?"

She bit her lip nervously, "Blake's mom called and invited us to a barbecue this afternoon. So after my last client I'm going to head over. I don't know what time you get in but it will probably be all day so you should come by if you're not too tired."

She added the last part to let him know she had nothing to hide. His silence lasted a little too long and it made her fidget.

"I doubt if I'll be able to make it, but enjoy yourself."

"Are you mad?"

He snapped, "Would it matter?"

She snapped back, "Derrick I think you're being absolutely selfish. Give me a break. These people are important to me. They are a part of my life whether you like it or not. I have done everything you've asked of me where Blake is concerned. Either you trust me or you don't."

"Jasmine, do whatever you want, I'm going back to sleep."

He hung up.

She wanted to throw the phone across the room but thought better of it. She got out of bed and got a pair of sweat pants out to put under her night shirt. She could feel the resentment settling in and she didn't know if she could fight it. She set out to wake everybody up and invite them.

∞∞∞∞

Despite how it started, Jasmine's day had been a breeze. When they arrived at the barbeque the guys got the drinks they'd bought out of the trunk while the girls headed toward the backyard. They were being led by their noses to the sweet smelling smoke of the grill. Jasmine opened the gate and saw her mom first. She hugged Jasmine.

"Hey baby."

"Hi ma."

The rest of the gang came in and everybody said their hellos with kisses, hugs and handshakes as they began to catch up. Blake's penetrating blue eyes locked on hers.

He left Amber to come over and hug her. With a conscious restraint he didn't kiss her nose and made sure to give her a side hug. She and Amber gave each other an amicable wave and nod.

Jasmine walked over to Frank who was sitting down talking to her father. She spoke and kissed her dad on the cheek. Frank shocked her as he stood up and gave her a huge hug.

He said, "It's good to see you."

Still in shock she smiled and said, "It's good to see you too."

Justin excused himself, "Why don't I give you two a minute to catch up."

Jasmine took a seat.

Frank asked, "How are you?"

"I'm really good and you?"

"I get stronger every day."

"That's great Frank."

"I'm so grateful for what you've given me. I hope you know the depth of what you made possible."

She smiled, "I'm starting to realize the depth of what God made possible."

He smiled, "Blake told me about how you came to decide to donate your kidney."

He saw the surprise pass through her.

"Yeah, me and my kid find all sorts of things to talk about these days."

She laughed.

"I've been going to church all my life and I think I missed the point. What you did for me forced me to take a hard look at myself. Now when I attend church I take a different perspective with me. I'm working on my relationship with God and any day now I will be ready to really clear my conscience."

She reached for his hand and smiled.

"That is nourishment for my soul Frank."

On the other side of the yard Blake and Amber were sitting on the wooden swing. He hadn't been able to take his eyes off his father and Jasmine. He was bursting with pride and joy. All his life he had waited for them to find common ground. Even though they weren't as close it still mattered to him that the two of them have a relationship.

Amber was battling a temper. She didn't mean to dwell on it but she was scared she was going to lose him. The way his demeanor changed did not escape her the moment he saw Jasmine. She knew he missed her. It wasn't that she couldn't sympathize but there just had to be a line. Every time Jasmine was around she was beyond irritated and she couldn't keep herself from voicing her frustrations.

Amber asked, "So are you going to stare at her the entire time?"

His temper flashed quick and hot. There was nothing he could do to stop it.

"Amber, are you kidding me? You need to just back off okay. Don't you get it? This isn't about you. I have waited my entire life for my dad and my best friend to even be in the same room without apocalyptic tension. Can't you understand what this means to me?"

She rolled her eyes. That pissed him off even more.

"That's just it Blake I don't understand because you don't share anything with me. Don't *you* get it? There are places inside your heart I can't have because she has them. You have no intention of giving them to me, ever."

He went on the defensive because he couldn't deny she was right.

"You can go to hell Amber. I have done every ridiculous thing you asked to try and make you feel secure about this relationship. I have practically moved out of my own house and you're still not grateful. I don't spend any time with her and you're still not happy. You need to understand the reality that she will never be completely out of my life. You can't just erase her."

She let her temper match his. Her fear wouldn't let her feel secure.

"Well, I guess you can only choose me when she's not around."

His face got very sober as he said, "I didn't have to choose. Jasmine gracefully bowed out."

The look of shock on her face told him his words hit the spot. He stood and walked away from her. He knew what he was implying, but he didn't care. It was the truth after all. Jasmine had removed herself from the equation giving Amber a false understanding of his choice. Lately he could feel himself starting to resent her and her complete disregard for his feelings.

Why should anyone have to apologize because they were fortunate to have one person in their life that loved and accepted them for who they were with no questions and no judgments? Giving her up was the hardest thing he ever had to do. He was beginning to feel like he would either fail as Jasmine's friend or Amber's man.

He was starting to realize there was no way he could do both. He was becoming quite uneasy about the one he was willing to let fail if given the choice. He now understood that it wasn't just Amber. Any woman he was with he would be right back where he started.

The awareness hit him hard in the gut that the only way he could be happy in a relationship and keep Jasmine in his life was for Jasmine to be the woman in that relationship. The problem with this line of thinking though was that he didn't see Jasmine like that. He never could. He headed up to his room to get his temper in check.

Jasmine didn't miss the heated exchange between Blake and Amber even though she was talking to both of their parents about their remodeling. Blake had gone in the house. She wanted desperately to go after him but she knew she couldn't. She wanted to slap the piss out of Amber. What more could the girl possibly want? She was tired of seeing Blake always unhappy.

Lisa hadn't missed the exchange either.

She turned to Jasmine, "Sweetie, why don't you go in the house and bring me a blanket out of the hall closet. It's starting to get a little chilly out here."

Jasmine stared at her blankly because it was *not* chilly outside.

Lisa said, "You should take your time and see all the changes I've made since the last time you were here. I'm gonna go and talk to Amber. I don't want her to feel unwelcomed."

Lisa winked at Jasmine. Jasmine grinned and excused herself as Lisa got up to run interference. Vanessa shook her head, but before she could speak Justin placed his hand over hers and shook his. Frank remained neutral but his wife's conspiratorial plans were not lost on him.

When she walked into the living room she saw him sitting on the top step looking quite upset.

She asked, "Hey, did you forget your room is downstairs?"

He looked up and smiled. He didn't want to be angry or confused anymore. He would put it all aside for another day and enjoy being with his friend.

"Yeah I did. What you came in here to remind me?"

She walked up and sat on the step below him.

"As a matter of fact I did."

"Well aren't you my saving grace."

"What on earth would you ever do without me?"

"I don't want to find out." He asked, "So I see you've got a new best friend in the Jessup family huh?"

She grinned, "As a matter of fact I do and you know he's easier on the eyes than you are."

"Really, because some people would say he looks just like me."

"Oh I beg to differ. He has those distinguished gray sideburns and all that wisdom in his blue eyes that you're not quite old enough to have yet."

He pulled one of her curls and laughed.

"Jaz, it was amazing to see the two of you laughing and hugging each other."

Her smile lit up his heart.

"I know right. It felt amazing. Your dad's actually a pretty cool guy. Who knew?"

They laughed.

"So, why didn't Derrick come?"

"Because he's out of town and mad that I did."

"Let's just not go there today."

"I'm with you there bestie."

"Just so you know, I'm coming back home tonight."

She couldn't hide her surprise.

"Really? How does Amber feel about that?"

"It's not going to matter, but I haven't told her yet."

"You haven't told me what," Amber said from the bottom of the steps.

Jasmine had to check that quick temper of hers and let Blake handle his own affairs. Jasmine stood up to leave but he grabbed her hand.

"You don't have to leave Jaz. We're just sitting on the steps catching up."

He looked at Amber, "I haven't told you yet that I'm moving back home. I think it will do us some good to have a little space."

Her eyes shot right to Jasmine but Blake responded before she could.

"This has nothing to do with her Amber. It's a decision that I made all by myself. If you want to blame someone, you can blame yourself. Jasmine didn't even know. How could she when I'm not *allowed* to talk to her."

She sent him a nasty glare.

"Looks like you're making up for lost time."

"Looks like."

Jasmine was about to slap both of them. She wasn't a pawn to be used.

"Blake can we talk in private please," Amber pleaded.

"I really don't want to talk right now."

She wanted to scream but remembered where she was.

"Fine. I'm leaving. Tell your parents goodbye. I guess I'll see you when I see you."

He didn't respond.

The moment she grabbed her purse and was out the door Jasmine pounced on him.

"Don't you ever do that again Blake! I am not a tool to be used to put your woman in check."

He frowned, "I'm sorry Jaz. She's really pushing buttons I didn't know I had. Nothing can get under her skin quite like you. I won't ever do it again I promise."

She hit him on the back of his head.

"Ouch."

"That's what you get."

He asked, "So can I have a hug? I mean it's been a month."

She rolled her eyes but opened her arms as he filled them. She squeezed him hard after she realized how much she missed him. He pulled back and kissed her nose. She smiled up at him.

He smiled too, "Come on, let's go get some food."

He grabbed her hand and led her down the stairs.

Chapter 27: Eyes Wide Shut

A couple months had passed. They were all falling back into their normal lives. Jasmine walked into the house excited about her new look. She had never felt so beautiful and so sexy in her life. She couldn't wait to show herself off to her friends. Maybe now she could have an identity independent of her wild natural curls. She needed a change.

When she left the salon she went to her favorite boutique and picked up a red dress. Her day was great but she was glad to be home. No one seemed to be buzzing about in the common area so she headed upstairs to her room to shower and dress for her big anniversary dinner with Derrick. She couldn't believe it had been three years.

After she showered and dressed she started applying her make-up. She took extra care because she wanted everything to be perfect. She added false eyelashes and dark smoky eyes. She put on red lipstick to make her full lips pop and then added on a shiny coat to top off the look that would keep Derrick drooling.

She barely recognized herself. She had gone from the big kinky curls of her natural hair all over the place to a short close cropped straightened style. It was sort of reminiscent of a Halle Berry cut. It brought out so much more of her face than she was used to seeing but she loved it.

She examined herself in her full length mirror and admired the way she looked. She put on her shimmering gold pumps, picked up her gold clutch and headed down the stairs. She had just enough time to model her new look for her roommates and then be ready to walk out the door because Derrick was nothing if not prompt.

As she glided down the stairs, Lucy, Damon, Carmen and Ahmed were sitting at the table playing a game of spades. Lucy saw her first and let out a whistle.

She said, "Well my, my, my, aren't we the bell of the ball. I'm dangerous with a pair of scissors."

"You sure are Lucy," Jasmine agreed.

Everybody looked up and gasped.

Damon said, "Girl, what the heck did you do to all your hair? You know a brotha's got the hots for your wild curls!"

She laughed, "Boy hush. It was time for a change."

Carmen said, "I could never cut all my hair off but it definitely looks good on you."

Jasmine smiled, "Thanks hun," and kissed Carmen on the cheek.

Ahmed said, "I think you're pretty too. Do I get one?"

She rolled her eyes but kissed him on the lips. His blush made her giggle.

Damon said, "Dang girl you're hot, I would try to holla fa sho."

Ahmed said, "Yeah I would too but I probably would embarrass myself by the time the dress hit the floor."

Everybody laughed and Jasmine threw the card box at him.

Blake came downstairs. Obviously he had been sleeping. He was rubbing his eyes into focus when he saw her. His mouth dropped open as he just stared at her.

"Jasmine, what did you do?"

She frowned slightly, "Ah B, what you don't like it?"

That was not exactly the problem, he loved it. She looked so *different*. Without all her big curly hair taking the focus off her face he could see how truly beautiful she was. Her eyes were so big and brown and her skin was practically glowing. As his eyes skimmed the length of her the red knee-length dress practically molded to her body. Oh my God, was she always that curvy? Her small waist made her curves that much more defined. She had never shown them like that before. Did he like curves? Her hips were begging his hands to be wrapped around them.

When he focused on those full, shiny, pouting red lips his body betrayed him. For the first time in 25 years he saw Jasmine as a woman. Not his best friend who happened to be a woman. Not just any woman though. The most beautiful woman he had ever laid his eyes on. He could feel his nature respond to his thoughts and the blood draining from his face. He had never been more embarrassed in his entire life. What the hell was he in Oz? Since when did Jasmine give him a woody? He grabbed his stomach like a sudden case of the runs had just transpired.

He mumbled, "You look fine," and ran back up the stairs.

Jasmine and the other girls looked innocently puzzled as Jasmine headed up the stairs behind him. When she left the room Damon and Ahmed fell out in hysterical laughter.

Lucy and Carmen just stared at them.

After they regained their composure, they both asked, "What?"

Ahmed said, "He totally just boinged!"

Damon laughed even harder. It took Lucy a second and Carmen a second longer to catch his drift.

Carmen said, "No way, not even."

Damon said, "Oh yeah he did and I'm guessing that is the very first time Jasmine was ever the cause of one."

He was now wiping tears from his eyes.

Lucy asked, "Are you guys serious?"

Damon said, "Oh yeah. We know that look. Now don't get me wrong, Jasmine is a pretty girl but she has never looked more let's say, grown up, than she did tonight. She obviously caught Blake off guard. He is used to seeing her in his sweats or jeans and a t-shirt."

Ahmed said, "This moment has forever changed the way he's going to see his best friend. Poor bastard is going to be in purgatory."

"So much for not being attracted to her," Damon laughed. He had no sympathy.

∞∞∞∞∞

Jasmine knocked on Blake's door.

"Hey love, you okay in there? What happened?"

Blake was sitting on his bed trying to think of every non-sexual thing to get himself back under control.

He yelled back, "Nothing, just my stomach. Thought I was gonna hurl. I must've eaten something bad."

She said, "Well can I come in?"

He yelled quickly and sharply, "No. I'm fine."

If she came in his bedroom he would be all over her. She was a little taken aback. Normally she would just barge in anyway but it was something in his tone that made her hesitate.

"Well okay. I will bring you back some Pepto or something. Feel better okay."

He said, "I'm fine, don't worry."

"Okay, good night."

"Have fun on your big date Jaz," he said trying to sound normal.

She struggled against going in because something was definitely off. Since when does Blake push her away? Yeah, they had been on chill mode for the last few months but not ice mode. She heard the doorbell and realized this would have to wait.

"Bye Blake."

She went downstairs to see Derrick looking beyond handsome in his gray pinstripe suit. His mahogany skin and dark eyes sparkled. She smiled that million watt smile and nodded her approval.

He looked up at her and smiled back, "Wow baby, you cut all your hair off!"

"Yeah, I did. You like it?"

"I love it actually. This style is more appropriate for that dress."

She didn't know how to take that but let it go because she was in such a good mood. He smiled as he pulled her into his well-defined arms and kissed her passionately. Her head swam. She had to refocus when he broke the kiss. She almost forgot where she was.

Damon said, "Okay people, get a room."

Derrick smiled and wrapped Jasmine in his arms, "Okay, we're out of here. Good night."

They all said, "Good night."

∞∞∞∞

When Jasmine got home from her date her thoughts were in so many places. Not at all the happy place she was before she left. She thought this night would be magical, but it turned out to be tragic. She knew that Derrick had something special planned.

In all her life when she dreamed of the moment a man proposed to her she never thought for one second that it would come with an ultimatum. She did not take too kindly to that ultimatum.

That fool had lost his mind, but he was also the fool that had her heart. She dropped the bag of soup and Pepto on her bed, peeled off her shoes and dress as she headed for the bathroom she shared with Carmen.

She washed off her make-up and put acne medicine on the two trouble spots that looked to be brewing. She was experiencing so many emotions that she didn't know which one was leading. She thought she should be crying because she had a sick feeling that her once very promising relationship was now a dream deferred.

How serious could she have been about marrying this man if she was willing to make a choice that would essentially mean choosing another man? She had been studying marriage in the Bible. She knew that according to it, she would have to forsake all others for her husband. She couldn't do it. In her heart she knew she couldn't.

The only person she could and had forsaken all others for was Blake. Hmph, wasn't that something? Life would be easier if she was with Blake. That thought made her pause and frown. Now where did that come from? She simply wasn't attracted to him. Why is that Jasmine?

The only reason you say you're not attracted to him is because he's white. Everything else you absolutely adore about him. Why was her subconscious attacking her? She wasn't prejudice, so that couldn't be it. She just wasn't attracted to white men. It was that simple.

She dressed in her pajamas and looked at the clock. It was 2 A.M. She didn't care if he was asleep. He would just have to wake up because Amber's car wasn't outside. She put on her slipper socks and headed across the hall to Blake's room.

She tapped on the door lightly and was shocked to hear, "Yeah, what is it?"

She said, "It's me love."

He didn't say anything, so she just walked in and closed the door behind her as she leaned against it. He looked a little off to her.

She said, "Hey love, what are you still doing up?"

Blake was hoping she would have just walked away but he knew better. Well at least she had on baggy pants and a shirt, his pants and his shirt to be exact. The make-up was gone. She had girl gunk on her face, but oh God she wasn't wearing a bra. Why was he noticing this all of a sudden? Did she not wear one at night usually?

Look at her face, Blake, just look at her face.

He managed to say, "Huh. What?"

She frowned, "Okay B, what's up with you, seriously?"

She put the Pepto and soup on his night stand, climbed into bed with him and lay facing him. She smelled amazing. He backed up a little bit.

Blake sighed, "Nothing Jaz. I'm okay, just a strange night."

She said, "Eww, your breath stinks."

He moved in closer to her face and blew his breath all in it.

She laughed and playfully punched him, "Boy move."

He pinched her nose, "So why are you in my bed instead of Derrick's?"

"I haven't been in his bed in several months."

She sighed and a tear fell. Her façade of strength always came tumbling down when Blake was around. She didn't have to always be strong with him. He was strong enough to hold her up.

"Hey, hey, what's wrong, what happened?"

She took a breath, "Well you were right. He did propose."

"Okay...but..."

"But it came with an ultimatum."

"An ultimatum for what? I thought you guys had finally gotten back on track."

She sarcastically laughed, "Yeah, so did I. Well apparently he loves me so much he wants to spend the rest of his life with me. What he won't do is allow me to spend the rest of my life with you!"

Blake stared at her for a long moment searching her eyes for laughter and then he blinked.

"Excuse me."

"Apparently he has a severe problem with our friendship and I quote, he will not have a wife who spends as much time with another man as I do with you."

"Wait, whoa, there is absolutely nothing going on between us. Jaz, we have done every ridiculous thing they have asked to make them comfortable."

"I know, but he says his instincts never lead him wrong. He says he talked to my mom. She told him that there was nothing going on between us and there never has been. She also said that I would never date a white guy so he didn't have to worry about that. Then she said that we did have a special friendship and I wouldn't be so quick to walk away from it. Obviously he ignored that last bit of advice."

For some reason unbeknownst to him Blake couldn't understand the profound hurt that manifested because she seemed to agree with her mom that she would never date a white man. Or was it just him she couldn't date because he was white?

She continued, "I just looked at him like he was stupid. I mean he couldn't possibly be serious. He never once said anything that final before to me about our friendship. How could he even ask me that? I always thought once we got married and stuff we wouldn't spend as much time with each other, but I never thought that us getting married would separate us forever."

Blake said, "Well I can understand him wanting to spend as much time with you as possible. So we cut back a little on hanging out, no biggie"

"Cut back, what else is there to cut out Blake? No, he doesn't want me to be around you at all. Once the vows are done I have to walk away from this lifelong friendship. How could I even consider marrying a man that would force me to give up the one person who means the world to me?"

She looked into his gorgeous blue eyes and said, "I would never walk away from you because someone wanted me to. We have been through everything. You have been there for me when I was at my lowest. If he feels that way then he cannot possibly be the man for me."

Blake felt the lump in his throat, but he cleared it.

"Jasmine, this man is offering you forever. Are you sure you want to walk away from that, I mean it's just me."

She sat up, "So what are you saying Blake that if a woman gave you an ultimatum you would stop being my friend to be with her?"

"Calm down, and no. Obviously we have already been down that road but I know how much you love this guy."

"Well, he is certainly not the guy I thought he was. There would never be anything like that between you and me. I would never date a white man and you like those bony lil white girls, which clearly I am not. We have never even kissed. It's just so asinine."

He swallowed hard. There it was again. Was he actually being prejudice by not allowing himself to see Jasmine like that? He didn't want to know the answer.

"Yeah, it's just so asinine."

Since she left for her date all he had been able to think about was her body wrapped around his. He had been driving himself insane trying to get back to just being her friend. He loved her more than he had ever loved another woman, but it was never like that. It was always untainted. Now he didn't know what territory he was in. It hurt like hell that she was emphatically saying it would never happen. There was a part of him that was starting not to care what color she was. He just wanted her.

For the moment though, he was grateful to have her all to himself. Even though Amber would probably cut him he wanted to hold Jasmine in his arms just for tonight.

He closed his eyes and took a breath, "Look Jasmine, let's just sleep on it okay and see how you feel tomorrow. We can talk about it then."

She looked at him and pushed his hair back from his face, something she always did. Suddenly her touch began to stir things in him that it never had before. When she gently placed her lips on his temple he had to suppress a shudder. He was scared to death. This could only end badly.

She asked, "You feeling better?"

She used the kiss to check his temperature. He felt a little warm.

It took him a moment to realize what she was talking about, "Oh yeah. Thanks for the medicine but I'm better now."

He kissed her nose, "Let's get some sleep."

She said, "Amber would kill me if she knew I was in here."

"And Derrick wouldn't?"

"Well as far as I'm concerned Derrick is no longer a factor."

"Jasmine what does it mean that you can walk away from forever just to be my friend?"

There it was, point blank in her face. She didn't have a clue how to answer it. His stare was so intense and hopeful. She took the cowardly way out.

"Like you said, let's just sleep on it."

His head was screwed up so he wouldn't judge her for evading the question. Blake opened his arms so she could lay her head on his chest. He ran his fingers through her hair and began to scratch her scalp as she moaned. He held her tight with the other arm. It felt so natural to him to have her in his arms. He had a lifetime of memories of her in his arms. She really was the only woman he ever really wanted, sometimes needed, to hold. Jasmine felt safe and loved. She wrapped her arms around his waist and willed her emotions to let her have a moment of peace.

He said, "Dang, I can't believe you got rid of the curls. Now what am I supposed to play with to put us to sleep."

She smiled and said, "This is the new me. Deal with it!"

They both fell victim to their own honest painful thoughts of a long overdue soul search as they tried to drift off to sleep.

Chapter 28: The Unexpected

Amber invited Blake to escort her to some formal event for a charitable organization her job sponsored. He really could care less about going. At one point he thought he was falling for Amber on a level that involved rings, houses and white picket fences. But having Jasmine pushed out of his life by Amber left a bitter taste in his mouth.

Their relationship had been on life support for the last few months. He knew he wanted out. He just didn't know how not to hurt her. She didn't deserve it because it wasn't her fault he just realized he was in love with his best friend. Nothing made sense anymore. Everything he thought he knew about his life changed the day Jasmine became a sexy woman in his eyes. He was tired of the ambiguity in his life.

That was nearly two months ago. He had been in perdition ever since. The fact that Jasmine was single now was not helping either. What the hell was going on? Why now? He was waiting for Jasmine to get home with his tux because he got caught up in court and didn't have time to pick it up. She was running behind. *Come on Jaz. You're going to make me late.* Just then his door flew open.

"Sorry, I'm late B. You won't believe the random stuff that happened to me today, but you know I would never let you down. So I'm here now. Come on Cinderelli let's get you dressed for the ball."

He said, "Ha, ha whatever."

He snatched the tux from her. He was thankful she had on jeans and a loose fitting t-shirt because lately her body had become his kryptonite. Jasmine popped him on the top of the head for snatching the suit as she walked to his dresser to pick out cologne. She hadn't actually looked at him as he walked into the bathroom.

When he walked back out he was wearing just the suit pants that were unbuttoned revealing the top of his black boxer briefs. She had never noticed his body was ripped because Blake was not one to be shirtless. That was Damon's thing.

She knew he, Damon and Carmen worked out regularly but still this was news to her. His v-cuts made her tilt her head and bite her bottom lip. *Oh my goodness, Jasmine what the hell? This is Blake. You can't look at him like that.*

"Hello, earth to Jaz." Blake asked, "Are you listening to me?"

She snapped back to attention.

"Huh? What did you say B?"

"Where are you?"

"I'm here. I just got lost in space for a minute. What did you need?"

"Well back on planet Earth I asked if you could pick out some cufflinks to go with this."

"Oh yeah right, cufflinks. Yeah, I can do that."

Her body was tingling for all the wrong reasons in all the right places.

Lord help me. What is wrong with me? All of a sudden it didn't matter much what color he was. All she knew at this moment was he was a very gorgeous man that she wanted. This time when he came back into the room he had on the crisp white dress shirt. He walked over to her so she could help him button up. She was thankful he was fully dressed. He extended an arm to her to fix the cufflink.

"Jaz, you okay? Why are your hands shaking? You're usually as steady as a rock."

She stammered because the man smelled edible.

"Uh yeah, I know. Just uh, low blood sugar I guess. Haven't really eaten today."

His raised a brow, Jasmine not eating, yeah right. He grabbed her chin to look into her face. She thought she would melt. His eyes were bluer than she had ever seen them. She could swear he could see into her soul.

She gulped hard, "Uh, you look nice."

"Thanks."

He gripped her chin a little tighter when she tried to pull away. "What's wrong Jaz, you okay?"

She snatched her face away causing him to take a step back. Since when couldn't he touch her?

"I'm fine B. Just get ready okay."

Carmen came into the room and said, "Amber's here. Do you want me to send her up?"

She looked back and forth between the two and could swear that Jasmine was blushing though it was hard to tell since her skin didn't betray her. He panicked. He didn't want her to see Jasmine in his room.

"No, tell her I will be down in five minutes."

Carmen looked at the two of them and thought Jasmine was telling herself a lie if she thought for one second that she was not attracted to that sexy man.

"No problem," she said as she closed the door.

He knew something was wrong with Jasmine, but he couldn't keep Amber waiting. He didn't want to give her any reason to complain anymore about their friendship. Jasmine quickly fixed his other cufflink and grabbed the bowtie off the dresser as Blake finished buttoning the shirt. She tied the bowtie on trying ridiculously hard to avoid his eyes. She was so unbelievably embarrassed about the thoughts she was having. Why was she ready to rip out Amber's hair just thinking about her touching Blake?

This was insane. She was ready to get out of the twilight zone and into the normalcy of her room. Blake looked himself over in the mirror and flashed that crooked smile of his she adored. But now it had a different effect on her. *Oh God Jasmine, get out, get out!* Blake was walking toward her. She knew he was about to kiss her nose but she swore if his mouth came within inches of hers she was going to nibble on that bottom lip like it was a chew toy.

She turned abruptly and said, "You look nice. Have fun."

She was out the door before he could react. His first instinct was to go after her but he knew Amber was waiting. He would deal with her later.

He went down stairs and saw Amber in a gorgeous lavender gown with shimmering emeralds dripping from her ears, neck and wrist. Her red hair was swept up into a messy chignon and those green eyes were as piercing as always.

He kissed her cheek, "You look amazing. You ready to go?"

She smiled, "Absolutely handsome."

∞∞∞∞

Later that night Amber ended up in Blake's bed because he couldn't think of a reason fast enough why she shouldn't be. It had been a long time since they made love. It was a very uneventful night because the whole time all he could think about was Jasmine and how he was somehow betraying her by being with Amber. He knew Amber could sense he was somewhere else but she was the one that insisted on staying over.

It was ridiculous. He couldn't sleep. He really wanted to know what was bothering Jasmine. He didn't like tension between them but it was three in the morning. He looked over at Amber who was lightly snoring. He gently slid out of bed, put on some sweats and a t-shirt.

He walked across the way to Jasmine's room. Did he knock? Normally if he knew she didn't have company he would just walk in, but things were so crazy now he couldn't depend on normal. He knocked lightly. No answer. He knocked again. No answer. He turned the knob and was relieved to find it unlocked.

He walked in to see her sprawled all over the bed. It looked like she had a rough night.

He sat down on the side of the bed and playfully poked her nose and said, "Hey, wake up."

She swatted at his hand. He laughed.

"Wake up Jaz."

She stirred, "What?"

He shook her, "Wake up."

She blinked several times, "Blake, what the...?"

He had no idea what he was supposed to say so he went for simple.

"I couldn't sleep."

"So take a pill and get out."

She rolled away from him.

He pulled the covers back.

"If I can't sleep then you have to stay up with me."

She slapped her hand down in frustration and finally just sat up.

"What Blake. What the heck do you want at," she looked over at the clock, "3:14 in the morning?"

He lay down in her bed, folded his arms across his stomach and looked up at her. She was definitely a grumpy sleeper. She was ready to knock him out. He had it so bad for her because all he could see was how adorable she was.

"You butt wipe, what do you want?"

He said, "Some pancakes. Will you make me some?"

She gave him a glare he hadn't seen in a long time. He braced himself because he knew she was about to hit him. She hit him three times with her pillow then rolled back away from him in an attempt to ignore him. He kept poking her and pulling her hair. She sat up again, this time her eyes were venomous.

"Now Jaz, you know the only way for you to get some sleep is to just get up with me and help me make some pancakes."

She threw a small tantrum and then got out of the bed. Blake had the patience to aggravate her until he got what he wanted. This was one of the things she despised most about him. All of a sudden she was extremely aware that Blake was in her bed. All she had on was a night shirt.

She dragged on shorts under her night shirt and slipped into her house shoes. To punish him, she jumped on his back and made him carry her down the stairs.

He groaned, "You been eatin' chicken and watermelon girl?"

She laughed and bit his neck though she wanted to do more than that.

"Shut up you triple K spawn."

He trotted down the steps to the kitchen and dropped her at the dining room table.

She said, "I'm not helping so don't ask."

"You don't have to. Just sit there and be pretty."

She rolled her eyes.

"You are so mean in the middle of the night Jaz. You know you should really work on your bedside manner."

She ardently extended her middle finger. He laughed as he got busy in the kitchen pulling out ingredients and pans.

"Blake, why are we here? What's wrong? Who did what?"

"Nothing. Can't a guy spend time with his best friend for no apparent reason?"

"Yeah, when the sun is up."

"I love you too."

"So how was the thing with Amber?"

"It was okay. She's upstairs asleep."

The mention of Amber being in his bed made her back stiffen.

With an attitude she couldn't hide, she asked, "Why is she still here?"

"Why you say it like that? You know she has stayed the night before genius."

She couldn't believe the twinge of jealousy that hit her in the belly.

"If she's in your bed, how come you're not?"

Because I would rather be in your bed, he thought.

He said, "Because I can wake you up in the middle of the night and you still love me, her not so much."

She rolled her eyes and started picking at the place setting to busy her hands.

"Besides, I needed to check on you. You were acting strange when I was getting dressed. What was up with that?"

She almost went into a panic. She felt the sweat dripping down her spine.

"Whatever Blake. You're paranoid. Just make your stupid pancakes so I can get back in my bed and you can get back in yours?"

He said, "You know I know you better than I know myself right? I know you're not telling me the truth, but whatever, keep your little secrets. You will tell me sooner or later."

Normally you would be right cutie, but not this time, she thought.

He said, "The truth is I didn't want her to stay the night. I'm sure I got a big fat zero in the lovemaking category tonight. My head was somewhere else."

She laughed, "And where was it? You know there are only so many holes it can go in?"

He laughed and threw an eggshell at her.

"Eww B, stop, that's nasty."

She got up to go in the kitchen to put the eggshell in the trash.

He put pancake mix on her nose. She stepped on his toe. He bumped her hip with his. She pinched him in his side. They kept laughing and playing around.

She said, "Shhh. You're gonna wake everybody up."

He laughed, "You started it. You do the eggs and I'll do the pancakes."

She got out a bowl, "You make me sick Blake. I said I wasn't gonna help."

"Yeah, but you love me and you know you're my slave."

"Is that a racist joke there buddy?"

He laughed, "Ha, no actually it wasn't."

She scrambled the eggs and added feta cheese just the way they both liked them. She put them over the heat as he was cooking the pancakes. They were moving as a unit and didn't even notice it. But they had an audience. Amber had gotten up to pee and realized Blake was gone. She heard voices downstairs. What do you know? Blake and Jasmine were in the kitchen flirting away like they didn't have a care in the world. How dare he? She was lying in his bed covered in his scent and he was downstairs with *her* cooking and flirting like she didn't even exist.

She watched him put the plates on the table. Jasmine was getting milk out of the refrigerator. They sat down to eat. Jasmine blessed the food. Amber rolled her eyes, *yeah pray for your food while you're screwing my man ten feet away from my sleeping body.*

She continued to watch them as they laughed and picked off each other's plates. It was something they always did that Amber could not stand, especially when they were eating the same thing. She'd had enough. She descended the stairs and headed into the dining room. They didn't even notice her so she cleared her throat.

Blake's head turned in her direction.

"Hey Amber. I'm sorry, did we wake you?"

She was stunned. He was caught red handed and acted as if this was completely acceptable.

She said, "No, the empty bed woke me."

Jasmine could tell this was a pissed off woman. By the way she was glaring at her she was partly the cause of it, once again. She was over Amber and her tantrums.

Jasmine said, "Hey Amber. You want some pancakes?"

"No, you back stabbing wench, I don't."

Blake's head shot up, "Whoa, now that was uncalled for."

He immediately reached to keep Jasmine in her seat because her temper was not to be underestimated.

Jasmine said, "Excuse you, what is your problem?"

"My problem is it's four in the morning and my man is with you and not me. Now if you don't back off we are going to have some problems."

Jasmine was literally speechless. As of that day, yeah, she had a couple of unexpected reactions to Blake's body but that was it. She was not now or never would be the other woman.

Blake stood up.

"Okay, we all need to just calm down."

Doors started to open because of the raised voices. Carmen said in a whiny sleepy voice, "Really guys?"

She looked down from the stairs and assessed the situation. She thought to herself, *Oh.*

Damon came out. He had a better view since he was on the bottom floor. When he saw the situation he shot Blake a sympathetic look. They both went back to their respective rooms.

Blake asked, "Jasmine, can you clean this for me while I go talk to Amber?"

She glared at Amber and said, "Yeah sure," without taking her eyes off Amber.

He said, "Thanks."

As an automatic reflex he kissed her on her nose.

Amber lunged for her but Blake was faster. His instincts had him putting his body in front of Jasmine and man handling Amber. Jasmine had had enough.

She stood up and said, "Lil girl, I don't know who you think you dealing with, but I will wipe the floor wit' yo scrawny behind. Now you better back the hell up before I act my color."

Blake dropped his head.

"Jasmine please?"

"Well then you better get her before I do. I don't have to apologize for hanging out with my best friend. If she had done a better job you woulda still been sleep." She pointed at Amber, "If you were up to par he wouldn't need me for additional entertainment. So don't blame me for your shortcomings."

Blake literally had to drag Amber screaming out of the dining room. Lucy and Ahmed came out this time, assessed the situation and went back to bed.

He looked back at Jasmine and mouthed, "Really Jaz?"

Jasmine shrugged, she was fuming. She was sick of everybody and their mama telling her she couldn't be friends with Blake. This was all a bunch of bull. How little was Amber's opinion of her to think she would sleep with Blake after she did? *Nasty heifa*, she thought. She began to clean up the kitchen and tried to calm herself down so she wouldn't go into Blake's room and show Amber a beat down she would not soon forget.

∞∞∞∞

Blake slammed the door behind him. The anger that was on his face frightened Amber. She had never seen him so mad. He was walking toward her so she backed up.

He said, "Don't you ever threaten to hurt my friend because you can't control your emotions. You will not disrespect her in her own house. You are a guest and you don't have to be here."

That's it. She was officially passed her limit.

"How dare you defend her to me when you left me naked in your bed to go and be with her?"

"Go and be with her? What the hell do you think we did? Do you really think that low of both of us that she would sleep with me knowing I had just slept with you and you were still in my bed? She is my friend, nothing more. I couldn't sleep."

"Well why didn't you wake me?"

"Because I chose to wake her."

She wanted to slap him with all her might.

"I am so sick of you and your *best* friend. That is such a load of crap. There is obviously something going on."

He felt a slight twinge of guilt simply because recently he had wanted something to go on. The fact still remained nothing had and nothing probably ever would.

"You are starting to sound redundant. I won't tell you again we are just friends."

"Oh yeah just friends. Whatever Blake. When you can't sleep you wake her not me. When you need something I am not the first person you call, it's her. Why do you need me, you have her?"

"I am not in a relationship with Jasmine. I am in a relationship with you?"

"Ha. Is that what you call this? Well obviously I'm just here for sex because she sure has your heart."

He was tired of defending his friendship to Amber and everybody else. How many ways could he say we are just friends? Tonight he would not be saying it again.

He said, "I will not have this conversation with you again. If you don't like it you can leave."

She gave into her urge and slapped him as hard as she could. It stunned him as his head whipped around. It made him flash back to his dad's hand slapping him across the face. Would she slap their children because she couldn't control her anger? Blake didn't hit and he would never allow anybody else to hit him either. He grabbed his jaw and gave her a cold steely stare.

His voice was dripping with ice.

"Get out of my house. Text me to let me know you made it home safely and then don't ever speak to me again."

She was taken aback by the sheer frost and finality in his tone.

"But Blake I'm sorry. I didn't mean that. I don't know what's gotten into me. Can't you understand why I feel threatened?"

He said one more time for good measure, "Get out now! When I come out of the bathroom, you better not be on my property."

He slammed the bathroom door and looked in the mirror.

"Blake, what the heck is going on in your life these days?" He washed his face and screamed into the towel as he dried it. He stood there for five minutes. He swore if this woman was not out of his house he would let Jasmine loose on her.

He walked into his room and she was gone. As he went to his bedroom door he heard the front door closing. He went down and locked the door behind her. He headed back up the stairs about to go to his room when he realized it wasn't where he wanted to be.

He turned and looked at Jasmine's closed room door. He tried to resist but there was such a pull, just to be near her. He didn't really have the energy to fight it. He didn't bother knocking just walked in and shut the door behind him.

She was sitting on the bed with her arms folded across her chest looking mad as a snake.

He said, "It's over."

She replied, "I know. Are you okay?"

"I will be."

She pulled back the covers and scooted over. He climbed in and turned his back to her.

"I don't want to talk about it."

"That's cool. Turn off the light."

He obliged. When he lay back down he shifted further to his own side away from her. It was beyond tormenting to need to be near her but want to be anywhere else. Jasmine couldn't remember a time when she was a million miles away from him, even though they were in the same bed.

It didn't bother her one bit that his back was to her because she wanted hers to him as well. She was scared by the relief she felt that Amber was out of the picture. That was something she didn't really know how to cope with.

Chapter 29: A Hate Filled Heart

It was early on a Friday morning. Jasmine was in a much better mood than she had been in for weeks. She was coping well over her break up with Derrick. Each day she was getting a little piece of her heart back. The thing that made her life difficult was this attraction she seemed to have to Blake. It was driving her crazy. For the life of her she couldn't understand where it came from all of a sudden.

Wherever it came from it must have been there for a long time because it hit her like a Mack Truck head on. She found herself avoiding him every chance she could manage unless there were other people around.

The fear she felt about her feelings for Blake was almost paralyzing. She only saw it ending badly. She couldn't see what so many other people saw. She didn't know why, but she was beyond afraid to act on what she was feeling.

As soon as she sorted through all of this and figured out what she was going to do about her attraction to Blake she would write Derrick a nice long letter filled with I-am-so-sorry, apparently-you-were-right anecdotes. As she stood in the bathroom mirror she shook her head at herself.

She ran her hands through her still short hair. Even though she loved her new look she really did miss her curls. She knew Blake missed them too. The thought of him playing in her curls made her smile and gave her butterflies.

"Jasmine, what is wrong with you? Get it together," she chastised herself.

Even though it was a Friday she didn't have any clients until noon so she wanted to just hang out and relax with whoever was at the house until it was time to go into the shop. She threw on Blake's sweat pants that were lying across her bed, his favorite t-shirt and headed out to the living room.

She walked out to find all of her roommates standing and sitting around the TV looking shocked. Lucy was crying. Jasmine got scared because she didn't know what was going on?

"Guys, what happened? What's wrong?"

When no one answered her she ran into the living room and stared at the TV. There was a breaking news report on.

As Jasmine tuned in she heard, "The gunman shot himself after he unleashed his rage on the college campus. His shooting spree lasted for twenty-two minutes before he killed himself."

They were showing shots of their college alma mater and the chaos that was left in the wake of the deranged gunman.

Jasmine gasped, "Lord, have mercy!"

The pain, agony, shock and fear on the faces of the people on the campus was heart wrenching. She couldn't believe this was happening and at their school none the less. She obviously missed the part about why this gunman killed all these people.

They were reporting the death of 35 people, including faculty and students. Even a child had been gunned down with countless wounded. If that wasn't bad enough the next thing shown on the screen put Jasmine on red alert. The panic that hit her was severe when they displayed a picture of the assailant who cowardly took his own life.

His handsome face showed dark olive skin that was flawless. His eyes were black and cold. His curly black hair was cut as neatly as his goatee. Jasmine's heart sank. She looked around for Ahmed and made eye contact with Damon. She knew he was thinking the same thing.

Ahmed was sitting on the sofa. Jasmine sat next to him as she picked up the remote and turned off the TV. She got protests from everyone except for Damon.

She said, "Guys listen, this is serious. What good is it going to do for us to keep watching this?"

Ahmed looked at her strangely.

"What is it Jasmine?"

She looked down and grabbed his hand. She noticed their skin was so similar yet so different. Even though some people looked at her with hate, she knew more people would look at him with hate, especially after today.

She swallowed hard.

"Ahmed, listen to me sweetie, you need to be careful when you go out today. If it's possible maybe you could call into work and not go anywhere on your own for at least a week."

He stared at her doubtfully, so did Blake, Carmen and Lucy.

Damon had her back though.

"You guys Jazzy is right. As wrong as it is, when people see you they don't know you're not a religious nut. They don't know that you're not some whacked terrorist trying to punish America. People's emotions are probably going to be out of control for the next few weeks. What Jasmine is saying is she doesn't want you to be caught in the crossfire of someone's misplaced anger."

Ahmed just stared at both of them for a moment.

Blake said, "I understand what you guys are saying, but I think you're being a little bit ridiculous."

Lucy nodded in agreement.

Damon spoke, "No disrespect guys but I believe Jasmine and I have a more intimate knowledge of racial profiling than any of you guys."

Ahmed said, "Damon, you're mixed, you're not the quintessential minority."

"Whatever man. You know I'm not fully black because you're my friend, but if you saw me in the street what would you assume?"

Ahmed didn't respond. Damon looked at Lucy, Carmen then Blake. Neither of them wanted to admit they would assume he was Black.

Smugly Damon said, "Exactly, that's my point. People assume and don't ask questions until after someone is hurt. Dawg, I know you're a grown man, but I really would feel better if you kinda kept it low key for a little while until this settles down."

Ahmed stood up.

"Look, I appreciate what you guys are trying to do. I am just as hurt as every other American to know that some psycho killed all those innocent people, but I can't stop living my life because people make bad decisions based on their skewed understanding of their religion."

Jasmine stood as well.

"Ahmed, please don't be so quick to think it can't happen to you. I'm telling you I just feel very strongly that you need to be careful. At least take one of Damon's or Blake's guns and keep it in your car."

Damon was so on Jasmine's side with this one.

Carmen spoke, "Okay guys let's everyone just chill out. Look guys, I remember how people profiled people who were or looked Arab after 9/11. It wasn't cool, but it was understandable. I think we are making too much of a big deal out of this. So let's everybody just calm down."

Lucy hadn't said a word. She couldn't stand to see that much pain and suffering and for no reason whatsoever.

She cleared her throat and spoke.

"Guys this house is a place where race isn't an issue. We all get along because we love each other for who we are not what we are. However, I think our acceptance of each other can blind us sometimes to what the world is really like outside of these walls."

She moved her arms in a sweeping gesture to encompass the idea of their home.

Lucy continued, "While some of us may think it's extreme and some of us think it's smart Ahmed just be extra careful and pay attention to your surroundings."

He started to say something. She put her hand up to stop him. "That's something all of us should do anyways, so don't get your boxers in a bunch okay."

Ahmed smirked, "Speaking of boxers, I have a hot date tonight. I don't plan on cancelling it so everybody just relax. I'm going to be late for work."

With that he left for his room. Lucy and Carmen followed suit. Damon gave Jasmine's hand a squeeze before he headed to his room. Left alone with no adult supervision Jasmine and Blake stared at each other. His first instinct was to comfort her. Even though he didn't agree, he could tell she was shaken and she was truly concerned for Ahmed.

Blake found a way to cope with his feelings for Jasmine. He wanted her but he didn't want to lose her as a friend so he decided to just continue being who he'd always been to her. He would deny himself what he truly wanted until he was ready to know if she felt the same way.

He walked around to where she stood in front of the couch. When he reached for her she took a step back.

His eyebrow shot up and he asked, "What's wrong?"

Jasmine couldn't believe she had just done that, but her fears made her avoid him at all costs. So she got defensive.

"Nothing Blake, I'm not a child. I don't need you to hold me every time I get upset."

This time he took a step back and stared at her like she had lost her mind.

"Is there something I've done that you need to tell me about?"

She saw the hurt in his eyes that she caused but there was no way she was about to let him touch her. She didn't trust herself to keep her true feelings to herself.

"What do you want me to say Blake, I'm fine. Can you just back off?"

He moved closer to her but there wasn't affection in his eyes this time, it was anger.

"I have backed off. Jasmine I'm so freakin' far from you these days I'm practically on another planet. So I'm asking you what the deal is. What have I done to you? You would think that with Amber and Derrick gone our friendship could go back to what it was, so what exactly am I missing here?"

"Nothing Blake, could you please just not make a big deal out of this. I don't need you to kiss my nose or play in my hair or hold me. I'm a big girl. You know I can handle my own emotions. I don't want you to touch me. I'm sorry I just don't."

Her mind was in self-preservation mode and she couldn't believe what she was willing to do to keep her feelings to herself.

Blake was heated.

"Well excuse me for trying to comfort a friend. I haven't *touched* you in weeks. You've been walking around here for weeks with this attitude and avoiding me like the plague. I'm sick of it."

She let her temper match his. They were unaware that because of all their yelling they now had an audience of four.

"Blake, we have been in each other's face since we were two. I'm sorry, but I need a break. Everywhere I turn you're in my face and I feel like I'm suffocating. I just need some space okay. You know since you're all done with your daddy issues I think I can have some time to myself now."

The moment the words left her mouth she regretted them, but what could she do? Words were one of those things you couldn't take back. He looked at her like she was a complete stranger. Even though it hurt her to see him look at her with such disdain the damage was already done. The pain of being rejected by the woman who meant everything to him almost made him lose it in front of her but his pride fought hard and long to keep that from happening.

The ache she caused him was ten times the ache he felt when Melissa and Amber made their exits from his life. He thought she was the one person in the world who would never hurt him. The realization that he couldn't have been more wrong crushed him. The agony he felt allowed some words to slip out that he regretted before they even left his lips, but misery loved company.

"Well I tell you what, since I'm suffocating you and you can handle your emotions all by your lonesome, how about you handle them all by yourself on June 8th."

His words sliced through her like a hot knife through butter. Her face cringed like she had just been given a swift kick in the stomach. She didn't have his control. A tear slipped out and ran down her cheek. For the first time since they were little her tears didn't move him.

She felt like she was going to be sick but her anger was quick and paramount. Before she could stop herself she slapped him as hard as she could. He knew it was coming and willingly took the slap. It didn't shock him because he knew her better than he knew himself. Somewhere deep inside he felt like he may have deserved it.

He got in her face looking her square in the eyes and said with barely controlled rage, "Go to hell Jasmine. That should give you all the space you need."

He sidestepped her and headed upstairs to his room.

She stood there in momentary shock. She'd hurt him and she did it on purpose. Was it really so shocking he would try to hurt her back? She couldn't believe she hit him. She knew how he felt about hitting. Who was this person she was becoming?

The pain was almost unbearable. She couldn't believe he would throw that in her face after all this time. She had to sit because she thought she would fall. She couldn't remember ever fighting with Blake let alone spewing words that could really end their friendship.

She was the mean one. Blake had never been a vicious person. How much pain must he have been in to push that button? What was going on in her life? Why was her world upside down? She couldn't believe she threw his dad in his face but all she could think about was pushing him as far away from her as possible because she was petrified of her true feelings.

Damon, Ahmed, and Lucy stood in their doorways and Carmen stood at the top of the stairs in shock. They had never seen Jasmine and Blake fight in all the years they had known them. They definitely made up for missed opportunities with this one though.

Jasmine felt the tears rising into her throat. Her anger was like setting fire to the rain. She was determined not to shed another tear for him.

Lucy was about to go over to her but Ahmed said, "Nah, I got her. Give us a moment guys."

It was at that moment that Jasmine realized they'd had an audience. They all obliged and headed back to their rooms to get dressed for the day. Ahmed grabbed her hand and pulled her off the sofa. She was beyond embarrassed. She kept her face covered with her hands as he pulled her into his arms.

"Jazzy, you know I love you but I have to say only people who are head over heels in love with each can hurt each other the way you two just did."

It was not what she wanted to hear. It only added to her hurt and fury.

"You know what Ahmed, even if you were right and I was in love with him, I'm sure as hell not in love anymore. As far as I'm concerned I don't even like him."

She stormed up the stairs to her room. Ahmed shook his head. Jasmine had to be the most stubborn person he had ever met. The four of them had a bet going about how long it was going to take those two to get together now that they were both single. It had already been close to two months. Looks like Damon was going to win. It would take a catastrophic event to get those two to realize how much they really meant to each other. He had a sick feeling that everyone's day was pretty much going to suck.

Chapter 30: Reality Check

Ahmed left his office early that day and went to the local park to hang out and absorb life. He sat on one of the benches in the middle of the park. He needed to see the beauty in the world because his temper had been on edge all day. It didn't surprise him that the buzz around the office was about the shooting on the campus. What did surprise him were the looks of disgust he'd received from people he had known and worked with for years.

He wanted to punch something, or punch somebody. It irritated him that Jasmine and Damon were right about people. When he'd gotten back from his three o'clock meeting there was a note someone shoved under his door. It suggested he was laundering money for a terrorist organization while claiming to be a proud American. After that he was done. If he hadn't gotten out of that office he would have terrorized someone with his fist.

It was just a bad day all around. He thought tragedy shouldn't bring out the worst in people. Instead he believed it should draw them closer. Now he could see that when people looked at him all they saw was the face of a man who could be a terrorist.

They didn't know that both of his parents were born in America as was he. It was true he was raised Muslim. But he was never raised with whatever beliefs terrorists were privy to in order to justify the brutal slaughter of innocent people.

Ahmed was a pacifist. He had no desire to cause harm to anyone or anything. He couldn't believe how quickly people turned on him. He turned his attention to a mom and her three kids playing not too far from where he sat. It looked like they had a picnic.

The mother was now blowing bubbles as the kids were chasing them. The littlest girl had to be about three years old. She was laughing and clapping her hands to burst the bubbles. Her chase led her toward him. She was looking up at the bubbles and didn't see the uneven patch of grass. When she stepped in it, she tumbled.

Without a thought Ahmed was up to help her get up as her mom was trying to make it to her. Her three kids had her really spread out. The little girl was lying in the grass crying. Ahmed bent down and reached out a hand to help her up.

"Don't cry little lady, it's okay."

Since her tears were already drying up he realized she wasn't really in that much pain. It was more about the theatrics. Her mom raced over to them with her other two kids trailing behind her.

"Blake honey, are you okay?"

The little girl looked up at Ahmed as if to verify with him that she was fine.

He said, "Of course you're okay because you're a big girl right?"

She gave him a big grin and nodded.

The mother said, "Thank you so much I saw her about to go down, but I couldn't get to her fast enough."

"She didn't go down that hard. I think it was more of an understanding that when you fall people expect you to cry. She just got some grass stains on her pants."

The mother laughed and picked up little Blake. Ahmed put his hand up for a high five. Little Blake obliged.

He said, "You know you have a very cool name. My best friend's name is Blake, except he's a boy."

Wide eyed with her tiny voice she asked in disbelief, "Really?"

"Yep, really."

The mother extended her hand, "Thank you sir."

He shook her hand.

"You're welcome. You guys enjoy the rest of your day."

Ahmed decided to walk around the park after the incident had restored some of his faith in people. She didn't know him, but she didn't shun him after he did what he thought any human being would to help a child in need. Meeting little Blake made him think of his Blake and Jasmine.

The thing that irked him the most about those two was how much time they were wasting, and for what? He was pretty sure that by now they had both figured out they had feelings for each other. He couldn't understand what their hold up was. He thought about all the people that lost their lives today. He wondered how many of them would have made different choices had they known that today would be their very last day on earth.

Blake and Jasmine could have the kind of relationship that people looked to for guidance. What was between them was so rare and so unbelievably perfect he wanted to shake both of them for being so stubborn. He wished he could find someone with half the potential those two had. If he could he would never let her go. His thoughts drifted to his date for the evening, Victoria.

She was great and had lots of potential. She just might be the one. They'd only been out five or six times so he hadn't brought her home yet. He was pretty sure that after tonight he'd make it a point to introduce her to everyone. They had known each other for years and had always danced around their attraction to each other. They recently ran into each other at a work function and reconnected.

They had plans to go out to dinner but he thought he might change it up and ask her over to his place so that he could cook for her. He didn't feel like dealing with people. He didn't want other people to ruin their evening. He took out his phone and sent her a text to see if she was up for it.

He would tell everyone he needed the house tonight and to go find something interesting to do. It's not like they could argue seeing as how they told him to stay home. She responded right away and said she would love to. He couldn't help the grin that spread across his face. He looked at his watch, it was after five. He needed to get to the store and get something to cook. He headed towards his car.

Chapter 31: The Domino Effect

Jasmine was at the shop. She had just finished her last customer. She was sitting in her chair lost in space while biting her nails. It was nearing seven o'clock. Though she was in no mood to go home she didn't want to be in the shop either. She had to wait for Lucy since they rode together. Her plan to let her work consume her was a bust. There wasn't a minute that went by that she wasn't replaying in her head the fight with Blake.

It made her sick and ashamed at how she'd purposely hurt him. She hadn't been able to eat all day and poor Lucy was getting snapped at about every little thing she could think to complain about. She knew she was wrong. She bought Lucy lunch to try and make amends, but she was still feeling irritated. She just wanted everyone to leave her alone. Most of all she wanted to punch Blake in his pretty face.

She had never been so mad at another human being. It scared her. She absolutely wanted nothing to do with him at the moment. Maybe for a lot longer than that, she hadn't yet decided. Of all the ways he could have hurt her going for the jugular on the first try had offended every sensibility she had.

She never thought that Blake could hurt her like that. Even though he had the right to defend himself against her rant, she felt he'd taken it too far. She asked for some space, but he dangled the end of their friendship in her face without a second thought.

She was too pissed off to cry. All three of their stylists avoided her all day once they got wind of her attitude. She tried to just keep quiet, but anytime someone said anything to her about anything she had a less than pleasant response.

She made a mental note to send each of them flowers and a card the next day to apologize. She realized what a horrible human being she had been that day. She tried to pray about it but that was annoying her as well. Every time she would pray it was like her feelings for Blake would be slammed in her face.

Having an honest conversation with herself she kept coming back to the same conclusion about why she couldn't be with Blake.

The only problem she had with him was he was white. What did that say about her? She was so frustrated and disgusted with herself that the only way she could deal with it was to ignore it.

If that was truly the case then there was something much bigger than being attracted to him that was becoming clear to her. She was head over heels in love with Blake Jessup but she hadn't a clue what to do about it. She was deep in thought trying to process her revelation and come to terms with the fact that she had racist tendencies when Lucy interrupted her thoughts.

"Jasmine."

She snapped, "What?"

Lucy shot her a glare that said she was done being her punching bag. She looked around. Her customer was the last one to leave while there was still one stylist cleaning up her station. Lucy didn't want to air their dirty laundry in public so she walked up and grabbed Jasmine's arm with quite a bit of force.

She said, "We need to talk."

This was a side of Lucy Jasmine had never seen. Sheer shock was the only thing that kept Lucy from getting slapped. After Lucy pulled Jasmine into the office she slammed the door and lit into her.

"Jasmine, what is your problem? The world is not to blame because you and Blake had one fight. How dare you treat me like that and in front of the entire salon?"

Jasmine was momentarily stunned. When she tried to speak Lucy put her hand in her face.

"No shut-up!"

Jasmine's eyebrow arched. She wanted to laugh more than retaliate because angry just didn't look right on Lucy. She was too sweet. She should leave the mean to her.

"I understand today sucked royally, I do, but that isn't any reason for you to use me as a punching bag because you're mad at the world. If you ever talk to me like that again I will smack you where you stand. Do you understand me?"

Jasmine gave a long stare, blinked and stared some more. She was completely outdone and could not help letting out the laughter that bubbled up. She sat down on her desk and had a much needed laugh. Lucy just stared at her like she had gone over the deep end. She waited for her to compose herself. When Jasmine finally looked up she was wiping tears from her eyes.

"Oh my God Lucy, that was hilarious. I know you meant it, but still you just can't pull off mean convincingly."

Lucy folded her arms across her chest and frowned. Jasmine stood up and wrapped her arms around Lucy.

"I'm so sorry for being a jerk. Yes I did use you as a punching bag, but that's only because I knew you'd still love me. I will never do it again."

Lucy was a softie so she just wrapped her arms around Jasmine and mumbled, "Forgiven."

Lucy grabbed Jasmine's face.

"Are you going to be okay?"

Jasmine nodded.

"I've never fought with Blake so I can't say how long it will take us to get through it. I know it won't be today."

Lucy laughed but her response was interrupted by Jasmine's phone ringing. Jasmine picked up the phone from her desk. She didn't recognize the number but she answered anyway.

"Hello. Yes, this is she, who is calling?"

Lucy watched as Jasmine's face went from light hearted to confusion.

She asked, "What is it?"

Jasmine shook her head as she listened intently.

She gasped, "Oh my God! Is he okay? Is he conscious?"

Now Lucy's heart began to race. Someone they knew was hurt.

"Okay, we are on our way right now. I will contact his next of kin."

Jasmine pressed the button to end the call. Her hands were shaking as she tried to call the first person that came to her mind, Blake.

"Jasmine what happened, what's going on," Lucy asked.

In a shaky voice Jasmine answered, "Ahmed is being rushed to the emergency room."

Lucy shrieked, "No! Was he in an accident?"

Jasmine was fumbling with her phone trying to call Blake again. He'd sent her to voicemail and brought her anger back with a vengeance.

"No he was attacked in the grocery store parking lot."

Lucy began to panic and Jasmine tried to dial Blake again while going to her desk drawer to get her purse. Lucy grabbed hers from her desk and headed out of the office. When Blake had sent her to voicemail for the second time her temper flashed so strong it gave her an instant headache. He knew she would never call him back to back unless it was important.

She quickly sent him a text telling him Ahmed had been attacked and was in critical condition at the ER. He was to meet them there ASAP. Lucy was already out of the shop, before Jasmine made it out she yelled for the remaining stylist to lock up because they had a family emergency to see to.

∞∞∞∞

It was approaching seven p.m. Blake did not want to go home. The fact that all of his friends lived in the same house with the one person he absolutely did not want to see made it even worse.

He never thought he would see the day he regretted not living alone. He was sitting in his office feeling like a man with no control over his own life. It wasn't like he was actually doing any work. He just couldn't bring himself to go home.

Maybe he'd call Damon and have him meet him for a beer. On second thought maybe a drink. He could not wait for this day to end, but tomorrow was not promising to be any better. He'd walked around all day with a heavy weight on his chest.

It was very hard to focus on other people's lives when his was in shambles. He was so infuriated with Jasmine. He knew she would never apologize first because she was too stubborn to be the first to admit error.

Now that he'd had time to calm down he realized she didn't mean it. She couldn't have. There was a reason she was pushing him away. He just couldn't figure out why. He was sick about throwing her abortion in her face. He still couldn't believe he'd let that come out of his mouth.

She was by no means an angel that deserved any mercy but still he would never forget the look he'd put on her face as long as he lived. He knew that was still an open wound for her. It was for him too. He didn't understand this wedge that was growing between them. He also knew she wouldn't get over this anytime soon.

He wasn't ready to talk about his change of feelings for her, but she was pushing him away like she blamed him for her break-up. Was that it? Was she regretting her decision to choose him over Derrick? The thought of that was too hard to bear. Nah, it didn't sound like Jasmine, but what could it be?

For the first time since he'd known her he couldn't figure out what was bothering her. Why was she avoiding him? Her resistance almost seemed like it was driven by fear. He had never known Jasmine to be afraid of anything. Somewhere something was foggy in the back of his mind about not having fear. He just couldn't remember where he'd heard it.

His phone rang. It was Jasmine. He didn't want to talk to her because he was still hurt. He sent her to voicemail. A few moments later she called back. It made him mad. He didn't want to talk to her. She usually didn't call back to back, but he was giving her the space she so desperately needed. Let her call someone who wasn't suffocating her for whatever she needed. His phone beeped signaling a text message. He wanted to ignore it but curiosity won out. When he'd read the message his heart hit the floor.

"Oh my God!"

He was up and out of his seat, reaching for his suit jacket as he ran out of his office in a panic.

∞∞∞∞∞

Damon was still in his office. His work was actually keeping him there. He was managing his first major project and wanted it to be successful. His bosses were putting a lot of faith in their youngest architect. He vowed he wouldn't disappoint. He was a little off his game today though. Everyone at the office was talking about the tragedy that happened on the college campus not far from his office.

The mood was very somber as he imagined the mood was all over the city. He'd heard countless anti-Muslim remarks by co-workers. It made him think of Ahmed.

He was glad he'd put his nine millimeter in Ahmed's glove compartment. He knew he would find it as soon as he got in because that is where he kept his sunglasses. He could be annoyed about it or he could be smart about it.

He could also attribute his dismal mood to Blake and Jasmine being at each other's throats. He couldn't believe how it went down between them that morning. He was more shocked at Blake. It was like Jasmine to pull out the dirty punches because she couldn't stand to lose, but for Blake to push whatever button he pushed meant his temper had to be well beyond his control. In all the years he had known him Blake protected Jasmine, he *never* hurt her. As a matter of fact, he threatened bodily harm to anyone who might try to cause her pain.

For years they had been trying to figure out what happened on June 8th between those two, but they wouldn't budge on the secret. Whatever it was it was definitely the wrong card of Jasmine's to pull. He honestly didn't know if they would be able to get past this. Jasmine was the queen of stubborn and Blake could be prideful when it wasn't smart to be.

He was wrapping up the last of the day's work. He had just locked his file cabinet when his phone signaled a text message. It was from Blake. He opened it. When he read it his heart stopped. He had to read it twice to make sure he'd read it right because it was a forward. When the reality of the text set in he hurried to the elevator. Wasting time wasn't an option.

∞∞∞∞

Carmen was at the house by herself trying to relax. Her shift at the restaurant was brutal. She had been in a sullen mood all day long. It was too much negative energy all around her. Everyone at the restaurant talked about the horror that plagued their college campus until she finally had to pull rank and tell them not to talk about it anymore in her kitchen. Being the head chef had its privileges.

Carmen plopped down on the couch in her sweats and propped her feet up on the ottoman with a buttery, salty bowl of popcorn to veg out in front of the TV. She avoided all the news channels like they were deathly contagious. She hadn't really watched the news with any consistency since 9/11. She tried again, but after Hurricane Katrina she was done with reality playing out on the news.

It made her physically sick to see such senseless death. She was struggling with her disdain for religious fanatics. She had some choice words to say when they first heard about it, but she bit them back because she didn't want to offend Ahmed or make him uncomfortable in his own home. Ahmed was one of the sweetest people she had ever met. She knew he didn't think like those zealous nuts, but she could definitely understand people's aversion to the Muslim community.

Ahmed was the only one she knew up close and personal even though she was acquainted with others. Carmen was an avid reader. She loved spy novels and political thrillers. They probably didn't help her paranoia for terrorists. If it hadn't been for her close friendship with Ahmed she would likely not give any of them the benefit of the doubt. She didn't want to add to the tension in the house because Blake and Jasmine left it ice cold that morning. It hadn't warmed up since.

She didn't understand the depth of the buttons they'd pushed for each other but she knew it was pretty bad. One thing about Blake and Jasmine, they protected each other's secrets like they were state secrets. They had always been fiercely loyal to each other.

She didn't think they would give up each other's secrets if they were tortured. She believed the only reason they heard what they did was because the two were unaware anyone was listening. She really hoped they could find a way to deal with whatever was going on between them. She just thought the tension between them was sexual. They should just bounce on each other and be done with it.

She didn't want the image of them getting their freak on in her mind so she nixed that thought process. She was about to change the channel when her phone vibrated on the couch next to her. She popped a hand full of popcorn in her mouth as she picked it up.

She opened the text from Lucy and began to choke on the popcorn that was now awkwardly lodged in her throat. She began to cough violently. Her mind was on what she'd just read. She thought meeting her demise because of a popcorn kernel was too much to fathom. She got down on her hands and knees and continued to cough.

Her eyes were beginning to water. She started to get scared that she would choke to death. She didn't have time to choke to death. She had to go and she had to go now. She knew she couldn't panic because she was all alone and she was her only hope. She tried to think.

She put her finger down her throat and made herself vomit up the popcorn. She plopped down on the floor trying to catch her breath, but she was still coughing. She put her head between her legs and took slow deep breaths.

The words from the text message were like a flashing billboard in her head. She knew the feelings of guilt would surface any moment. She got up to get a wet paper towel to clean up her mess. When she finished she shoved her feet in Lucy's flip flops by the door and headed out.

Chapter 32: In the Blink of an Eye

Ahmed was waiting for the clerk in the seafood department to hand him his order. It was the last thing on his list. He was more than ready to leave. His confidence in people had once again been tested. As he walked through the aisles of the grocery store minding his own business he got a variety of nasty looks from every race and every gender.

There was even a woman who actually pulled her kid closer to her when he walked by. That was the last straw. He would never harm a kid. The assumption that he would completely destroyed his faith in his fellow human beings. He could feel the bitterness settling in. That couldn't be a good thing because he would be just like the people that were ticking him off.

At least the clerk in the seafood department who handed him his food was pleasant enough.

He grabbed it and said, "Thank you."

When he turned to leave there was an African-American woman standing not too far from him. He made eye contact with her.

She said, "You might want to hurry up and get home. It's probably not safe for you."

His mouth went slack. Was she threatening him or warning him? He didn't respond, just walked toward the check-out lines. He was so irritated he just wanted to go home. When he got to the front of the store there were quite a few short lines but he chose the long one because it was the lane of his favorite cashier Alyssa. He needed to see a friendly face and hear a friendly voice to restore his faith in humanity. As he patiently waited for his turn he purposely ignored everyone around him because he wasn't sure how much longer he could contain his resentment.

Alyssa didn't disappoint. Her beautiful smiling face was just what he needed.

She greeted him, "Hi Ahmed. How are you today?"

"Not so great, but I'm sure it's about to get better."

Alyssa looked at his purchases.

Her gray eyes sparkled with mischief, "Looks like someone has a hot date."

Ahmed smiled genuinely for the first time all day long. "Looks like."

"Well, when you come in here next week I want to hear all about it."

"Well maybe just the PG highlights."

She laughed, "Ahmed you so are crazy."

He grinned and paid for his purchases.

She said, "Get home safe. See you soon."

"Bye."

He walked out feeling slightly better. He remembered his night promised to be amazing. He couldn't wait to see Victoria. Even though his day royally sucked he walked out the store with a smile on his face. He was crossing the parking lot to get to his car. As he began to pull his keys out of his pocket something struck him hard in the back of his head.

He dropped the bags and automatically reached back to touch his head. Fighting hard to keep his balance he saw the can of soda laying on the ground near him spewing out its contents. His head began to throb. He turned around slowly to see three young men quickly approaching him. He saw them in the store a few times. Had they been following him? Panic began to set in. He couldn't figure out exactly what was happening.

His car was only three parking spaces away. He knew he had to get there and fast. His keys never made it out of his pocket. He reached to grab them and started moving as fast as he could towards his car. He remembered the gun in his glove compartment. God help him because he would use it today.

He heard three sets of footsteps approaching behind him. He was trying to fumble for his cell phone in his breast suit pocket. He looked around to see if anyone was in the parking lot that could help him. He pulled his hand away from his head because he needed both hands and saw his own blood stained them. He really began to panic. There was no one in the parking lot except him and his attackers.

As he approached his door his keys slipped from his hand because it was slicked with blood. He was also starting to feel dizzy.

He bent down to pick them up and saw the kick coming for his face. He went down. He felt fists and shoes hitting him all over his body.

All he could do at this point was try to protect his head. He heard and felt something snap. The pain was a hellish burn that caused his consciousness to initiate retreat. He was slipping quickly.

He heard a scream coming from a distance yelling, "Stop! Stop! Somebody help him please!"

It was the last thing he heard before everything went black.

Alyssa had noticed the three guys loitering outside the door as Ahmed was heading out, but her attention was taken by the toddler in the basket screaming at the top of his lungs. When she looked back outside she saw one of them throw something. She couldn't really see what it was or where it landed. Something felt off to her so when she finished ringing up that customer she excused herself to get a closer look. That's when she saw it.

She ran out of the store screaming for them to stop. She couldn't believe it. They were beating Ahmed. She had never seen anything so horrid in her 21 years of life. She fumbled for her cell phone in her pocket and dialed 911.

The dispatcher answered.

"Yes hello. They're gonna kill him."

"Ma'am, can you calm down and tell me what happened?"

Alyssa felt helpless.

"My customer is being beat up in the parking lot. He's not moving. Help him, someone please," she screamed into the phone.

"Ma'am what is your location."

Alyssa yelled out their location and said, "Please hurry."

The three young men were running away from Ahmed's limp body. Alyssa rushed over to him. She had to stop herself from vomiting. There was blood everywhere. She could barely recognize his face. With great effort she reached down and touched his neck to see if she could find a pulse.

"Ma'am are you still there," the dispatcher asked.

Alyssa took a deep gulp.

"Ye...Yes, I'm here."

She was crying now and seeing his blood on her hands was a bit too much for her.

She softly said, "He has a very weak pulse. You guys need to hurry."

"The paramedics and police are on their way ma'am. Can you tell me your name?"

"My name, uh...my name is Alyssa."

Alyssa was terrified and she didn't know CPR. She was afraid to even try to move him.

She whispered a silent prayer and said, "Hold on. Help is on the way. I'm so sorry I didn't get out here sooner."

"Ma'am can you describe the people who assaulted him."

She reached out and held Ahmed's bloody hand because if it had been her she would want to know someone was there.

"Um yes, not good though. There was a white guy and a black guy and I'm not sure about the other guy."

"Can you give any other additional descriptions?"

Alyssa was getting annoyed. Who cares, Ahmed was literally dying in the street.

"Um, no I can't I was trying to help my friend not get details."

"I understand Alyssa. We just need to get all the information we can to help your friend."

Alyssa could hear sirens in the background heading her way.

She whispered, "Hold on Ahmed. They're almost here." An idea occurred to her. "Wait, we have cameras that monitor the parking lot. You can have them pull the tapes."

Alyssa stood to frantically wave down the paramedics. She was jumping up and down. Patrons were beginning to crowd the front of the store as the EMT and two police cars pulled up.

The paramedics pulled up to her and hopped out. They began to work. She heard them say he was still breathing. When they lifted him to put him on the stretcher she saw his keys were on the ground. She bent down to pick them up and a glint from under the car caught her eye.

She got down on her hands and knees and pulled his cell phone from under the car. It was surprisingly intact save for a little blood. The paramedics were loading him and the two police officers were coming toward her. She looked down at herself and saw the blood on her shirt and all over her hands. It made her outraged. She couldn't understand how anyone could do that to another human being, especially one as sweet as Ahmed.

He had been coming to her register for over a year now. He was always polite, always had a smile, and never treated her like she was beneath him even though she knew he made a lot of money doing whatever he did. He was always impeccably dressed in a tailored suit whenever he came in on a weekday.

The police officer asked, "Ma'am, could you please tell us what happened?"

Before she could respond, her boss, a portly man came running over.

Sweat poured from his face from the run.

"My God Alyssa, are you alright? What in the world happened out here?"

The other officer responded, "Sir we need to ask her some questions if you could just let us speak with her first."

He nodded.

"Sure officer, I'm sorry."

Alyssa ran down everything that she remembered trying her best to remember every detail, but her emotions were all over the place. They asked her question after question and she answered them the best she could.

One of the officers asked her boss, "Sir, can we get the surveillance tapes please?"

"Yes sir officers. Please give me just one moment." He turned to Alyssa. "Listen honey, why don't you go on home, try to get cleaned up and maybe go see Ahmed at the hospital."

She wiped at the tears that never stopped running down her face. She realized she had just smeared Ahmed's blood on her face. The nausea she'd been fighting won out this time. She turned, bent over and was viciously ill. Her boss pulled her curly blonde hair away as her system purged itself. This whole ordeal disturbed him to no end. He couldn't imagine what would possibly make someone do something like this. Ahmed was a nice young man who they saw every week. He really hoped he would make it.

Alyssa apologized and told her boss she would be okay. When he and the officers headed back to the store Alyssa followed to get her purse and keys. She made herself have tunnel vision. She ignored the questions, the stares and the murmurs. She could only imagine that she looked like a walking nightmare, except this was her reality.

All she could think about was if Ahmed was going to die. She realized she still had his phone in her hand. She had given the keys to the officers but kept the phone. She remembered that he had a very close group of friends. She met all of them on one occasion when they all came in for a big party they had one time.

Sitting in her car now she tried to remember the name of the friend she saw Ahmed with the most. She was a black woman with big curly hair.

"Come on Alyssa think, what was her name?"

She pressed a button and made the phone light up. She was so grateful it wasn't locked. She began to scroll through his call log and when she saw Jasmine Monroe she remembered her name. She took out her cell phone and dialed Jasmine's number.

She answered on the second ring.

"Hello."

"Hello? May I speak to Jasmine?"

"This is she, who's calling?"

"My name is Alyssa and I have Ahmed's phone. He was attacked tonight in the grocery store parking lot."

"Oh my God! Is he okay? Is he conscious?"

"I'm not sure. He lost a lot of blood but he has been rushed to University Hospital. I am on my way up there now. I didn't know who else to call."

"Okay, we are on our way right now. I will contact his next of kin."

The phone hung up and Alyssa just stared at it. She sent up prayers and turned on her car to head to the emergency room.

Chapter 33: The Trials of Life

As Lucy drove them to the emergency room Jasmine called Ahmed's parents which she regretted because she didn't have enough information to do anything except scare the crap out of them. They told her they were going to book the next flight out. She promised to update them as soon as she got to the hospital.

With every extra second she had Jasmine prayed for Ahmed. She knew something like this was going to happen. She wished she had spent the day praying for him instead of being caught up with Blake drama. Lucy came to a skidding halt in the parking lot of the emergency room. They were both slamming car doors and breaking their necks getting inside the hospital.

Jasmine beat Lucy to the nurse's station by two steps. The short, brown-skinned nurse looked at them like they were mental.

Out of breath Jasmine said, "Our friend Ahmed Dossari, was just brought in by ambulance. He was attacked. We need to know anything you can tell us about him."

The nurse took her time looking for the information.

"What did you say his name was?"

Jasmine wanted to choke her. She responded through clinched teeth.

"His name is Ahmed Dossari. He was brought in by an ambulance."

The nurse got snippy in return.

"There is no need for your attitude. Besides if he just arrived by ambulance he's probably not even in the system anyways."

Today was not the day. She was all out of patience, grace and mercy. Jasmine was about to reach across the desk and snatch her up by her shirt.

Lucy discerned her friend's thoughts and said, "No Jasmine."

Just then Damon and Blake ran up behind them. Blake knowing her as intimately as he did could read her body language.

Without thinking he grabbed her and restrained her arms down by her side.

"Jasmine, this is not the time or the place," he whispered in her ear.

Jasmine felt like Blake was once again trying to chastise her and treat her like a child. Her emotions were overloaded. He was the last person she wanted anywhere near her. She snatched herself away from him with force.

"Didn't I already tell you that I don't need you coddling me?"

Blake wasn't in the mood. He had better restraint over his tongue so he just sent her a steely glare and walked away. He saw Carmen rushing in.

She ran up and grabbed him.

"Blake, what's happening? Is Ahmed okay?"

"We don't know anything yet sweetie. Jasmine's probably ruined any chance we have of getting that information anytime soon."

Carmen looked at Jasmine who looked ready to spit fire. She opted out of saying anything to her.

Damon said, "Okay everybody just calm down. Everyone go have a seat in the waiting room. I will talk to the nurse."

Jasmine started to protest.

"Jazzy, not now, go sit down."

They all found a seat in the waiting room. Damon began to work his magic on the nurse. He found out that Ahmed had just been put into the system. She would go find out his status. He walked back over to the group.

"Okay guys she is going to go find out what's going on and give us an update. Jasmine, you stay away from her."

Jasmine rolled her eyes when a young lady rushing in from the entrance caught her attention. She was a young blonde wearing a uniform of some sort. Her shirt, hands and face were stained with what appeared to be blood. Her gray eyes were bloodshot. She looked whiter than white. Jasmine realized she was pale as if something had frightened her. She just stopped in the middle of the room looking confused.

Alyssa was looking for Ahmed's friend with the big hair. As she scanned the waiting room she didn't see her. She took out her cell phone to call Jasmine again. When she heard a cell phone ringing she looked over at the group of people sitting in the waiting room. Jasmine pulled out her cell phone and answered quickly recognizing the number from earlier.

When she said hello Alyssa ran over to her.

"Oh my God, are you Jasmine? What happened to all your hair?"

Stunned Jasmine said, "Yes. I cut it. Are you Alyssa?"

Alyssa began to cry again and nodded her head. Jasmine just stood and wrapped her arms around her. She let her get it all out. The poor girl was shaking like a leaf on a tree. The others just stared waiting for information.

When she finished Jasmine asked her, "Okay, who are you?"

Alyssa gave her a watery laugh.

"I'm sorry. According to Ahmed, I'm his favorite grocery store cashier. That's where he got attacked. I know it's a lot to ask but if you could give me just a moment to go to the bathroom and clean up. I came straight from the scene. I will tell you guys what happened."

Jasmine gave her shoulder a squeeze, "Sure."

Alyssa handed her Ahmed's phone and left to find a bathroom. She was grateful she found a t-shirt balled up in the back seat of her car. Jasmine took her seat again and let out a deep breath. Everyone sat around with nothing to say to each other worried about their friend.

Lucy sat straight up, "Hey guys didn't Ahmed have a date with someone tonight?"

It took a few moments for everyone to come out of their fogs and register what Lucy was asking.

Carmen said, "Oh my God, you're right. She is probably supremely upset with him right now."

Damon said, "Well, let's call her."

Blake asked, "Uh, who is she?"

The question stumped everyone. They all just stared at each other waiting for someone to remember.

When it dawned on Jasmine that they couldn't remember what they never knew she said, "Guys we don't know her. I don't even know her name."

Blake said, "Okay let's look through his phone, likely the text messages."

Jasmine picked up the phone but when she pressed the button the phone was locked.

"It's locked, does anyone know his code?"

All four of them said, "2-1-3-3."

Jasmine looked at them and laughed, "Oh right."

Ahmed being a numbers man always loved how their birthdays lined up. When you added the months together they equaled 21 and when you added the days together they equaled 33. The strange part about them was that they were consecutive. Jasmine's birthday started in January on the third. Blake's was in February on the fourth. The rest all flowed consecutively through June for the month and the eighth for the date. Jasmine input the code and pulled up his text messages. The last message was from someone named Victoria.

"Hey guys I think I found it, her name is Victoria. Oh and yes, she's pissed. So do I just call her?"

Lucy asked, "Well does anyone know how long they've been dating?"

Carmen said, "Does it matter? Regardless she should know he's in the hospital."

Damon replied, "Uh, I think we should know how serious it is before we decide how much to disclose."

Blake asked, "How are we going to do that if we can't talk to either one of them?"

The nurse from earlier walked into the waiting room and Alyssa was on her heels.

She stood in front of Damon and said, "Your friend was badly beaten. He lost a lot of blood. He has some broken bones but they are more concerned with the damage done to his head and to his kidney. He is in emergency surgery. If something were to happen and decisions needed to be made who is his next of kin?"

Jasmine said, "His parents are out of state. They're flying in, but I'm listed as his in case of emergency person."

The nurse barely acknowledged Jasmine. She kept talking to Damon, "That's not exactly the same thing."

Blake interjected, "Actually Ahmed had a living will. He listed Jasmine as his power of attorney should he ever be unable to make a decision for himself."

Everyone stared at Blake.

Jasmine asked incredulously, "What are you talking about? I'm his what?"

"Come on guys you know Ahmed is a planner. When you had surgery a few months back he decided to do a living will so he came to me. Jaz, he gave you the right to make the tough decisions because and I quote, "You are the most responsible person in a crisis. You will always do the right thing no matter what.""

Damon said, "Yeah girl, you are good to have around in a pinch, but talking about wills and power of attorneys is not cool right now."

Carmen said, "I second that."

The nurse said, "I will keep you guys posted. It's also customary for friends and family to donate blood."

She walked back to the nurse's station.

Alyssa spoke, "Um guys, I had a thought. I don't know if you guys are aware but Ahmed was going to cook dinner for his girlfriend tonight. Does she know yet?"

Jasmine said, "We were about to call her. You said it's his girlfriend?"

"Well, I assumed she was. He was very excited about the date."

That brought on new tears for Lucy. Damon pulled her in for a hug and kissed her forehead. Jasmine went back to his phone and began to scroll through the text messages between Ahmed and Victoria to find out how serious they were. She was speed reading through the text messages that Ahmed apparently never erased.

"Okay guys, I think he really liked her but they haven't slept together. So how serious does that make them?"

Blake asked, "How do you know that?"

"Their sexual innuendos are unrealistically optimistic."

Carmen snorted.

Jasmine continued, "They've known each other for years though. They made reference to things that happened a long time ago. I wonder why we haven't met her. I'm going to call."

Jasmine dialed her number and waited.

The voice on the other end said, "How dare you call me two hours late? I texted you and called with no response."

"Uh Victoria, this is Jasmine, Ahmed's roommate."

"Oh...oh, okay well why are you calling me from his phone?"

Jasmine hesitated and Lucy prompted her to tell her.

"We're at University Hospital right now because Ahmed was attacked tonight. He's in surgery right now and we are waiting to hear something. We're sorry we didn't get in touch sooner but we just remembered he had a date."

The shriek Victoria let out caused Jasmine to pull the phone away from her ear.

When the screaming stopped she asked, "Hello? Hello?"

Victoria was sobbing now, "Is he going to be okay? How serious is it?"

"We're not sure but you can come to the hospital and wait with us. We're going to be here until, well just until."

"Okay, okay, I'm on my way right now."

Jasmine hung up and let out a deep breath. She looked up and met Blake's eyes. She swore they could see into her soul. She turned her body and let her back face him. The suggestion was not lost on him, but now was not the time to address it.

Damon asked Alyssa, "So, can you tell us what happened?"

She laid out the incident as humanely as she could. The Asian lady was in tears and Alyssa could tell the two guys were barely hanging on to their restraint. Jasmine's and the Hispanic woman's face were stoic.

"I'm so sorry. I got distracted by this crying baby that was in my line. I didn't see it in time to stop it before it happened."

Lucy asked, "So you're basically saying this was just a hate crime?"

"Yeah, I think so because I doubt they were robbing him. It seemed malicious and almost personal. With what happened on the college campus today I guess it has everyone on edge."

Jasmine snapped, "That's not an excuse!"

"Oh no, sorry, I didn't mean to suggest it was. I'm sorry, I didn't mean it like that."

Blake grabbed Alyssa's hand.

"It's okay. She knows you didn't mean it like that."

Jasmine cut her eyes at him.

Blake continued, "Thank you so much for being there for our friend. You may have saved his life."

A gentleman holding on to a crying woman from the other side of the waiting room angrily spoke toward them.

"If he was one of those religious nuts I hope he dies. My daughter is fighting for her life and for what? If she loses her life he deserves to lose his."

They all stared at him dumbfounded.

Damon said, "Yo homie, you don't know us like that. I suggest you chill before it really gets ugly in here."

Lucy stood between Damon and the distraught man.

She pleaded, "Damon no. This isn't gonna help. Ahmed would never be okay with it going down like this."

The man stood and said, "You are a traitor to your own country defending the likes of his kind."

Jasmine stood, "His kind? And what kind is that, an American citizen who is completely innocent and who was attacked in a grocery store parking lot because of who he was perceived to be? So I guess you deserve to be dealt with for every wrong every white man has ever done. Our friend is fighting for his life just like your daughter. They are both innocent victims of crazy people. How can you be so hateful?"

The woman with him was an emotional wreck.

She managed, "Please stop. Just stop."

Blake grabbed Jasmine and turned her away from the couple. "Jaz, you need to walk away."

Jasmine wanted to punch Blake in his mouth. She could barely control her anger where he was concerned. But she couldn't deny he was right.

She said, "Whatever, I'm going to try and reach Ahmed's parents and update them on what's going on."

She excused herself and went around the corner.

The man looked at Blake and spit at his feet.
"Traitor!"

Carmen got between them lightning fast as she saw Blake's fist clinch by his side. She knew his temper was actually worse than Jasmine's if the wrong button was pushed. The man's wife pulled him away to wait somewhere else. It was over as quickly as it had started.

The tension in the waiting room had escalated to biblical proportions. Carmen hugged Blake fiercely. She struggled because she understood where the man was coming from but because she knew Ahmed she knew it was the wrong way to be. Lucy held on to Damon trying desperately to convince him not to go after the man. Alyssa sat down and cried she couldn't understand all the hate.

Jasmine made the call but didn't get an answer. She assumed they were already on a plane headed there so she left a detailed message. When she turned to walk back into the waiting area Blake was blocking her path.

She froze and her entire body tensed.

"Can you please move out of my way?"

"Look Jasmine we need to talk."

"No, actually we don't, I know I said all I have to say and trust me you've said enough."

She attempted to walk past him but he grabbed her arm to stop her. Her stare was vicious.

"Get your hands off of me. I don't ever want you to touch me again."

"Jaz, you know you don't mean that."

"Like hell I don't. Let. Me. Go!"

He tightened his grip on her arm and stared her intensely in the eyes. There were so many things he wanted to say to her. He was so mad at her and so miserable that they were fighting at the same time. It disturbed him that all he wanted to do was kiss her. God help him, this was too much. He had every conflicting emotion a person could have all at once.

In a rare moment of contrition she pleaded.

"Blake please. I can't handle you and this right now. I just can't."

He didn't release her but his stare became more intense because he saw the real plea in her eyes. He knew she was hurting. He couldn't help his desire to want to fix it.

"If you don't get out of my face I will make you get out of my face."

Well her vulnerable moment was clearly gone and her claws were back out. He wasn't in the mood to deal with it.

He smirked.

"Whatever Jasmine. You want me gone, then I'm gone."

It sounded so final it stung, but she wasn't about to let it show. She couldn't get mad that she got exactly what she asked for.

When they returned to the waiting area there was a petite dark haired beauty standing with Lucy and Carmen. She had onyx eyes and her golden complexioned face was stained with tears.

Jasmine walked up to her.

"You must be Victoria."

She nodded.

"Sorry to have to meet you under these circumstances."

She sniffled, "I don't understand why this happened."

Damon said, "This happened because Ahmed was a victim of a hate crime."

Blake said, "You guys, we need to contact the police and find out if this was something random or if Ahmed was targeted because of his race. It can totally change the charges that will be brought against his attackers. We shouldn't speculate and add to the madness."

Disbelieving Jasmine asked, "Are you blind or is your head just thick. Once again you're not listening. I warned all of you this morning that this could happen but you were just determined to see the world through your rose tinted glasses. Wake up Blake, the world is full of racist pricks that are so full of hate and ignorance that innocent people are victimized everyday simply because they exist."

He fired back, "Jasmine, I'm not discounting that. I'm just saying let's get the facts before we speculate."

"There isn't anything to speculate. The writing is on the wall in Ahmed's blood. What more do you need a note signed by his attackers saying that they attacked him because he looked like the psycho who killed all of those people this morning."

"Is it really necessary to be that morbid Jasmine," Blake asked.

"I'm being real Blake. Just because all of your friends are minorities doesn't mean you will ever understand what it is to be a minority in this country. So don't try and placate me with your reasonable doubt theories. Can you be a compassionate friend and not a cold lawyer?"

Blake's temper flashed white hot.

"Jasmine, you can kiss my white behind. Don't tell me I can't understand this. He is my friend too or are you two closer than he and I because you are both minorities? It does not matter why this was done because the fact remains that our friend is fighting for his life. At the end of the day I don't care why it happened just that it happened."

Carmen said, "Okay you guys that is enough! This isn't going to help anything, our being at each other's throats. Can you two not do this in front of Alyssa and Victoria?"

Jasmine snatched her purse.

"I'm out of here. I'm heading to the police station to find out what is being done to find out who did this. Regardless of why this happened I want these bastards behind bars. I don't care if they're skin is red, white or blue. Damon, will you take me? I don't have my car."

Damon nodded. He realized this was the first time their personal racial frustrations had ever come into their friendship and caused discord. He wondered if they would ever be able to get past it. Maybe Jasmine was right. Their friendship may have clouded their perception of what each person actually felt about race.

Blake said, "Jasmine, you're Ahmed's power of attorney. You need to stay here just in case there is anything that has to be decided. I'll go with Damon to the police station and handle that."

It angered her that she couldn't argue with it.

"Fine, whatever. One of us needs to leave immediately."

Chapter 34: Breathtaking Moments

They had waited for hours. The only report they got was that he was still in surgery. Everyone was restless and worried. Jasmine had tucked away all of her Blake crap and gone into the hospital chapel to pray for Ahmed and his safe recovery.

She didn't know what was wrong with her. She felt as if something outside of herself was fueling her anger. Everything Blake did grated on her nerves to no end. Spending time with God gave her new perspectives. Even though she was still upset with Blake she would try a lot harder to check her attitude.

No one could get under her skin quite like her best friend. When she walked back into the waiting room she saw that Blake and Damon had returned and was handing out food to everyone. She took a seat next to Lucy. Damon handed her a sandwich and a drink.

"Thanks."

Blake walked up to Jasmine and handed her a set of keys.

"We picked up your car. I know how you don't like to be without your own transportation."

It was so sweet and just like Blake, but she wasn't willing to fold that easy.

She said, "It wasn't necessary, but I appreciate it."

It irritated Blake, "A simple thank you would suffice."

"Well I didn't ask you to do it."

"That's not the point Jasmine and you know it."

Carmen interrupted them exasperated with their antics.

"Guys seriously? Ahmed is fighting for his life. Put all your crap away! Blake, what did the police say?"

Blake took a seat as far away from Jasmine as possible.

"They have the whole thing on video. They released their images and are waiting for someone to turn them in while they are canvassing the neighborhoods surrounding the grocery store. So now it's just a waiting game."

Silence settled over everyone as they picked at their food.

Damon asked, "Have you heard any more about Ahmed's condition?"

Victoria shook her head, "No, but his parents should be here soon."

The nurse that was Jasmine's adversary came into the room accompanied by a surgeon.

"Hey guys, I have some news."

She immediately received their undivided attention.

The tall doctor with the well-worn face said, "Your friend has made it out of surgery successfully, but it was touch and go there a few times. We had to resuscitate him twice. He suffered some pretty intense injuries. There was internal bleeding along with a broken arm and a broken leg. If he makes it through the night his chances of survival increase by fifty percent. In my opinion it's a miracle he survived at all. He is in recovery right now."

Lucy asked desperately, "When can we see him?"

"You can see him in about an hour, but not all of you at once," he warned sternly.

There was a collective sigh of relief from all of Ahmed's loved ones. It seemed like everything was falling into place.

The doctor said, "I will have the nurse get you when you can see him. It won't be that much longer."

Victoria, Lucy and Alyssa broke down in tears. Jasmine was still holding her breath. When she finally released it she fought hard not to cry. She wanted to stay strong because she could see that all her friends were taking this pretty hard.

Blake watched Jasmine fight her emotions. He knew her so well it was chilling. He could practically see the thoughts running though her head. He knew she was trying to stay strong. As tough as she was she too had a breaking point.

He knew it was only a matter of time before she broke because she and Ahmed were very close. They all were, but Jasmine loved so hard. He wanted to wrap her in his arms and take her away from all of this. He didn't want to think about losing Ahmed. The thought was too painful so he kind of numbed himself to it like he did his feelings for Jasmine.

The hour came and went. Like she promised the nurse was back to escort them to see Ahmed. His parents had just arrived shortly before and everyone agreed that they should go first.

They left the waiting area of the emergency room and headed to a waiting area closer to where Ahmed was now being kept. They all took a seat and waited patiently, except for Victoria.

She paced the small room back and forth as if that would make time go faster. When his parents came out a short while later his mother was wrapped securely in his father's arms as she wept. His father's face was just like Ahmed's. He didn't cry. He just led his wife to the other side of the waiting area.

Disregarding the doctor's orders the five of them went in next. Victoria understood her place. She didn't resent it because she knew how much they all meant to each other. She would get to see him next. Alyssa quietly waited her turn. She knew she was last on the list. She was just grateful he had made it out of surgery.

Blake and Damon were the first to enter the room. They both took in a sharp breath at the sight of Ahmed lying there so still and broken. Blake stood to the left of his bed and Damon went to the right. Jasmine came in next and unconsciously gravitated to Damon because of her simmering anger just below the surface.

When she saw his face all bruised and battered she thought she would toss her cookies. She bore down to stop it. Carmen and Lucy stood at the foot of his bed. Lucy was silently weeping as Carmen rubbed her back fighting back her own emotions.

Ahmed's head was bandaged in gauze that was stained with blood. One side of his face was swollen and sporting black and blue coloring, the eye swollen shut. His right arm was in a cast lying across him. His left leg was in a cast propped up on some pillows.

Ahmed groggily said, "Well, I guess I ruined everyone's night. Sorry about that."

No one laughed at his poor attempt at humor. With his single eye he could see the fear and trepidation in each pair of eyes that looked back at him in horror. He thought he must've looked as bad as he felt. This was not the group that was about to lie to him about his chances of survival.

Damon said, "Asking you how you feel seems pretty stupid. Man what happened?"

He whispered, "Water."

Jasmine hurried over and put the straw from the cup of water sitting on the bedside table to his lips.

Like a mother she cooed, "Drink it slow sweetie."

When he'd finished he said, "Jazzy you were right. All day long I had been getting dirty looks, talking behind my back and nasty notes left in my office. I took off early because it was really starting to get to me. He shifted his eye to Blake. I went to the park and met the cutest little girl when she fell down right in front of me. She had to be about three, her name was Blake too."

Blake found a small smile.

"She made me remember the fight you two had this morning."

Jasmine said, "Ahmed we don't need to talk about this right now. You should get your rest."

He concentrated his eye on her for a long moment and made her squirm. Then he looked at Blake.

"You two are still fighting aren't you?"

Carmen said, "Like hell cats and rabid dogs. They are so ridiculous."

Jasmine and Blake both felt like children being tattled on. They avoided eye contact with each other.

Ahmed continued, "Look guys I thought I was going to die tonight and what flashed in my head in those very painful moments was all the people that I loved. You guys, my parents and Victoria."

Stunned by the last name they all stared at him. He gave a little chuckle that turned into a cough. Jasmine was there to give him more water.

"You two need to remember all the people that lost their lives today. They have no more chances. It's so obvious to everyone in this room including the two of you that you two are very much in love with each other. What are you waiting for?"

They stared at each other. Their silence spoke volumes. They managed no answer for Ahmed.

He said, "Well, I tell you what, you guys are making the biggest mistake of your lives. Whatever reason you think is a valid one it's not. Nothing is worth denying what is truly in your heart. Tonight I am faced with my own mortality. What I am regretting the most is that I didn't try harder to share my life with someone special."

The weight of Ahmed's words was breaking Jasmine down slowly and mercilessly. She knew he was right but there was just too much to be figured out in one moment. It scared her to think that she didn't know, none of them did, how many moments they had left to waste or enjoy.

Ahmed had made her his power of attorney because she was calm in a crisis but that tiny grip she had on her control was quickly unraveling. She didn't want him to think she couldn't handle it.

She managed, "I need some air. I'll be back."

Even though her back was to him as she headed to the door she felt it in her bones that Blake's instinct was to come and comfort her. She shook her head because she knew he would be watching.

Blake got her message loud and clear. The fact that she predicted his move only made the ache stronger. He looked up at Damon. Damon immediately got the message and nodded his understanding. He walked out behind Jasmine and shut the door. She was a few steps ahead of him.

He called out gently, "Jazzy."

She turned tears running down her face.

He went to her and held her as the gut wrenching sobs racked her body. She was sickened by the sight of her friend. She was so angry at the world they lived in. How could they do that him? Then on what could possibly be his death bed he asked her to do what was in her heart.

She couldn't bring herself to honor his wish. What kind of person did that make her? She didn't understand any of this. She begged for God to have mercy on her, on all of them. Damon sat them down and let her get it all out. Victoria and Alyssa looked on in a panic.

Damon said, "He's okay. You two go ahead in. Jazzy and I will stay out for a while."

Inside Ahmed's room he had been telling them what happened. Lucy was now in Blake's comforting embrace because she couldn't stop crying. Carmen, stoic as ever, just stood and fought her anger as Ahmed recounted his horrendous ordeal. The door opened and Victoria and Alyssa came in.

Victoria was by his side in a flash gently kissing the few spots on his face that weren't bruised.

He said, "I'm sorry I stood you up."

She gave him a watery laugh.

"Yeah, I can't even argue with your excuse."

He managed a small smile and reached for her hand with his good one.

"I love you Victoria."

Tears spilled out, "I know because I love you too. I know it hasn't been that long but I think it was already there from before."

He nodded, "Yeah it was. Five years is a long time to dance around an attraction."

She stood and pointed to Alyssa.

"There's someone who wants to see you."

Even though it hurt his busted lip he smiled.

"It was you wasn't it, the one who held my hand?"

She nodded.

"I thought that if it were me I would want to know that someone was with me. I'm so sorry I didn't get there sooner. I'm sorry. I'm so sorry."

"It's not your fault. It's okay, thank you for being there."

Lucy found her voice, "She was the one that called Jasmine and got us here so fast."

With tears in his eye he said, "Thank you."

Jasmine had pulled herself together and told Damon to go back in to spend some time with Ahmed. She headed to the bathroom to wash her face. Damon went back inside and stood at the foot of the bed with Carmen. She reached down and squeezed his hand really tightly. Even for Carmen that was a lot of emotion. The nurse from earlier came into the room to check his vitals.

"Now y'all know it is too many of y'all in here. Get out, every one of you. Only one at a time. If I catch y'all in here again I will put all y'all out of the hospital."

She laughed. They all found some small chuckles for her.

She went on, "But seriously you guys one at a time."

Alyssa, Carmen and Lucy kissed his cheek and whispered their affection to him. Blake and Damon dropped their egos and told Ahmed that they loved him before heading out. The last to leave was Victoria.

She gently kissed his lips and said, "Get better baby."

He said, "I'll do my best beautiful."

The nurse asked him how he was feeling.

"Much better now that I got to see everyone."

"Well your vitals are strong so that's good. Let me know if you need anything."

"Actually, can you send Jasmine in here please?"

Suspiciously she asked, "The one with all the mouth?"

Even though it hurt, Ahmed laughed, "Yeah, that's the one. I'm kinda soft on her."

The nurse shook her head.

"I'll let her know, but then that's it. You need your rest."

"Okay."

When the nurse walked out she saw Jasmine heading towards everyone waiting.

Though it pained her to talk to her she said, "Your friend is asking to see you."

Jasmine nodded, "Okay, thanks. I'm very sorry for earlier. My emotions were just out of control. I'm sorry for being rude."

The nurse simply nodded.

Jasmine stood at the door and took deep breaths. She hoped she didn't look like she felt. She lifted her head and for a moment her eyes met Blake's. The pain reflected back at her was too much to behold.

She wished she could stop hurting him but she didn't know how to. She cut the eye contact and walked into Ahmed's room. His eyes were closed. She didn't know if he had fallen asleep. She pulled up a chair to his bedside and held his good hand until his eyes opened.

He said, "Hey Jazzy."

"Hey sweetie, how are you?"

"I'm trying to work through it."

She nodded.

"I guess Blake told you about my living will."

She nodded.

"Ahmed I don't understand."

"Jasmine, when you decided to donate a kidney to Frank you changed my whole life."

"What do you mean?"

He took a labored breath.

"You know, I've always been searching when it came to religious stuff. There were pros and cons to each one of them. After seeing you give your kidney to one of the most hateful people I have ever known because that's how God loved you really made me stop and think."

The tears stung Jasmine's eyes.

He continued, "It made me very curious about the God you chose to serve. I actually stole one of the bibles you have on your bookshelf."

She smiled, "I've been looking for that one."

He gave her a little smile with great effort.

"I started reading the New Testament. I looked up the chapter about love in 1 Corinthians. After reading it over and over and over again I felt like something outside of myself was giving me understanding of what I had read."

Realization started to sink in for Jasmine.

He went on, "About a week ago I went to church with Victoria. When they made the call for salvation at the end, I went."

Jasmine put her head down on top of the hand she was holding and wept. After a few moments she sat up and wiped her face and smiled at her friend.

"Ahmed, that is really wonderful. Do you believe that He can heal you?"

"Actually Jazzy, I do but I don't think He will."

She stared at him in a state of panic, "What are you talking about?"

"I believe He can but I'm really tired Jasmine. I really feel like it might just be my time. I don't understand it but I'm not mad about it because I no longer fear death."

"How can you just give up like that?"

"I'm not giving up, I'm just accepting it."

He could see Jasmine was about to go into an all-out protest.

"Listen Jazzy, I need you to listen to me. I know Blake told you about my will. Everything will be well taken care of. Blake has all the information but I want you to do something for me."

She defiantly shook her head.

"Jasmine don't make me regret making you my power of attorney. You're supposed to be the rock in a crisis."

"This isn't a crisis Ahmed. It's insanity."

"I want you to do something for Alyssa. I don't know pay for her education or help her find a better job but get her going on a promising path. She was there for me when I really needed someone and I don't want that to go unrewarded. She has a little girl and I know she struggles to care for her. I found out some time ago where her little girl goes to daycare and I've paid the bill up for a year but she doesn't know it was me. I don't want her to."

Jasmine was crying frustrated tears.

"Well just save your strength and you can do whatever for her yourself."

Ahmed simply stared at Jasmine until she calmed down. She could see such a peace in his eyes and it scared her like nothing else she had ever feared. When she stopped crying she could feel it. Somewhere deep inside her heart was preparing for the inevitable. A spiritual connection they shared in that moment. Ahmed saw it in her eyes that she realized it too.

He said, "Jasmine, if I'm wrong and I survive the night I will never let a day go by that I don't live my life to the fullest. I would spend every moment I could with the person I love the most."

She knew where he was headed and she looked away.

"Jasmine, don't be like me looking back over your life with regret. You have nothing to lose, only everything to gain by finally being honest about what you feel for Blake. I love you Jazzy and I want to see you happy whether I'm looking down from heaven or staring at your pretty face here on earth. The only person who can truly make you happy is Blake. You and I both know it."

She didn't respond. How come no one seemed to understand how hard it was to just change everything you knew about your life to something so ridiculously different? There was a paralyzing fear gripping her by the throat.

What if they acted on what they felt and it didn't work? She could lose Blake forever. That is something she knew she couldn't handle. It would shatter her heart into pieces that could never be mended.

After everything they had been through to keep their friendship, how tragic would it be if they were the ones to ruin it. She hated her fear but there didn't seem to be anything she could do about it this time.

Because her fear made her vulnerable she did her best to mask it with anger rather than to expose herself. This was a big decision and people didn't seem to get that. She had too many emotions strangling her every breath.

Ahmed said, "I'm really tired now Jaz and I want to go to sleep. I love you. Tell everybody that I love them."

Jasmine sat holding his hand for a few minutes until he fell asleep. She kissed his hand and held it against her face for a long while. Before she left she gave a hard look at her friend praying it wouldn't be the last time she saw him alive.

Chapter 35: Tick, Tock

When Jasmine stepped out all eyes were on hers. She was thankful she had composed herself. She didn't want anybody to have to handle the burden she felt. She kept her face indifferent.

Victoria asked, "How is he? Is he okay?"

Jasmine said, "He's tired and he's asleep."

She nodded, "I think I'm going to go sit with him."

"That would be good."

Victoria headed into the room. Blake could tell with one look at Jasmine that there was something heavy weighing on her heart even though he knew to everyone else she appeared to have everything under control.

He wanted so badly to go to her but he knew that wouldn't happen anytime soon. Too much had happened between them in the last 24 hours. Everyone's nerves were on end.

Damon said to the group, "Hey guys, why don't we go home and get some rest then come back first thing in the morning, or maybe we can take shifts so that someone is always here."

There were murmurings of agreement when Jasmine spoke. "No, you guys, I think we just need to wait a little longer."

The way she said it had Blake taking a harder look at her.

He asked, "Why is that?"

She said, "I just think we can give it a few more hours."

His parents looked on with concern.

His mother asked, "Jasmine is everything okay?"

Jasmine couldn't tell them what she felt in her spirit so she said, "It means a great deal to him that we're all here. I think we should just give it a little longer before we call it a night."

They were too tired to argue. It was unlikely they would get any sleep at home so they agreed. Jasmine went off to the far corner of the waiting area to sit alone. She silently prayed for Ahmed and she prayed for everyone who loved him. She had no idea how they would handle this if Ahmed was right.

She looked up and met Blake's very concerned eyes. She just lowered her head discouraging any approach he may have attempted. She wanted to be in his arms so bad it burned but now was not the time. There was something much more pressing to do. She didn't need to fall apart in his arms right now. He had always been her tower of strength but this was one time when his strength could break her. She couldn't afford to let that happen.

It didn't take a couple of hours, it only took one. An hour after Jasmine left out of Ahmed's room they heard the machines screaming their declaration that his heart had stopped beating. A frantic Victoria ran out looking for help just as a nurse and a doctor were heading toward his room.

Everyone except for Jasmine stood as they watched helplessly outside of his room door as the doctors did everything they could do. Jasmine covered her ears because she didn't want that incessant beep to be stuck in her head, but she didn't cry. She couldn't at the moment as the realization really set in.

She heard his mother's and Victoria's wail. She saw his father break down and cry. Lucy slid down to the floor as Carmen, her face void of any emotions, sat down beside her. Jasmine saw Blake wipe a stray tear away. The angry rush of tears coated Damon's face without shame. Alyssa stood there completely still staring and watching the end unfold.

When some time had passed and it was all over, Ahmed had been pronounced dead. Jasmine went into administrator mode. If she couldn't do all that Ahmed asked of her because she was simply too afraid, the least she could do was this.

She first went to Ahmed's parents and offered them words of comfort. They told her that they preferred a hotel instead of going back to Ahmed's place stating it would be too painful to be around his space.

Since Carmen looked to be the most stable she had her drive them. She didn't want to put them in a cab with a stranger. She told Victoria if she wanted to she was more than welcome to come back to their place if she didn't want to be alone. She was in a slightly catatonic state so Jasmine just gave her to Blake to make sure she got back to their place safely. She would arrange to have her car picked up in the morning. She also reminded herself to send flowers to her stylists to make up for her rude behavior.

Alyssa assured her she would be fine and would call her to let her know she made it home. Lucy was a little difficult but said she was going to head over to a friend's house. Jasmine knew it was the guy she had been keeping a secret but told her to let her know she made it safely. Damon headed out too. Jasmine completed all the necessary paperwork to have Ahmed's body released when they knew the next step they were going to take.

∞∞∞

Hours later when Jasmine finally arrived home she was exhausted. She had yet to let herself feel the inevitable. She walked in to see Damon, Carmen and Blake at the dining room table.

She asked, "Where's Victoria."

Carmen said, "She's tucked away in Ahmed's room for the night."

Blake said, "Jaz, you must be drained, why don't you come sit down."

"No, I'm fine. I'm just going to go to my room. Good night."

She got no response. She didn't expect one as she headed to look in on Victoria and then up to her room. She wanted to throw something, she wanted to scream she wanted to single handedly strangle the men who had done this to their friend. She wanted to start this miserable day all over again and do everything differently. If she could do that then maybe it would have a different outcome. Tears fell relentlessly as the sobs shook her body.

Later that morning she was awakened by a constant tapping at her door. She didn't know how long she had been out. She looked at the clock; it was 10:08 a.m. Clearly she had passed out from fatigue because she didn't think she'd get sleep for days. Her head was hammering ruthlessly. She cracked opened the door. No surprise it was Blake. His eyes were red-rimmed. She could tell he hadn't been as lucky as her to get a few hours down.

He asked, "Can I come in?"

She really didn't have the energy for this right now. This was something she wasn't prepared to handle. There was no way she could think clearly with her head throbbing to a mad African drum beat.

She looked into his sad eyes.

Though it pained her to do so she said, "I can't do this right now Blake."

He asked, "Did you know Jaz? Did you know he was going to die?"

Ashamed she nodded. There was no need to ask her why she didn't say anything, he already knew. All the pain he had endured that day had stripped him of his pride.

He confessed, "I need you Jasmine."

"I needed you when you sent me to voicemail twice. Even after everything that happened between us you were still the first person I *needed* to reach out to when I found out about Ahmed. I'm not going to insult you by lying and act as if I don't need you too. We're better than that but I can't do this right now. I'm sorry, please just go."

It may as well have been a kick to the groin. His jaw clenched as his eyes sent her daggers. He backed away. The look on his face broke her heart but she didn't have any more room for anyone else's pain. She gently closed the door in his face. She slid down the door and wept. She wondered if her tears were ever going to stop.

Chapter 36: Closure

After the funeral everyone came back to the house to gather comfort in numbers and for everyone's favorite pastime, eating. A week had passed since Ahmed's death. Blake looked around at the sea of people in his home there to celebrate the life of his friend and roommate. There was some laughing, some crying and some just standing around looking lost.

Ahmed's parents shared a look of absolute devastation that broke his heart. He watched Victoria try to busy herself in the kitchen. He wondered if it hurt more to have experienced a great love and lost it or to always long for the potential that you knew you could never have. Alyssa stood off to the side by herself looking as if she was trying to absorb everything she didn't know about Ahmed through the people who knew him.

He didn't have the energy to mingle or whatever was the appropriate behavior for the host of something like this. He made eye contact with his mother. She was of course manning the food in the kitchen with Jasmine's mom. She blew him a kiss. He smiled but he needed to get out. He nodded at his dad and Justin on the way out. He felt like he couldn't breathe.

He went outside to the backyard to get some peace and quiet. Closing the door behind him he stepped out onto the white wooden porch and took in a gulp of fresh air. He loosened the black tie that felt like a noose around his neck and leaned against the column after he gave it a good kick to rid some of his frustration.

Life really sucked at the moment. Once again racism had reared its ugly head and brought pain into his life. It just wasn't fair. Ahmed was one of the nicest people he knew. He wasn't a terrorist. He wasn't like the whack job that shot up the campus and slaughtered those innocent people. This is the kind of stuff that exasperated him where God was concerned. Why in the world would He let someone like Ahmed pay for the feelings people couldn't handle?

He wished he could be like Jasmine and just accept God as sovereign, but it was hard. At the moment his heart was broken because he'd just lost a friend. The only relationship he'd had in years was over. He was in love with his best friend and she acted as if the sight of him revolted her. The thing that upset him the most about it was if he hadn't been so close-minded he and Jasmine would probably be married with 2.5 kids by now. He could see their lives so clearly.

He was such a hypocrite. He was no better than the people responsible for taking Ahmed's life. He didn't choose violence but he'd hurt people in the process like Amber, Derrick and hell Melissa. Had he really been in love with Jasmine even back then?

In his heart he knew he was. If he could pinpoint the moment it would've been that night his father beat them. The moment he realized she still wanted to be his friend after knowing and living through the truth about his father. She had him bound to her for life. He was back to his first thought. Life sucked and the choices he'd made that got him here sucked too.

He heard the door open and close behind him. He didn't bother to look because he didn't care who it was. He wasn't in the mood. He looked down at the hand on his arm. It was Amber's. Well, he didn't expect that.

She smiled, "Hey."

"Hey."

"Can we talk just for a minute?"

He didn't want to deal with this at the moment.

His face must have expressed that because she said, "I just need some closure. Give me a few moments of your time, please?"

He nodded. It was the least he could do. He headed out to the wooden picnic table sitting in the middle of the yard. Amber followed.

She looked really nice in her black dress. He didn't remember seeing her at the service but there were so many people he'd probably missed more than just her. Since she called the meeting he waited her out.

After a few moments she finally spoke.

"First, let me say this. I am so sorry for your loss. I adored Ahmed. He was actually my favorite of the group."

Blake laughed because that he knew.

She continued, "Look, I'm really sorry for the timing but I need to move on. I doubt I'll ever see you again."

He nodded.

"I watched you today. Knowing you the way I do I realize you're no longer hiding the fact that you're in love with Jasmine. It's all over your face."

His head snapped up. She put her palms out in surrender.

"Wait, I'm not trying to start a fight. I guess it's my roundabout way of asking are you ready to admit that you're in love with her?"

He didn't see the point in lying to her now, "Yeah I am."

"Does she know?"

"I haven't told her yet if that's what you're asking?"

"Why not?"

Defensively he asked, "Why do you care?"

She sighed.

"I'm sorry, I guess I'm just feeling a little smug that I was right," she smiled.

He relaxed a little and decided to get this over with.

"Amber, I am so sorry for all the pain and heartache I caused you. I want you to know I never set out to purposely hurt you. I really didn't know that I was in love with Jasmine. I wasn't trying to play you. Nothing has ever happened between us. I never cheated on you."

"When did you realize it?"

"It hit me the night of her anniversary dinner when she hacked off all her curls."

She laughed.

"Don't tell her I said this but I like her new haircut."

He laughed too.

"Actually I think it looks nice, but I still prefer the curls. It was such a dramatic change that it just got my attention and caught me way off guard."

"So the night we went to the charity ball you knew?"

He wanted to squirm but he resisted.

"I knew I was attracted to her. The realization of being in love with her came later."

She rolled her eyes, "Well that explains a lot."

He felt horrible.

"I never meant to hurt you Amber. You were the first woman I felt a real connection with after my break up way back in high school. You're the only person since my first love that I even wanted to let in. I honestly thought you were it for me, but that day at the barbecue I realized that it didn't matter who I was with. They would have a problem with Jasmine. The truth is Jaz has had my heart since we were nine years old. You forcing me to give her up made me realize how much she meant to me. That was the hardest thing I ever had to do. Honestly, I started to resent you for it."

She frowned.

He continued, "I'm not saying I was right because I was dead wrong. Your instincts were right on the money. I just couldn't see it because I was blinded by my own BS."

Amber said, "I would love to blame you and say this was all your fault but I can't. I played my part too. I should have gotten out when I first realized you two had something that I just couldn't compete with. That was pretty early on. I was just arrogant and thought if given enough time I'd win your heart."

He asked, "Are you going to be okay?"

She waved him off.

"Yeah I'm gonna be fine. I've cursed you and Jasmine to hell and back a few times. Now I've moved on to more grown-up ways of coping."

He laughed.

She smiled, "I know this is going to shock you but I think you should tell her how you feel. I'm 99 percent sure she's going to tell you she feels the same way."

He eyed her suspiciously.

"So now me and Jasmine have your blessing?"

"I know right. It's hard to believe, but to be honest you two have something I didn't even know existed. You have this total and complete intimacy that's not even marred by anything physical. You're like the perfect team. It used to drive me insane because even when she wasn't around her presence was there. In the last few months my pride kept me in the relationship not my heart. I wanted to win. Now that I've had some time to be honest with myself I've realized that. What you guys have has given me hope that I can find it too. The next guy I date, however, is absolutely, positively not allowed to have any close female friends that are not blood relatives."

He smiled. All the things that Amber thought they had no longer existed. It hurt so bad to know it. He had to get Jasmine back. He just had to.

He grabbed her hand, "Thanks for this. I feel better."

She said, "Me too," and stood.

He stood also as she walked around the table to give him a hug.

She smiled up at him, "Good luck with everything."

He kissed her cheek, "You too."

Before she turned to leave she asked, "Hey, I need clarification on something Jasmine said the night of the charity dinner."

With a puzzled look Blake said, "Okay."

"What does don't make me act my color mean?"

Blake threw his head back and laughed.

"That just means don't make her play into the stereotype that would have been appropriate to display at the time."

"Oh. Ha!"

She headed back inside and passed Damon on his way out.

Blake looked up to see Damon heading towards him with a couple of beers.

He walked up and said, "Here, I thought you could use one of these when Lucy said Amber had you cornered out here."

Blake accepted the beer and laughed, "You guys are priceless."

Damon took a seat, Blake followed his lead.

Blake asked, "So you needed some fresh air too?"

"Nah, I really just came to check on you."

"Me? Why?"

"Because I know you man and I know you came out here to sulk. So what are you going to do about Jasmine? You two have been walking around on eggshells for a week trying to avoid each other and for what? If we can learn anything from Ahmed it's that you never know when your time is up."

Blake took a sip of his beer.

"I hear you. I want her so bad my balls are perpetually blue."

Damon choked on his beer.

"That's TMI man, TMI! Man you can hang that up. Jasmine ain't gon give you none until you jump that broom homie."

Blake sighed, "Yeah you're right about that, but that's not a problem. I would marry Jasmine in a heartbeat if I knew she felt the same way or if I could get her to speak to me."

Damon paused mid sip, "Whoa, whoa, whoa! Wait a minute now, you're ready to pop the question?"

"You said life is too short and you know better than anyone how much time me and Jasmine have wasted. I'm tired of being mad. The two of us really have no reason to drag out a relationship. We've practically been dating since we were two."

"True, but I guess your other relationships wouldn't have been as entertaining had you guys hooked up back in high school."

Blake laughed.

"So what do I do Damon? This is big. It's going to change everything for everybody."

"Man don't worry about everybody else. After all this time you and Jasmine deserve to snatch your little piece of happiness. Jazzy's a strong black woman. You're gonna have to put your foot down and be like...Woman," Damon said, in a faux macho voice. "Look here, we need to talk and I don't want no lip. I'm taking you away this weekend. We got some stuff to deal with it so be ready when I call! And then just walk off."

Blake laughed hard.

"Dude, you're an idiot. How about I translate that to say, we should take a trip, get away from everybody and finally have a heart to heart about all of this."

"Okay fine, if you wanna do it the soft way. I think my way would be more entertaining for me, Carmen and Lucy though."

Blake just shook his head.

Damon continued, "Now remember, Jasmine is still pretty wounded. She can be a beast when she's like that. Don't take no for an answer. You're going to have to force her to deal with this because she's avoiding it."

"Why do you say she's avoiding it?"

"Man come on, why do you think Ahmed made Jazzy his power of attorney? Because she is always cool, calm and collected and she's smart. She makes good decisions."

Blake nodded in agreement.

"For the last two weeks she's been a mess and so unlike herself. Only love or fear can fluster somebody like Jasmine into being this off her game. It might be a little of both."

There it was again, that word, fear. He remembered Jasmine's dream and Nurse Ashley's warning. Could that be it? Was she warning them of their fear all along?

"Do you really think she's in love with me?"

Damon just shook his head in exasperation.

"Okay, let me ask you this. Do you think she is attracted to me because Jasmine has always been adamant about her non-attraction to white men? I've never flat out ruled out dating black women, I just don't do it."

Damon put down his beer.

"Look man, if she's in love with you then she's attracted to you. I'm not the one you should be asking. You should be asking her all of this."

"I know man but she's so annoyed with me right now I keep thinking it's just going to blow up in my face."

"Man you know Jasmine better than anyone else in this world. If you can't figure out how to get through to her then it simply can't be done."

Blake changed the subject. He was sick of thinking about it.

"So how are you doing?"

Damon responded, "I'm dealing man, though I have been doing some strange things lately."

Interest piqued, Blake asked, "Like what?"

"Like I slept with Carmen."

Blake spit out his beer.

"You what? When?"

"The night Ahmed died. It was crazy man."

Blake simply stared waiting for an explanation.

"We were the last to go to bed that night, or should I say that morning. After I went to my room she knocked on my door about five minutes later."

"Just like that, she just came and offered it on a platter?"

Damon laughed, "No fool. She just said she wasn't ready to be alone. Lucy wasn't there and you and Jasmine had your own issues to contend with that night."

Blake nodded, "So how did it happen?"

"It was pretty innocent we were just lying in my bed and she asked me to hold her. Being the gentlemen that I am you know I wrapped her in these big strong arms for safekeeping."

Blake snorted, "You're an idiot."

Damon smiled, "You know Carmen, she's all hard and stuff. She won't cry under any circumstances but that night I saw a different side of her. She was all soft and feminine instead of her usual ball busting self."

Blake laughed.

He continued, "So you know I'm wiping her tears and comforting her and what not then she kissed me."

"Whaaaattttt?"

"I know right! At first I pulled away and was like, girl, stop, what you doing? She said being comforted by a friend. You know me Blake, I was like bet dat up. Carmen is sexy as hell."

Blake nodded, "Yeah she is sexy. I think it's the hair."

Damon nodded, "No!, it's not like that dude. The terrifying part is I'm really feeling Ms. Carmen. Truth be told we've been sneaking around every night since then."

"Wow. So if you're feeling her why are you guys sneaking around?"

"Man it's too much going on in the house right now for us to add in our mess to the mix. You and Jasmine are at war so everyone else has to be Switzerland and not add to the drama."

Blake laughed, "Okay now you know I have to get all big brother on you because I really care about Carmen and Lucy."

"Don't even go there man I would never hurt her like that. Besides I'm not even fooled up with anybody right now. I've been chillin' for the last couple of months. Trust me when I say, Ms.

Carmen done put something on ya boy. She's definitely got my undivided attention."

Blake shook his head, "You're whipped after a week. Man come on, that's just sad."

"Hold up playa, at least I got some before I was whipped. Jazzy got your nose wide open and you ain't even kissed her yet."

Blake laughed, "True. I am so gone over Jaz man I'm bout to go insane."

"So bite the bullet man, tell her."

"You're right. I'll talk to her tonight about going away. I'll make plans."

"That's my boy."

They clinked bottles.

∞∞∞∞

Jasmine was sitting in the front yard in their gazebo. She was enjoying the balmy breeze trying to sort through everything in her life, a life that no longer made any sense. The fact that she knew Ahmed was okay was giving her peace but she missed him so much. She didn't know if it would ever not hurt. She put her feet up on the wooden bench, leaned her head back and closed her eyes. She could sense the light around her go dark. A familiar scent wafted near her nose.

She felt the wood give way under his body weight as he sat.

Without opening her eyes she said, "Hi Derrick."

"Hi Jasmine."

"Thanks for coming to the funeral."

"No problem. Ahmed was cool people. He wasn't the one in the house I didn't like."

Jasmine opened her eyes only to roll them as she stared at him.

"Derrick, please don't go there."

"You're right I didn't come for all of that. Seeing you today made me realize how much I've missed you. I know we had a lot of issues to work through, but you're obviously not with Blake so maybe I was wrong about you two."

She wanted to crawl under the gazebo and bury herself.

"Derrick, you weren't wrong about me and Blake. I have very strong feelings for him but I doubt I'll ever do anything about them because I don't want to lose my friend. Relationships are messy and full of the unexpected. I can't risk losing him the way I lost you. With that being said I know it's not wise for me to be with anyone right now as long as I have these unresolved feelings for Blake. I'm sorry. I never meant to hurt you."

"I knew it was a long shot but thanks for being honest about it. When did you realize your feelings for him? Never mind. I don't really wanna know."

Jasmine reached for his hand.

"From the bottom of my heart I truly apologize for any pain or embarrassment I caused you. I honestly didn't know what I really felt for Blake until it was too late. I would have never willingly led you down that path."

"It's water under the bridge now. There is nothing to do but move on. I will say this though, you've never been afraid of anything. That's one of the things I loved most about you. Don't start now. It's not the Jasmine everyone knows and loves."

It hit her hard, Nurse Ashley's words. She realized now they had been a warning. She also thought about when Blake said that God was trying to get both of their attention. Could this be God getting them to finally realize what was between them? If that was the case, why was this union divinely ordered?

Jasmine leaned in to hug Derrick.

"Thank you so much. I wish you nothing but the best in life. You deserve it and you deserve a woman who can be totally devoted to you. I was so wrong. I am so sorry."

"You're forgiven."

Derrick indulged himself one last gentle kiss. She smiled as he stood up to leave.

"Take care of yourself Jasmine."

"You too Derrick."

Chapter 37: The Hard Truth

Everyone had gone home. The house was all cleaned up. Ahmed's parents had been taken to the airport. They were trying to find their new normal. Carmen, Lucy and Jasmine were in Jasmine's room hanging out. They were in their pajamas and eating huge bowls of ice cream on Jasmine's bed.

Carmen said, "Anybody want to hear something that's totally gonna take our minds off Ahmed?"

They both raised their hands. Carmen had been dying to tell them about her and Damon.

"I slept with Damon, and more than once."

Jasmine choked on her ice cream and Lucy screamed.

Lucy said, "Okay, start from the beginning right now!"

Carmen grinned.

"Okay so the night Ahmed died I was feeling really vulnerable. I didn't want to be alone. Luce, you were gone and Jasmine you had your hands full with your own stuff so I went to Damon. I told him I didn't want to be alone."

Jasmine said, "You slut! You just went in there and offered him the goodies like that?"

Carmen and Lucy laughed.

"No I didn't. I asked him to hold me then I broke down and cried." They just stared at her. "I know. I know I never cry but you know I adored Ahmed. We all did. It was just so random and unexpected. I just couldn't deal."

"So then what happened," Lucy asked.

"So I'm lying there with him and he has these huge arms that made me feel so safe. You know Damon is a very nice looking young man. My goodness, the man smelled delicious."

Jasmine smirked, "He sure is. I think it's the green eyes against his skin tone, but I reiterate, you slut!"

Lucy laughed, "Well I ain't mad at you. Who made the first move?"

Carmen sheepishly confessed, "I did. He tried to do the noble thing and back off but I wasn't having it."

"So you guys have just been humping like bunnies for a week," Jasmine asked.

"Pretty much."

Lucy gave her a high five.

Jasmine said, "Please do not encourage her. So Carmen, are you two just being nasty or do you guys really like each other?"

"Well to be honest I really am feeling him. I think it could be something, but you guys know Damon. He's a ho. He is not the settling kind."

"Yeah he's been that way since we were in high school. I refuse to believe that he would play you like that though he loves you."

"As a friend," Carmen protested.

Lucy chimed in, "I have to agree with Jasmine on that. Damon wouldn't use you like that. He hasn't really been dating that much lately. On to more important things, how was it?"

Jasmine laughed and said, "I'm with Lucy. Spill it!"

Carmen blushed, "I think I'm sprung."

They all fell out laughing.

Lucy said, "While you're playing Jasmine you need to start bouncing like bunnies with Blake. You guys are so overdue. That's why you're being so mean to each other."

Carmen laughed, "Jasmine I will give you 100 bucks right now if you can look me in the eye and tell me you don't want Blake."

Jasmine didn't have to answer because there was a knock at the door.

Jasmine gratefully said, "Come in."

Blake walked in and took her breath away. God, what was she going to do about this thing she had for him?

Lucy said, "Speak of the devil."

He smiled and Jasmine thought she would melt.

"Ladies, I need to talk to Jasmine alone. It's kind of important."

Carmen smirked and looked to Jasmine for her answer. She was working through her fear but she was still mad at him.

"I'm busy Blake."

Lucy said, "No, actually you're not because we were just leaving. Weren't we Carmen?"

Carmen mischievously replied, "Of course. Your timing could not have been more perfect."

Jasmine rolled her eyes at Lucy as they began to gather all of their ice cream bowls.

"Good night Jasmine."

Blake decided that the weekend was too long to wait. He'd gone out to look for her when he saw Derrick kiss her. The jealously that hit him was dangerous. He wasn't about to waste any more time. He would do this right here and right now. She was about to officially be off the market.

He was sick of her attitude. He knew just how to play his hand. Damon was right. He knew her better than anyone. He was the only one who could put a stop to this nonsense. This space between them was going to end now. He was putting his foot down. He'd let her dictate this game between them for too long.

Blake closed the door behind them.

Jasmine climbed off her bed and headed towards him.

"Blake, you need to leave. I don't want to talk to you about anything."

She tried to maneuver around him and open the door. He gently but firmly grabbed her by her arms and shifted their positions. He had her up against her bedroom door trapped with his body. He felt her tremble but he didn't know if it was anger or fear.

He backed away slightly because he didn't want his body to betray his intentions before his mouth could tell her the truth. She stared up at him wanting to fight it with everything in her. It really was pointless. She was hopelessly head over heels in love with this man.

"Jasmine, if I hit women you would be the first one I'd deck. Why do you have to be so stubborn?"

The fear of losing him rose up again. She turned her head to break the eye contact.

He gently shifted her face back to his.

"Look at me Jasmine."

She didn't respond.

"Look at me."

She made eye contact.

He said, "I'm sorry about everything. I'm sorry about what I said. I'm so sorry about hurting you. Jaz, this isn't us. I'm not happy about the way I've been behaving. I *know* you're not happy with your behavior either. I miss you. I miss us. I *need* you back in my life."

Stubbornly she said, "So just like that forget everything that happened and go back to being best friends."

"Well no not exactly. First you need to apologize."

She gave him a nasty glare.

"Jasmine you're starting to tick me off. If I can come in here and swallow my pride then you can definitely suck it up and show some kind of contrition. I mean you're the one who started this wedge between us in the first place."

She squirmed. She wanted some breathing room. He had her trapped but she knew he wasn't going to back off until she confessed it all. What angered her the most is she knew he knew he just wanted her to say it.

She said, "Blake, can you please back up some, you're..."

"I'm what? Suffocating you? Well that's too bad Jasmine because you're *hurting* me. So let's just get to the bottom of what's going on. *Then* I'll back up but not before."

She wanted to scream.

Irritated he asked, "Why can't you just apologize? I know you didn't mean it so what's the big deal?"

She felt her resistance slipping. She knew fear was a trick of the enemy. She had to put it behind her.

"If I say I'm sorry then I have to tell you why. I don't think I can do that."

He relaxed. She was beginning to cave.

"Jaz talk to me. What is going on with you?"

How could she tell him?

"I think you already know."

His voice was almost a desperate whisper when he said, "I need to hear you say it."

"Why don't you say it?"

"Because you're the one who started this little war and this is how you're going to wave your white flag," Blake said.

She rolled her eyes and took a deep breath. It was so lawyerly of him to punish her on a technicality. She stared up into his dark blue eyes.

Nervously she admitted, "I think maybe...lately...well I've realized that I might be...okay it's like this, I think I'm falling in lo..."

She didn't finish her haphazard confession because his lips were on hers. The kiss caught her off guard. She didn't have a chance to brace herself for it. His soft mouth so perfectly fit onto hers. She reached up and fisted her hands in his hair.

Blake wrapped his arms around her so tight. The punch he felt in his gut was incredible the moment his lips touched hers. Everything about his world steadied and was starting to make sense again. Her lips were soft, warm and inviting. The fact that she was no longer pushing him away but pulling him into her gave his heart a peace it hadn't had in a long time. Reluctantly he pulled away. He needed to see her beautiful face to know it was real.

She buried her face in his chest.

"Blake, I am so sorry for everything. Please forgive me for being so mean and stubborn. I was afraid of what I felt for you the only way I could think to deal was to push you away. I wasn't entirely sure what to do about it. All I could think is that if it didn't work I would lose you forever. That I could not handle. When I put that look on your face the morning we fought I was so ashamed but my temper was working overtime. Everything happened so fast. There was safety in my anger. I'm so sorry I pushed you away. I will *never* do that again. I'm sorry, I'm so sorry Blake. The night Ahmed died was so unbelievably painful. Then I realized too late what I had done by continuing to push you away. I'm sorry."

It meant the world to him that she wished she could take that one moment back.

"I gave out some pretty hard blows myself," he said.

"Let's never fight again."

He smiled, "I am definitely on board with that idea. It took 25 years for us to have our first fight. I think we can make it another 25 without incident." Blake caressed her face. "Jaz, I've been in love with you since we were nine. I've just been blinded by my own prejudices because I didn't understand that it was okay to look for love with you."

"When I realized the same thing it made me sick. So what do we do now?"

He grabbed her face with both hands.

"I've waited a long time to do this, so let me do it right this time."

He gently placed his lips on hers again and kissed her with such exquisite tenderness it made her want to cry. They explored each other through their kiss for a long while. When the kiss was broken she was shocked to see unshed tears in his eyes.

He put his forehead on hers, "Jasmine I love you so much. I don't want to be just your friend anymore. I want you as my friend, my lover and my future."

She couldn't hide her shock. Her mouth fell open. He chuckled.

"You're so adorable." He kissed her all over her face. "Jasmine, I love you more than I ever thought I could love another human being. My love for you runs very deep. It's rooted and grounded in this friendship. It's more important to me than anything else. It was always untainted and innocent. I never thought for a moment about you in a sexual way, not once. You were just one of my boys, with excellent tits."

She laughed.

"But that night of your anniversary dinner it's like once those curls were gone I could see your face so clearly. It was the most beautiful face I had ever seen. That dress made you look like a woman for the first time not just my friend who was always in my baggy clothes. I've seen you dressed up before but not like that. Then those lips of yours, I literally couldn't think. For the first time ever my body reacted to yours. It traumatized the heck out of me. All I could think to do was run."

She laughed.

He pinched her nose, "Oh so that's funny?"

She laughed again, "Heck yeah it's funny because I didn't know what was wrong with you."

"I can't tell you how relieved I was when you came to me that night because it meant that you weren't with Derrick. The thought of you with him made me insane with jealousy. I have done everything in my power to go back to the way it was before that night, but I can't. I notice everything you do. Whenever you touch me you're doing things to me that's not supposed to come from you. I find myself doubting my abilities to please a woman for the first time ever. I'm stressing because you being a black woman never mattered before. Now I'm nervous about would I satisfy you, am I enough man for you? Will I measure up to her expectations? How am I supposed to approach all that booty?"

She choked on her surprised laughter.

He smiled now too, "Don't laugh, I'm serious."

She asked, "What about...what about everything else? Blake this will change everything in our lives and in other people's lives. What if it doesn't..."

He put his finger over her lips and said, "Shhh. Tell me how you feel about me. Do you want more than this friendship with me?"

She felt the heat in her cheeks. Did she ever.

She cleared her throat and said, "I never even thought about dating a white guy. It was always ingrained in me by my mother. Treat them fairly but don't trust them. For me it was bring home a man that looks like your dad. When we were little I really didn't see your color. You were just this boy that was my friend. Like you said it was so pure and innocent there was no point in even acknowledging other people's opinions. I just knew that I felt safe with you, that you had my back. Even though you knew the worst of me you loved me anyways. I've never enjoyed being with one person the way I enjoy being with you. I always had someone. You always had someone so it never occurred to me to look for anything more. Then that night you got all sexy to take Amber to that thing, with your perfectly tailored tux, I dern near jumped your bones. I was appalled like Jasmine what the hell? Your mouth was driving me crazy."

He smirked.

"I felt like I violated something sacred. It terrified the crap out of me especially the little twinge of jealousy toward Amber.

You know me, I'm not the jealous type, but I couldn't stand the thought of you in her arms or her bed. I realized that I had been in love with you for a really long time. I honestly was so blind to it because I never thought to look there for love."

He let out a deep breath. For the first time in months he began to relax.

He laid his forehead on hers.

"I'm just glad this isn't just a physical attraction but something real.

She laughed, "Now I'm wondering how in the heck I'm going to react to pink body parts!"

He threw his head back and laughed hysterically.

Sober now he looked into those big brown eyes and said, "Jasmine I love you so much it alarms me because I know it can only grow. You're the woman that gave my father your kidney just so he would have more time to make it right with me. That man treated you worse than any person should ever be. No woman can take your place in my heart. I'm sorry I couldn't see past my own preconceptions to see it sooner, while true happiness evaded you."

She responded, "You're the man who was willing to raise my child as his own. You're the man who held my hand through an abortion that you didn't want me to have. You're the man that held me on every birthday my child never had because I couldn't stand the guilt. You're the man that loved me through it all and never judged me. No man could ever love me the way you do. I'm amazed I have the capacity within me to feel what I feel for you. I'm so sorry I let the color of your skin keep you from being loved the way you deserve."

He kissed her again because it was quickly becoming one of his favorite things to do.

He broke the kiss and whispered, "How much do you want to bet that those three are on the other side of the door trying to listen?"

She laughed, "Can't take that bet because I believe you're right."

He pulled her to his side and snatched the door open. Lucy almost tumbled in but Damon grabbed her with one arm to prevent it. They all laughed.

Carmen screamed, "Oh my God you guys, I'm so happy. We couldn't exactly hear all the words but we figured the long pauses involved kissing."

They laughed. This had been a long time coming. Lucy and Carmen hugged Jasmine. Damon gave Blake's fist a bump. When the girls released Jasmine they jumped into Blake's arms and kissed him all over his face.

Damon kissed Jasmine, "I'm happy for y'all baby girl."

"I know, thanks Damon."

Blake said, "Okay now that we have shared this moment with everybody, I need y'all to find something else constructive to do because me and my lady have a lot of things to uh...discuss."

Jasmine's eyebrow shot up, "So I'm your lady now?"

He kissed her hard and said, "Absolutely."

Carmen and Lucy gushed with oohs and aahs.

Damon said, "Come on ladies. Let me take y'all out for a movie or something. No chick flicks! There is too much romance in the air."

They laughed.

Blake said to him, "Thanks."

"Anytime bro."

Chapter 38: No Time to Waste

Blake grabbed Jasmine's hand and led her back into her room. He closed the door. He lay across her bed and pulled her down on top of him.

She smirked, "Now as bad as I want you, you know you're not about to get none right."

He laughed, "Yeah I know that."

"Good."

"I just really want to hold you. It's seems like forever. It means so much more to me now to be able to put my arms around you knowing that you're mine."

He rolled so that they were now facing each other. This was all happening so fast. Jasmine felt like she was trying to catch her breath.

She asked, "Babe, so after our first kiss we're in a committed relationship with each other, just like that?"

"What? Don't tell me you want to date me and get to know me to see if we're a good fit?"

She laughed, "No, but this is just happening so fast. I feel like I'm dreaming or something."

"Okay, well do you have a problem being committed to me or something? Is there another guy in your life that I have to knock out?"

She rolled her eyes, "No of course not. He wouldn't last anyways. That much we know."

He pulled her closer to him.

"You know this could go a lot faster if you would just say yes."

She gave him a puzzled look, "What are you talking about?"

He looked her deep in her eyes, "Marry me Jaz."

To say she was speechless was an understatement.

When she found her voice she gasped, "Oh my God. You're serious aren't you?"

Without a hint of doubt or disinclination he said, "Yes."

"Blake isn't this too fast I mean..."

He kissed her to stop her denial then said, "Tell me Jasmine, what are we waiting for? How much time have we wasted? I'm so ready for this I just had to know that you felt the same way. If you can give me *one* reason why we should wait I will oblige."

She gawked at him taken aback. She couldn't think of any reason. She knew no one would ever love her more. She recognized she would never love anyone else. She believed that she could take him for better or for worse, for richer or for poorer, in sickness and in health without hesitation. This was so big, but her heart, her mind and her spirit was screaming yes.

She whispered, "Yes."

His smile was so big it made her laugh, "Really?"

"Yes really, unless this is just a plot to get in my panties?"

He laughed and kissed her cheek, "Well of course it is."

She laughed. He sat up and dug into his jeans pocket. He pulled out a small black velvet box.

Her eyes got big.

"Oh wow, you really were serious."

"Jasmine, if Ahmed made me realize anything it's that tomorrow is not a guarantee. I will not waste another minute of my happiness for anything or anyone."

He opened the box to reveal a three-carat princess cut diamond in a platinum setting. He slid it on her finger.

She held her hand up to admire it and exhaled, "Blake it's so beautiful. Oh my God, I can't believe you did this."

She looked at him with such love on her face he felt like the luckiest man in all of creation. She kissed him with so much passion it took his breath away. She broke the kiss to catch her breath and to look at her ring again. He laughed. Proud that he'd gotten the ring right.

She said, "I'm struggling right now."

"With what?"

"With my morals. When a man gives you a flawless three-carat diamond you give him the goodies."

He laughed hard.

"Girl, you are crazy. I've waited all this time. Besides, I know you'd be worth the wait."

Their eyes met and the love between them took on its own personality. She reached up and ran her hands through his hair. She kissed his temple. It sent a shiver through him like nothing he'd ever felt. He leaned down and kissed her nose, her lips and the scar his father left on her jaw. He kissed her neck. His hands began to roam. Jasmine's body simply yielded. His touch was electric. It was blowing her mind that it was Blake's hands that had this effect on her. She'd never felt more completely in tune with another human being.

He brought his lips back to hers and kissed her like his life depended on it. She felt her control slipping. She was surprised that she wanted it to slip. That's when she knew she had to stop. Jasmine pulled away trying to catch her breath.

"Blake wait. We have to stop now or I won't be able to."

His eyes were on hers. They were dark and smoldering with a yearning for her. His mind was in agreement but his body not so much. His breathing was labored.

He said in a husky voice, "Okay babe, but just give me a second okay. Don't touch me for the next few minutes."

She laughed and moved away from him, "Thanks."

They lay beside each other in silence for several minutes. Jasmine began to cry uncontrollably.

Blake sat up alarmed, "Hey what's wrong?"

Her heart couldn't handle the emotional roller coaster it was on. Something had to give.

She said, "I miss him so much Blake. It's not fair. He didn't deserve it. He was a good person. How do we just walk around this house knowing he will never come home again?"

His heart sank. He knew exactly where she was coming from. He hadn't really grieved either. How could he when they were out of sync. He wrapped her in his arms as his own pain slid quietly from his eyes.

"Shhh baby, it's okay. I miss him too. We just have to take it one day at a time."

"Blake, I don't know how to do this."

"I thought you were the one who said even if you don't agree with God's plan you accept it."

She sniffled, "I'm not angry with God. I'm angry with the people that killed him. I'm angry at him for going out alone. Even though I'm willing to accept that God allowed it to happen it still hurts. I still have to miss him every day."

Blake let that marinate for a little while as he continued to comfort Jasmine. After a while her sobs began to ease. He continued to stroke her back.

He said, "I'm sorry baby I know this is hard. It's going to be hard on everyone but we will be okay. The five of us will be okay."

She nodded and continued to hold on tight.

He said, "I really don't understand how you cannot be mad at God. After everything we've seen and been through why do you keep letting him off the hook? I mean if he's God then this kind of stuff doesn't' have to happen. So why does it?"

Jasmine knew Blake struggled with his relationship with God and she understood why. She knew this was an opportunity to be a witness for Christ. She didn't want to mess it up. Jasmine sat up and wiped her eyes.

"Listen honey, I get your frustration, I really do. One of the main things I try to remember about my relationship with God is that He is in control. Everyone has the freedom to make their choices. We're given information and then we make a choice. Some people think they don't really have a choice but in actuality they do. They just don't want to deal with the consequences of the harder choice."

"Okay, we have a choice. What does that have to do with God being in control?"

She knew she needed another tactic.

"Look at it like this. The same God that told me to give your father my kidney is the same one that for whatever reason did not stop this from happening. I believe some things God causes and some things he just allows to happen."

"Meaning?"

"Look at what happened when I gave your father my kidney. At first it seemed like all hell was going to break loose and nothing good could come out of it but look at all of us now. You're relationship with your father is better than ever. I actually have a relationship with your father and your parents act like they're on their honeymoon these days. That one thing changed all those other things."

"Okay so you're saying that whenever something bad happens I should try to find what good can come out of it."

"Yes, that's what I'm saying."

"Whatever good I can find that came from Ahmed's death won't make me feel better about losing him."

"I agree with that, but that's the part where you just have to accept that God is sovereign and that there is a master plan."

"So what good things can we say came from losing our friend?"

"Me and you. We finally let go of all of our fears and are giving love a chance. Losing him made us realize just how precious life truly is. We shouldn't waste it on stuff that doesn't really matter in the grand scheme of things."

"Okay. I'll add Carmen and Damon."

"Right, now is he playing with her or does he really like her? I love my Damon but, I will cause him great pain if he hurts her," Jasmine said with no humor.

"Oh trust me, he is definitely into Carmen. I don't think he would ever hurt her like that. She means too much to him. Jasmine is any of this worth Ahmed's life?"

"No, I don't think we will ever see it that way. In my mind I wish we could have it both ways, Ahmed to see us all together. But see, that's just it. We can't know what's ahead in the future. We can't know if this hadn't happened if any of these things would be. We also can't know what is in the future for these relationships or what they will bring into the world. We don't know what our children will be or who's lives we will touch and how. I heard a pastor say once you don't marry a person you marry a destiny. Who knows what we are destined to do as a couple."

"I guess that's one way to look at it."

"See that's the advantage that God has over us, He knows. There's always going to be little things in life that trigger great things. Just like I'm grateful for what God did through me donating my kidney I'm not going to pick and choose which of God's plans I like and don't like. With Him it's all or nothing."

"I understand what you're saying baby, but I think it's going to take me a little longer to get to acceptance."

She stroked his face, "I know baby. Let me give you one last thing to think about. I'm not mad at God about his death because his grace and mercy is so sufficient."

"What do you mean by that?"

"God made sure that Ahmed knew Him and accepted Jesus as his personal Lord and Savior before he left this earth. That's God. That's sovereign. So his eternity is taken care of. That's what really matters."

He stared at her for a long moment while he let it all sink in. As it did, something began to prick his heart. He didn't exactly know what it was though.

He confessed, "I am so grateful for whatever brought you to me like this because I don't think I could have kept going if I couldn't be with you."

She kissed him softly and lay on his chest.

"I love you Blake, more than you will ever know."

"I may have an idea because there are no words for the way I feel about you."

Chapter 39: Heart to Heart

Blake and Jasmine were in the kitchen making breakfast which consisted of bacon, eggs and grits. The breakfast was coming along very slowly because they kept stopping to kiss, tickle or hug each other. Damon descended the stairs and headed to the kitchen for some juice. What he saw caught him off guard. He had to remember what had transpired the night before.

Jasmine and Blake were blocking the refrigerator as they were locked in an intimate embrace. He noticed that Blake's hand rested possessively on Jasmine's backside. Damon cleared his throat. Blake looked up and smiled. Embarrassed, Jasmine buried her face in Blake's chest.

Damon asked as his eyes landed on Blake's hand, "I thought you weren't into that dawg."

Blake grinned, "A very wise man once told me that one could learn to get into that."

Damon laughed and extended his fist for a bump.

"Now can y'all please get from in front of the fridge? I'm thirsty."

Jasmine asked, "Hey where is Carmen and Lucy? We have some important stuff we need to discuss."

Damon replied, "Carmen should be down any minute. I don't know if Lucy is here or not."

Blake picked up a cell phone that was on the counter and dialed Lucy.

"Hey are you home?" He waited for her response. "Okay see you soon."

When he hung up Damon and Jasmine stared at him waiting for an explanation.

Blake said, "She is actually on her way home now, about five minutes away. Enough already. We need to meet this guy she's been creeping with."

They both nodded. As Damon was sipping his juice Carmen descended the stairs with a Cheshire cat grin on her face. Jasmine gave her a knowing look and laughed. It made Carmen blush. Damon poured her a glass of juice and brought it to her as she sat at the table. The two of them joined them at the table with breakfast to wait for Lucy.

Carmen asked, "Why does everyone look so serious?"

Blake answered, "Serious business to discuss."

His somber look gave Carmen pause. Before she could ask Lucy popped her head into the front door.

She looked to be in a good mood.

"Morning guys! Why is everyone sitting at the table staring at me?"

Damon said, "We were just discussing who you been tiptoeing with and why we don't know him."

Lucy rolled her eyes as she sat next to Carmen. She stole Carmen's glass and took a sip.

Jasmine said, "Let's say grace people."

They all bowed their heads as Jasmine blessed the food.

As they began to dig in Blake said, "Okay guys it's time to have that talk. Jasmine and I were discussing some things last night about Ahmed's final wishes. It's about time we dealt with it."

The mention of Ahmed's name brought a very somber, painful mood on the moment of breaking bread together.

Lucy asked, "Do we have to do this now?"

Jasmine responded, "Yeah sweetie, we do."

Carmen said, "Okay then, just spit it out."

Blake took the floor, "Okay guys as his attorney you were made aware that Ahmed made out a living will. Ahmed was a very well off young man. He was very risky in his investments and it paid off. You know how much of a stickler he was about finances and saving for his future. It was his desire to pay off the rest of this house. I sent the check over-night yesterday and we should be getting the deed to the property any day now."

There were stunned faces all over except Jasmine because she already knew.

"He also left $10,000 to each of us to be used to start a college fund for our first born."

More shocked faces.

Damon asked, "Dude seriously?"

Jasmine nodded, "You know how Ahmed was about planning."

Blake said, "So now that the house is paid off there are some decisions that need to be made."

He got up and went to a drawer in the kitchen and pulled out four manila folders. He handed each of them the one that had their name on it.

He said, "So over the past week I kind of buried myself in work trying to avoid dealing with the Jasmine drama." She elbowed him and they all laughed. "But since I knew I was going to pop the question it got me to thinking about where we will all go from here because I know you guys don't want to be here with me and Jaz all over each other."

It took a few seconds for them to comprehend what he said.

Lucy choked on her eggs, "Oh my God Jasmine you're wearing a freakin' diamond!"

Carmen dropped her fork and snatched up Jasmine's left hand.

She said, "How in the world did we miss this iceberg sitting on your finger?"

Jasmine grinned in response.

Damon shook his head and said, "I see y'all two ain't playing no games."

Lucy chastised, "How could you not call us and tell us the moment this happened?"

Jasmine smiled, "Um, I was a little busy hanging out with my fiancé."

Lucy rolled her eyes, "I just bet you were."

Damon gave Blake a hopeful stare.

Blake shook his head and said, "Still blue."

The two men shared a laughed that was lost on the women.

Blake asked, "Can we please focus on the business at hand?"

Carmen demanded, "We want details immediately following this meeting."

Jasmine replied, "Deal."

"Anyway," Blake continued, "So I got to thinking our original plan was to turn this place into a bed and breakfast. It looks like we will meet our goal a year early. In your folders you will find real estate listings. Ahmed made sure that we were all financially secure and made good decisions with our money. We've been living here for almost six years so our expenses have been pretty minimal. I have found each of us, well me and Jaz's are together, three listings to choose from. We will all be still within fifteen miles of each other and this place."

Each of them opened their folders and began to look at the listings.

Jasmine asked, "So you just knew I was going to say yes, huh. That's why I don't have my own folder?"

He laughed, kissed her hard and gave her a cocky grin. She smiled and rolled her eyes.

He went on, "Knowing each of you the way I do I think you will see that I picked some great prospects based on what I knew you'd like." He kissed Jasmine again. "See, being annoyed with you made me very productive."

She gently pinched him.

He said, "Carmen each of yours has a huge kitchen. Lucy each of yours is very modern in design and Damon each of yours are architectural works of genius."

As each of them browsed they were nodding their approval.

Carmen asked, "You guys know what this means? I can't believe we're not going to be living together anymore."

Lucy leaned her head on Carmen's shoulder and wrapped her arms around her waist.

Lucy said, "Growing up is so not fun."

Damon said, "Well at least we won't be that far away from each other and we can just rotate whoever's house we hang out at that week."

The moment was bittersweet for each of them.

Damon asked, "So what's the plan to turn this place into a B&B?"

Jasmine said, "Okay this parts my turn. Let me just get this off my chest now. You guys, Ahmed knew he was going to die."

She paused to let them absorb it. She could tell by the look on their faces that they needed a moment.

She gave it a few more beats then said, "When he called me into the room he told me. Please don't be mad that I didn't tell you guys. How could I when I was praying that it wouldn't be true. There were a couple things he told me that I want to share. One is that a week before he went to church with Victoria he gave his life to Christ, which has given me so much peace in my time of grief. Even though I know we are all in different places where that is concerned I hope it gives you all some peace as well. He's okay. He's actually better than okay."

Carmen, Lucy and Damon all shared a look that had Blake and Jasmine aware that they were missing something.

Blake asked, "What is it?"

Carmen said, "Well Jasmine, with everything that's been going on we've all kind of been thinking that maybe we should give this church thing a try."

Jasmine's mouth involuntarily fell open.

Lucy laughed, "We decided that we want to start going to church with you on Sundays."

Jasmine's hand went to her heart. She put her head down to say a silent prayer of thanks for yet another answered prayer.

Damon said, "It's about time we give this God of yours a try, maybe find out where you get your resolve from to stay so strong."

Carmen added, "Jazzy, you were never preachy to us and you don't judge us because we're not living by the same standards you try to. Even though we know you feel some of the things we do are wrong you've still remained a great friend to each of us. You led by example and that's something we can respect."

Blake was shocked as well. That same tugging he felt on his heart the night before was back.

Jasmine said with unshed tears in her eyes, "Oh my God, you guys don't know what this means to me. I'm so happy. I'm so excited about what God is going to do in each of your lives."

Carmen smiled, "Was there a number two?"

Jasmine was momentarily flustered, "Oh yes of course, sorry you guys completely threw me off my thought process. The second thing was he wanted to do something for Alyssa. He said she saved his life and he wanted to do whatever he could for her.

He said she has a little girl and I think he wanted to get her out of her situation of just being a grocery store cashier. So here is my suggestion. You guys let me know if you're down. I was thinking that we set up a scholarship in Ahmed's name for Alyssa and the five of us put her through school for him."

She paused to gauge their reactions. They all gave her poker faces.

"You guys I know we don't really know her but Ahmed adored her. We are all so fortunate. We won't have to pay for her room and board if we offer her the position to manage the B&B. We can afford to give her a decent salary. It was Ahmed's financial planning that put us in a position to be able to do this. We may have never gotten the chance to see him alive again if it wasn't for her. Okay, somebody say something."

Jasmine was nervous. She had discussed it with Blake. Of course he was on board. He always had her back, but she waited patiently for her roommates to respond.

Lucy said, "I'm in."

Carmen replied, "Me too."

They all looked at Damon.

He said, "If we send our family to stay here when they come to visit do you think she'll let us get a discount?"

They all laughed.

Damon said, "Of course I'm in. I can't think of a better way to acknowledge Ahmed's legacy."

Blake said, "Great, then it's settled. The realtor is expecting calls from each of us next week to set up times to go view the houses."

Damon looked at Carmen and asked, "Wanna look at houses together?"

She goggled at him.

He laughed and said, "I'm just playing relax."

Truthfully he was half serious but he wanted to see where she was. Carmen had him by the heart strings and he didn't know what the next step was. This was all brand new to him. He didn't think he was ready to put a rock on her finger like Blake had done but he knew the thought of losing her was one he didn't want to entertain. Would she feel like she didn't mean as much if he offered to move in with her versus marrying her? This was the first time he'd ever felt bad about sleeping with a woman and not being married to her. Where had that come from? He'd have to give that some serious thought. With this new approach they were taking to know God he knew that was something he had to take very seriously.

Lucy interrupted his thoughts, "So you guys, what's the time frame for all this to happen. How soon are you guys trying to get married?"

They both responded, "Soon."

Everybody laughed.

Lucy asked, "How soon?"

Jasmine said, "As long as it takes me to plan it."

Blake added, "She means as long as it takes my mother to plan it."

Carmen was so happy for Blake and Jasmine. She found herself for the first time thinking of a future with Damon in a forever kind of way. Is that what she wanted? If she was honest it definitely was but she didn't think it was what Damon wanted.

If he did it wasn't anytime soon. They had a good thing and it was still so new. Even though it was like starting on the 100th date they shouldn't rush into anything.

She didn't want to mess it up by putting pressure on him. She thought he had to be playing when he asked her about moving in. She decided to table all that for now and just focus on Jasmine's long overdue wedding.

Jasmine said, "I'm going to go call Alyssa and see if she can come over so we can tell her in person."

Jasmine excused herself to make the call.

There was something else that was weighing on Carmen's heart that she wanted to discuss with the group.

"Okay guys, since we are having a come to Jesus meeting as Jazzy would say there has been something bothering me."

Damon asked with concern, "What is it baby girl?"

She smiled hearing Damon's new pet name for her.

She sobered her face and said, "This is about to get real honest real quick so don't judge me."

They all nodded.

Jasmine walked back to the table and saw their serious faces.

She said, "Alyssa will be here in an hour. What did I miss?"

Carmen said, "I was a little bothered about that scene at the hospital when racial tension for the first time hit us hard. I know we recovered from it, but I've been feeling guilty as hell since Ahmed was attacked because even though I would never physically attack a person that wasn't an immediate threat I do understand the aversion people have to that particular ethnicity. I know it's wrong, but I'm just saying outside of Ahmed and his family I look at them sideways when I see them in public places."

She held her breath as everyone processed her words.

Damon said, "I feel you on that, but because I've traveled all over the world and met so many different people race doesn't bother me. Plus there was no racial tension in my home. Only in America is racism and prejudice so paramount."

Jasmine said, "I don't think profiling is wrong in all situations. In some cases it may save your life. What I have a problem with is people who react on their fear when they profile and cause innocent people to lose their life. If your common sense is telling you the situation is dangerous then walk away."

Blake asked, "Okay, but what if you walk away and because you didn't do anything about it innocent people are hurt?"

Damon said, "I'm with Jasmine on that because as a black man if you call in the authorities because you profiled me they are known for being trigger happy. I could lose my life over a misunderstanding because I looked like a threat. I'm not a fan of the po-po. I think most black men would agree."

Jasmine said, "Yeah I've seen it with my dad and all my brothers. Black men are treated differently."

Lucy chimed in, "With the exception of Blake, we are all minorities. We all deal with some type of profiling or pre-judging."

Carmen said, "Oh, I profile, but I profile every doggone body. I mean if I see a group of bald head white men or some in trench coats I'm out."

Lucy said, "If I see a group of black men standing around with gold teeth and their pants saggin' I'm out."

Jasmine said, "Ah hell after the economic crash in 2008 and all the Ponzi schemes men in blue tailored suits and red power ties are the new thugs. If I see a group of them chillin' over coffee, I'm out."

Everyone laughed.

Carmen said, "Okay, so what is the one thing that upsets you about how people judge you because of your race."

Blake said, "People assume because I'm a white man that my life is perfect and every day I live a life of privilege which could not be further from the truth. Yes, my dad's family had money but I think my mom and I would have forfeited it in order to not have gone through the pain that was in our home."

Lucy confessed, "I hate it when people mistake me for Chinese, Japanese or Korean. They should just ask if they don't know. I hate how people assume that I can only do nails just because I'm Vietnamese and that we are taking over. That's just good business strategy to come in and saturate a market. It's also good sense as a group of people to support one another and build a dynasty."

Damon said, "Uh Luce, you do, do nails."

They all laughed.

"Yes, but it's not all I can do. It's what I choose to do because I had experience in it from my parent's salon. Why not make money off of a skill you have that's in high demand. I am also a hair stylist and I get sick of black women coming into the salon and automatically avoiding my chair because I am the only non-black stylist in the shop. I can actually do hair just as good, if not better than the other stylists. Not to mention that I am part owner of my very own salon. I went to school and trained to do it."

Carmen said, "I get tired of the slick comments about my citizenship by upset patrons or even my own staff. Every time someone has a problem with me that is the first attack they go to. I worked my butt off to run that restaurant. How do you get to assume I'm not a citizen just because I'm Mexican? Screw that. I was born here. I earned every single thing I have. I'm also sick of other Hispanic ethnicities looking at Mexicans like we are the bottom of the barrel. I speak correct English and I am a proud

American, but I am also proud of my heritage. I don't think I should have to choose between the two."

Blake said, "Well Carmen, I get that you're proud of your heritage. Because I've gotten to know you and your family I understand it and I can embrace it, but why do I have to press one for English and two for Spanish. I mean you're in America and the language is English. You can't go to other countries and expect them to change their standard because you made the choice to make it your home."

Jasmine said, "That irks me too. As a black person when I'm around my family and other black friends the way we talk with all the slang and Ebonics most people would not understand it, but I don't expect it to be a standardized language. When I'm dealing with other races or in a professional setting I speak correct English. That doesn't make me less of a black person because I can speak well. We're not saying don't speak Spanish we're just saying learn to speak English. If you're a proud American, embrace all of it."

Carmen said, "I agree with both of you. I'm actually fluent in Spanish. However, I understand this is the country I chose to live in. It doesn't bother me but some Hispanics just don't get that. I speak whatever language is appropriate for whatever situation I'm in. If I'm with my people and we're speaking Spanish among ourselves don't look at me crazy and think I'm wrong because you can't understand me if I'm not talking to you."

Jasmine said, "I see the injustices that are done to my race. I honestly hate when people try and say racism doesn't exist and that it's all in our imaginations. However, I am also not one of those black people who try to use racism as an excuse every time something doesn't work out. It sucks that sometimes we have to work twice as hard as other races to get less. I wish we could come together and get over all of our infighting to stop being the race of consumers that keeps all other races in the money-making business and ours out. I hate how we put the weight of our entire race on a child that doesn't know any better. Like if they mess up they are letting down an entire race. It's not fair."

Damon said, "I feel you on that Jazzy."

Blake said, "Uh, you're not Black Damon."

Damon chuckled, "You see Mr. White man, I don't agree with that. Don't get me wrong, I think my mom is beautiful and being exposed to her culture and family has made me a well-rounded person but when the world looks at me they see a black man. When I look at me I see a black man and I'm proud of that. What I'm sick of is that all of sudden we get a black prez and now people want to recognize him as biracial. Whatever happened to the one drop rule?"

Lucy asked, "What is the one drop rule?"

Jasmine responded, "It was a rule back in America's less than politically correct days where if you had one drop of black blood in you, you were deemed black and therefore a second class citizen no matter what your skin tone looked like."

Damon said, "Exactly. So bump it, I'm black. Don't change the rule now because you want to believe that it's not actually a black man in the white house."

Blake said, "I don't think that's the rationale behind it. I just think maybe in this rapidly evolving world people are trying to embrace who they really are and move on from the ignorance of the past."

Damon said, "Okay I can respect that. The world is evolving but if he himself considers himself a black man, who are we to argue with him? I mean it is his choice. That's an issue I have as a biracial person. You don't get to dictate to me which race I choose to embrace. You don't get to criticize me if I choose to pick one over the other. Maybe I want to say I'm biracial. Maybe I want to say I'm white. Maybe I want to say I'm black, but look at my skin. If I say I'm white people gon be looking at me like I'm touched, delusional or have some kind of warped psychological issues of self-hate?"

Blake said, "I don't think that everyone is a racist but I do think that everyone is prejudiced. We all clearly are. We just sat here and prejudged how many groups of people? I had to own up to my own assumptions about someone that I loved very deeply. Because of the world I live in and what I've been fed by whoever is controlling the conversation to the masses, I almost missed it."

Jasmine grabbed Blake's hand, "I think when it comes to racial issues you have to be careful about what's being passed down from generation to generation. Thankfully we each had one parent with some sense because clearly my mom and his dad are racists. Now my mom is a closet one and his dad was open with it. I can respect that more. At least he was honest. I'm glad he's changing, but you have to be careful about whose perception you allow into your heart even if the person is someone whose intentions are good towards you. Hate is not innate, it's taught. No child knows how to hate. They have to be taught how to do that. So that burden lies on the ones who are there to shape their lives. We have to put all this foolishness to the side and just enjoy people because they are people."

Carmen said, "You're right Jazzy. We feel the way we feel or we fear what we fear because of what we are taught. If we would take the time to get to know everyone for ourselves and then make a decision about whether this is someone who should be in our lives the world would be in a much better place."

Damon said, "That's good in theory, but how are we gonna make it happen. It happens in this house because we've created this oasis but outside these walls it's a different ball game."

Lucy said, "I hear what you guys are saying. But there are some genuinely bad people that do play into the stereotypes out there. I don't want to be made to feel like a racist because I'm letting common sense win out and walking away from a potentially harmful situation."

Damon said, "I got two words for you why that is a dangerous combination. Trayvon Martin."

Jasmine added, "Or Sean Bell."

Carmen said, "It's like a catch-22 right there. Where do you draw the line between personal safety and racial fear? Blake, I want to ask you as the only non-minority what issues you have, if any, where you think white people get the short end of the stick?"

Blake said, "Well if your people keep making babies I'm not gonna be the majority anymore." They laughed. "Seriously, one of the things that genuinely bother me is affirmative action. I get why it was started but I don't feel like it's relevant now-a-days. I mean everyone is afforded the same opportunities. Should we even still be talking about it?"

"See let me stop you right there," Damon said. "Affirmative action was designed to help *qualified* minorities. It's still not fair out there. Yes, it's a lot better than it was but black people are disproportionately affected in almost everything. Now it's too many black people out there living their lives, being educated and moving forward in the American dream for people to say, they're all lazy and don't do anything. True, there are some who won't help themselves but that's in every race not just black people. To suppress a whole race to the proportions that the black race is suppressed you gotta consider the system at large. Just like black people of today have been disadvantaged by the racism of the past, today's white people are the beneficiaries of the racist system of yesterday. The remnants of the past still remain and still have impact today."

Blake said, "Okay, but how long are white people going to be punished for something that was done decades ago. I'm not responsible for enslaving your people so why am I the one who gets burdened with the fallout. Why do you assume I'm a racist just because I'm white? White people don't own the patent on being racists. Other people can be racist as well."

Jasmine joined in, "The sins of the father."

Carmen asked, "Meaning?"

Jasmine responded, "The bible says you reap what you sow. The world would call it karma. So look at it this way. I can't say as a black person I'm for or against affirmative action. I understand the purpose and I agree with Damon the playing field is not quite level so it may still be needed. But no matter what you do karma will one day come for its due. If you die before you have reaped what you have sown then it falls to your children. This is why we have to be so careful about what we do and how we treat people. We can never know the depth or the reach of the ramifications."

Lucy said, "That's food for thought."

Jasmine added, "I know y'all aren't bible readers but there is a story in there that is relevant. I'll break it down for y'all. So you got this couple right, Abraham and Sarah. God promised them a child even though they were old and her eggs was powdered by this point. He was in his seventies and she was in like her sixties I believe."

They laughed.

"The promise took 25 years. So he didn't have the promised kid until he was like 100. During this wait Sarah was like dude this ain't gon happen so why don't you go on in there with my hand maiden, Hagar, and put it down one good time so we can get this kid and keep it moving."

Everyone was tickled by Jasmine's updated version of the story.

"Then Abraham knocked her up. The kid, Ishmael, is like twelve now and wifey starts to trip. Abraham bonded with him because he loved his kid. Then the promise finally comes to past and Isaac is born. So wifey is like dude, this baby mama of yours is getting on my nerves. I'm tired of her and her kid clowning my son with all this nonsense. Put her and the little bastard y'all made out. He will not be joint heir with my baby."

Lucy said, "Jasmine you are crazy. The bible does not say that!"

She laughed, "I promise y'all this is how it went down. So anyways, Abraham is all heartbroken like God, seriously, this is my kid and I love him. God told him to do what his wife said to do because the promise was in the seed he bore with Sarah not Hagar. So he put his kid and his baby mama out the house with like a loaf of bread and a bottle of water. So baby mama is out there in the desert bout to leave the kid to die because she doesn't want to watch him die once the food and water runs out. But God sent an angel that told her its gon be alright boo. I got you and your kid. I'm gonna make him great because he is still Abraham's son. He will be a great nation. So you know the Lord provided for her and her kid."

Blake said, "Baby you are silly."

"For real I have a point, just listen. So like because Abraham did not wait on God for his promise but took matters into his own hands, or rather his own loins Ishmael and Isaac were fighting all throughout the bible and still to this day all that conflict over there in the middle east is Ishmael and Isaac fighting over the birthright land because Ishmael was the first born but Isaac was the promised son."

Damon said, "Now *that's* deep."

Jasmine said, "I'm not saying it's right but there are consequences to our actions. Sometimes it's just karma coming back around and innocent people get stuck in the cross hairs because no matter how much good you do in the world you cannot stop karma from coming to collect. Treat people right because your children may have to repay the debt of your sins."

The doorbell rang interrupting their philosophical discussion. Blake got up to answer the door. Alyssa came in carrying a beautiful three-year old spitting image of herself. The little girl's explosion of blonde curls framed her cherub face.

Jasmine said, "Oh my goodness Alyssa she is so beautiful. What's her name?"

"Her name is Samantha."

Carmen said, "Please come in and have a seat."

Alyssa obliged and held Samantha in her lap.

Jasmine said, "Well, we brought you here because we wanted to offer you an opportunity."

Alyssa looked shocked and confused.

Jasmine continued, "Ahmed absolutely adored you and he wanted us to do something to help give you a leg up in the world."

"Are you serious," Alyssa asked puzzled.

"Yes I am. The five of us want to offer you a scholarship to go to college. We will pay for all your expenses. We were kinda hoping you would attend somewhere locally because we are turning this place into a bed and breakfast and we were hoping you would run it?"

Alyssa's mouth fell open. They laughed.

Damon added, "I could actually draw up some specs to add on to the place to give you and Samantha a little more room so you're not crammed in one room. That way you have more rooms to rent."

"Are you guys serious?"

Lucy beamed, "Absolutely."

Alyssa's tears fell on their own volition.

She said, "I wondered for a while who paid the daycare bill in full for me and now I know. It was Ahmed wasn't it?"

Everyone looked to Jasmine.

"He didn't want you to know he did it but yeah that was him."

Alyssa put her head down on the table and silently cried grateful tears. Carmen got up to stroke her back. Samantha started crying too. Carmen reached down and picked her up. Samantha buried her tiny face in Carmen's neck as she comforted the little child.

"Don't cry sweetie. She's happy," Carmen cooed.

Alyssa sat up and wiped her face.

"Thank you so much and yes I will go locally. I would love to run this place. I've always wanted a job in hospitality management but with everything I've been through I didn't ever think it was going to happen."

Blake said, "We are more than happy to help. You gave us the last precious moments with our friend. We will never forget that. We have been very fortunate in our lives. It is our pleasure to help make your dreams come true."

"I don't know how to thank you all."

Damon said, "Make us some money with this bed and breakfast, shoot."

Lucy playfully punched him in the arm as they all laughed. Samantha had her thumb in her mouth as she asked Carmen what her name was.

Carmen said, "My name is Carmen."

Samantha said, "You're pretty."

Carmen gushed, "Oh I love her!"

They laughed.

Carmen took a seat and sat Samantha down in her lap. Samantha seemed to have taken a liking to her. She laid her head on Carmen's bosom. Carmen never really thought of herself as maternal but this little girl was quickly capturing her heart. Carmen stroked her hair, kissed her on her head and began to rock her since it was obvious that the little girl was sleepy.

Watching Carmen with the baby stirred something in Damon he wasn't even aware was in him. She had never looked more beautiful than she did holding that adorable kid. He knew he would look back at this instant and know it was the moment he fell in love with Ms. Carmen Sanchez.

Blake hadn't missed Damon's reaction to seeing Carmen holding Samantha. His boy was beyond smitten. He knew there was no going back now.

Blake said, "Well guys me and Jasmine need to head on over to our parent's house to give them the news about this wedding."

He lifted Jasmine's hand and kissed it. She was all smiles.

Alyssa said, "Oh my goodness! You guys are getting married? Congratulations! I wondered about you two."

Lucy said, "So did everyone else. Just be glad you didn't have to live through the process."

They all laughed.

Chapter 40: Me and You against the World

As they were headed to dinner at Jasmine's parent's house she asked, "So can you see the hand of God working through our tragedy in the lives of so many people?"

He looked over at her and then back at the road.

"Yeah I can. Especially with Alyssa, and that kid is just too cute."

"She is so adorable. For me it was seeing how all of this led Carmen, Lucy and Damon to want to know who God truly is. That is amazing. It's bittersweet though I can see God's hand moving through our loss of Ahmed."

He reached for her hand.

"You're right. Seeing all of this does bring a little comfort and some clarity to seeing the big picture. Still hurts like hell though."

"It will for a while. It might always."

Jasmine looked over at Blake adoringly and said, "That felt amazing to do something like that for someone."

He grinned at her, "I know. I think she is going to do a great job with the B&B."

"Me too. Uh oh, we are almost there. Are you nervous about telling our parents?"

"Not really. We know we have half their support with my mom and your dad. I can't imagine what your mom and my dad could possibly have against it. I know they've had their racial hang ups, but still they can't deny that this is perfection."

"Yeah you're right. Clearly this moment has been building for 25 years, but just to play devil's advocate what do you want to do if we don't get their blessing?"

"I'm not going to lie and say that thought hasn't crossed my mind." He reached over, grabbed her hand and kissed it. "I am not going to let anything or anyone else come between us ever again. I don't care who it is. So Jaz, if they try to stop this we move on with our lives and do what we have to do."

She stared at him for a moment knowing he was dead serious.

"Okay baby. I'm with you."

He kissed her hand again.

"That's good because it's show time."

He pulled into her parent's driveway. He got out and went to open her door.

As he helped her out of the truck she asked, "Should I hide the ring?"

He smiled, "Good thinking. We want to pick the right moment to drop this info, but we drop it today no matter what."

She laughed and turned it around so the diamond was faced down. He grabbed her hand as they walked to the door.

She rang the bell and said, "Uh, don't you think us holding hands is going to tip them?"

He laughed and let go but said, "Well, that glow on your face is screaming I'm in love."

She lightly punched him in the shoulder. Her mom came to the door.

"Hey y'all. You are just in time because your father is about to drive me crazy trying to eat that peach cobbler."

Jasmine hugged her mom, "Everything smells great mama."

Vanessa kissed Blake on the cheek and said, "Come on in baby. How are you?"

"I'm good Mrs. Monroe and yourself?"

"Oh just fine thank you. I'm so happy to see you two with smiles on your face." She took a moment to stare at Jasmine. "Baby what's going on with you?"

Jasmine tried to dim her smile, "What do you mean ma?"

"You've got like this glow. You look really happy. What am I missing?"

"Um, nothing. Just happy to be here with you guys."

Her mother gave her a sideways glare and said, "Mmmm hhhmmm."

Blake gave her a wink and she concealed her laugh with an awkward cough.

Her mother looked behind her at Blake and asked, "And what are you grinning for?"

He sobered his face and cleared his throat.

"You know I'm always happy when I'm eating your food."

She rolled her eyes and said, "Cute." As she walked away she said, "I know you two are hiding something. Y'all have had the same look since y'all were two when you know you did something you ain't have no business."

They snickered and headed into the dining room where his mom stood up to hug them both.

"You guys, I'm so happy y'all are here. I'm just so grateful to be able to put my arms around both of you."

Lisa had ached for Ahmed's parents. She felt so blessed that her two babies were healthy and from the look on their faces, happy. She wondered, could it be after all this time, they had found their way to each other? Nothing would make her happier.

Justin kissed his daughter on the cheek and shook Blake's hand. Frank kissed Jasmine's cheek and hugged his son. It warmed Jasmine's heart to see such genuine affection between father and son. There was so much love in the room she couldn't wait to break the news. She just knew it would only add to all the love and happiness of the moment.

They each took their seats, Justin and Vanessa on each end, Frank and Lisa on one side. Jasmine and Blake sat across from them. Justin said grace and they began to dig into a honey glazed ham, homemade macaroni and cheese, green beans, and dressing. There wasn't much chatter going on as everyone was enjoying Vanessa's labor of love.

Justin noticed that Blake and Jasmine were in their own world. It wasn't unusual to see them picking off of each other's plate, but there was something else there this time. There was a new kind of intimacy between them, deeper than what they normally shared. He knew that could only mean one thing.

Frank was the only parent completely oblivious to what was unfolding before him but that was because his relationship with them was less than a year old. Vanessa knew they were up to something but she had no clue what it actually was. She would never let her mind go where Lisa's and Justin's stayed. That was simply not an option.

Blake and Jasmine were trying very hard to conceal their love for each other. They wanted to make sure they didn't spill the beans too soon since they could not be completely sure how their parents were going to react. Little did they know they were doing a very poor job. They looked at each other with such love and affection Stevie Wonder would know they were in love. A touch here, a glance there, they were once again oblivious to those around them.

Vanessa had had enough. That's when she noticed the silver band on Jasmine's ring finger. Her daughter wasn't one for rings so it caught her attention. Jasmine was giggling at something Blake whispered to her so she didn't know she was being watched like a hawk.

Vanessa said, "Jasmine sweetie."

She came to attention like a kid caught with her hand in the cookie jar.

"Yes ma'am?"

"Can you pass me the green beans please?"

Relieved that she wasn't caught Jasmine grabbed the basket with her left hand and handed it to her mother. As her mom took the basket she saw a glint of light hit something on the inside of Jasmine's palm. She reached for her hand. Realizing her mistake too late Jasmine tried to snatch her hand, but her mom's grip was no joke.

"Jasmine, what is this engagement ring doing on your hand? Why are you hiding it?"

Every head popped up to attention and focused on the mother and daughter who were now staring each other down.

"Mom, I can explain, can you please let my hand go?"

"No I cannot. Can you please tell me why you're wearing an engagement ring and just who are you engaged to?"

Finally realizing what she had been sensing Lisa asked, "Blake did you propose to Jasmine?"

Blake now had the pleasure of being the focus of four pairs of eyes.

"Mom, just let us explain. Yes it's an engagement ring and yes I did propose but..."

Vanessa interrupted, "You did what?"

Jasmine begged, "Mom please let us explain."

She replied, "How exactly are you going to explain something that you were evidently trying to hide."

"Mom we were going to tell you guys when it was the right time."

"The right time would have been before you came over here trying to intentionally mislead us."

"Okay now, let's just everybody calm down and let the kids talk," Justin interjected, always the voice of reason.

Blake looked to Jasmine's father first.

"Pop, I'm sorry that I didn't come to you first for your permission but it just happened last night. We came over here to tell you guys today but we wanted to wait until the right moment."

He grabbed Jasmine's hand and smiled at her.

"It took us a really long time to figure this out and we didn't want to waste anymore."

Justin nodded his head, "Son, you've always had my blessing. You're the only man who ever did."

Blake visibly relaxed, but Jasmine was still looking at the scowl on her mother's face.

Lisa sprang up, "Oh my goodness, you guys I am so happy. Finally my prayers have been answered. Jasmine let me see the ring!"

Jasmine could not tear her gaze away from her mother's penetrating stare. Vanessa stood and threw her napkin down on the table.

"Jasmine you are making the biggest mistake of your life. You will never have my blessing. Do you hear me? Never! You will not taint my bloodline with his blood. If you marry that boy I will have nothing else to do with you."

Lisa and Blake were taken aback as Vanessa stormed out. Justin knew why his wife reacted that way, but that was drama for another day. Still stunned all eyes turned to Frank who had remained silent throughout the ordeal. His eyes were sad as he looked back and forth between Jasmine and Blake.

"I'm so sorry you guys, but I have to agree with Vanessa. This is a mistake. I don't think you should do this."

He stood and headed towards the front door.

Lisa sat back down in shock and asked, "Now what exactly just happened here? How did one of the proudest moments of my life turn into this?"

Jasmine wanted to cry. She couldn't understand how anybody could believe that she and Blake were a mistake after everything they had all been through. Couldn't they see how perfect they were or did it all come right back down to black and white?

Lisa was so hurt by the words that so cruelly flew out of Vanessa's mouth. She thought they were friends.

She gathered her strength and said, "Let me go find out what stick your father has up his butt now." She kissed both of them on their cheeks and said, "I am so happy for you two. We will figure this out, I promise."

Blake was hot. How dare her mother look at him with such disgust? He had never been anything but good to her daughter. His dad's reaction didn't shock him as much as it hurt him.

He thought they were past this, but at least he didn't look at them like the sight of them made him sick. Or was the way he looked at them worse? He looked at them like he pitied them. Neither of them had said a word since her mother's outburst. Justin stood and put his hands on both their shoulders.

"You kids listen here. You two deserve to be happy and you will always have my support. You can't live your life for other people. If you two want to be married then I say do what your heart is telling you to do. They will come around eventually. Even if they don't you two will always have each other."

Jasmine asked teary eyed, "But daddy why?"

"Baby girl, that's your mom's burden to tell you when she's ready, as far as Frank, well I suspect he carries a heavy load too, but it's up to them to deal with it. It's not your problem and don't you let their burdens stop you from living your life."

She wiped her eyes but nodded.

He said, "Blake, you're a good man. I would be proud to have you as a son. Y'all go on home now and let me do damage control. You can come back when cooler heads prevail. We can discuss all of this then."

Jasmine stood and hugged her daddy. His heart ached for both of them. He knew it wasn't the ideal way to start their life together, but he trusted that God would make a way. God clearly had His hands on the situation if the two of them had finally realized they were soul mates.

He knew they would always face opposition because of their skin color but that was the world they lived in. It didn't bother him one bit. Blake hugged him too and then he took Jasmine's hand and led her out to his truck.

Inside the truck Blake punched the steering wheel.

Jasmine jumped.

"Did you see how your mom looked at me like I disgusted her?"

"Baby I know and I'm sorry. I don't know what to say."

"What did I ever do to her? What the hell is this bull about *tainting* her blood line?"

"Baby, I know how you feel but please don't get so upset."

"How can I not be upset Jasmine?"

She was hurt because she knew exactly what it felt like because his father had looked at her like that so many times.

"Does she really have that much of a problem with white people that she would disown her own daughter because you chose to be with me?"

Jasmine asked, "Why is this so hard?"

Hearing the pain in her voice Blake realized that Jasmine was hurting too. He realized what she would be giving up if she chose him.

He reached over and pulled her into his arms, "I'm sorry baby. I'm so sorry."

He loved Jasmine more than he wanted his next breath but he didn't want to ask her to choose between her mom and him. It broke his heart to know they were so close to realizing their happiness. To have it snatched away or put on indefinite hold was too much.

He was so over everybody and their opinion about who he should love and who he should be with. Why did they need anyone's permission to love each other? He lifted Jasmine's face to his and kissed her nose.

He wiped her tears and said, "Tell me now, are you in or out. I'm sorry that I'm asking you to choose, but Jaz I cannot give you up. I just can't. I just need to know."

She stared at him and saw the fierce love for her in his eyes. How could she walk away from a man willing to love her like that? She didn't want to give him up either. She had never been happier than she had been for the last 24 hours. She had to be true to her heart. She had her own life and she had to live it.

She said, "I'm in baby. Me and you against the world, right?"

"Right!"

He kissed her and pulled out of the driveway. He held her with one arm and drove with the other not wanting to be separated from her even for a moment. He meant it when he said he would not let anyone or anything stand in the way of their happiness. He knew exactly what he needed to do.

Chapter 41: From Now until Forever

Five days later, Blake and Jasmine were sitting on the side of the bed in a hotel room. She was wearing a satin white night gown and he was wearing a t-shirt and boxers. Jasmine was nervous and digging her toes into the plush carpet.

She asked, "So do you have protection?"

"No, I don't want there to be anything between us tonight."

She nodded.

He said, "I've actually never done this without protection, this will be the first time."

Her head popped up, "Are you serious?"

He nodded.

"Really, I mean even with Amber?"

He put his right hand up, "I swear."

"Wow, well that's interesting."

He asked, "What about you?"

"Oh after that disaster of my first time I never left home without it."

"Are you on birth control?"

She shook her head, "There was no point once I chose to abstain."

She shrugged her shoulders.

"So that means you could get pregnant tonight."

She asked, "And how do you feel about that?"

He grabbed her hand and ran his finger over the wedding band she now wore along with her engagement ring.

"Well Jaz you are my wife now and nothing would make me happier than to have a child with you."

Jasmine and Blake had gone to Vegas for the weekend and eloped. The only people who knew were their roommates. They were tired of letting other people's feelings dictate their relationship or prevent them from the happiness they knew they deserved that could only be found with each other.

Jasmine asked, "So you really don't care if I get pregnant."

"No I don't, Jaz. I told you I'm ready for this, all of this. There is no way I'm using a condom with my wife on my wedding night. So whatever happens let it happen. I mean how cute would our kid be? A little baby with my blue eyes and your wild curly hair and skin somewhere in between ours would be perfection. To know that our love created that would be the ultimate validation."

She smiled, "You never cease to amaze me."

He kissed her nose.

She wondered, "Don't you think it's crazy that we know just about everything there is to know about each other but we have no idea about this kinda stuff?"

"Well there was never a need to know any of it."

"I have a confession to make. I'm nervous, like really nervous right now," Jasmine said.

"Why?"

"Why aren't you?"

"Well, I mean, I have a few reservations but I'm not nervous anymore because I remembered I'm actually quite good at this."

She laughed, "My, aren't we arrogant."

"I prefer the term confident."

She rolled her eyes. He noticed her hand trembled slightly.

He said, "Hey, you really are nervous."

"Uh didn't I just say that?"

He stood up, "Come here."

She stood.

"Tell me why you're nervous and be honest."

She hesitated and he gently lifted her chin to look her in the eyes.

"Blake, I'm not the type of woman you're into. What if you don't like what you see?"

He relaxed, "Oh is that what this is about? Jaz, trust me when I tell you I have never wanted anyone more. I'm looking forward to getting to know your body like I know your heart. You are beautiful and I love all your curves. I'm trying to figure out why it took me so long to appreciate them."

She tried to smile.

He asked, "Do I have to kiss you all over your body like I did your nose to let you know that it's perfect?"

She laughed as he'd hoped she would.

He pulled her into him, "Dance with me beautiful?"

"But there's no music."

He laid her head against his chest.

"Just listen to my heart then. It beats for you."

Jasmine closed her eyes as Blake swayed them to the rhythm of his heartbeat. He stroked her back and she started to relax. She started to let all of her fears and worries dissipate as she enjoyed being in his arms. After a while she felt herself being lifted and then Blake laid her on the bed. She felt him slipping her out of her gown. She couldn't believe this moment was finally here.

Blake said, "Look at me gorgeous."

She opened her eyes.

He said, "I love you."

"I love you."

He kissed her nose and then her lips. She fisted her hands in his hair letting everything go except her husband and this moment. Blake shifted his body and put his weight on Jasmine.

He asked, "Are you ready?"

"Yes."

He kissed her passionately. When he joined their bodies they both gasped. It seemed like time stopped. They stared at each other frozen in the moment. Jasmine had never felt anything like it and the tears spilled out from the pleasure.

He whispered, "Am I hurting you?"

She shook her head.

"Am I too heavy for you?"

She shook her head and said, "It's a..."

"...Perfect fit," he finished her thought.

She nodded. He kissed her again and began their first dance of love.

Blake took his precious time loving his new wife. He wanted this to be a night they would never forget. He explored everything he didn't know about this woman that he loved so dearly. As she experienced the dance Jasmine was drowning in the pleasure he gave her over and over and over again.

Blake stared down at his wife and was rewarded by the gratification on her face. The glow of her skin was breathtaking. He studied the contrast of their flesh and it didn't bother him anymore. It was comforting to see it now as he let all of his reservations about it go.

It felt so amazing to know she was his in every way a woman could belong to a man. The mere thought that he got to spend the rest of his life with her, pleasing her, protecting her and making her happy made him feel favored by God himself. He knew what a precious gift she was and that this moment was priceless. The fulfillment she gave him was unlike anything he had ever experienced.

Jasmine was astounded by the connection she felt to her husband, mind, body and soul. Nothing could separate them now. Their dance felt like it had been divinely choreographed from the beginning of eternity. She wanted him to feel what she felt. She wanted him to give himself to her in every way she had given herself to him. She grabbed his face, his eyes bore into hers.

She whispered, "I'll always be yours and no one else's."

Her words were the perfect finale to the dance. Knowing and believing that he would never have to give her up made him lose the tiny grip he had on his control. She ran her hand through his hair and kissed his temple gently causing goose bumps to saturate his flesh. He buried his face in her neck and let go as her name gently danced off his lips.

Jasmine held on to Blake as tight as she could while he trembled in her arms. She never wanted to let him go. After his breathing slowed and he gained back control of his limbs he placed soft kisses all over her face and then shifted to lay behind her. He kept his arms wrapped tightly around her.

She asked, "Oh so you like to cuddle huh?"

"Uh, not really. I never did before. You're the only woman I've ever really wanted to hold. I'm just not quite ready to let you go yet."

She smiled, "I know the feeling."

"Jaz, that was amazing. I will never buy another condom again."

She chuckled, "I know, I guess you have earned the right to be arrogant. I feel so free and satisfied."

He whispered in her ear, "Next time I'll go for four."

She smiled, "You were counting?"

"I aim to please. I need to keep my stats up."

"Boy you are so silly."

He stroked her belly.

He said, "I'm really kind of hoping we made a baby tonight.

"Really, why is that?"

"Every kid should be conceived out of this kind of love. Though there is something that I've been thinking about since we had that talk with the guys."

"What's that baby?"

"What if we have a son and he looks like Damon then will I have to live with the fear you do every day for the men in your life? Will I have to wonder if my kid is going to make it home? How do I tell him that even though he's my son when we walk down the street together people will judge me one way and him another? Will he pull away from me because I don't know what it's like to be him?"

Jasmine grabbed his face, "Baby, the fact that you even considered that makes me love you even more. We will just have to cross those bridges when we get there. I tell you what though. If you love your children with half the effort you love me they will never pull away from that kind of unconditional love no matter what the outside world is telling them."

He smiled, appreciating her so much in that moment, "I love you baby."

She grinned, "Blake I'm so unbelievably happy right now."

"It does seem like a dream doesn't it?"

"Too bad it will only last for a couple of days?"

"I know. What are we going to do about those parents of ours? They are going to freak. My dad and your mom are probably going to disown us. My mom and your dad will be eternally indignant because I think they wanted this more than we did. They didn't get to be a part of our wedding."

"Well you know what, we can have a formal wedding when we get this all straightened out. I've been thinking about it and I think I have an idea."

"I am all ears."

Jasmine said, "You remember when I went to hang out with my cousin Tameka in Tallahassee for homecoming a few years back."

"Yeah."

"Well, my cousin took me to her church. I think it's called Kingdom Builders or something."

"That's when you decided to give your life to Christ right?"

"Yeah it was. It was something about that church, something was different. The first thing that drew me in was the music. The songs were so powerful but I had never heard any of them before. When I asked Tameka she said their minister of music, Seth, wrote almost all the songs they sang. After church she introduced me to him so that I could tell him how one of his songs prompted me to give my life to Christ."

"Uh Jaz, what does church songs have to do with getting our parents to come to their senses."

She smiled.

"Shhh. I'm getting to that. So when I met him I also met his wife. Her name was Sheridan. We got to talking and I asked her what she did. She told me she was a psychologist. That made me curious because I asked her did she include Christian principles in her counseling and she said yes, that her practice was faith based."

"Okay, you want our parents to go see a church shrink."

"No I want all six of us to go and see a Christian counselor."

He stared at her for a long moment.

"Why do you think we need to see a psychologist?"

"Because you told me yourself your dad said there was a reason why he was the way that he is but he wasn't ready to deal with it. Right before my surgery my dad said my mom had issues that she hadn't dealt with. I've been praying about this and I think those two have some deep rooted issues that go back to way before we were even a thought. Until we get to the bottom of that we can't have any real peace between us."

He propped himself up on his elbow.

"Okay, I'm not thrilled about going to see a shrink but how do you suppose we get my dad of all people to go see one."

"Okay, see that's the part that will get a little tricky. I've been thinking about this. The only thing I think will work with absolutely no resistance is for us to threaten them."

He laughed.

"Jasmine you're funny. So what are we going to do, hold them at gunpoint and make them go?"

She hit him.

"No. We are going to tell them that we will no longer be a part of their lives unless they agree for all of us to get counseling."

He frowned.

She continued, "To really pull their heart strings we will tell them that grandbabies are inevitable but as long as they refuse to work out our differences we cannot subject our kids to that kind of discord."

He blew out a breath.

"Wow Jaz, that's dirty."

"I know that's why it's going to work. We have to make them see they are risking everything to hold on to the past. Your father needs to know he will be jeopardizing his new relationship with you and any future relationship with his grandchildren. I think your mother will be the key."

"What do you mean?"

"She has wanted this relationship practically from birth. If she can't enjoy us being together she will make your father's life miserable until he agrees."

"You got a point. Your dad will draw the line as soon as he knows there's a baby in the picture and he will insist your mom goes."

"We both know when my dad makes a decision that's the final word on the matter."

He asked, "So do we recruit my mom and your dad as co-conspirators first or do we wait to see if we will need to?"

She thought about it for a moment.

"Let's wait and see if we need help. First, we're just going to ask them to go."

"So when do you plan on doing this?"

"Well honey, I'm glad you asked. I contacted her office last week. She called me back. She agreed that we needed an entire afternoon, a four hour session."

"Why do I feel like you've already made this appointment?"

"Because you know me so well. The appointment is in a month."

He shook his head, "Jaz, you are a mess."

"Baby just trust me, this is going work. I just need you to have my back on this."

"I've always got your back. You know that, no matter what."

"Have a little faith baby. God has brought us this far. He won't leave us now."

He lay back down and turned her so that they were facing each other.

He began, "Speaking of how far God has brought us, I need to tell you something important."

She didn't like the way his face got all serious all of a sudden.

"Baby what is it? What's wrong?"

"Nothing's wrong, I just made a decision that I need to tell you about."

Nervously she said, "Oh okay."

"Jasmine you know I think you're an amazing person. I always have. But ever since your operation I've been noticing something very different about you. I have been paying attention to your faith in God. Watching your life I've come to the conclusion that He must be real. I've finally found the faith to believe. I still struggle with some aspects of Christianity but I know for a fact God is real. It's really real to me because you are so not a perfect person. You're flawed and you're mean and you're stubborn when you cannot get your way."

She stuck her tongue out at him. He smiled.

"But for me that's the beauty of it. Even though you're not perfect He still loves you. It's very obvious from your life that He does. I see you work every day to be a better person. I see how your life has changed others. God has to really care about you to do all this stuff in your life just because you chose to give Him your life. What happened with you and my dad and what's happening with me and my dad I know without a doubt was nothing but a miracle. I wanna be the best possible man I can be for you. I realized that I can't do that if I don't have a relationship with Jesus."

She gasped and silent tears fell down her face.

He continued, "You know I don't really get all caught up in church but I remember you telling me a long time ago that when I was ready I could give my life to Christ wherever I was. I've been reading my Bible a couple times a week and some things are beginning to be clear for me. I wanted to do it before we got married so yesterday when you were at the salon getting your hair done, which I've now ruined," she gave a watery laugh.

"I sat down in my room and had a conversation with God. I asked Him to forgive me of all my sins and for His son to come into my heart. I asked Him to make me a better man so I could be everything you needed me to be and to help me give you the life you've always dreamed of having."

Her tears continued to spill. He wiped them.

"It's hard to explain but I know that I wasn't alone in that room. There was this warmth that spread across my chest that I just can't explain. I knew He heard me and accepted me with open arms. You remember when you said He was trying to get my attention?"

She nodded.

"Well, He got it. I didn't even realize He was using all these obstacles in my life to talk to me. So when we get back home, I want to start going to church with you. I also want us to pray together. You can help me study the Bible until I get better at it."

She stared at him in shock and awe. The rush of emotions that surrounded her was too much to keep inside. This is what God meant about blessings that would overtake you. She had been praying for Blake's salvation for years. Now she was married and more in love than she ever thought she could be. God had given her so much more than she could have ever imagined. When she found her voice she hugged him tight.

"Oh baby, I love you. Thank you, thank you so much. You don't know the kind of peace you've just given me. Thank you Lord, thank you so much for hearing and answering my prayers."

Blake lifted her head and smiled his crooked smile that made her heart melt.

"You know what? You are so beautiful when you cry happy tears."

She wiped her tears away and smiled.

"I feel so blessed right now. I just don't have the words to show my appreciation."

"Then show me without words."

Her eyebrow arched, "You know what, salvation is really sexy on you."

He laughed hard.

"Only you Jasmine would say something like that."

"I hope you got your second wind because you're gonna need it."

He stared at her in surprise.

"Really?"

"Yes really. My appreciation is really great at the moment and I need to show you what you mean to me."

He made a face she couldn't interpret.

"This is throwing me off seeing this side of you."

Her voice took a dip and got deep and throaty.

"Oh honey you haven't quite seen this side of me just yet."

His body came alive.

"Is that so?"

"Absolutely."

Jasmine slid on top of Blake and then pulled him up to meet her. They sat facing each other as she ran her hands through his hair and put her lips to his ear.

"You're gonna wanna hold on tight for this baby, mama's bout to take you for a ride you won't soon forget."

She pulled back to look at his face. His jaw dropped. She laughed and then devoured him. Once they were finished with their second round Jasmine collapsed on Blake's chest in a satisfied exhaustion. He felt like he had just run a marathon and was trying in vain to catch his breath. She could show him how she felt about him without words anytime she wanted to.

After several minutes he said, "I shoulda got saved a long time ago."

Her laughter was a purr of amusement.

Still breathing hard Blake said, "You know I tried to clown Damon for being sprung after a week. Now I'm gone for life after one night."

With great effort she picked up her head to look at him.

"That's right. You're all mine baby."

"After that I don't want to be anybody else's."

She laughed.

"We probably should head for the shower."

"Yeah in theory that sounds great but I don't really trust my legs to support me right now."

"Good point," she agreed.

He reached over and pulled the sheet across them. Moments later they both dropped into sleep.

Chapter 42: Back to Reality

The next morning Jasmine and Blake had just gotten out of the shower. They were both wearing plush white robes compliments of their hotel and were brushing their teeth.

Jasmine said, "Babe I'm starving. We definitely need to get food."

She eyed him in the mirror when he didn't respond. He was looking at her like she was a stranger.

"What? Why are you looking at me like that?"

He shook his head.

"No reason."

"Yes it is why are you looking at me like that?"

He spit.

"Okay I'm sorry but it's like I don't even know you."

She spit.

"What do you mean?"

"Now don't get mad but I'm seeing a whole other side of you that I didn't even know was there."

She grinned. She knew exactly where this was going.

"Jaz round two last night literally blew my mind. Then you woke me up around two for round three."

She replied, "So you woke me up around sunrise for number four *and* returned the favor of blowing my mind."

"True. Don't take this the wrong way but you're a freak."

She laughed, rinsed her mouth and toothbrush out then put the toothbrush down. He followed suit.

She asked, "Is that a bad thing?"

"Heck no, but I never really thought about you like that. You always seemed to be kinda..."

"Kind of what? A prude?"

He laughed, "No, but I mean Jaz, come on, you never talk about this kind of stuff and you're like a church girl."

She laughed.

"Well church girls gotta keep their men too right?"

"Yeah well you can teach a class to church girls about how to keep their man because I'm not going anywhere."

She laughed hard. He turned her around to face him and sat her on the bathroom counter.

He said, "So you're basically saying that you never kiss and tell."

"I believe what is between two lovers should stay between those lovers. Just because I don't brag about it doesn't mean I'm not good at it."

He smirked and started kissing her. He skillfully undid the belt on her robe.

"So you mean to tell me that when we get home and Lucy and Carmen say tell them all about our weekend you're not going to give them any details about how your new husband put it down, as Damon would say."

She laughed.

"Do not quote Damon. The world should only have one of him. I don't know, maybe I'll give them a general synopsis. You never tell another woman in detail what your man is working with. I will be keeping your skills to myself because I don't want to have to slap anybody about my man. However, I will tell them my white boy has rhythm."

He bit her neck and chuckled. He picked her up. She wrapped her legs around him.

"Okay I'd say that was fair. A little possessiveness is kinda sexy on you," he said.

She just noticed that her robe was undone.

"Baby, we just got cleaned up."

He laughed.

"There is more hot water you know."

"Well clearly I'm not the only freak. Your stamina is amazing."

She bit his lip. He laughed and gently backed her into the closed bathroom door.

"You're amazing and I am a very lucky man."

"What is it with you and backing me up into doors?"

"It's good for leverage."

He was kissing her neck.

"Are you sure you can hold me up?"

His head popped up and he looked insulted. She laughed.

He said, "You just enjoy the adventure and leave the heavy lifting to me."

"Only if you promise to feed me after this."

He covered her mouth with his. In her first act of submission to her new husband Jasmine relinquished her control and obediently enjoyed the adventure. She left the heavy lifting in his very capable hands.

∞∞∞

Blake was getting their bags out of the trunk of the cab while Jasmine paid the driver. They were finally home. They had an amazing weekend of making love and discovering new things about each other. She was pooped. Blake didn't let her get much sleep. They barely got enough food. She was sure they broke some kind of record. As the cab driver pulled off Blake walked up to her dragging the two bags.

She smiled.

"You look as tired as I feel."

"Yeah, my new wife took advantage of me. She deprived me of sleep and food."

She laughed.

"Okay, if that's the way you remember it."

He kissed her nose.

"That is exactly how I remember it. That is my story and I'm sticking to it."

"What, no kiss on my lips? Don't tell me you're getting tired of kissing me already."

He let go of the bags and pulled her into him.

"Your lips drive me insane and are quickly becoming my favorite pastime."

She smiled as he gently placed his lips to hers.

"Ahh come on, I would say get a room but y'all just left one. Y'all all in the front yard with this mess. Stop it."

They laughed and turned to see Damon standing near the front door.

Blake said, "Stop hatin' and help me with these bags. A brotha is tired."

Damon laughed.

"Oh, so you marry a black woman and now you a brotha?"

They all laughed. Damon gave Jasmine a hug and a kiss and grabbed one of the bags. They headed inside. Jasmine was so grateful to be home, she couldn't wait to see Carmen and Lucy. Knowing that soon all of their lives would change and they would no longer be living together she wanted to spend as much time with them as she could before they had to grow up and everything changed.

She walked in and dropped her purse on the sofa table sitting near the door. Lucy and Carmen were sitting at the dining room table. They looked up and saw her.

Lucy said, "Well don't you look all tired and worn out."

Jasmine laughed, "An excellent observation."

Carmen said, "And look Luce she even walks a little different."

Lucy laughed. They both stood up and hugged her. Blake and Damon were a few steps behind.

Blake said, "Uh, I was gone too you know."

Carmen and Lucy went over and greeted him with a hug and kisses.

Carmen grabbed Jasmine's hand and said, "Okay girl time. We want to hear all about it."

Jasmine looked at Blake and he gave her an "I told you so" look. She laughed. She was dragged to Lucy's room since it was on the bottom floor. Lucy's room was full of color and plush pillows. Jasmine dove on the bed that was covered in a deep purple satin comforter. She lay down in the middle.

"Oh my goodness guys I am so tired. Sleep was not a priority."

Lucy and Carmen lay in the bed too on either side of Jasmine.

"Well it's your honeymoon. You're not supposed to sleep," Lucy said.

Jasmine gushed, "Y'all, it was amazing."

Carmen said, "Bump all that mushy crap. You got some, how was it?"

Lucy laughed, "Amen to that."

"I am a married woman and I do not kiss and tell."

Carmen said, "Whatever heifa, you gon tell this. You know how long we been waiting for this to happen?"

Lucy said, "Well it had to be good. Even though you're tired you're lit up like a Christmas tree."

Carmen pinched Jasmine, "So were you a good girl or were you a slut and freaked Blake out because he didn't know how you got down?"

Jasmine laughed.

"Both. You know the first time it was sweet and romantic and he made me feel like I was the only woman in the world. He also scored three times on the first try." The girls squealed and giggled. "Then on round two I showed out. The look on his face was priceless. So the next morning he was like, okay, I don't even know you."

They laughed.

Jasmine grabbed each of their hands, "Oh, and you guys could be aunties soon."

They both shouted, "What?"

"Okay relax. We are not actively trying but we are not actively trying to prevent it either. I'm just giving y'all a heads up. This is something we both want. I can't wait to give Blake a house full of babies."

Lucy said, "Wow, you guys aren't wasting any time are you?"

"Nope, we've been doing that all our lives. Y'all I am so freaking happy I don't know what to do with myself. I am so in love with that man of mine. He is even more amazing than I ever realized. I feel so blessed to have someone that can love me so completely and so selflessly."

Lucy hugged her, "Jazzy, that is so great."

"I don't know why you two didn't convince me sooner that I should do this?"

They both stared at her like she should be Baker Acted. They grabbed pillows and started to beat her with them. Jasmine laughed and used her arms to protect her face.

∞∞∞

Damon and Blake were sitting at the table.

Damon asked, "So how does it feel to be a married man?"

"Ah man, it is the best feeling in the world. Marrying Jaz is the best thing I could have ever done."

"Wow, I didn't think you could be more sprung than before you left."

Blake laughed.

"Man, am I ever! Let's just say Ms. Jasmine put something on ya boy."

Damon laughed at Blake's use of his phrase.

"I am truly gone. I am more in love with Jasmine now than I ever was before. I honestly didn't think that was conceivable."

"Well dang dawg, did you let her get any sleep."

"She didn't let me get any either."

They laughed.

Damon asked, "Well, so how was Vegas?"

"Uh, I can tell you what the airport looked like."

Damon shook his head.

"Man did you even take her out for a romantic dinner?"

Blake frowned.

"You know we had the best room service had to offer."

Damon shook his head.

"That's a sin and a shame."

"Trust me. She has no complaints about this weekend. I promise you that."

"I guess not, she came in here glowing and grinning like she just won the lottery or something."

Blake gave a cocky grin.

"I'm going to take her on a real honeymoon in a few weeks. I will wine and dine her then."

"Does she know?"

"Nah, it's a surprise so do not tell Carmen."

He laughed.

"I got you. You better hurry up. The way y'all going at it Jazzy will be knocked up on that honeymoon."

"Oh believe me every chance I get I am planting a seed and she gives me plenty of chances."

"Whhaaaaattttt?" Damon laughed. "Man, y'all off the chain."

"We have wasted so much time man. I'm ready for it all. She's ready for it all. I can't wait to make a baby with Jasmine."

"Well dang, I guess Uncle Damon it is then."

"So what's going on with you and Carmen?"

Damon couldn't hide the grin that spread naturally across his face.

Blake smiled, "Enough said. Now who's off the chain? Me and Jaz played around for years. Y'all have been at this for mere weeks."

Damon laughed.

"Yeah, let's say we have learned from your mistakes."

"I feel you on that. Love looks good on you man. And if I'm correct this is the very first time I've ever seen it on you."

"Yeah but I haven't told her yet so don't tell Jasmine."

Blake laughed.

"I got you. So what are you waiting on?"

"I'm going to do it tonight when we take you and Jasmine out for a surprise."

"A surprise?"

"That's right, so I suggest you and the missus get some rest because we are leaving here at seven on the dot. And wear something nice."

Blake's brow shot up.

"And where are we going?"

"Dude, what did I just say? It's a surprise!"

Jasmine and the other ladies walked into the room.

Jasmine asked, "What's a surprise?"

She slid onto Blake's lap. He wrapped his arms around her. It was now a natural reflex.

"Apparently our friends are taking us out to celebrate our nuptials," Blake responded.

"Aww really? That's so sweet you guys."

Carmen walked up behind Damon, slid her arms around him and kissed his cheek.

She said, "It was Damon's idea. Isn't he a sweetheart?"

Jasmine looked shocked.

"Damon are you blushing?"

He looked away. Jasmine laughed.

"Carmen whatever you doing you need to bottle it up and sell it. It works miracles."

Damon gave Jasmine the middle finger. They all laughed.

Blake asked Lucy, "So are we finally going to meet this mystery man you've been creeping around with?"

Now it was Lucy's turn to blush, "Tonight as a matter of fact."

Carmen asked, "So why the big secret Luce? You've been keeping him under wraps for a few months now?"

Damon asked, "It is a he isn't it?"

Lucy and Carmen punched him.

"Of course it's a he. I just didn't want to bring anyone into our circle unless I felt strongly that they would stay. I've had a string of bad relationships. I wanted to be sure this one was a keeper before he got attached to you guys."

Blake patted Jasmine on her backside. She stood. He stood also.

He said, "Okay guys we are really beat. If you want us to make it to our own celebration then we need to sleep."

Carmen said, "Yeah right, sure you're gonna sleep."

Jasmine said, "Oh no, cross my heart, we will definitely be sleeping."

Blake asked, "Can you make sure we're up by five because Jasmine doesn't know what she's wearing and I can't know what I'm wearing until she decides? She's going to want to coordinate."

He rolled his eyes. Jasmine sighed.

"It's nice to have a man that knows you so well."

They laughed. Jasmine looked up at the stairs.

"Oh my, they may as well be Mount Everest."

Blake said, "You can hop on my back since I'm partly responsible for your state of weariness."

Lucy said, "Aww you guys are so cute."

Blake laughed.

"Now in all honesty I might drop us both."

Jasmine bit his neck.

"Boy hush."

Blake took them up the stairs and asked, "My room or yours?"

She said, "Yours babe, my bed is still covered with the clothes that didn't make the cut for our trip, which was a waste because we never left the room."

He chuckled and headed to his room. He sat on the bed and she climbed off his back and curled up on the bed. He slid in behind her and pulled the extra cover from the foot of the bed over them. He pulled her in close to him and kissed the back of her neck.

"I love you gorgeous."

"Love you too handsome."

Sleepily he said, "Oh, before I forget, can you please grow your curls back. I miss them."

She yawned, "Sure babe."

"I have a fantasy in my head that requires my fingers being in those curls."

Too tired to laugh she let out a small chuckle. Within minutes they faded into sleep.

Chapter 43: Not in a Million Years

Everyone was buzzing around the house getting ready to celebrate the marriage of their friends. Damon was the time keeper. He had been frequently yelling at Carmen and Jasmine because they were the most likely to be late.

Jasmine yelled out, "What is the big deal? What happens at exactly seven p.m. on the dot?"

Damon said, "The limo arrives to pick us up. Where we are heading they will not wait for us to get there. Now hurry up Jazzy."

"Don't get your panties in a bunch. I will be ready with five minutes to spare."

Blake walked into Jasmine's room to see if she had finally picked a color. He had resolved that he was wearing all black and would put on a tie to match whatever color dress she wore. There was a siren red dress laid out on her bed. He walked into the double bathroom she shared with Carmen where they were both applying their make up in their robes. He leaned against the door jamb looking handsome as ever in all black.

Jasmine eyed him through the mirror.

"Well don't you look delicious?"

"I'm glad you like what you see."

"I love what I see."

Carmen said, "Uh gag me!"

They laughed.

Blake asked, "So baby are you sure you're wearing this little red number on the bed. I wanna finish getting dressed."

"Yes. I remembered the effect I had on you the last time I wore red."

He laughed.

"Not fair."

"All's fair in love and fashion baby."

He kissed her shoulder.

"Okay, y'all hurry up before Damon has a conniption fit."

Carmen said, "You tell him I will be worth the wait."

"Yes ma'am."

With ten minutes to spare Jasmine walked out of her room wearing a red knee length strapless dress that managed to compliment her curves without being tight. Her black patent leather pumps were set off by the patent leather clutch and the dangling rubies that sparkled in her ears. They had been a birthday gift from Blake years ago. She never really had an occasion to wear them. Tonight seemed perfect. She was rewarded with an approving smile when he stepped out of his room. They met at the top of the stairs.

He said, "I am such a lucky man. You look so sexy baby."

She grinned.

"You sir wear black very well. You will definitely get lucky tonight."

He leaned down to press his lips to her shimmering red ones then hesitated.

She asked, "What?"

"Um, Amber never let me kiss her with fresh lipstick on."

Jasmine smirked and straightened his red and black tie.

"Well I'm not Amber and you can put your lips on mine anytime and anywhere you please. I can always reapply."

"See that's why I married you. I can't wait to get you back home."

He pulled her into him and kissed her like she was his last meal and he was on death row.

Carmen walked out of her room and said, "You guys get a room. Can't you stay apart for more than five minutes?"

Blake reluctantly broke the kiss and said, "No."

He did a double take.

"Wow Carmen, I'd say you were definitely worth the wait. Damon's tongue is going to fall out when he sees you."

A big grin spread across her face.

Jasmine turned to see, "Oh sweetie you look so beautiful."

She was wearing a white halter dress that hugged her athletic but curvy body. She did a little spin and showed off the plunging back of the dress that featured a sparkling silver rope that stretched from the neck to the waist. Her butterscotch skin was the perfect contrast. She'd pinned her ridiculously long hair onto the top of her head. Her hair cascaded out in curly tendrils. She wore strappy sandals that sparkled and carried a white clutch with rhinestone accents.

Damon called up, "Are you guys ready?"

Blake said, "Heading down now."

He grabbed Jasmine's hand as they walked down the stairs together. When they reached the bottom they looked up to see Carmen basically teasing Damon with her slow seductive descent.

Jasmine whispered, "She is gonna give the poor guy heart palpitations."

Blake laughed.

Damon stood in his white linen suit and just stared.

"Uh. Wow. You um look...wow Carmen you literally have me speechless right now."

She smiled and walked into his waiting arms.

Carmen said, "If you can't talk with your mouth find something else to do with it."

He obliged and kissed her. Jasmine and Blake teasingly oohed and aahed. Jasmine thought they were so cute together. She had never really seen them together like this. It was a sight to behold.

Lucy cleared her throat, "Can we please go and get my man because I am so over all these public displays of affection."

They all turned to see Lucy also dressed to turn heads. Her long, lean frame sported a black jumpsuit set off by gold peep toe booties and gold accessories. Her jet black hair was now cut into a razor sharp bob that framed her face. In the back, it was short to the nape of her neck and hung two inches below her chin in the front. She was dazzling.

Jasmine walked up to her.

"So while I was sleeping you were cheating on me and letting someone else cut your hair."

Lucy laughed.

"Sorry, it was a last minute decision. I know you needed your beauty rest."

"It's fierce. Who did it?"

"Sharon. She is the only one I could convince to meet me at the salon on a Sunday."

"Oh yeah that young lady has skills. That's why I hired her."

Damon said, "As fascinating as this is, and Lucy you do look amazing, I believe the limo is outside. So can we go?"

They rolled their eyes at Damon but obliged. Jasmine hooked an arm in Blake's and he extended his other arm to Lucy.

"Shall we ladies?"

Damon said, "You look like a pimp dawg."

He got dirty scowls from the ladies, he just laughed.

Outside the driver held the door open to the black stretch limousine. Blake helped Jasmine and Lucy into the limo while Damon helped Carmen. Jasmine and Blake were on the left side of the limo. Lucy sat across from them. Damon and Carmen took the rear seat. Through the intercom Lucy gave the driver the address of their next stop.

Damon handed out glasses and popped the top on the champagne that rested in the bucket of ice.

Once everyone had a glass he raised his and said, "To my best friend, my brother and the woman that God himself created just for him. I'm so glad you two finally came to your senses and stopped ruining other people's lives."

Everyone laughed.

"Ever since I met you guys back in high school, I thought there were no two people more perfect for each other. It took y'all long enough to come to the same conclusion, but I wish you both every kind of happiness there is, long life and peace of mind. I look forward to seeing your relationship blossom into whatever God intended it to be."

Jasmine said, "Carmen, what did you do to my Damon. You got him all soft and gooey now."

They laughed.

Blake said, "Thanks man, we love you."

Lucy said, "Ah shoot, they have started in with the 'we' talk."

Laughing they clinked glasses.

As they waited to meet Lucy's new beau they sipped their champagne and made small talk about everything. Each of them skillfully navigated the topic away from anything Ahmed.

Individually they were finding their own way to deal. They all wanted to keep the mood celebratory. After about 20 minutes the limo came to a stop. Lucy tried to look through the dark tinted windows but not with much luck.

She pulled out her cell phone and dialed.

"Hey sweetie. We're outside. Okay."

She hung up.

Blake was whispering in great detail what he wanted to do with his wife when they got home. She was giggling and not paying any attention to what was going on around them. Carmen and Damon were pretty much in their own world too. Lucy just rolled her eyes when the door opened. Her face lit up as the handsome face of her man smiled at her.

"Hi baby," she gushed.

He gave her a long hug and complimented her on her new hair. Since Blake and Jasmine were still ignoring everybody Lucy began the introductions with Damon and Carmen.

"Baby these are my roommates, Damon and Carmen."

Jasmine realized there was someone new in the limo. When she looked up her heart stopped for a couple beats. She'd heard Lucy say his name to Damon and Carmen but she thought there was no way it could be him. Then he looked at her and she knew it was him because she saw the instant flash of recognition on his face that he quickly masked.

Blake still had his face buried in his wife's neck. He felt her body go rigid all of a sudden. She gripped his hand so fiercely that her strong nails were digging into his flesh. Instinct had him trying to pull his hand out of hers but her grip was vice and that was not about to happen.

He was about to get mad but something in his gut told him there was something very wrong. He studied her profile then followed her gaze to where it was stuck. He looked at the face of the man sitting next to Lucy. He knew he recognized him but he couldn't quite place it.

Lucy was bubbling.

"These are my friends that just got married. This is Blake and his wife, Jasmine. This is my guy, Jeremy."

Blake was beside himself to know that the man who got Jasmine pregnant and discarded her was sitting across from them with his arm wrapped possessively around one of their closest friends.

Blake recovered quickly and said, "Nice to finally meet you."

Jasmine cleared her throat and just smiled. She was officially speechless. Jasmine turned and stared at Blake. To play it off he grabbed her face and kissed her. Then he whispered in her ear.

"It's gonna be okay baby. Just breathe. I'm right here. I'm right here Jaz."

She squeezed his hand. She still couldn't find her voice.

"Just breathe baby and let me think."

She nodded. He pulled her into him to steady her, to keep her grounded.

Damon asked, "So how did you two meet?"

Jeremy had to clear his throat and get his bearings. Coming face-to-face with the woman he abandoned was not the way he imagined this evening would start.

"Uh, actually we have a mutual friend that introduced us, Ahmed."

Jasmine's head snapped up. Her voice was back.

"Ahmed did what?"

Lucy, Carmen and Damon stared at her shocked by her outburst.

She said, "I'm sorry I just, that's just a little strange because Ahmed never said anything to any of us about it."

Jeremy was still as handsome as ever. His cocoa brown, six-foot-one frame was decked out in a grey suit with the vest only and a black dress shirt underneath. The matching tie pulled it all together with hints of light blue winding through it.

He said, "We worked for rival finance firms but Ahmed and I hit it off at a conference. He told me several months back he had a roommate he thought I would really like."

Blake asked, "So why is this our first time meeting you?"

He tried to hide his derision for the man but he didn't know if he was quite pulling it off.

"Actually, I've been living on the West Coast. I've been flying back and forth because I've just accepted a position on the East Coast. Lucy has been a doll about understanding a hectic schedule and transition."

He kissed her hand and looked at her adoringly, she blushed.

"I was out of the country when Ahmed died. Lucy had a key to my place so she just crashed there for a few days. He was such a great guy. I have him to thank for bringing this beautiful woman into my life."

He kissed a blushing Lucy on the lips.

Chapter 44: A Haunting Past

Jasmine wanted to retch all over Jeremy. She felt Blake's grip on her tighten. Thank God he knew her so well. She was ready to pounce on that bastard. She'd never wanted so badly in her life to hurt another human being with her bare hands. She felt like the walls of the limo were closing in on her. She never knew she was claustrophobic. She wanted out. She looked away from Jeremy and tried to take deep breaths without being obvious.

Oh God, she thought, *what kind of sick joke is this?*

Blake was trying to figure out how in the heck they were going to get through this evening without him knocking Jeremy the hell out and without crushing Lucy. This was bad. This was very, very bad. His first priority was Jasmine. He needed to make sure she was able to handle this. He knew he had to be the one with some sense because her common sense was likely to be very far removed.

All the memories of that horrible weekend came flooding back to his mind. He didn't want to go back. He wanted to move forward with their lives. Why was God allowing this to happen now? His concern was for his wife. She still had yet to relax. He didn't know how far they had to go or how much longer she could stay trapped like this. He knew that she needed to get out and fast.

Blake asked, "Hey guys are we almost there?"

Damon looked at his watch.

"We should be there in like five minutes or so."

Blake nodded.

Carmen asked, "Blake are you alright?"

"Yeah I'm fine. Why do you ask?"

"Your face looks a little flushed."

He thought quickly on his feet.

"Aw, well you know Jasmine whispered something nasty in my ear."

He laughed it off and everyone seemed to buy it.

The limo came to a stop. Blake and Jasmine were beyond grateful. They still had no idea where they were going but they let everyone exit before they did. Carmen was the last out. Jasmine put her head between her legs and took a few deep breaths. Blake rubbed her back. He felt so helpless. She sat up and he saw the tears shimmering in her eyes.

"No baby don't. You can't cry. We have to figure this out. It's going to be okay."

She willed the tears away and frantically asked, "How is it going to be okay? She's basically in love with him and she has no clue about any of it."

"Jasmine stop! Look at me."

She complied.

"Trust me to handle this okay. Just hang on to me and I'll make sure you get through this night."

She was so grateful for him. She nodded.

"Okay baby."

Damon popped his head in, "Y'all coming?"

"Yeah sorry we got caught up."

"Man y'all are just nasty," Damon laughed obliviously.

Blake held out his hand to help Jasmine out of the limousine. They realized they were about to board a dinner cruise. Jasmine walked into his arms.

She tried to focus on something else.

"You guys, this is so beautiful. Thanks."

Damon asked Carmen for the tickets. She dug them out of her purse. After a brief wait they were on the ship and looking for their table. The table covered in white linen was elegantly set for six. Blake tried to hesitate before taking their seats. He wanted Jasmine as far away from Jeremy as possible, but good luck with that at a table with an even number of chairs.

Carmen and Damon sat. Jeremy sat by Carmen and Lucy sat next to him. Blake took the seat next to Lucy and held out the chair between him and Damon for Jasmine. Next to him, Damon was the only other man he trusted without hesitation to protect her. A waiter came around, filled their water glasses and took their drink orders.

After he left, Lucy asked, "Jazzy you okay. You're awfully quiet tonight? I thought for sure you'd be the one to ask Jeremy a million questions."

Under any other circumstances Jasmine would have laughed at the irony. She knew plenty about him.

Jasmine looked at Jeremy, "I'm sorry I'm not my usual chatty self. It's just that I feel a bit nauseous right now."

Blake gently kicked her under the table. It looked like she had found her bearings and her claws were about to come out.

Carmen laughed, "Maybe you're knocked up."

Jeremy choked on his water. Everyone looked at him.

Lucy patted his back, "Are you okay honey?"

Embarrassed, he coughed to clear his throat.

After a few moments he couldn't help but stare at Jasmine when he said, "I'm fine sweetie. That sip was just bad timing I guess."

Blake glowered at him.

Jasmine said, "No it's too soon for me to know I'm pregnant, but if I am I know my husband is going to be there for me every step of the way."

Blake kicked her a little harder under the table. She looked at him and smiled letting him know she had no intention of stopping.

Damon said, "Ah man, I hope you don't get sea sick."

Blake said, "I'm sure she will be fine guys."

He gave Jasmine a look that begged her to chill out.

Lucy changed the subject, "You know guys, I just thought of something. Each of us is together one way or another because of Ahmed."

The table became silent. After a few moments Jasmine raised her water glass.

A single tear fell from her eye.

"To Ahmed, he was a friend who always wanted to help everyone around him and make them better. Even in death he's still looking out for us."

They each raised their glasses and took a sip.

Jasmine stood and said, "I need a minute guys, I'll be back."

She grabbed her purse and headed toward the back of the ship in search of the bathroom. When she went in she checked the stalls and was grateful to find herself all alone. She leaned down on the counter and took a deep breath. She fought with everything in her not to let the tears come. She observed her reflection.

"This is not happening God. This is not happening! I have to see Your hand in this because I do not believe in coincidence. I can't hurt Lucy like that. She has finally found happiness and I can't be the one to take it from her. Is he even worthy of her? It's been a long time. I know I'm not the same person I was back then so maybe he isn't. Father, you have to help me. I can't do this alone. I don't know what to do? I really want to go out there and show my natural black behind. I have so much anger in my heart for that man. Please help me get through this night and guide my steps."

Her cell phone signaled a text. It was Blake asking if she was okay and if she needed him. She smiled. She loved him so much. She didn't know why God saw fit to give him to her but she was grateful. She texted back that she was okay and she would be out in a second.

She checked her make-up and refreshed her lipstick. She took a deep breath and headed back towards their table. She spotted Blake hovering near the dance floor. She smiled when he saw her. He opened his arms and she gratefully slipped into them.

A soft love ballad was playing.

He began to slow dance with her and said, "I thought maybe you could use a little time away from the group with your co-conspirator."

She laughed, "You're a genius."

"Is that why you married me?"

"It is indeed."

His face got serious.

"You okay baby."

"Yes. I just had a consultation with God so I'm waiting for Him to kick in before I act up."

He laughed.

"Yeah I thought I was going to have to step on your toe to shut you up."

"Bringing Ahmed into the conversation was a splash of cold water on my anger."

"Lucy has no idea you guys ever dated, though I'm sure she knows he went to school with us."

"I was thinking Lucy is already in love with him. I don't want her to know about what I did and I don't want her to know we ever had a relationship."

"Baby, don't you think that's a little dangerous. What if he tells her?"

"I don't think he will."

"I'm more worried that he is still a jerk. If he hurts Lucy I will have to put my hands on him since you wouldn't let me do it back in college."

She shook her head. Blake would always have that temper so it was pointless to argue.

"Baby listen, what if he's changed. I mean we have?"

"Babe he just dropped you like you were nothing and left you alone to deal with what you both created. He never tried to contact you to see if you were okay or anything. I'm sorry, but I don't care who he is now. I will always see him as who he was."

Jasmine didn't want to go back to that dark time in her life but she knew it was inevitable.

"Let's hit pause on this and go back to the table. I'm not quite ready to have my sins on display."

"Okay baby."

They walked back to the table hand-in-hand. There was a conversation underway when they took their seats.

Carmen said, "Jeremy was just telling us that he went to school with us."

Jeremy locked eyes with Jasmine.

"I transferred to another college after my first semester."

Blake knew exactly why he'd transferred too, the coward.

He asked him, "What made you transfer?"

Jasmine didn't miss Jeremy's jaw clinch before he answered.

"I just thought Tallahassee was a better environment for me."

Blake nodded and resisted saying something nasty and completely inappropriate.

Damon said, "Guys, they say they will be serving dinner in about forty five minutes, so this is the perfect time to go and check out the deck. I would love a moment alone with my lady."

Carmen blushed. Damon and Carmen were the first to leave the table hand-in-hand.

Lucy gushed, "Oh my God you guys they are so cute."

Blake said, "I've never seen Damon quite like this. Carmen has definitely put a spell on him."

Jasmine chimed in, "Well when it's real, all bets are off. Damon's trifling ways are no match for true love."

Jeremy asked Lucy, "Shall we go and check out the deck?"

She smiled, "We shall."

Jasmine looked at Blake, "I could actually use some fresh air."

"Then let's get you some."

∞∞∞

Damon and Carmen were leaning against a rail out on the deck. The breeze was perfect as they looked out over the sparkling water in the moonlight. He looked at her feeling like a pretty lucky man to have her in his life. He ran a finger down her cheek.

"I have a gift for you."

She lit up.

"Really? What is it?"

He pulled a long velvet box out of his pocket.

She grinned, "Oh wow that looks like jewelry."

Damon laughed.

"Just open it."

She opened the box and a one carat white gold diamond tennis bracelet twinkled up at her.

She gasped, "Baby it's so beautiful. What is this for?"

"Just for being you."

She was shocked to know she wanted to cry. This man brought out sides of her she thought she had long ago buried.

"You look like you're fighting back tears."

She chuckled.

"Don't remind me. You know you're setting the gift bar pretty high if you start off with diamonds."

He laughed.

"You're worth it. I'm pretty sure I can afford to keep you spoiled for years to come."

Her face held surprise when it registered what he was saying.

She asked, "Damon what are you saying?"

"I'm saying that for the first time in my life I'm in love."

She couldn't fight the tears now and they spilled out.

He wiped them with his thumb and asked, "Why do you try so hard not to show any emotion?"

She took in a deep breath and responded, "When I was a little girl my dad was so hard on us. See he was an immigrant and once he became legal he worked very hard to make a good life for his family. He was strict about us speaking correct English and the one thing he drilled into us was never to be weak. He didn't want anyone to have any reason to automatically assume we were lazy or that we didn't earn our own way. He said crying was a sign of weakness and his children would never be weak."

Damon could understand her father's drive but he definitely took it too far. He held her a little closer.

She continued, "I remember I fell off my bike and scraped my knee once. Of course I cried. My dad said if it didn't kill me, it made me stronger. He told me he never wanted to see a tear again. He said I was not weak but strong and I could do anything I put my mind to."

Damon let out a whistle.

"So he built up your confidence. He just took all the emotion out of it for you."

She let out a sad chuckle.

"Something like that. All of his kids are successful and we are all productive citizens of society but we all have one failed relationship after another because we never learned how to deal with our emotions."

He said, "Well this relationship isn't going to fail because I'm not going anywhere. You're free to show all your emotions whenever you need to.

Her heart overwhelmed she said, "I love you too Damon. It's really throwing me that after all this time we could find something real with each other."

He kissed her very gently and hoped she could feel just how much he truly loved her.

∞∞∞

Blake and Jasmine were on the other side of the ship so they could discuss their options in private.

Blake said, "Jasmine, I've realized something tonight that I never really thought about."

"What's that baby?"

"You haven't forgiven yourself for having that abortion. That's why this is such a challenge for you."

She looked away. He gently pulled her face back to his.

"Jaz, you need to deal with this. You can't torture yourself for the rest of your life."

"Blake, my baby is dead. I know that God has forgiven me but I feel like I just shouldn't be let off the hook that easily. If God sees fit to give us a baby then that's enough for me. Forgiving myself is just not a priority."

"Jaz, that is crazy. You can't continue living like this. Jeremy may be in our lives forever. What if they get married? He will always be around. What if they have kids? You will have to see him loving those children and not the one the two of you made. You need to free yourself from this otherwise you will snap and Lucy and everybody else will want to know why."

A little defensive she asked, "Don't you think I've tried?"

A little snap in his voice, "Obviously not hard enough."

Her face instantly showed attitude. He threw his hands up in surrender.

"Okay, wait. I'm sorry but Jaz listen. We need to deal with this and you know I'm right."

"I took a life, how am I supposed to just forget that?"

This is the moment he feared all those years ago. He knew her compassion would always outweigh her logic no matter what she tried to make herself believe. Suddenly a thought came to him.

"You also gave life Jasmine."

She looked at him confused.

"What do you mean?"

He laughed a little because it was just like her not to even give herself credit for it, one of the main reasons why he adored her.

"Did you forget you gave my father your kidney and saved his life?"

She blinked and said, "Oh yeah. I mean but..."

"But nothing Jaz. You saved his life and you saved mine."

She shook her head.

He said, "Stop it Jasmine. No you're not perfect and yes you've made mistakes. Everybody has. We're human. You are going to let this go once and for all because you have to."

He rubbed her belly.

"You need to make sure your heart is ready to love the beautiful babies that God is going to bless us with. You've punished yourself enough. It's time Jaz."

She said, "I feel like a fraud. Ahmed gave me the power to make life or death decisions for him because I always did the right thing. If he knew what kind of person I truly was I'm sure he would have made a different decision."

It broke his heart to see her like this. Even though he could understand her thought process he didn't agree. He reached out and hugged her. He just held on to her for a while. He didn't have words but he hoped his touch would comfort her as he silently prayed for her.

She knew he was right. She wanted more than anything to be a good mother to their kids. She couldn't bring this baggage with her. Was this why God was allowing this all to happen now to prepare her for the seed she would soon be carrying.

She said, "You're right baby. Today is the day that I am going to start putting this behind me. If God can forgive me surely I can forgive myself."

He pulled away to wipe the tears that he knew were there but was shocked to see there were none. He loved that she had that kind of strength whenever it was needed most.

She smiled at him.

"God, what would I ever do without you?"

"Lucky for you you'll never have to know," he said.

She kissed him.

Their kiss was interrupted by the clearing of someone's throat. Jasmine turned to see Jeremy staring at them looking very uncomfortable. Blake turned and prayed hard that he wouldn't knock him out. Jeremy cleared his throat again.

Jasmine asked, "Where's Lucy?"

She is talking to Carmen about some bracelet Damon gave her. Jasmine made a mental note to find out about this bracelet later.

"What do you want?"

"To talk to you," his eyes shifted to Blake, "Alone."

Blake's temper flashed instantly.

"That's not gonna happen buddy. So go ahead and say what you need to say."

Jeremy looked over to Jasmine as if she could change his mind.

"You've met my husband Blake right?"

Jeremy smirked.

"I see you're still as feisty as ever Jasmine."

"Get to the point or get the hell on," Blake said.

Jasmine ran a hand over Blake's arm to calm him.

"It's okay baby."

Reluctantly Jeremy said, "I was just as stunned to see you in that limo as you were to see me but to be honest I'm really grateful. Jasmine some time ago I gave my life to Christ. I've been trying to be a good person but there was one thing I always carried with me, a regret I had. That's the way I treated you."

Still pissed Blake said, "Well you should have felt bad, knowingly taking advantage of her innocence and then tossing her aside like she was nothing."

As busy as Blake's sex life had been he had never bedded a virgin. He knew he was full of crap back then and so he required a consenting adult that knew exactly what she was getting herself into.

Remorse showed on Jeremy's face.

He said, "I know I took advantage of you and I'm sorry. I was young, stupid and arrogant but there hasn't been a day that I haven't regretted what I did."

Sarcastically Jasmine said, "Oh really there has been several days gone by that I haven't heard you express that regret."

"I deserve your anger and so much more, but Jasmine I prayed that God would let me find you so that I could apologize and make it right."

"There isn't anything you can do to make it right Jeremy. Our baby is gone and it's not coming back."

He took a deep swallow and was staggered at the sudden sadness he felt. He'd assumed as much but knowing was different. He found his voice.

"Jasmine, I can't imagine what that must have been like for you and I won't try. I'm sorry for whatever part I played in your having to make that decision but we can't go back. All we have is today. I'm here and I'm sorry. I hope you can find it in your heart to forgive me."

"I forgave you years ago but that doesn't mean I have to like you or be friends with you."

"No it doesn't, but the fact remains that I am very much in love with Lucy and I want to spend the rest of my life with her."

Jasmine felt like the wind had been knocked out of her.

Blake said, "If you hurt Lucy we are going to have some problems."

Jeremy was sick of Blake. He wanted to punch him in his face but he couldn't blame him. He was just protecting his loved ones. It's not like he hadn't given the man plenty of reason to dislike him.

"Look, I understand where you're coming from but let's just chill. I love Lucy and I am not the same person I was back then. Lucy means the world to me. I want a life with her, kids the whole nine."

Jasmine took a deep breath.

"Do you plan on telling her about us?"

"Yeah, that's why I'm here. I don't want anything to be between us. I can't keep something like this from her. I know you guys are practically best friends but I don't want my marriage built on lies."

Jasmine said, "Okay look, you can tell her about our very *brief* relationship but the part about the baby is mine to tell and I won't be telling her. I won't be telling anybody is that clear?"

Jeremy showed reluctance on his face. He honestly wanted full disclosure.

He said, "I can't agree to that. You're asking me to lie to the woman I love."

Jasmine got into his face lightning quick.

"I am not asking you to lie to anybody. I am telling you that you do not have the right to give anyone information you know nothing about. The woman you love? Be careful how you throw that word around because your track record says you don't know what love is. Do you honestly think Lucy will stay with you if she knows the truth about what you did?"

She saw the confidence he so passionately spoke with fade a little.

"Not so sure are you? Is it really worth the risk Jeremy? Let's face it. This isn't about you being honest with Lucy. This is about you clearing your conscience. Nothing you say or do is going to bring our kid back or the moment you put your hands on me. You want to make this up to me? Well fine, this is how you do it. You tell Lucy we had a very *brief* relationship freshman year in college. You can tell her we had one sexual encounter that was only satisfactory for you and we broke up shortly thereafter. For your sake I'd stay away from the fact that I was a virgin who you said you loved but clearly didn't. I would also avoid telling her it resulted with the conception of a baby, that you hit me and that you discarded me and your unborn child like we were yesterday's garbage. Are we clear on how this story goes down?"

Jeremy stared into her eyes. Through the bravado he saw the very real plea in her eyes. It wasn't what he wanted but he did owe her a debt he could never repay. What good would it do for Lucy to know about that? He was not that person anymore. It still pained him to know that he hit her in a moment of anger. Under the heavy weight of his misguided youth he hung his head for a moment and then looked her in the eyes.

"Okay. You got it. You have my word. I won't tell her about the baby, just that we briefly dated and slept together once but it didn't work out."

He saw her visibly relax.

She said, "Thank you. Lucy will want to talk to me after she talks to you. For the record I'll tell her to not let this stand in the way of her happiness. It's ancient history that means absolutely zilch to me."

Defeated, Jeremy nodded and turned to walk away. Jasmine turned to Blake.

"Tell me I'm doing the right thing?"

"This is a sticky situation baby. You're doing what you feel you have to do to protect everyone involved."

"If she finds out one day who will she blame?"

Blake swallowed hard.

"She will feel betrayed by both of you. It's hard to say who will get the brunt of her anger but neither one of you will walk away unscathed. You will likely be the one to lose her because she would have pledged to him two days past forever."

Jasmine nodded. Her heart was so torn. She didn't know if she was protecting Lucy or herself. She couldn't tell if she was being a true friend or a selfish one. She prayed she was doing the right thing.

She slid her arm into Blake's and said, "Let's head back."

As Jasmine and Blake approached the other side of the boat they passed by a smiling Carmen and Damon heading in for dinner. Carmen held out her wrist that displayed a very fabulous diamond tennis bracelet. Jasmine gushed with Carmen while Blake nodded his approval to Damon.

Behind Carmen a little farther away Jasmine could see that Lucy and Jeremy were having an intense conversation. Lucy did not look happy and Jeremy looked very distressed. Lucy looked up and caught her eyes as Jeremy was heading towards them.

Blake caught the eye contact and said, "Hey guys why don't we head in for dinner?"

Jasmine said, "I'll be there in a sec. Let me go have a girl moment with Lucy."

Carmen looked back at Lucy and asked, "Is everything okay?"

"We will just be a few minutes."

The men headed in and Carmen reluctantly left her girls out on the deck. Jasmine tried to place a comforting smile on her face as she approached Lucy. Lucy had her arms folded tightly across her small chest. Her lips were paper thin with the scowl she wore.

Before she could speak Jasmine said, "Lucy, I promise you it was nothing. We went out for a couple months and we slept together once and for your sake I hope he has improved in that arena."

Jasmine tried to laugh it off but Lucy didn't even chuckle.

"Jasmine, how can I go out with a guy that you slept with?"

"Okay Lucy, you're not going out with this guy. You're in love with him and you guys are trying to have a future together. You didn't even know either one of us when it happened. I don't even think that should count as actual sexual intercourse."

This time Lucy did laugh but said, "Jasmine I love him so much. I finally feel like I've met that one person I could really be happy with. He is the kindest man I've ever known. He's so thoughtful and respectful of me. I don't want to give him up but this is weird."

"If it helps I wasn't even completely naked."

Lucy laughed and lightly punched Jasmine in the arm.

"Jazzy, I'm serious. Does Blake know?"

"Yeah he knows but it doesn't bother him because Blake knows no one else matters to me. Do you feel like anyone else matters to him besides you?"

"No I don't. I know he loves me. Jasmine, I've never been this happy. He supports my dreams. He wants a big family too because he's an only child like me. You know how important it is to me because I always wanted a huge family."

Jasmine didn't know why it stung just a little to know he wanted kids with Lucy but he turned his back on the one they would have had. It didn't matter now, everyone deserved a second chance.

Lucy asked, "Jasmine, are you sure there isn't anything else I need to know?"

Jasmine did not want to lie to Lucy but she could not ruin her happiness. So he was a bastard when he was eighteen that had nothing to do with the man that put that amazing glow on her friend's face. She had her happiness. There was no way she could willingly take Lucy's from her.

She said, "Lucy, you know everything you need to know. Nothing that happened then has any bearing on what's going on now."

It wasn't an actual lie. Jasmine would just have to find a way to make her peace with it. Lucy's happiness was more important than her nine-year-old wound. Lucy jumped into Jasmine's arms and gave her a big hug.

"Thank you Jasmine for being okay with this. I really didn't want to give him up but I would have because you are my family."

That choked Jasmine up a bit, "Well it's a good thing you don't have to choose."

They walked arm in arm to join their friends for dinner.

Chapter 45: Group Therapy

The Monroe's and the Jessup's, the old and the new, had just arrived in Tallahassee, Florida at the offices of Dr. Sheridan Richards for their family intervention. It had been two months since Blake and Jasmine wed. Jasmine finally convinced them that this was necessary. She was so grateful how understanding Dr. Richards had been to adjusting her schedule to suit them and their changing needs. Jasmine was nervous. She had her hand in Blake's as they were led down the corridor to the room for the group sessions.

Jasmine was feeling very nauseous as they neared this long overdue moment. She didn't think she would be this anxious because she was so ready to get to the bottom of all the hate and bitterness that lurked in the branches of her immediate family tree. Blake was glad this day was finally here, but he was worried about if it would it bring them all closer together or drive them further apart?

He had never prayed so much in his life as he had prayed for this day and the hour that was upon them. Jasmine always talked to him about his faith. He believed that God wouldn't bring them this far to let them down, so he was about to see if he had what it took to trust in the God he now served.

Frank's hand was also in his wife's. He knew she could feel the cold sweat pooling in the palm of his hand. The sweat that dripped down his back also tickled him but he could find no humor whatsoever in this moment. His soul was weighed down so heavily it took great effort to even make each step. He had no idea what his family would think of him once they found out his truth. He couldn't stand it, so how could they?

He too had been praying but he couldn't forgive himself so he wasn't expecting God or his family to. He would do what he came there to do though. The least he could do was tell them the truth. He would enjoy the last hours with his family and the moments he got to see his son truly happy. He decided to accept that when this was over he would lose them. He was prepared to accept punishment but there was no punishment on this earth that could have been enough for what he'd done.

Vanessa was mad. She didn't want to be there and she didn't want to air her deepest pains in front of a stranger and these white people. She wanted to choke Justin. Every time she scowled at him he just kissed her hand and told her it was going to be okay. She did miss her daughter though. She hadn't seen her since that awful Sunday dinner that went awry.

She hadn't hugged her baby since Blake had stolen her from their lives. If this was the only way she could get her child back she supposed she was going to have to do it. She had not allowed herself to go back to that pain in a long time, but today she would relive the worst day of her life all to supposedly heal her family. Now on what planet did that make any sense?

Sheridan's assistant Stacy held the door open and extended her hand to point in the direction of where they should each sit. The room was done in warm earth tones and the furniture was very plush. The room screamed comfort. The pretty brown skinned Stacy directed Blake and Jasmine to sit on the love seat in the middle. She pointed to the one on the left for Frank and Lisa and the one on the right for Vanessa and Justin. They each took their seats.

Stacy said, "Dr. Richards will be here in just a moment."

No one said a word. They were all dealing with the magnitude of what this day could mean. Each couple had a truth they had to share with everyone. None of them were looking forward to bearing their souls, but they had all agreed and were at the point of no return.

Sheridan walked in wearing a red pantsuit and brown pumps with her hair swept up into a sassy tail. She exuded confidence and a serenity that put them all at ease.

She said, "Good afternoon everybody."

They murmured their tense greetings. Sheridan strode to the chair directly in front of the sofa that held Blake and Jasmine. She took a seat and crossed her legs then picked up the pen and pad on the table next to the chair.

She said, "Well guys we have a lot of ground to cover today. Even though four hours seems like a lot, it's really not. Let me go over a few house rules. When someone is talking we don't interrupt because everyone will get a chance to talk and everyone needs to feel free to express themselves. There are boxes of tissues under each sofa on each side. After the first two hours we will take a twenty minute break to let everyone take a breather and go handle whatever they need to. Are there any objections?"

Everyone shook their heads.

Sheridan smiled, "I see you guys are nervous huh?"

They let out uneasy chuckles.

"Well let me just say this one last thing and then we will get started. I know you are aware that this is a Christian counseling center. I have to be honest. When Jasmine contacted me I was very intrigued about your family. But the closer we got to today the heavier my heart began to get. I started praying for this session like I always do and the Holy Spirit led me to go on a fast. I am not sure exactly what God has planned for this day and for this family but I know it will be amazing. I can tell you with strong conviction that there is healing in the air for this family and all you have to do is be willing to pull it down."

Jasmine was astonished to hear that she had prayed for them. She was feeling more and more confident that God had truly led them there but her stomach was still in knots. She hoped she could keep down the lunch she'd had.

Sheridan stood and said, "Can we all stand, hold hands and pray before we begin."

Everyone stood and grabbed the hand next to them.

Sheridan began, "Dear Lord, we thank You for this day that You have made. We know that it was ordained before the foundations of the world to bring healing and wholeness to this family. Lord I ask that You open hearts and loosen tongues. Let honest communication flow and Your peace that passes all understanding comfort this family as they rebuild the foundation of who they are. Let them know Father that there is nothing too hard for You to do. It doesn't matter what they've done or what they've been through. You are there for them and You love them. We give You praise and honor for what is about to take place on this day. In Jesus name I pray, amen."

A chorus of amen followed.

Sheridan took her seat, "Okay so here is how I want to do this and this is why I had you seated this way. Vanessa and Justin, I want you to go first. Then I want Blake and Jasmine to go."

Blake said, "Uh there isn't anything that we have to tell."

Sheridan smiled and said, "I think there is. She looked at Jasmine."

Blake's confused expression turned to Jasmine.

She timidly said, "We go second baby."

Blake's heart sank. What could Jasmine possibly have kept from him? Jasmine wished that Sheridan hadn't said it quite that way but she knew it was time he heard it all.

Sheridan said, "Frank, you can go after the break okay."

They nodded while Frank wiped his damp hands on his jeans. His throat was so dry he thought he would cough up dust. Sheridan relaxed and sat back in her chair. She slid on her rimless glasses and looked over at Vanessa.

With her pen and pad in her hand she asked, "Vanessa, I want you to take a deep breath and when you're ready I want you to tell us why you have a problem with Blake marrying your daughter."

Vanessa gave a startled look.

A very somber Sheridan with no smile said, "We need to get right to the heart of these matters. It's going to be okay. I promise you. Aren't you tired of the burden that is drawing a wedge between you and your daughter?"

Vanessa began to fidget and Justin grabbed her hand to steady her.

He whispered in her ear, "Sweetheart, it's time to tell Jasmine. It's okay."

She nodded.

In a shaky voice she began, "It's not that I have a problem with Blake per say. It's that I have a problem with what he represents."

Sheridan asked, "And what is it that you feel he represents?"

She looked up at Blake and then looked back down at her hands.

"I think he will betray her and take advantage of her when she's vulnerable. I have a hard time believing he's sincere in what he claims to feel for my baby."

Blake wanted to defend himself but Sheridan signaled for him to let it go.

Sheridan asked, "Why do you think that?"

"Because that's what they always do," Vanessa snapped.

It took Jasmine by surprise. She had to rub Blake's leg to calm him down. His face was turning red. She knew this must be hard for him to hear, but she knew they couldn't judge her especially not knowing the root.

Sheridan saw where this was heading. She'd had her suspicions but now she knew what it was. Now she just had to figure out when and who.

She asked, "Vanessa can you tell us how old you were when someone you trusted took advantage of you when you were vulnerable?"

Vanessa put her head down for a moment and began to shake. When she lifted it tears were streaming down her face.

She squeezed Justin's hand a little tighter and said in soft whimper, "I was sixteen years old when that sorry excuse for a man raped me."

A collective gasp came from everyone in the room except for Sheridan and Justin. After all these years it still broke something in him to know his wife had been violated and to know the great deal of pain it had caused so many people. Jasmine and Lisa immediately felt the pain as women and their tears of anger, fear and sympathy began to silently flow.

Sheridan asked, "He was a white man?"

In a soft whisper with her head hung low, Vanessa answered, "Yes."

Chapter 46: Getting to the Bottom

The realization of where Vanessa was coming from struck Blake like a slug to the chest. He was angry and the thought crossed his mind of someone doing that to Jasmine. He saw red. He knew he would kill him with his bare hands without a moment's hesitation should he ever be given the chance. He pulled Jasmine closer to him just to assure himself she was safe.

He could imagine even a peaceful man like Justin would have done the same had he had the opportunity. Frank now took an understanding to how and why Vanessa had always treated him with kid gloves. Even before the beating, he knew she didn't trust him. Now he couldn't blame her because he understood better than anyone in the room how something horrible from your childhood could mess you up for life.

Sheridan asked, "Vanessa can you tell us what happened?"

Vanessa took in a very deep breath and let it out very slowly.

"I used to work at the little store in our neighborhood. Mr. Matthews was the sweetest man you ever wanted to meet. He treated black people with dignity and respect. You couldn't find anyone to say a bad thing about him. On my 16th birthday I had to work the close shift. It was a Saturday. I had been working there almost a year. I came in with my hair done and make-up on for the first time. I was feeling really beautiful."

She smiled at that part of the memory.

"I had my first date ever that night and I was so excited. Mr. Matthews closed up the store. I was counting the money in the register."

She started to tremble but Justin wrapped her in his arms as she continued.

"He came over and told me how beautiful I was and how much I looked like a woman. Being young and naïve I smiled and thanked him for the compliment. He stroked one of the curls in my hair and there was this look in his eye that made me realize something wasn't right. I tried to hurry up and finish with the register. He came around the counter and put his hand on my shoulder. When I eased out of his grip he said, don't run, it will only make it worse. I stared at him confused and scared out of my mind. I did exactly what he said not to do and turned to run."

She took a deep breath as she had to relive this. She never told anyone but her husband and that was because she had to explain to him why on their wedding night she froze. He was so understanding and patient with her. She loved him severely for that. He'd waited until she felt safe. Then he showed her what sex was meant to be between a man and a woman.

Jasmine felt sicker as her mom went on with the story. She didn't want to hear it but she knew this was such an important part of the process. She didn't know if this was such a good idea after all. Everyone in the room was silent and patiently waited for Vanessa to unburden her hidden truths.

Justin rubbed her back and whispered, "It's almost over sweetheart. It's okay. I'm here for you."

She nodded, took a deep breath and said, "He grabbed me by my hair and pulled me down behind the counter. I screamed and he slapped me. He told me if I screamed again he would kill me and I believed him. I tried to fight back but he was so much stronger than me. It seemed like the fight in me made him more excited. He ripped my underwear and he violated me."

Jasmine buried her face in Blake's chest and wept. He held her a little tighter knowing there was really no real comfort he could offer her. Sheridan was a bit choked up but managed to keep her voice steady.

She asked, "What ever happened to Mr. Matthews? Did you report the crime?"

Vanessa let out a sarcastic chuckle, "I never told a soul except for my husband on our wedding night. Mr. Matthews told me that no one would believe me because his reputation would never be tarnished by a slutty nigger. Foolishly I believed him. I ran home and scrubbed my skin until it was raw. I quit my job. I used to have nightmares, but they stopped when I met Justin in my early twenties. Every now and then I can still smell his smoky breath and his lustful sweat. It makes me sick to my stomach."

She looked at Jasmine, "After that I never wore another stitch of make-up or made any fuss about my hair or my clothes. I wanted to be as plain as I could manage and to never stand out for any reason. In my mind bringing attention to myself only brought unspeakable pain and suffering. If it wasn't for your father intervening I would have had you looking like an old maid. That's why I never complained about you running around like a little tom boy with Blake. I'd honestly hoped you'd stay that way. I can admit now that I was jealous of what you had with Lisa."

She glanced over at her friend. Lisa's face showed she was startled by the revelation.

"It hurt me so bad that Jasmine had to go to you to learn how to embrace being a woman but it was something that I just couldn't give her. I didn't want to stand in her way. That's why I never said anything about it. I knew you truly cared for her so that gave me comfort."

Her eyes shifted to Blake, "I'm so sorry about what I said to you. I can't imagine how that must have made you feel. Deep within my heart I know that you've always been the best thing for Jasmine but my life taught me to look at you a little differently. I'm sorry that I couldn't put that aside and let you two be happy."

Blake cleared his throat and said, "It's okay now that I understand why you felt that way. It won't be held against you. I promise."

Vanessa took a moment to hold on to Justin and to get herself together.

Sheridan asked, "Justin, how has this affected you?"

A little alarmed Justin cleared his throat. He took a nervous glance at his wife. She rubbed his leg giving him reassurance that it was okay to speak his mind.

He began, "I love my wife with all my heart and I never wanted to push her into anything that she wasn't comfortable with. I was so happy just to have her that I was willing to accept her as she was because that's who I fell in love with."

Sheridan saw the reluctance and prompted, "But..."

He smiled and said, "But..." He hesitated.

Sheridan said, "It's okay Justin we are all married adults here."

He sheepishly smiled and continued, "I would have loved to see her in a sexy dress every once in a while or some high heels, maybe a little red lipstick sometimes."

Blake grinned. He knew exactly where the man was coming from. There was nothing like seeing your woman all glammed up just for you, especially in a sexy high heel.

Justin turned to face his wife, "Sweetheart, it's not that you need it because you're gorgeous without it and your body is still incredible after all these years but one of the things I'm hoping for is that you will embrace being a woman and flaunt your beauty just a little."

Frank let out an understanding chuckle, Lisa elbowed him. Vanessa blushed, but didn't respond. Jasmine stood and walked to her mother. She knelt down in front of her and looked in her eyes.

"Mama, I'm so sorry this happened to you and I'm sorry I didn't try sooner to understand you instead of always picking a fight."

Vanessa grabbed her daughter's face, "It's okay baby. You could never understand something that I wasn't willing to let you see. I'm sorry too."

She hugged her for several moments. When she let go Jasmine stood, wiped her face and took her seat next to Blake.

Vanessa looked at Blake and Jasmine and asked, "There's something I've been curious about for a long while now. Since we are sharing our deepest secrets I believe you and Blake have been keeping a secret for years and I really want to know what it is."

Lisa said, "I agree, something happened between you two freshman year in college and whatever it was it changed both of you."

As a memory came flooding back, Justin asked, "Does this have anything to do with that weekend you just showed up at home upset and you were hiding from your mother?"

Disbelieving Blake asked, "Jasmine, you went home during those three days? Is that what changed your mind?"

All eyes were on Jasmine and her queasiness kicked into overdrive. It was now her turn to bare her soul.

Chapter 47: The Whole Truth and Nothing But

Jasmine could feel a headache coming on as all eyes were on her. Usually Blake was in her corner but she'd left him in the dark on this one as well. The thought of telling their parents that not only was she stupid enough to get pregnant her freshman year but she chose to abort their grandchild was very depressing.

Sheridan asked, "Jasmine, is this the same thing that you shared with me during our telephone consultation?"

Jasmine was surprised at how perceptive their parents were. All this time they knew something happened, they were just not sure what. Jasmine nodded.

Blake asked, "Jaz, what is she talking about?"

"Baby you know this. You just don't know all of it. I don't think I can do this Blake, oh God, I think I'm going to be sick."

She put her hand to her mouth and took deep breaths. Because of what Blake had just learned about Vanessa he reserved his anger and decided to wait her confession out before he got mad. He knew she would struggle telling their parents this and he was prepared to break the news for her. Wherever she was weak he had to be strong. This had always been and probably would always be her Achilles heel. Jasmine hid her face with one hand from pure shame and grabbed Blake's hand with the other. He knew she was asking him to do this part.

He cleared his throat and said, "Yes, there was something that happened freshman year of college and it did change our friendship. This is really hard for Jasmine so I'll just get this over with. Jasmine had an abortion our first semester of college."

While their parents gasped, Jasmine broke down in tears and she could not bring herself to look any of them in the face.

It took a moment to sink in, but Lisa jumped up and got in Blake's face.

"Boy did you get her pregnant in college?"

She started hitting him really hard with a pillow from her sofa.

"Blake Michael Jessup I will have your hide for this."

Blake was taken aback by his mom's outburst and was using his arms to block his face. The only other time he had seen her angry like this was when she pulled a gun on his dad.

Sheridan said, "Lisa calm down, please, calm down."

Lisa's outburst snapped Jasmine back to attention. She would defend Blake against anybody even his mother.

She stood and got in between them, "Stop! Ms. Lisa wait, it wasn't Blake's baby. It was not Blake's baby."

Lisa barely heard Jasmine's words the first time but the second time it registered. She was breathing hard and staring at both of them like they were strangers.

Panting hard she asked, "Okay, what exactly happened between you two?"

Jasmine pinched her nose and took a deep breath. The look on her parents face broke her heart. She knew without a shadow of a doubt that she had officially been a disappointment to them.

Jasmine said, "Everyone just calm down, take your seats and let me explain."

Vanessa was livid, "Explain what Jasmine, I don't think there is any explanation needed. You had sex, got pregnant and killed the baby. Does that about sum it up?"

Her mother's words felt like a slap that would sting for a while.

Blake interrupted, "Now wait just a minute. It wasn't like that."

Vanessa stood, "You stay out of this Blake. You better be glad you didn't have anything to do with this."

Sheridan decided not to interrupt and let this play out. She knew what tipped Jasmine's decision. She wanted to see how her decision would be perceived once that was made known. She began quickly jotting down notes of how each parent reacted. Of all people Frank came to her defense.

"Vanessa, please take your seat and give her a chance. This room is supposed to be free from judgment. Let's give the kids a chance to tell us the whole story."

Justin's heart was broken because he regretted not pushing harder that day to find out what was wrong.

He grabbed his wife's hand and said, "Calm down Vanessa and take your seat, please sweetheart."

She obliged her husband's request.

Justin looked at his daughter, "I am so sorry baby girl that I didn't push harder that day for you to tell me what was wrong."

Vanessa rolled her eyes, "What are you talking about Justin?"

He said, "I could have stopped this. We both could have."

Blake looked at Jasmine and asked, "Baby, is that why you changed your mind because you went home?"

Jasmine said, "Blake I was so grateful to have your support. I really wanted to believe it was possible. Even though I knew I had you in my corner I knew I couldn't do it unless I had my parents in my corner as well."

She stole a glance at her parents and then continued, "I came home that day to tell you guys that I had gotten pregnant and that I wanted to keep the baby. I just hoped that after your initial disappointment we could put our heads together and figure it out. But when I came home, mom you were on the phone and..."

Vanessa's hand went up to her mouth as she gasped, "Oh my God, that was when we found out about Rachel getting pregnant and having to come home."

Jasmine nodded.

The realization of what pushed her daughter to make the decision floored Vanessa. She began to weep.

"Jasmine, I am so sorry. I can't imagine how scared you must've been with me ripping that girl to shreds for being stupid and what I said about no child of mine better bring home a bastard child."

Jasmine said, "Mom, I can't pin it all on you. It was just so many reasons why I decided to do it. Ms. Lisa, you will be happy to know that your son did everything in his power to get me to change my mind. It is a decision that I regret daily, but there you have it. That's our secret."

Blake stared at her, "So that's what happened. That's what changed your mind. I've wondered about that for years. I just didn't want to bring it up. Why didn't you tell me?"

She responded, "I really don't know why I didn't tell you but her reaction to Rachel scared me so bad I couldn't tell them. Without their support I just couldn't do it."

Blake grabbed her face, "Ah baby, I wish you would have told me that. We could have found a way to work through that."

With much regret she said, "It's water under the bridge now. There's nothing that can be done about it."

She was right and he knew it but it brought a fresh sting to a very old wound.

Lisa asked, "Well Blake, if you're not the father then who was it?"

The question startled both Blake and Jasmine.

Jasmine said, "You guys, it doesn't matter who he was. He didn't want anything to do with us. That was also one of the factors weighing into my decision. There isn't any good that can come from revealing the father."

Vanessa asked, "What else are you hiding Jasmine? I mean what is the big deal about giving us his name."

Jasmine swallowed hard, "I'm not hiding anything mom. I just don't see the point. He is irrelevant."

Sheridan interrupted, "Jasmine this is an opportunity for everyone to get everything off their chest. Are you sure you don't want to disclose the father?"

Jasmine nodded her head, "Yes I'm sure."

Blake whispered to her, "Why don't we just tell them baby."

"No," she said in a hushed voice, "Think of the consequences for other people. Let's just leave it where it's at. Please, I gave him my word."

He stared at her for a moment and realized it wasn't just their secret it was someone else's and they couldn't risk the potential fallout.

He put his forehead on hers, "Okay. I got your back babe."

Blake said, "I'm sorry but Jasmine is right. We have our reasons so please don't be mad. Respect that we know what's best in this situation. We have enough on our plate to deal with so all the details don't really matter."

Sheridan saw their parents weren't too thrilled about his answer. She decided now was a good time for a break.

"Okay guys I think it's time for a break. A lot has been revealed, emotions are raw but truth is coming out and that's the important thing. Please don't be discouraged. I promise you won't feel this way when it's over."

She took a look at her watch and said, "Let's take about thirty minutes and meet back here. There are very nice grounds to the office that you can walk to stretch your legs or regroup and think about any questions you may have so far. I need to take a break to fine tune some of my recommendations. Does anyone want to say anything before we leave?"

She got no response, "Okay, I will see you all in thirty."

Frank, Lisa, Justin and Vanessa all stood and headed out the door.

Jasmine told Blake, "Baby, I don't feel good. I feel like I'm going to be sick. I don't know what's wrong."

Sheridan noticed that Jasmine has begun to look a little green.

She asked, "Are you okay sweetie?"

Jasmine said, "I don't feel so good. I think I literally can't stomach all the confessions in this room."

Blake stood and extended his hand to her, "Come on baby, let's get you some fresh air."

They headed out to the hallway and Jasmine felt the vomit rising. She shoved her purse at Blake and took off running looking for a bathroom. Finding one a few doors down she ran in and headed into the handicap stall and retched everything she had eaten that day. Blake was very close on her heels, not caring that he was in the women's restroom. When she finished and flushed the toilet he helped her up.

She headed out of the stall to the sinks in the front of the bathroom and began to rinse out her mouth and wash her face. Blake placed his hand on her forehead to see if she had a fever.

She dried her face with a paper towel and took in some deep breaths.

Blake asked, "Well, did that make you feel better?"

"A little but not much."

"Do you think it's something you ate?"

"No I don't because I didn't eat anything new or unfamiliar today. I don't know baby, I've been feeling sick all day."

"This is so unlike you babe. Do you think it's just because today is so stressful."

"I have no idea, but can you get me a ginger ale or a sprite?"

"Yeah baby sure."

"I'm gonna stay in here just in case I'm sick again."

As he headed out the door, something occurred to him and he turned to ask, "Is your cycle late?"

Jasmine blinked like he was speaking Portuguese.

"What?"

"Baby did you miss your period?"

"Oh my God, Blake it is late."

"How late?"

She started counting on her fingers, "Like five days late."

"How about I get that ginger ale from the drug store on the corner that I saw when we came in and pick up a pregnancy test too."

"Baby, are you crazy? I am not going to take a pregnancy test right now."

"Oh yes you are. You don't think we are going to be able to wait to know this especially at a time when our focus cannot afford to be split."

He flashed her favorite grin and walked over to her and kissed her forehead.

"Jaz if you're pregnant then I just need to know and I can't wait."

Her mind was blown. This was the last thing she expected from today.

"Okay baby, go get the test but hurry because we don't have much time."

"Okay be right back."

Jasmine dug through her purse for some gum and went to the waiting area in the restroom as Blake ran out. She knew this was what they both wanted but her mind was on the first child she carried. She was so grateful that God may have seen fit for her to carry another one but her heart ached for the child that never was. She wanted to be a good mother. She placed her hand over her belly.

"Please God, if I'm carrying a child, please take care of my baby and let it be whole and healthy. I will spend the rest of my life loving it and cherishing it for the beautiful gift that I now know it is. Please take care of my first born that's up there with You and help me to forgive myself so that I can love this baby with no limits."

Lisa and Vanessa came into the bathroom. Vanessa saw her daughter sitting there looking despondent.

"Baby is everything alright?"

"Yes mama. I'm okay just a little nauseous."

Lisa and Vanessa shared a look then took a seat. Lisa put the back of her hand on Jasmine's forehead.

She said, "You're a little warm sweetie."

"I'm okay just been a rough day I guess. An emotional roller coaster."

"Yeah it has been but are you sure that's the reason you're sick."

Not wanting to go into detail about their suspicions Jasmine nodded.

"Yeah I'm sure. It's just a bug."

Vanessa rolled her eyes, "Yeah the kind of bug that lasts for nine months."

Jasmine's head popped up, "What, why would you say that?"

"Uh perhaps because I have four children."

Lisa laughed, "How late is your cycle Jasmine."

Beyond embarrassed she blushed.

Lisa said, "Do you really think that we don't know you and Blake are consummating your nuptials every chance you get?"

Vanessa laughed, "We were newlyweds once upon a time too."

Jasmine smiled, "Guilty as charged and I'm five days late. Blake just went to get me a ginger ale and a test."

Silence enveloped them until Blake walked into the restroom ten minutes later carrying a plastic bag. He stopped in his tracks when he saw his mom and Vanessa sitting with Jasmine.

He said, "Uh, hi. What are you two doing in here?"

Lisa said, "Oh we could ask you the same thing, this is the women's bathroom."

Jasmine said, "Baby we're busted just give me the test so I can go and take it. He handed her the test and she went into the stall. Blake was beyond mortified with both of them staring at him while his wife was peeing on a stick a few feet away.

Jasmine came out of the bathroom and said, "Well we gotta wait three minutes."

Lisa looked at her watch, "That gives us just enough time to find out and then get back to our session."

Blake set his phone timer for three minutes. Jasmine walked into his arms.

He put his forehead on hers. In a low murmur he asked, "Are you excited baby?"

"Well I was until the puking reared its ugly head."

He laughed, "Listen, I know today isn't the ideal day for this, but maybe in the end it will be the glue that keeps us all together as a family. Remember how you told me to trust God? Well you need to trust Him too."

Vanessa looked at how in love her daughter was with this man and said, "Lisa, why don't we give them a minute. I feel like we're intruding on a private moment."

Lisa smiled at their kids, "I know what you mean. We will know soon enough."

They slipped out and a minute later the timer beeped. Jasmine walked back into the stall and picked up the test she'd left sitting on a paper towel on the sink.

Blake followed closely behind and asked, "Are we pregnant?"

She turned with a huge smile on her face and nodded. He picked her up and spun her around. He put her down, grabbed her face and kissed her.

She grinned, "Oh my goodness Blake we're gonna have a baby!"

"Jasmine I'm so excited about starting our family."

"Me too baby, but we're going to have to cut this party short. We're late!"

The door opened and an older woman walked into the restroom alarmed to see Blake. Seeing the way they were hugged up her mind deduced what they must have been doing. She gasped aloud and looked at the door again to make sure she had the right restroom.

She said, "Now I know sometimes you just gotta have it but in a bathroom honey. That's just tacky."

They ran out of the bathroom laughing.

Chapter 48: A Very Dark Past

Everyone had returned to the session except for Jasmine and Blake.

Sheridan checked her watch and said, "We will give them a few more minutes before we send out the search party."

Lisa and Vanessa shared a look. They decided not to say anything to their spouses but to let the kids share the news. They didn't want to get any hopes up if they weren't with child. Frank wanted the kids to hurry up while he had the nerve to share his pain. He had no idea how much longer he could keep this courage.

A minute later Blake and Jasmine walked in with smiles from ear to ear and apologizing for keeping everyone waiting. Sheridan wanted to ask if they'd just had a quickie but she knew it wouldn't be professional. Jasmine didn't look sick anymore. For some reason she felt strongly that she should let Frank tell his story before she addressed whatever Blake and Jasmine had going on.

She began before anyone else spoke, "Okay guys let's keep this moving. In order to be mindful of the time we're going to move right on over to Frank and after he's done then we can have open discussions about everything that has taken place. I will give my recommendations for how to move forward from today, okay."

Everyone said their agreement.

Lisa reached for Frank's hand but he gently pulled away as he stood up. He walked over to the window on the far side of the room. He could feel every eye in the room on him just as he could feel the bile rising in his throat. How was he supposed to do this?

He knew he would keep his back to them until he finished because he couldn't stomach watching their faces as he uttered the unspeakable events from his past. Sheridan didn't want him to feel rushed, but she had a feeling this was going to take some time.

She said, "Frank, whenever you're ready. Remember this is your family. They care a great deal about you. This room is free of judgment."

He let out a cynical chuckle, "I'm not so sure that's even possible."

Lisa had no idea what it was but she wanted desperately to know. She knew this day had been weighing on her husband because his sunny disposition as of late was now a distant memory. She hoped this day would unburden his soul so they could live out the rest of their lives finally in peace.

With his back still to his family Frank took a deep breath and spoke, "What happened to me was a lifetime ago. It was so horrible I honestly convinced myself it wasn't real. When I was a teenager some kind of way I was able to block it out. I honestly forgot all about it."

He had everyone's undivided attention. Sheridan sat up in her chair, intrigued.

She asked, "What triggered this memory back into your life Frank."

He hung his head and said, "Blake's friendship with Jasmine."

There were a few sharp breaths taken. Jasmine inched a little closer to the edge of her seat.

Sheridan asked, "So what happened to you happened when you were just a child."

He nodded and said, "The nightmares started coming to me when the kids were around seven. It's when I realized that what they had was a true friendship that could last forever. I started having flashbacks. I thought it couldn't be real but I knew it was. I could hear the screams in my head. So I started drinking to block out the nightmares and it helped for a while. I never had nightmares but now that it had been brought back I couldn't escape it. Every time I saw the two of them together it would bring it right back."

Sheridan could tell he was struggling for composure so she asked the question, "What was it about the time you beat them that pushed you over the edge?"

Frank took a deep breath, "I now know differently but through my alcohol induced haze I thought they were kissing. It triggered a moment from my childhood that I couldn't stand to remember. Jasmine was my pain. She had to be the one to go. When Blake stood in between me and her to protect her I lost it."

Sheridan asked, "Why Frank?"

"Because he stood up for her something I couldn't do."

Frank began to weep. It wasn't hysterical, it was quiet and dignified. Lisa was so lost. She had no idea what he was talking about but she knew whatever it was, it was bad. She stood next to him and held his hand. She turned her back to him because it seemed like he needed to not look at them in order to release his truth.

Sheridan asked, "Frank who did you fail to protect?"

It took several moments but he said, "When I was five years old I used to visit with my grandparents on their plantation in the summer. My great-grandparents owned slaves."

He paused to let that marinate considering his audience. Jasmine gave a look at her parents. Their faces remained blank. Lisa held Frank's hand a little tighter as he began again.

"The children of their slaves were of course freed but they still lived on my grandparents land and worked for them. They had a daughter. Her name was Beth. We were inseparable that first summer. We did everything together. My grandparents never had a problem with it for whatever reason. It was likely because my grandmother was so fond of Beth. I taught her how to read and she taught me pretty much everything else," he said with a smile in his voice.

"It almost broke my five-year-old heart to leave and go back home when the summer ended."

He let his mind drift back to a time when his innocence was at its most perfect.

"The next year when I came back we picked up right where we left off. We were the best of friends playing together every day, getting in trouble for running through the house and what not. We were only six but we shared our first kiss. It wasn't anything inappropriate though, just a friendship peck. It was really innocent and it only happened once. I guess she learned affection from her parents because mine certainly didn't show any. One thing you all need to know about Beth's parents is that they were so in love with each other. It was in every interaction they shared with each other.

Anyways, one day about halfway through that summer my grandmother would not let me play with Beth. I didn't know why. I thought it was because she found out we kissed. It was a big uproar going on but at the time I couldn't comprehend. Apparently Beth's father Joe was said to have made a pass at my mother when they came for a visit. It was hard for me to believe that because he was devoted to his wife but I believed what had been told to me. Late that night I heard screams and it startled me awake. I knew for a fact one of the screams was Beth's voice."

Everyone in the room began to fidget. Lisa held on a little tighter as tears began to roll down her cheeks. Sheridan began to doubt her ability to keep her professional composure. This was brand new territory. Jasmine felt the burn in her belly. This was the kind of stuff you saw in movies. She never thought she would know someone who actually experienced it.

Blake was ashamed at what had transpired in his family and for some reason it made it hard for him to look at Jasmine at the moment. Justin just hung his head not knowing exactly where this was going but knowing he wouldn't like it. Vanessa felt her resistance against white men building back up. It was going to be a task to separate them from Mr. Matthews.

Frank continued, "A short while later my dad came and got me and we left in his truck. I asked him where we were going. He said to do what men do when one of their own is disrespected. I had no idea what was going on but I remember being really afraid of my dad for the first time ever. He had this look in his eye that even at a young age I correctly interpreted as dangerous. We arrived at another plantation down the road. There was this mob of men yelling and cussing and throwing their fists in the air. My dad took me out of the truck and he maneuvered us to the front of the mob. That's when I saw the most horrific thing I had ever seen."

Frank began to weep, "It was Beth's dad hanging from a tree. He had been beaten bloody and I knew he was almost dead. I screamed. I asked my daddy why he was hanging like that. He told me because he deserved it. Someone handed my dad a torch. He turned, handed it to me and said you finish him to do your part in honoring your mother. I was shaking. I cried and said no I didn't want to. My daddy backhanded me and said boy you will defend your mother. I got up and picked up the torch that fell out of my hand. My dad lit it. Because I was too scared to do anything else I set it to his foot and was forced to stand there and watch him burn. I was violently ill. In my tiny mind I literally thought I was throwing up my insides."

The silence that hit the room was deafening. It was so quiet they could hear a cockroach take a tinkle on a cotton ball. Frank could not see the stunned expressions on the faces of his family or Sheridan. There wasn't a dry eye in the room.

Frank managed to compose himself, "I can still hear his screams and smell his flesh burning in my nightmares. I fell to the ground until my dad dragged me to the truck and beat me because he said I was weak. About a week later I saw Beth. She told me that she didn't have a daddy anymore and that she didn't know why. Beth was my best friend in the whole world. I'd had a hand in killing her father. I didn't want to see her and her mother kept her away from me after that anyway."

He felt his wife's hand tremble in his. When he managed the courage to look at her and only her she stared back with a blank expression and a face ravaged with silent tears. She was shaking uncontrollably. He didn't know if it was from fear, horror, anger, or disgust. He wanted to hold her but he was afraid to touch her.

He found some courage deep in the recesses of his soul to look up and face everyone else in the room. His eyes bore into Blake's.

"Son, I'm so sorry. For a long time I thought if I hadn't been so close to Beth then my father would have never made me do that. I felt as though he wanted to sever my ties with her once and for all. I know now he was passing down his hatred to me, making sure it stuck. He was a very mean and intolerable man. You guys don't know this because I kept him as far away from you as possible but he died when you were eight years old Blake. I went to see him on his death bed and he confessed to me that he'd overheard my mom coming on to Beth's father. He'd beat her silly for it, but his pride couldn't take it and Joe had to pay for it. He said it wasn't like killing a real man, he was an animal. He wept. It was the first time I had ever seen my father cry but I didn't care because I still lived with the nightmares of what I'd done. He was about to be free of his because death was knocking at his door. I hated him even more. I didn't think that was possible. I know you and Jasmine's relationship was nothing like that but still the familiarity of it hit too close to home. I was determined to do everything in my power to stop it. The truth is Jasmine the reason I hated you so much is because you represented something I was conditioned to despise. It was easier to hate you and see you as less than human than to hate myself. It was easier to see you as the problem than see myself for who I truly was, a coward, a murderer and a racist. As long as you were less than me then I could live with what I did. The moment I saw you as equal is the moment I would have to face what I did so I always kept you and all other black people beneath me. I can see that now. For that I am truly sorry."

Blake had no response. He just stared at his father not even sure of what he was feeling. Jasmine didn't know how to comfort her husband. There was no instruction manual for this kind of emotional bomb when dropped at your feet. She stared at Frank he looked so much like a broken man her heart bled for him and the six year old that was still in there screaming for understanding and forgiveness.

Jasmine stood up and walked over to Frank.

She wrapped her arms around him and whispered, "I forgive you Frank. You are not a coward. It took great courage to tell your story."

Frank held Jasmine tight and said, "Thank you."

A few moments later Jasmine released him and took her seat.

Sheridan took a tissue and wiped her face, "I apologize for my lack of professionalism but that one took me by surprise. Frank, my heart breaks for that six year old you were and the burden you can't help but carry with you now."

It pained her to be objective. She wanted to lash out at him for that life that was carelessly disposed of.

She cleared her throat, "You're no different from any other abused child out there. This tragedy was not your fault. Even though you knew right from wrong the people who were responsible for guiding your life distorted that sense of morality."

She had to wipe her eyes again.

"I cannot imagine what this has been like for you but you have to find a way to forgive yourself and embrace your family."

She paused again to wipe her face.

"You must also find it in your heart to forgive your father. You've been blinded by your hatred for so long that you can't see you've turned into someone like him. Even though he's dead and gone you have to free yourself from the grip he has on you. That spirit of hatred was passed down to Blake as well but thankfully that issue has already been resolved between you two. It's very important that you all can recognize the pattern."

She needed to take a break. She checked her watch and realized they only had thirty minutes left in their session but she was willing to stay for however long it took.

She cleared her throat again and said, "Why don't we take another break guys. What do you say we meet back here in 20 minutes? Let's not be concerned with the time. It isn't a factor."

She excused herself from the room. Frank sat down on the floor right where he was. He brought his knees up to his chest, hung his head and cried for everything he had been holding on to for over fifty years. Lisa sat beside him not believing there were any words she could utter to him to make either of them feel better. So she did the next best thing. She sat there with her husband and cried with him.

Justin pulled Vanessa out of the room and said, "Let's give them their privacy."

Vanessa nodded still stunned. Her heart was shattered and it was sad. No one, let alone a child, should ever be forced to do something so unspeakable. Jasmine held Blake's hand having no clue what she could possibly say to him. She was having a war within herself. She was so grateful to finally understand why and how Frank could have hated her for so long but the explanation was even worse than his acts. She needed time to process it.

She whispered to Blake, "Can we step outside."

His body registered his response by standing up and being led out by her hand but he was on auto pilot. He was so broken knowing what had taken place in his own blood line. How could he look his child in the eye and tell them about their family history. He knew their kid would face additional challenges because of its mixed heritage but how would the kid feel if he knew that one side of his family tree slaughtered a representation of the other half of the tree.

They stood just outside the door where the session was held. Jasmine seemed to be handling this better than he was.

She asked, "You okay?"

He shook his head and pulled her into him. He was grateful that her hair had begun to grow back and was just a shorter version of her wild curls. Burying his face in her curls felt so normal and grounded him just a little bit. She held on to him tight trying to absorb his pain. She knew it would take some time to get through this.

∞∞∞

Pacing in her office Sheridan was struggling to hold it together. She herself had never been a fan of white people. She never treated them unfairly. She just didn't really care for them as a whole knowing all of the injustices they seemed so heartlessly willing to participate in, even in this present day.

The ironic part is that God had saw fit to give her a black man that had been raised by white people. It had taken some time but, his parents had found a solid place in her heart and she loved his family dearly. She never considered herself anti-white just pro-black and she didn't think that they were synonymous.

She was struggling hard with her current clients because she never cared for interracial relationships. Be it a black man or a black woman she didn't care. She had a problem with the separation of the black family.

She shocked herself by taking on Jasmine's case, but it was something so sincere and real in her voice the way she pled for help to keep her family together. Listening to the way Jasmine talked about Blake and all they had gone through to be together softened her heart and forced her to widen her perception.

Seeing them together was a sight to behold. They weren't like so many other interracial couples she'd seen where one seemed to be pretending they were the other race. That annoyed her to no end. Blake was just your average white guy and Jasmine was your average sista. They weren't pretending to be something they were not. They were just simply in love. They seemed to actually be one person. They epitomized the phrase, "the two shall become one."

They were so in tune to each other it was remarkable to watch. There was an intimacy they shared in their marriage that crossed every color line and she found herself falling in love with the purity of their relationship. Watching the way he'd anticipated what would hurt her and how he was right there to hug or stroke or kiss away the pain she was feeling.

She noticed how her hand would blindly reach for his whenever something was too much for her to handle and his hand was always right there waiting on hers. She noted the way Jasmine so passionately protected him while at the same time still allowed him to lead her. It was like they could feel each other's needs and respond before the need was even expressed. She counted it a blessing to be able to witness it.

She recognized the spiritual battle they had to endure to get to this day of healing and forgiveness in their family. She recognized how the enemy had used fear and racism to stunt the progress of their love that had the power to heal so many. Jasmine told her they wanted to start their family but were afraid of what they were bringing the child into.

They were prepared to deal with the outside world and its prejudices but they didn't want it to come from within. Knowing what Vanessa experienced at the hands of a man she trusted was bad enough, but then hearing Frank's confession had pushed her past her limits. This family and all their secrets were forcing her to deal with her own prejudices and perceptions.

If it wasn't for the love of their children Frank and Vanessa might have gone their entire lives with those horrible burdens. The psychologist in her was excited and encouraged with the opportunity to work with them, but the black woman in her was none too thrilled about the rape, the hanging or the interracial marriage.

What did that say about her? These people had valid understandable reasons for their seeds of hate that were planted but she couldn't say she had ever been through anything personally with anyone of another race to warrant her dislike of them.

In the middle of her floor she kneeled, "Dear Heavenly Father, I need Your help like never before. I need Your help right now in this very moment. I know You brought them to me specifically so that means that I can handle this, but I don't see how at the moment. I need You to guide my tongue and deal with me to rid myself of ill feelings I carry for people I don't even know because they look different than me. I can see Your hand in this Father, in my life and in each of theirs. Help me to guide them to a healing that will last and expand into other lives. Please forgive me of my sin and the resentment I hold in my heart. Thank You for opening up my view point to realize I need to discern each individual tree by the fruit that it bears and not unfairly assume anything about others I don't even know. Thank You for softening my heart. I give You all the praise and the glory, in Jesus name. Amen."

Sheridan waited there patiently listening for God to tell her what to do and how to handle this situation. She sat in silence on the floor for about ten minutes meditating on what God was placing in her heart. She got up, cleaned her face and straightened out her suit. She took a look in the mirror and headed back to the session.

Chapter 49: The Resolution

When Sheridan strolled into the session everyone was relatively composed and sitting in their assigned seats. Her stroll was confident and she was back in control.

She took her seat and said, "Let me apologize once again for my emotional response but I'm human too and I don't think anyone could hear a story like that and not be affected. However, I would like to say I'm sorry."

Frank said, "It's okay, really I understand."

"Thank you."

Sheridan looked around the room at the solemn faces. She was ready to share with them what their next steps should be.

She began, "Does anyone have anything to say before I get to my recommendations?"

Lisa raised her hand and spoke to her husband, "Baby I am so sorry that you had to endure such a horrific experience, but I'll always be here for you and with you no matter what. I love you."

Frank hugged and kissed his wife passionately shocking everyone by his very intimate public display of affection. Blake had never seen his parents do more than peck in his presence growing up and even in adulthood. It was a beautiful thing to see. Jasmine squeezed his hand understanding exactly what this moment did for him.

Sheridan began, "Anyone else?"

No one responded.

"Okay so moving on. Vanessa let's deal with you first. You must recognize the love that Blake has shown to your daughter and realize that it is sincere and without prejudice. You must have had some type of affection for him in order for him to have still been in her life. I'm sure it would have been much easier to separate them as children than now. You have to work on seeing Blake and Frank for how they are now, for who they are to you and your family. From this moment on the past is the past and you are letting it go."

Vanessa nodded.

Sheridan continued, "One thing I want you to do and this is something you can do with Lisa and Jasmine. I want the three of you to go to a spa. Spend the whole day being pampered and spoiled and enjoying being a woman. Get your toes, nails, hair and make-up done and go out somewhere where you can be seen."

Vanessa squirmed a bit and made Sheridan smile.

She continued, "Trust me. It's going to be okay. For you Justin, I want you to take your wife on a shopping spree. Buy her all the kinds of outfits you've wanted to see her in but never put much emphasis on."

Justin smiled and Vanessa looked petrified.

Sheridan laughed, "It's okay Vanessa because what I want you to do is wear the clothes at home on dates with your hubby until you feel comfortable enough to go out. Then when she does Justin I want you to take her out and wine and dine her at least once a month. Show her the rewards of embracing her femininity from the man she trusts the most. Vanessa, what you should understand is that even though you were blessed to have a husband who was very understanding and very supportive he had to deny himself some very basic pleasures as your man and your husband. It's only natural for him to want to see you that way. Now don't panic, this is a process. You shouldn't rush into it but at least once a week really try to embrace something new and look forward to experiencing being a newlywed all over again."

Sheridan winked at her mischievously.

Vanessa liked the sound of that. If she was honest she was always intimidated by women who could embrace their beauty and show it with such confidence. She knew she was beautiful and she knew her body was well in shape. She didn't want that sorry excuse for a man to have power over her life anymore. She wanted to finally overcome it all and be who she was meant to be. She wanted to show her husband how much his patience had meant to her. She leaned over and whispered something to her husband that had his very brown face show a tint of red. Vanessa smiled a very wicked grin and focused back on Sheridan.

Sheridan laughed and said, "Now for the healing."

She handed Vanessa a list that her assistant had printed out.

"Here is a list of rape counseling centers in your area. One of the ways for you to heal is to share your story with others who have been through it and showing them that there is life on the other side of this horrible experience."

Vanessa's eyes popped out, "I don't think I can do that."

"I think you can. Look at what you've overcome in spite of what happened to you. Someone else needs to hear that. We don't always understand why we go through the things that we do but God can turn it out for good. What if you're the person that talks a rape victim out of suicide? What if a young girl needs to hear your story in order to decide to keep following her dreams and become who God created her to be?"

Vanessa nodded. She had never thought what happened to her could help someone else but she was beginning to believe that she could do that.

She said, "Okay I'll give it a try."

Sheridan looked at Frank and let out a breath.

He laughed and asked, "So doc, what'd you come up with for me?"

She smiled and said, "Well now Frank I have to say I am just so proud of you for coming in here and sharing such a deep dark secret to help your family heal. I want you to remember that courage and strength that you found within yourself to be able to release that burden. Now for you I'm not sure if telling people about your past experience is going to help you because people as a whole can be unforgiving and judgmental. So use your discretion and the direction of the Holy Spirit before revealing it. You have a beautiful family and I know they will always have your back."

They all nodded in agreement letting Frank know he had their support. The weights that fell off of him felt miraculous. He took a moment to let his emotions show as Lisa rubbed his back. Everyone was silent and afforded him this time. After a few minutes he looked into Sheridan's warm brown eyes.

She smiled and said, "Frank I know you feel guilty. The truth is you have no reason to but I know changing your mind is easier said than done. What I want you to do is volunteer your time with urban at-risk teens and become a mentor. Now of course all of them won't be black teens but most will likely be minorities.

There will of course be some white ones but this isn't about race. Contrary to what you think, this is about knowing and accepting all kinds of people for who they are especially if they are different from you. This task is meant to expand your view of the world. To learn and empathize with the life experiences of other people you don't know. Just by sharing with them the obvious compassion you have inside of you, you can change the course of their lives."

He looked at her like he didn't quite understand.

She said, "Oh yes you have plenty of compassion inside of you, that's why it hurt you so deep being forced to do what you did. I want you to find that compassion again and use it to help those whose lives have been hard and unfair to help them find a reason to believe in themselves and a future that is far removed from their past. They too are trying to cope with things forced on them that were out of their control. Don't be afraid to share your diverse family with them. In doing this they will be more likely to trust you. Through you it can change their perception of the big bad white man. So many minorities are taught to blame white people for the hand they've been dealt. Now I will be the first to say I have and can see the injustices but it cannot define a person or be an excuse not to prevail and become who God created them to be. This country's racial divide has got to be healed, but we will do it one person at a time."

Frank let out a breath and said, "Well I just recently became a people person but I will give it a try. After what Jasmine did for me I have wanted to return the favor to someone else. I believe they call it paying it forward to do something selfless for someone else because you never know if that will be the one thing that changes their lives forever."

"I also feel that it would be good for you to try and locate your friend Beth to bring closure to both you and her. It's going to be really hard for you to forgive yourself but in doing this you can free yourself from the burden of not being there for her. If she is still alive I'm sure she has many questions about that horrible night that you could answer for her. I believe that it would bring you closure as well. I know that would open up a whole new can of worms so definitely pray about it and if there is anything I can do to help I'm more than willing."

Frank let that marinate for a while. It was actually something he'd thought about several times but he just didn't know where it would lead.

He said, "Okay doc, I'll give it some thought and some prayers."

Sheridan handed him a list of agencies that were in need of volunteers in his city.

She smiled and said, "This has been one of the most incredible sessions I have ever had. This family has forever changed my life for the better. Thank you so much for allowing me in your lives. I almost hate that our time has to come to an end."

They all laughed as they each stood up. Sheridan looked at Jasmine and Blake and asked, "Isn't there something else you two would like to share before we leave."

She gave them a knowing smile and Jasmine's mouth fell open.

She asked, "How did you know?"

Sheridan just shrugged.

Lisa and Vanessa were all smiles.

Justin asked, "Well what is it?"

Blake said, "Jasmine and I have an amazing reason for this family to stay close and connected. We're having a baby!"

Frank's eyes got huge as he just stared at his son and new daughter. The joy he felt in his heart was both shocking and comforting. Justin in a very rare show of emotion shed a few tears as he embraced his daughter and then Blake. There were lots of hugs and tears.

Sheridan said, "Now Jasmine I need you to recognize the second chance that God has given you. With the birth of this child you need to finally let go of your first born. That child is in God's hands now. Do not allow your past to keep you from embracing your future entirely."

Jasmine smiled and nodded.

"Blake," Sheridan said, "Make sure she doesn't regress. You guys have your whole lives ahead of you and that's plenty to focus on. I also want you not to let what your father revealed keep you from building that relationship okay."

He nodded intrigued that she could see the resistance in him. But she was right their future was bright. There was no point in letting the past cast a shadow over it. Sheridan counted herself blessed to be able to have a front row seat to the healing and miraculous power of the awesome God she served.

Chapter 50: Here and Now

They were on Ponte Vedra Beach and the sun was due to set in moments. The salty breeze teased their faces and whipped through their hair as they stood to watch the people they love vow to love each other two days past forever. Carmen stood in her strapless white gown with intricate detailing on the bodice and the train. Her long hair was in a perfect French braid that touched the top of her backside. It had beautiful white flowers threaded through it.

She had a crown made of white flowers sitting atop her head. Her skin was glowing with pure happiness. Her smile was endless. Damon stood across from her in a white tuxedo and stared into her eyes as his heart fluttered. He never thought he'd see the day he wanted to be standing in front of a woman vowing to love her forever. Now that he was it made him happy beyond his wildest dreams.

Blake stood by his side in a white tuxedo with a silver vest smiling. He couldn't be happier for his friends. Jasmine and Lucy stood next to Carmen and continued to wipe tears from their eyes as they had been since Carmen came down the aisle. They were wearing matching silver halter gowns. Lucy's hair was pinned up with spiraling curls and decorated with a band of white flowers. Jasmine's hair had grown back and was pulled away from her face with a white flower tucked behind her right ear. Jasmine's dress had to be adjusted for her nearly nine month protruding belly. She had two more weeks to go. She and Blake would be welcoming their daughter into the world. They couldn't wait to meet her.

The minister said, "You may now kiss your bride."

Damon made sure to make a show out of their first kiss as husband and wife. He dipped Carmen back and took his time sealing their vows with a kiss. They received many laughs, hoots and whistles from the intimate audience.

Jeremy was in attendance. He couldn't take his eyes off Lucy's smiling face. He was so in love with her. He couldn't wait until the day they shared their vows with their friends and loved ones. Alyssa sat next to him smiling at the newlywed couple. She smiled as Samantha had a serious look on her face taking her job as flower girl to heart.

Alyssa was so grateful for the people that had been brought into her life. It amazed her how life turned out. She missed Ahmed dearly but being around those who loved him most was helping her make peace with the tragedy that had befallen them that dreadful day. The soulless monsters that killed him were behind bars and awaiting trial, one she would not miss.

She was learning a lot about her new friends. It was the little things she noticed that made her understand their love dynamic. Like how only Blake called Jasmine, Jaz and the rest of them called her Jazzy. It also tickled her that Jasmine referred to Damon as "my Damon." She admired how Damon and Blake were protective of all the girls. She hoped one day to have men in her life like that to care about her. She was grateful for her new job and her new outlook on life. Her first occupants were due to arrive in two weeks. She was so excited.

Vanessa and Justin were also in attendance. Justin couldn't take his eyes off his beautiful wife who had her make-up professionally done for the occasion and was wearing a black halter dress that hugged the curves she never lost in all the years he had loved her.

The strappy silver heels she had on gave him a nice view of her freshly painted toes. He was in heaven and felt like it was his honeymoon. Lisa and Frank were also there hugged in an intimate embrace as they watched the beautiful couple head down the aisle. They had never been so close. Their marriage was finally free of pain and secrets.

Everyone was on their feet cheering and wishing congratulations as they blew bubbles over their heads. Blake took Jasmine's arm in one of his and Lucy's in the other and they followed the couple down the aisle.

Once the pictures had been taken everyone was ushered and seated into a white tent as they listened to the waves outside. Lucy, Jasmine, Carmen, Damon and Blake were seated at the head table and enjoying the meal of filet mignon, red roasted potatoes and fresh green beans.

Blake tapped his champagne glass and stood to give the best man's toast. All eyes were on him as he stood.

"I am so grateful to be a part of this momentous occasion. Damon has been my friend since high school. He has remained loyal, trustworthy and always had my back no matter what. Carmen this is the kind of man you're getting. I know that he will love and cherish you for the incredible woman you are. I pray God blesses you both beyond your wildest dreams as you embark on this new life together. I love you both without limits."

He raised his glass, "To the bride and groom."

The audience echoed his sentiments and they took a sip.

It was Jasmine's turn for her speech because Lucy hated public speaking even though she knew everyone in the room. She backed her chair out and required a little assistance from Lucy to get up.

She laughed and blew out a breath, "This kid better hurry up because mommy has lost all of her gracefulness."

Everyone laughed.

Jasmine raised her glass of sparkling cider and said, "Oh my gosh you guys, I have practically been in tears all day long. I am so happy for the two of you. Who knew all those years ago when we met at college that this was what God had been planning all along while we were as clueless as we could possibly be? Carmen, I am so grateful for the friend that I found in you and Damon you know we go way back."

Carmen and Damon smiled up at her.

"I knew that one day Damon would find a woman that would completely knock him on his butt. I waited patiently for that day."

There was light laughter.

"I couldn't have been more pleased that it was a woman of inner and outer beauty, as well as a woman of substance and integrity. I have no doubt that you will make my Damon happy and you will be there to keep him in line because Blake and I are tired of being the ones to keep him on his best behavior."

Everyone laughed.

"Now if you two could hurry up and start making babies so our little one will have someone to play with."

Everyone laughed when Carmen's eyes got big as saucers and Damon was struck with a sudden coughing fit.

Jasmine smiled, "I love you both more than you'll ever know."

She raised her glass, "To the bride and groom."

The crowd echoed.

Everyone was mingling and enjoying the reception when the DJ announced it was time for the first dance. Damon stood up and took his new wife by the hand and led her to the dance floor. They began a slow dance to Luther Vandross' "Here and Now."

Damon said, "Baby you have made me so happy. Thank you for agreeing to spend your life with me."

Carmen let the tear spill down her face with no shame as she smiled, "Thank you for asking me. I love you so much."

"I love you."

He kissed her with so much passion she trembled in his arms. The audience hooted and hollered as they laughed.

The DJ told the rest of the couples to join them on the dance floor. Blake went to help Jasmine to the floor as Jeremy stood and headed for Lucy. Justin and Vanessa went as did Lisa and Frank. Both Damon's parents and Carmen's parents also joined them on the dance floor. Jasmine's brothers and their wives joined them as well. As that love ballad faded, the DJ played another one.

Blake stared down at Jasmine's belly, "I can't wait for you to get here sweetie."

Jasmine said, "Me either. This child will not stay out of my ribs. I can barely breathe right now."

Blake laughed. He had always thought his wife was beautiful but the glow she wore as she carried his child made her breathtaking. He ran his fingers through her curls and kissed her nose.

He said, "Okay then let's sit the next one out."

Before Jasmine could respond a commotion behind them got their attention. When she turned around to look she saw Jeremy down on one knee with a sparkling diamond in his hands and Lucy with fresh tears in her eyes smiling from ear to ear. Jasmine could not believe what she was seeing. Damon and

Carmen laughed because they knew it was coming as others started to cheer.

Lucy was jumping up and down as she said yes. The intimate crowd began to cheer and Jasmine smiled. She made her peace with their relationship but knowing that it was now going to be forever was a different story.

Jeremy stood and kissed Lucy. Blake was about to give his congratulations when Jasmine let out a little scream. Blake was by her side in a flash.

He asked, "Jaz are you okay?"

She reached for his hand her other hand over her belly.

"Baby I think my water just broke."

"Oh my God are you serious?"

She took in a deep breath as a contraction hit her, "Oh yeah it's time. Somebody please get me a freakin' towel."

Everyone was now focused on Jasmine as Blake was trying to get her to a chair. Damon took over.

"Okay people, here is what we're going to do. Blake you drive Jazzy to the hospital. Alyssa you go to the house and get her bag. Jeremy can you stay here and get this wrapped up?"

He nodded and said, "Yeah no problem."

Damon asked, "Luce, you wanna go with me and Carmen or stay here with Jeremy?"

Before she could answer Jeremy said, "Honey you go ahead with them I will see you there shortly."

She smiled and kissed him hard. He smiled and slid the ring on her finger since his proposal was interrupted.

Damon said, "By the way guys, congratulations."

Blake had left to get the car and was heading back in to get Jasmine. She was taking deep breaths and said, "I'm so sorry guys. I didn't mean to ruin your wedding."

Carmen said, "Oh no darling the fun doesn't start until tonight."

She winked at Damon and he gave her a wicked grin. Staying celibate had been a huge challenge and they were ready to make up for lost time. Jasmine managed a small smile through the growing pain.

- 356 -

Blake helped Jasmine out to the car. He didn't even argue when Vanessa was right on their heels hopping in the back seat. He was surprised at how calm he was.

∞∞∞

By the time everyone arrived at the hospital Jasmine was full on in labor. Blake was by her side and her mother flanked her other side. They were encouraging her and coaching her through the process. Since the baby started coming so fast she did not have time to get an epidural. She was trying her best not to cuss everyone out and to remain calm.

Blake cooed, "Come on baby. I know you're tired and I know it hurts but just one more. I can see the head. Just one more big push and she will be here."

Jasmine squeezed her mom's hand as tears ran down her face. She didn't scream but pushed with all her might hoping and praying that this would be it. She thought she would pass out from the pain.

Suddenly she heard her baby's voice crying out. She thought that had to be the most beautiful sound she had ever heard. A teary eyed Blake cut the umbilical cord as Vanessa kissed Jasmine on the forehead. Jasmine reached for her daughter and cried as she pulled her safe into her bosom to make sure she was complete with ten fingers, ten toes, two eyes and a nose.

She was making a mental note of everything about her baby girl. The pain was forgotten and she didn't even mind that she hadn't been cleaned yet. No words were spoken as the nurse came and took her.

Blake kissed his wife, "I love you so much baby. Thank you for giving me this precious gift."

"I love you too, thank you."

Her mom smiled and said, "I'm going to go so you two can have a minute. I'll bring everyone in when the nurse says it's okay."

They nodded.

Jasmine said, "I love you mom."

"I love you sweetie. I'm so proud of you."

Blake kissed his wife.

"What are we going to name this little beauty?"

"I really wanted to name her after Ahmed but his name doesn't exactly make for a user friendly girl version," Jasmine said.

Blake laughed, "That's true. What about Amy but spell it with two e's instead of a y?"

"Well that will definitely be her black side."

They laughed.

Jasmine asked, "I've been thinking about Amadi."

"I don't hate it. We can call her Madi or Di for short," Blake said.

Jasmine said, "Let's just stick to Amadi for now. Now you go watch that nurse. Do not let my baby out of your sight."

He laughed and said, "I'm on it baby."

About an hour later everyone was in Jasmine's delivery suite laughing, crying and cooing over the new addition to their family. Frank was holding his beautiful granddaughter with tears shamelessly falling down his face. He was so honored to know her and to be in her life. His family had come a long way. He was so grateful to be here for this moment. He looked around at everyone dressed up in their best. To him it seemed appropriate that this is how his first grand was welcomed into her family. He looked over and kissed Lisa.

Justin was smiling taking it all in. He was a proud dad and granddad. Vanessa and Blake were busy fussing over Jasmine. She was so tired and could barely keep her eyes open.

She said, "Okay guys, I'm gonna pass out pretty soon so can I hold her just one more time before I fall asleep?"

Lisa stood to bring Jasmine the baby.

Carmen said, "We'll leave Jazzy so you can rest."

"Your fast tail behind just trying to get to that honeymoon," Jasmine teased.

Damon said, "You better know it!" He handed Jeremy the garter and Lucy Carmen's bouquet. "Y'all were going to be next anyways."

Everyone laughed. As they all started to say their goodbyes Jasmine held on to her baby girl as Blake stood over them.

Seeing Jasmine hold her daughter made Jeremy feel some kind of way. He couldn't exactly place his emotions but he knew he had them. He grabbed Lucy and held her a little tighter praying and hoping that he and Jasmine's secret would never see the light of day. What he had with Lucy was as close to perfection as he would ever get. He didn't want to even entertain the thought of losing her.

Jasmine said, "Come on precious open your eyes. Let mommy see how pretty they are."

Blake said, "Baby she is like two hours old, she is not going to open her eyes."

Jasmine laughed and gazed down at her baby. She had a perfectly round face with chubby cheeks and a head full of brown curly hair just like hers. Her skin was the color of sun-tinted beach sand. She was gorgeous. Jasmine wanted to see her eyes. She wanted to see if they were hers or Blake's but she knew it was too soon and she probably wouldn't open them.

Suddenly a breeze came through the room that had everyone looking around for the source and understanding. Jasmine looked down at the baby and she saw a little smile tug at her face. Then Amadi opened her eyes, stared up at the ceiling and gave a big toothless grin. Moments later she closed her eyes again but kept the smile.

Jasmine and Blake immediately looked up at the ceiling trying to figure out what exactly their daughter saw. Jasmine felt a warm calm come over her and she found herself smiling.

Blake asked, "Okay, what just happened?"

The door opened and in walked Nurse Ashley. Blake and Jasmine gasped. She smiled, her hazel eyes sparkling even more than before.

She said, "Ahmed told me to tell you all congratulations on the marriage, the baby and the engagement. He loves you very much. He says Blake, your baby girl is beautiful and Jasmine he hopes you can get some rest now that you've seen her striking blue eyes. He wants you to know he will always watch over his namesake."

Everyone just stared as she walked out.

Carmen was about to go after her when Blake said, "Trust me, she's gone."

Letter to the Reader

Hello Reader,

I want to first say thank you for taking the time to read my book. I am very passionate about this book and I think it's time we in this country have an open honest discussion about race. Let's not be afraid to expose wounds and let's not judge others perception but offer them the tools to help them adjust to reality.

The bible tells us whoever does not love does not know God, because God is love. One of his commandments is to love your neighbors as you love yourself. Therefore, all this hate among us is NOT pleasing to God. We need to suck up our differences and realize all life is precious and should be treated with dignity and respect. There is just one race, the human race.

If you do not know Jesus Christ as your personal Lord and Savior and you want to, right now is your opportunity to do just that. It doesn't matter who you, where you are or what you've done. He loves you and He has a plan for your life. You can accept Him right here and right now and ask Him to come into your heart. It's as easy as your ABC's.

A = Admit you are a sinner, ask for forgiveness
B = Believe in Jesus Christ, that he died and rose again
C = Confess, I accept Jesus as my personal Lord and Savior

Romans 10:9-10—That if thou shalt confess with thy mouth the Lord Jesus, and shalt believe in thine heart that God hath raised Him from the dead, thou shalt be saved. For with the heart man believeth unto righteousness; and with the mouth confession is made unto salvation.

Sincerely,

Melinda Michelle

Discussion Questions

1. Who were you more upset with for not realizing their true feelings or their divine purpose, Blake or Jasmine?

2. Did you get tired of Jasmine's resistance to their love? Has there ever been anything you knew was right that you resisted?

3. How do you feel about what happened to Ahmed? Do you think this was an accurate depiction of our country?

4. Did you sympathize with Frank all along or not until the end?

5. Do you feel Vanessa was a true racist? Why or why not?

6. How do you feel about the parents' reaction to their children being beat by Frank? What do you think you would have done?

7. Has reading this book softened your heart to another race or will it make you less likely to judge based on what you think you know?

8. How do you think God feels about racism?

9. Have you had a relationship with God and then walked away from it because of life's tragedy? Has this book made you realize that maybe you should give God another try?

10. Do you think Jasmine was wrong for not telling Lucy about what really happened between her and Jeremy? Why or why not?

11. Do you feel that Dr. Sheridan Richards was wrong for allowing her emotions to come out in a professional environment? Why or why not?

12. Do you like the diversity of the characters represented in this book? Why or why not?

13. Do you have a problem with interracial relationships? Why or why not?

14. Were you offended by anything said in this book by a particular ethnicity about another ethnicity? Why or why not?

15. Do you think the intimacy of Blake and Jasmine's relationship is attainable in reality? Why or why not?

Author Biography

Gwendolyn *Melinda Michelle* Evans (GMME) was born in Jacksonville, Florida. She was raised in Sanford, Florida and was introduced to reading at a young age. She has been a lover of reading since she could put two letters together to form a word. Growing up in a family of readers she was exposed to different genres of writing and developed an eclectic taste in books.

She is a graduate of Florida A&M University with a bachelor of science in accounting. She went on to pursue her MBA with a concentration in finance and accounting at American Intercontinental University. She has worked for financial institutions for the past nine years only recently stepping out to write full time. She is the owner and founder of Global Multi Media Enterprise (GMME) a free-lance writing and publishing company. She currently resides in Tallahassee, Florida.

Through the encouragement of family and close friends she turned her passion for reading into a passion for writing. She can always be found with a book somewhere within her reach. Once she realized it was a gift from God it was easy to see the purpose behind it. Being able to combine her faith and her passion to tell a good story is something she counts as a blessing.

It is her hope and desire that she can shed a positive image on the church, which she feels is viewed negatively by the world because of the actions of a small percentage of Christians. It is her desire to be able to tell a story that connects with Christians but also connects to people who just like to read. She tries to create a captivating story with powerful testimonies about the power of God.

Melinda Michelle's other published works include the short story "You Can Never Leave." It can be found on Amazon in e-book only. Her novel "Surviving Sunday" is the first of seven in a series. Book two, "Monday Madness" is due out in the summer of 2013.

Made in the USA
Charleston, SC
15 June 2016